FEAR
THE STARS

Also by Christopher Husberg

Duskfall
Dark Immolation
Blood Requiem
Fear the Stars

FEAR THE STARS

THE CHAOS QUEEN QUINTET

CHRISTOPHER HUSBERG

TITAN BOOKS

Fear the Stars
Print edition ISBN: 9781783299218
E-book edition ISBN: 9781783299225

Published by Titan Books
A division of Titan Publishing Group Ltd
144 Southwark Street, London SE1 0UP

First edition: June 2019
10 9 8 7 6 5 4 3 2 1

Names, places and incidents are either products of the author's imagination
or used fictitiously. Any resemblance to actual persons, living or dead
(except for satirical purposes), is entirely coincidental.

A CIP catalogue record for this title is available from the British Library.

Printed and bound by CPI Group (UK) Ltd. Croydon, CR0 4YY.

What did you think of this book?
We love to hear from our readers. Please email us at:
readerfeedback@titanemail.com, or write to us at the above address.

To receive advance information, news, competitions, and exclusive offers
online, please sign up for the Titan newsletter on our website:
www.titanbooks.com

FOR MOM

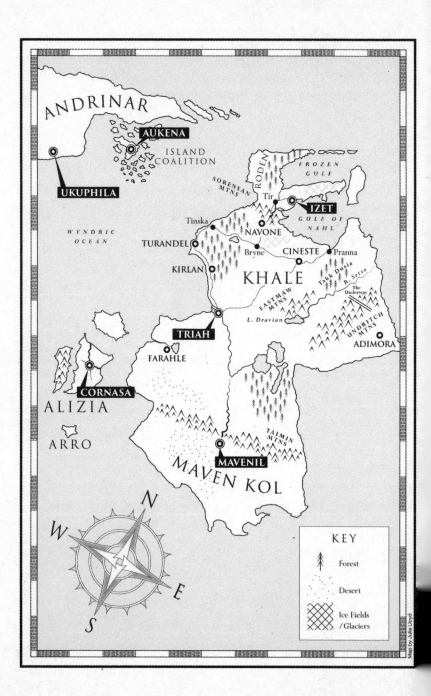

PART I

THE CHAOS QUEEN

1

173rd Year of the People's Age, Tiellan City of Adimora,

BLOOD SOAKED THROUGH THE side of Winter's black leather leggings as she rode at the head of a long column of horse toward the hidden city of Adimora. The tiellan riders, though smaller in stature than most humans and of finer features, nevertheless looked formidable in worn battle gear and tight formation. As well they should; they rode to Adimora after another victory.

The blood on Winter's leggings was not hers, but that of the commander of the Khalic force she and her Rangers had just decimated. The sack that contained his head knocked against her leg again; she had given up trying to adjust it. If the cursed thing wanted to bleed on her, let it. It seemed a small enough revenge.

"Urstadt, has word been sent to alert the city to our arrival?" Winter asked the human who rode beside her—the only human in her otherwise tiellan Ranger force.

"Yes, Your Majesty," Urstadt said. "They are expecting us."

Winter nodded. The force that rode behind her—over five hundred of her best fighters—would have taken hours to meander down the gorge through the main entrance to the underground city. Their chosen route led to a wider and less imposing entryway—horses could traverse it easily. Like all routes in to the city, it was well hidden, and led to a subterranean passage that would bring them into the city itself.

"Are they aware of our victory?" Winter asked.

"They are, Your Majesty."

Winter's lips pursed as she glanced at Urstadt. She still couldn't get used to the appellation on her companion's lips, but she had conceded that anything more familiar would imply weakness. And in the delicately balanced situation, she couldn't afford a challenge to her leadership from within her ranks.

"Some victory it was," Winter muttered. The head in the sack, bleeding vengefully on her leg, was for show. The soldiers they had destroyed had been hardly more than a guard force for a merchant caravan. But Grand Marshal Carrieri of the Khalic Legion had all but pulled his major forces back to the city of Triah, and victories were hard to come by. Her own Rangers had not begun the year as warlike people—they were for the most part refugees from the city of Cineste who hadn't even seen a weapon until they had been forced to flee. But the clanspeople of the plains encircling Adimora were a different matter; they lived and died by the sword. Once the clans had joined their numbers to her own, their respect for the honor of the battlefield had infected the Rangers, and Winter herself. And after the devastating losses Winter's army had faced at Carrieri's hand, and then in the battle with the Daemon Mefiston's army of shadowy Outsiders three months ago, Winter needed to give her people victories. For now, this was the best she could do. A head that refused to stop bleeding.

The air chilled, despite the sun beating down on her. On the journey home, the leaves had turned from green to red and orange. Ahead of her, a series of hills rose above the valley of the River Setso, like waves frozen in place. This was the easiest path for the horses to follow, but even here large outcroppings and boulders lined the water. Looking back, Winter was pleased to see Selldor, her lieutenant, had already lit his torch. Using the light it cast, she spurred her horse closer to the narrowing river's edge, following it until it bent between two hills. Once the river had been wider, cutting a gorge into the hillside, now artfully hidden by overhanging trees. Behind her, she saw more torches being lit as the company followed her into the ravine, descending gradually until the sky disappeared.

The path to the city twisted and turned, with many false trails to waylay travelers. They soon emerged into a large cave, where a pair of armed guards awaited them. Other Rangers were placed at strategic points on the plains above, keeping a watchful eye on the area surrounding this entrance. These two, a man and a woman, knelt when they saw Winter.

"Welcome home, Your Majesty," the woman said.

Home. Adimora was not her home, no more than the Rodenese city of Izet had been when she had been an unwilling guest there, and no more than her hometown of Pranna was now that the tiellan population had fled the prejudice and dangerous arrogance of their former human neighbors. "Home" had little meaning for her these days. Especially when, at the heart of Adimora, a Daemon was lurking.

Leaving her commanders to see to the disbanding of the company, and gladly relinquishing the bloody head to Urstadt's care, Winter wound her way on foot through the busy city, dodging the attention of her fellow warriors, Rangers and clanspeople both. Whereas on the surface Adimora was silent and sparsely populated, below ground it teemed with life, lit by torches and natural lightwells. The thousand or so tiellans who called Adimora home had carved their homes out of the underground rock. Now that the day was drawing to a close, traders were packing away their goods, calling out to passers-by in the hope of one last sale. Children darted past her in a complicated game. She refused to wear a crown or change her wardrobe, and her lean, powerfully built frame looked like any Ranger's. If anyone noticed Winter, she was just another returning soldier—without her army, nobody recognized her.

The rock dwellings were mostly small, tightly packed affairs, and the one she sought was no exception. But neither the tiellan inhabitant nor the Daemon he allowed to share his body was of this city.

Ghian answered his door with a smile, as if there were no enmity between them, and nodded her toward a seat at the small table at the center of the room. As the leader of the Druids of Cineste, he had been one of the few newcomers to procure a place below ground; the rest of the refugees Winter had brought from Cineste, Druids and Rangers alike, camped above ground, either in the meager huts that made up Adimora's above-ground facade, or in tents surrounding them. Ghian had retreated from his old companions since Winter had been declared queen. Many would have put this down to thwarted ambition; Winter knew better. Inside Ghian another presence lived: the Daemon Azael, the Fear Lord.

"What news do you have for me, Ghian?" Winter asked.

"News? I'm afraid there is not much to speak of. The Cracked Spear—"

Winter waved a hand. "Their missives have followed me into battle and back out again. I don't need to hear any more about the Cracked Spear and their trade arrangements." The Cracked Spear had led the tiellan clans until Winter wrested power from them. They liked to pretend they still had a say, but Winter did not care for pretense. "Tell me about you, Ghian. About Azael."

12

Ghian shrugged. "Even if I knew…"

"You wouldn't tell me," Winter finished for him. "You do this every time. You insist on your inability to communicate with me, until suddenly you speak up. Can we just skip to that part this time? I've had a long day, and I still have blood on my clothes. I'd like to get cleaned up."

"Blood on your clothes." Ghian's eyes rested on Winter thoughtfully. Something in Ghian's demeanor shifted. An image flashed in Winter's mind.

A black skull, wreathed in black flame.

"You cannot escape blood," Ghian said, with the skull's dead smile.

Fear closed in on her, but she pushed it away. Burning skull or not, she had a duty to her people.

"Why are you here, with us? Why did you choose Ghian?"

"Because you refused me." Something about his voice had changed, or his choice of words; Winter was now speaking with Azael, the Fear Lord, who called himself the master of the Nine Daemons. "And I want to keep an eye on you. I thought you would understand that by now. The Fear Lord, and the Chaos Queen," he added, chuckling. "What a pair we make."

"The Khalic Legion may call me by that name in their ignorance," Winter retorted. "But that title is out of an old tale—it belongs to another, if she ever existed." Since Carrieri had left her forces to be decimated by Mefiston's army of Outsiders, Winter's own combined Ranger and clan force had been reduced to roving the countryside in smaller bands, picking fights with other equally small groups of humans. Sowing chaos and disorder. But she could not afford to meet the might of the Khalic forces in open battle, not with her numbers.

Her words only made Azael laugh harder.

"Either way," she said, meeting Ghian's eyes and the Daemon beneath them, despite the swelling fear in her throat, "a queen commands a lord."

Ghian's laughter faded. "No one commands Azael," he said. "Not since—"

"No one has commanded Azael since what?" Winter asked.

"I do not have the capacity to speak of it."

A shadow passed over Ghian's face, and for a moment Winter knew she was speaking with the man again, not the Daemon.

Fear burned in Ghian's eyes. He still had his ability to choose, she was almost sure of that, but whatever Azael threatened him with was enough to shut Ghian up. Ghian had allowed himself to become Azael's avatar in the first place because he was scared, frightened for his people. It had been a stupid decision, and Winter hated him for making it, for making this Daemon a part of her life again, but there was a small part of her that understood it.

"Ghian, you cannot enjoy being connected to this… thing," Winter said. "You're invoking terrible danger. Not just to yourself, but to the whole movement you've been trying to—"

"You know nothing of the movement," Ghian rasped— himself again, it seemed—standing up so quickly he knocked his chair over backwards. "You joined us with no intention of *helping*. You don't care about the Druids, you don't care about the tiellans at all."

Winter looked away. After Lian's death in Roden she had not cared about anything for a long time, not until Eranda was killed in the battle against Mefiston. That loss of one of the last tiellans from her hometown—a woman who had known her from infancy—had changed things for her.

But how could she express that to Ghian?

"You were bored, that was all. You had nothing else to do

with your life, so you joined us. Your powers helped us at first, but all they've done is corrupt the Druid movement. So many have died, human and tiellan, who did not need to die. Those deaths are at your feet, Winter. Those deaths—"

Ghian cocked his head to the side, as if listening. After a moment, he bent over and picked up the overturned chair. Slowly, he righted it, and sat back down.

"I'm sorry," he said. "My outburst was uncalled for. What I said... does not matter."

You might not think it matters, but it is still true, Winter thought. And another voice whispered in her head.

Murderer.

"These little skirmishes you fight, these miniature victories, they are useless. They accomplish nothing."

Winter looked hard at Ghian, trying to discern who really spoke now, the man or the Daemon. She could not be sure.

"They raise morale," Winter whispered.

"But they do not inspire fear."

The thought had crossed her mind more than once. Carrieri had been winning the battle against her troops when Mefiston and his Outsiders had entered the field. In the heat of the battle, they had briefly fought alongside one another to save themselves from being overcome—but Carrieri had broken the pact and fled the field, leaving her and her people to be slaughtered. The human army did not see the full blossoming of her psimantic strength, when she had accessed the powers of the huge standing stone—a *rihnemin*—that towered over the battlefield, and slaughtered the Outsiders and Mefiston himself in an attack of liquid fire. Her people knew of her powers; the humans were ignorant of it. And these small skirmishes did not bolster her reputation. The Chaos Queen was a derogatory name. She needed to do more to regain her reputation, to make people *fear* her again. Only then could she bring about change for the tiellans. They had been enslaved and oppressed, downtrodden for far too long. Winter would assure them a place alongside the humans. She would end the oppression, the fear.

But she could not end those things here, in Adimora.

"I must go to Triah," Winter said softly. "Carrieri is hiding there, like a fox in a hole. I'll drag him out and make him pay." And in so doing, show how powerful the tiellans could truly be.

"*Yes*," Ghian hissed. The black skull flashed again. "Go to Triah. That is where all of this will end. Make people notice you again. You need their fear. And for that, you need me."

Winter closed her eyes, remembering the words of her friend Galce: *The only order is Chaos.* It seemed a long time since she had consulted Chaos, as Galce had told her the legendary Chaos Queen had done. As she closed her eyes, the sphere of Chaos waited patiently in her mind as always. This time, it was black and ominous.

2

Triah

THE GATE TO FAMED TRIAH, the great Circle City, was nowhere near as impressive as Cinzia remembered it. A wave of embarrassment washed over her as she checked her sister's face. She had told Jane of Triah's grandeur numerous times, but this gate was no better than the gates they'd grown up with in Navone. Of course, Jane didn't know that this was just the outer gate, or that there were two grander gates beyond; but, then again, Jane didn't seem to be paying much attention to the gate, anyway. Instead, her eyes repeatedly looked to the city beyond.

Farmlands and homes sprawled outward from the wall that encircled the greater city, spilling into the valley along the river toward the cliffs to the north. Cinzia felt the excitement stirring within her at the thought of seeing the city: the Trinacrya, the Crystal Pyramid, the trim tower-houses and apartments, and of course God's Eye overseeing it all.

But Triah was no longer her home, she reminded herself. Just as her family had fled Navone, and would likely never return, her life here—the chapel she had once run in the southwestern corner of the city near the harbor and the Cat District, her apartment at the seminary, her friends in the Denomination and in her congregation—was no longer hers. Her former Goddessguard, Kovac, was dead. Everything had changed when she had returned to Navone and discovered her sister had become a heretic, the Prophetess; and soon she had joined in the heresy, had become a disciple in the new Church of Canta, an Odenite.

Perhaps there was nothing left for her in Triah at all.

And yet Jane had dictated they come. Cinzia obeyed, dutifully, but her own feelings warred within her the closer she got to the Center Circle. Not only her misgivings about returning to the city itself, but her misgivings about Jane.

She looked over at Knot, walking beside her. The three of them—Cinzia, Jane, and Knot—had come to the city alone, leaving the other four Disciples behind, for now. "Do you feel anything, being here?" she asked. "Lathe was from Triah. What about your other sifts?"

Knot grunted. "It's all familiar to me. That's Lathe's doing for the most, but others're responsible for it, too. The investigator, and one other, I think. The warsquares champion."

"But do you feel anything?" Cinzia asked.

Knot looked up at the gate before them. He only shook his head in response.

Cinzia sighed. Knot had been quiet lately—ever since their confrontation with the Black Matron, where he had evaded the trap laid for him by the sift Lathe and the Daemon Bazlamit.

The gates opened before them as they approached. Inside was a squad of Khalic soldiers, waiting for them. The men wore full armor and plumed helmets, each carrying a spear, shield, and sword. The captain, his plume red instead of white, asked to see their papers.

Cinzia reached into her satchel for the documents they had been given by the parliamentary representative to secure them entry into the city, and showed them to the captain. He examined Knot, Cinzia, and Jane closely; he must have been given descriptions of their appearance.

"Very well," he said. "You may enter the city."

The soldiers parted, allowing Cinzia, Knot, and Jane entry into the city. But before she could enjoy being in her city once more, another group of armed men greeted them just inside the gate.

Sons of Canta.

Cinzia recognized them easily; their red-and-white livery made them stand out even more than the Khalic Legionaries. There were a half-dozen of them, but they parted to make way for a woman and man. She wore the robes of the priesthood, but they were trimmed with gold, and a long gold chain hung from her neck. A high priestess—one of only nine on the Sfaera. Cinzia recognized her—she would recognize any high priestess in person—as Garyne Hilamotha. Her Goddessguard, an older, grizzled man with high cheekbones covered in scruff and a higher hairline, walked beside her.

"Cinzia Oden," High Priestess Garyne said, frowning as she met Cinzia's eyes. The woman's dark hair sat atop her head in a towering bun, and her dark eyes were ready to pierce whatever they locked on to. She was almost a full head taller than Cinzia.

Cinzia and Knot exchanged a glance, then Cinzia stepped forward. "Yes?"

Garyne looked Cinzia up and down, then handed her a large envelope. "This is for you," she said. She and the Sons turned and walked away.

"Well, that was short and sweet," Knot said, puzzled. The last time they'd been confronted by Sons of Canta, back in the city of Kirlan, they'd nearly been slaughtered on the spot. Now they didn't seem interested in the Odenites at all. "We could have done with more of that back in Kirlan."

"Cinzia, are you all right?" Jane asked.

Cinzia had not taken her eyes off the envelope since Garyne had handed it to her.

"What's that?" Knot asked. "What'd she give you?"

"These are my papers of excommunication," Cinzia said softly. She knew they could not be anything else.

Slowly, she broke the seal of the High Camarilla—the familiar circle-and-triangle of the Trinacrya embedded on a blazing sun. The excommunication of someone who held the priesthood had to go through the highest bodies of the Denomination. Cinzia unfolded the note, and began to read.

A tear dropped from Cinzia's face onto the paper, and she quickly brushed it away, wiping her eyes with one sleeve. A plain, brown linen sleeve. No crimson and ivory; no robes of priesthood. She'd thought she had come to terms with the idea of never being a part of the Denomination again. It was corrupt, after all. Flawed.

And yet, for years, it had been her home. The Denomination had taught her so much—in addition to Cantic doctrine, she had learned history, sciences, and medicine at the seminary. She had made friends in the Denomination—Goddess rising, she had met Kovac there. The thought of him, of everything they had been through and everything she had been through since he died, racked her body with pain and regret. She could not feel her fingers, she realized. She could see them, gripping the letter in both hands, white-knuckled, but only the slightest tingling sensation made her aware that they were attached to her body.

"Silly of me to get worked up about this," she said, her

throat dry. "I have not been part of the Denomination since we left Navone; no reason to let it affect me now."

She felt Knot's hand on her shoulder. "Grieving ain't something we can control," he said. "Comes at us in different ways. Usually when we least expect it. Sometimes we think we're over a thing, but turns out that's far from the truth." Knot glanced at Jane, then back to Cinzia. "Nothin' wrong with being sad about losing a part of your life, something you thought would be with you for a long time. Doesn't do us any good to wallow in it, either, but ain't nothing wrong with acknowledging the grief is there."

Cinzia met Knot's eyes. Whether the words were his own, or dug up from one of the buried sifts that made up his soul, or from somewhere else entirely—she loved him for saying them. The embarrassment heating her face faded, just a fraction of it.

"Of course," Jane said quickly. "Knot is right. You are part of something new, now, something greater than you've ever been a part of before, but… it's all right to acknowledge that you miss the past."

You're better than this, Cinzi.

Cinzia almost jumped at the sound of the voice echoing within her mind. Only she heard it; it came from Luceraf, the Daemon of Pride, who now festered inside Cinzia, seeing and hearing just about everything Cinzia did. Every time Luceraf spoke, Cinzia felt a jolt of horrible realization at what she had done.

She had made a deal with a Daemon. It had been to help those she loved, but the Denomination had been right to excommunicate her. Even if all the other charges weren't true, or if she could explain them away, there was one she could not.

She consorted with Daemons.

You're better than this, and you know it. You're better than the

21

Denomination—you were too bright a star for the likes of them. But you're too bright for your sister's little charade, too.

Luceraf didn't know what she was talking about.

If you don't see it now, you'll see it soon, Luceraf hissed at her. *Trust me, Cinzi. I know what I see.*

They parted company from Knot in the city—both he and Cinzia had old contacts to find, in very different worlds. Cinzia and Jane spent the day in search of people and organizations that might support their cause, but didn't make much progress. Now that she had been officially excommunicated, Cinzia was cautious in who she approached. Not everyone would be willing to even speak with her, let alone help or offer support. She certainly could not contact anyone else in the Denomination.

She also regretted bringing Jane. People had heard of the Prophetess of the new Church of Canta, and even if they were interested in such a thing, they were extremely cautious about showing it. The Denomination had all but threatened excommunication, at best, to any who sided with Jane and the Church of Canta.

Walking about the city had been a small comfort at first, but then it had become just as painful as reading the papers High Priestess Garyne had delivered to her that morning. She saw the seminary, and her apartments where she had lived—where she would surely have no place anymore. She wondered what happened to the meager belongings she had left at the seminary, but was too frightened to ask after them, or to even approach anyone in the Denomination. It made her think of the friends she still had there, and thinking that she had given all of that up hurt. Even seeing Canta's Fane from a distance was painful.

The memories were too strong, the pain too fresh. With

time, she hoped, like anything, it would heal. But she was glad to leave the city as the sun set.

"Well, today could have gone better, I suppose," Jane said as they passed through the outer gate alongside homebound merchants and farmers, and turned off the road to find the Odenite camp.

"Yes," Cinzia said quietly. "I suppose it could have."

"Will you translate with me tonight?"

The two had not translated anything from the Codex of Elwene since they had left the city of Kirlan. Since before Cinzia had made her bargain with Luceraf.

You fear translating, Luceraf hissed in Cinzia's ear.

But it had been long enough since she had translated. They needed to get back to work.

"Absolutely," Cinzia said, filled with resolve.

Jane smiled. "Wonderful. Let's get set up."

The Odenite camp was almost a town in itself; they had brought hundreds of followers on this journey, and many more had joined them on the way. Their tent was located toward the center of the bustling camp, alongside the tents belonging to the rest of the Oden family. It was larger than most, made of waxed canvas that did a fair job at keeping out the weather. The two women nodded at Alidar, the Prelate guard assigned to guard their tent. The translated pages of the Codex of Elwene were kept in their tent, and the two had agreed it was best not to risk losing them. A Prelate guard was posted at their tent at all hours of the day. Alidar's long face, patchy beard, and bright eyes were familiar, and Cinzia smiled at him as she ducked into the tent.

The inside was cozy, and barely high enough for them both to stand without stooping. Two cots lined two of the walls, while a small traveling desk stood opposite the entrance. Jane approached the desk quickly. Stacks of paper covered the ground around the desk as well as its surface, and Jane began to go through them.

Cinzia went around lighting candles. It was still light outside, but nightfall was imminent. And she wanted to do anything possible to avoid even touching the Nine Scriptures.

You're afraid because you think I'll learn something I shouldn't, Luceraf said, a hint of realization hanging in her voice.

Again, Cinzia refused to answer, but again, Luceraf was right.

Finally, after primping her pillows—she usually sat on one of the cots during translation—and changing into a more comfortable dress, Cinzia had nothing else to do to avoid what came next. Jane sat at the desk expectantly. With a sigh, Cinzia reached for the bag beneath her cot that housed the Nine Scriptures. The Codex was not light, but considering the pages themselves were made of metal, it was not as heavy as it should have been.

Cinzia heaved it onto her cot. She sat cross-legged, and ran her hand over the leather cover of the book before opening the Codex of Elwene on her lap. She marveled, as she always did, at the strange, dark metal pages as they shimmered in the candlelight, a wave of crimson often appearing to ripple across them.

"Very well," Jane said, a broad smile on her face. She was clearly excited to be back in the process again. "We were in the Book of Elwene, were we not?"

The Codex of Elwene, also called the Nine Scriptures, was a collection of scripture written by Canta's original Nine Disciples shortly after her Reification. The writings had been compiled and abridged by a woman named Elwene, and her words served as a coda for the collection. Despite her fear,

24

Cinzia was curious to see Elwene's commentary.

"We were," Cinzia said, scanning the pages. Odd. She had gotten used to opening the book directly to the spot where they had most recently left off, but right now she was having trouble finding her place.

"Cinzia?"

"I..."

Cinzia did not know exactly how her ability to translate worked; the Codex was written in Old Khalic, a dead language that no one understood anymore. The characters and words appeared as strange symbols and patterns etched into the metal. Cinzia did not speak or understand Old Khalic, but over the past year, she had been able to discern what the symbols meant. If she simply read through the Codex, she could read uninterrupted, as if the book were written in Rodenese. But if she examined any word or character too closely, it blurred back into Old Khalic dizzyingly.

But now, as she looked at the words on the pages of the Nine Scriptures, Cinzia had absolutely no idea what they said. She could not read them at all.

"Jane," Cinzia said, a lump forming in her throat. As she turned the pages, she realized she was shaking.

She had been unable to translate once before; it was the first night she had spent in Izet. The night Azael had possessed Kovac, and Cinzia had been forced to kill her own Goddessguard. Her old friend.

She feared, now, that at any moment something similar would happen. A Daemon might possess Jane, or Alidar, still standing guard outside. For all she knew, Azael might descend from the heavens himself.

Luceraf's laughter echoed inside Cinzia's skull.

"Something is wrong," Cinzia whispered.

"What is it? Can't you translate?"

Cinzia shook her head. "No," she said softly. "I do not think I can."

It's because of me, Luceraf sneered. *You've figured that out by now, haven't you? Took you long enough.*

"I am sorry, Jane," Cinzia said. Sorrow pierced her. She did not belong with the Denomination. She could no longer translate; her place in the Church of Canta was lost now, too.

If she did not have either of those things, what was left for her?

Without another word, Cinzia rose and swept out of the tent, not sure where she would go.

3

Odenite Camp, East of Triah

As THE SUN CREPT lower on the horizon, the camp lit up with the friendly glow of cooking fires, and people bustled from one to the other exchanging meals and stories. Astrid sat alone at one of the fires with her feet up, sharpening a dagger. The slow slide of the whetstone against the blade soothed her. She felt the graininess of each movement, the way the vibrations moved up her arm, and she lost herself in the motion until a voice brought her out of it.

"Hello there."

Astrid looked up to find a family of five standing at her fire. The children watched her wide-eyed with awe; the father had a simple grin on his face.

"Astrid, is it?" the father went on. "I have heard much about you."

Astrid focused on sharpening her blade. She made no effort to hide her frown. The Odenites had started to recognize her more, lately. While she had to imagine most of them suspected something strange about her—a girl of nine or so, occupied with fighting and sharpening weapons was far from normal—there had yet to be any talk of vampires, thankfully. She had been around people she thought would accept her before, when they found out. It almost never ended well. Knot, Cinzia, and even Jane, to a lesser extent, were rare exceptions to the rule.

"Well, I hope you don't mind if my family and I join you."

27

He sat down at the fire, and Astrid's head snapped up, a scowl on her face.

"I am Jusef," he said, still smiling at her. Idiot.

She ignored his outstretched hand, but Jusef seemed not to mind. He nodded to the woman with him, then to his children— two boys and a girl. "This is Umia. And these are our children, Daves, Jonef, and Hild. Hild is about your age, I think."

Hild was actually taller than Astrid by just a bit, but the man was right: she looked to be in her ninth summer, give or take. The girl smiled at Astrid shyly.

Astrid turned back to sharpening her dagger without a word. She was vaguely aware of Jusef and Umia exchanging a glance. But instead of speaking further, Umia sat down near Astrid and pulled out an item of clothing that needed mending. She quietly worked on the garment, head down, while her husband prepared food for their children.

Astrid stopped the movement of the whetstone. Her dagger would be sharp enough, now, and the sun was getting low.

"What do you think you're doing?" Astrid asked.

Umia didn't look up from her sewing. "Warming ourselves by your fire," she said quietly.

"Out of all the fires in the camp, you choose mine?" Astrid asked. "That either makes you stupid, or…" *Or you have some other agenda.* Astrid doubted it was the latter; this family seemed just strange enough to be normal. If these two adults had brought children along with something nefarious in mind, Astrid was quite capable of tearing them to pieces. But she did not get that impression. Jusef was helping Hild hold a frying pan over the fire. The little girl was smiling, her father's hand on her back. Astrid immediately looked away.

"Jusef is not the brightest star in the sky, I'll admit that."

The woman glanced at her husband with an affectionate grin, and Astrid had to stop herself from giggling.

Jusef scoffed from across the fire. "Least you could do is save that kind of talk until the children are asleep." But there was a smile on his face, too, and the children giggled as he said it, and Astrid hated the way this family made her feel at ease.

"But I don't see how we are stupid for sitting with you," Umia continued. "We are grateful for all you have done for us. We watched you lead the Prelates at Harmoth; we saw you fight those monsters that attacked outside of Kirlan. You saved Jusef's life, that night. He was by the central fire when it happened."

Astrid had heard enough. She hadn't done any of those things for the praise of mortals. Umia's words only made her more uncomfortable.

Astrid felt Umia's hand on her shoulder. "Look, we know you aren't like other children. But we want to say that... whatever it is about you, whatever is different, that's all right. I'm grateful for it, actually. We wouldn't be here without you."

If you knew I'd kill you and eat you as soon as look at you, I don't think you'd feel the same way.

Astrid shrugged out of the woman's touch.

"I'm not doing this," was all she said. She got up and left.

Back in the tent she shared with Knot, Astrid wished, again, that he had taken her to Triah with him. But the People's Parliament had given leave for only specific Odenites to enter the city, and Astrid was not among them. Any attempt to get a nine-year-old girl on such a list would be met with high suspicion, at best.

But still. She was *bored*.

Not to mention the fact that Cinzia and Jane had already returned. She had stopped by their tent to check, now that the sun had set. Astrid had half a mind to sneak into the city on her own—easily done at night—and find out exactly what Knot was up to, alone in the city, but she had refrained. Knot could take care of himself.

That didn't make the waiting any easier, though.

Finally, Astrid heard movement outside her tent.

"About time, nomad," she muttered. She jumped up, but froze the moment her tent flap opened.

Eerie red light poured into the small tent. Astrid frowned. "Trave, you need to be less sneaky about visiting me. I might accidentally kill you one of these days."

But the tall figure that stepped into her tent was not Trave. Instead, in the dim light of the single candle that lit her tent, strode Olin Cabral. He'd cut his blonde hair short once again, but his tall, muscular build, and abnormal beauty—the hard lines of his jaw and the way his skin seemed to glow—gave him away.

Astrid instinctively took a step back. Her mind raced through her options. She could tear through the back of her tent if she needed to. But that might slow her down too much, and Cabral was faster than her. And if he chased her through the camp itself, even if the Odenites wanted to help her, there was not much they could do to help against a vampire like Cabral. He was far too strong and too fast for any of them, especially at night. Cabral probably *wanted* Astrid to run. He would love to kill a few others in addition to killing her.

"Cabral," Astrid said, taking the only option that seemed reasonable in the moment, "what brings you to my humble tent?"

Cabral smiled, but his eyes remained the same: dead red lights, staring straight at her. "You, my dear Astrid," Cabral said, his voice low. "I'd like to say I've missed you, but… well, the truth is I've been rather peeved. The attack that you and that castrated fool Trave perpetrated on my tower-house was most unwelcome. Some way to show your gratitude for all I have done for you both."

Cabral might be alone. Astrid and Trave had killed his latest crop of Fangs, but a vampire like Cabral always had more followers. He could have gathered them to make his approach to her, if he did not want to take any chances. Outside of her tent, Astrid heard nothing.

She hoped Knot would not return for some time. He could not help her in a fight against full vampires at night; no one in the Odenite camp could, with the exception of Jane if she was filled to the brim with Canta's power, or Cinzia, if Luceraf chose to empower her with strength again. But their powers were unreliable. Astrid was on her own. Even Trave, who was in the camp somewhere, could not stand against Cabral. Astrid had seen him try, and fail, too many times.

"What do you want?" Astrid asked again.

Cabral stared at her, unmoving. "Isn't it obvious? I want you, Astrid."

Astrid shook her head. "There are powerful people in this camp. People who could defeat even you."

"Even if I did believe you," Cabral said, "how would such people discover me? Your camp has no real defenses. Sneaking into it was as simple a thing as I've ever done. No, my dear Astrid, I don't believe anyone will come for you." He shrugged. "And if someone does, I'll just kill them."

He lunged at her, and Astrid shot away. At night, she could run many times faster than a human, and she tore through the cloth at the back of the tent easily with her claws. She burst out into the night, her green eyes glowing—and something rammed into her from the side.

Astrid tumbled into the dirt, rolling a dozen rods, miraculously missing the tents around hers.

Don't wake up, Astrid pled to the unsuspecting Odenites, all likely sleeping around her. *Don't come out to see what is happening.*

As she got to her feet, the form that had tackled her rose, too, its eyes glowing red. This one was tall, taller than most humans or vampires Astrid had seen, and thin, its limbs long and wiry. Her heart sank. If Cabral had been alone, she might've had the smallest chance of escaping him.

Another red glow appeared over her shoulder. She turned too slowly, and a blow knocked her to the ground. "You're coming with us, Astrid," she heard Cabral say, as if from far away. "Do us a favor, and come without a fight." As she struggled to lift her head, another blow fell, and she sank into blackness.

4

Triah

KNOT HAD NEVER BEEN in Triah before, but, as he'd told Cinzia, some of the sifts that had formed him had lived here all their lives—most significantly Lathe, the Nazaniin whose body he now inhabited. Lathe would have known the city like the back of his hand, so Knot let his instincts take over. It had worked in the past: In Navone, he'd come across a network of people Lathe had used—a guard captain and an alchemist among others. In Tir, he'd found an inn where Lathe had contacts and a safebox. He hoped to find something like that now, in Triah.

This city had been Lathe's home, after all.

Not long ago, when he'd been captured by the Black Matron, and when Lathe's sift had attempted to steal back this body, he'd had a revelation, of sorts: a vision while he was trapped in the Void—he had seen Winter, the wife he'd thought dead, fighting—winning—a battle. She was a *leader*. Soon afterward on the road to Triah, word had reached him of a woman leading a tiellan force against humans, and of a series of battles that had been fought. Grand Marshal Riccan Carrieri had been present for the last one, and the story went that he had defeated the tiellan woman and her forces. But now the tiellans had crowned her their queen. The Chaos Queen, people were calling her. He could only guess that she might be Winter.

How Winter had survived the collapse of the dome in Izet,

33

and become involved with this tiellan rebellion, Knot could not guess, and how she could possibly have become their queen, he could not fathom. She'd not been the type to seek out power. All of it, however—the vision in the Void and the rumors of a Chaos Queen psimancer over the tiellans—was enough to give him hope that she was alive.

Now, he just needed more information, something Triah had in abundance.

The inner city of Triah at night was unlike anything Knot had ever seen. And yet, it felt familiar to him, as if he'd seen it countless times before. Whereas most cities shut down after dusk, with only a few shadier business transactions happening at night, this city was different.

At night, Triah came alive.

Triah was a particularly beautiful sight at night when viewed from the cliffs that overlooked the valley. The inner city consisted of the first fifty concentric circles or so that surrounded the Trinacrya at the city's center. It was a swathe of metropolis larger than most cities themselves, but that only made up a third of the greater area of Triah. Ring after ring of oil lights illuminated the inner city, like a field of stars right there on the Sfaera.

Knot walked with the confidence of a local, filled with a knowledge that was not his own. Where he walked now, for example, along the Radial Road between the Ninth and Fourteenth Circles, was a lively spot, full of tea houses, inns, and shops. The students of the Citadel, their classes over for the day, were just beginning to gather. Knot had a vague memory of coming here as a student, drinking into the early hours of the morning.

Not his memory, though. Lathe's, most likely. Knot pulled

his cloak down further over his face; it would not do to be recognized as Lathe before he got his bearings.

Knot left the Radial Road and moved south along the Ninth Circle into Little Alizia.

He walked past bath houses and meditation centers, Alizian restaurants, and even a chop house—an Alizian specialty restaurant, where the chefs cooked meals directly in front of their patrons in a show of acrobatic cutlery.

He let his instincts guide him as best he could. He wanted to go someplace where his face would mean something, but not somewhere that the wrong people might recognize him. Such a thing was impossible to discern when his only guide was intuition, but he figured he'd best avoid the Trinacrya at the center of the city, and the Citadel most of all, where the Nazaniin had their base. While his only hope for real information might indeed be the Nazaniin, he was loath to contact them. He'd thought his business with them had concluded at Harmoth, but if it meant helping Winter, he would contact them again.

The thought of her out there somewhere, alive, still brought on a host of competing emotions. Hope that he might see her again. Fear that she would hate him for leaving her for dead, and guilt that he had. He'd made the wrong choice, back in Roden. Or Astrid had made the wrong choice for him—and that had saved him. If Knot had stayed to try to find Winter's body in the ruins of the imperial dome of Izet, he would likely have been captured or killed.

But Astrid had taken that choice from him. Once, he thought, he might have asked her to meet him in Triah to help, or even as a protection against a possible Nazaniin confrontation. But right now he was still angry with her for telling him, back in Roden, that Winter was dead. What suffering had Winter gone through as a result of it—a tiellan injured in a nation that had banished all her kind on pain of death?

Eventually, he would let go of this anger—Canta knew he'd forgiven that damn girl for enough already—but tonight it lingered. Astrid would survive one night without him in the Odenite camp.

After some time wandering, Knot found himself in a bustling area on the south side of the Seventh Circle. Inns and elegant apartments dominated the area.

Walking along the street, seeing the lights and hearing the people inside the common rooms laughing, talking, shouting, hearing the music, it was all… it fit his mind like a glove. With any luck, he'd find an innkeeper that recognized him, that might even lead him to another safebox.

Knot stopped outside of one of the inns. This one, like many others, offered outside seating that spilled onto the cobbled street, even in the increasingly chilly fall weather. A faded sign above the entrance read *Swordpoint Inn*.

A woman drinking alone at one of the tables outside marked him immediately, and stood up.

"You," she said. While she wasn't quite drunk, Knot could tell she'd had more than one drink. She had the kind of beauty that took a moment to recognize, but once seen remained; haunting, inescapable. Her dark red hair was cut short to just above her shoulders, and sharp hazel eyes stared out at him from beneath a strong brow.

The more he looked at her, the more familiar she seemed to him. He had had dreams about this woman, he realized. Nothing specific, nothing concrete, but she'd been there, in his mind.

A low, haunting tune began to play from inside the inn—a lute, guitar, and violin joining together.

"You have a lot of nerve, coming here first," she said.

Knot had trouble reading her expression. In one moment, her eyes flashed in anger, but in the next they softened, shifting to something like affection or concern.

"Sorry," Knot said, unsure what else to say.

"Damn right you're sorry," she breathed. Knot caught more than a hint of alcohol. "He'll know you've come here."

She looked down the curving street, then back into the inn, then up at the windows above them.

Knot frowned. Either this woman was mad, or they were both in danger.

"Come with me," she said, grabbing his arm.

Knot hesitated. Just because he recognized this woman from his dreams did not mean she had his best interests at heart. She could be leading him into a trap. She pulled on him in an effort to get him to come with her, but Knot stood his ground, not budging.

The woman rolled her eyes. "Look," she said, "I know you don't know who I am. I know you probably don't even recognize me, but—"

Before finishing her sentence, the woman twisted Knot's arm, using his weight against him to slam him face first into the wall. Knot reacted quickly, stamping down on her foot with his own and then shoving backwards. He wrenched his arm around and tore it from her grasp, but she was already coming after him.

She was *quick*, almost as fast as a vampire, but her eyes would have given her away by now. Astrid had explained to him that while a vampire could keep up its glamour under normal circumstances, it was almost impossible to do while fighting or doing anything that took a level of concentration.

Knot blocked a jab, and then she had somehow swept

37

his legs out from under him. As quickly as Knot moved, this woman moved quicker. He hit the ground hard on his back and all the air rushed out of him. She was on top of him before he could move, a dagger point at his throat.

"Er... Sirana, is everything all right?"

Sirana. Knot knew that name, it echoed within him, but he also *knew* it. A member of the Triad—the lead body of the Nazaniin, the guild of assassins and intellectuals that practically ran the Sfaera.

Knot swore under his breath. So much for avoiding them.

He shifted his eyes to see the innkeeper staring at them, wide-eyed.

"Is that—"

"It's no one," the woman, Sirana, said quickly. Then, down at Knot, "You would have known better than to go up against me before. Now get up, and *come with me.*" She hoisted Knot up, and Knot let himself be led. Wasn't much else he could do with a dagger at his throat.

"Sirana..."

"I'll pay for the damage, Fenton."

Sirana directed Knot away from the inn, the knife digging into his back now as she walked closely behind him.

"Go where I tell you to go," she hissed in his ear.

Knot had no choice but to obey.

"You're not taking me to the Citadel," Knot said after they turned down a side street, headed toward the Eighth Circle.

"Of course I'm not," Sirana said. "I'm not taking you to him. Not yet."

Not yet. What other use could this woman have for him?

Lamps lit the way as she eventually led him to the entrance

of an apartment on the Eighth Circle. The building was tall, at least three stories, made of stone and wood.

Sirana pressed the dagger deeper into Knot's back, forcing him up the steps until they were standing before a wooden door.

"I know this house. There's an anteroom just past this door, with a painting in it," Knot said. He knew this place in the same way he knew the height of Triah's three sets of walls, or the distance between the Citadel and the Parliament building, or that he could move at an all-out sprint for just under three minutes before he collapsed. "A painting of Cranen's Bridge—by a woman named Hracen, I think." Cranen's Bridge spanned the river at its widest point in Triah—he could picture it in his head. Large stone pylons jutting into the water beneath it, and towers rising above.

Oddly Sirana did not respond. Instead Knot heard the jangling of keys, and for a moment considered making a move while Sirana fumbled with them. But he knew this place. He knew *her*.

Sirana opened the door, and they walked into the anteroom.

In the light from the street, Knot saw the painting hanging on the wall to his right. He felt a curious sense of displacement at the sight of something he both had and hadn't seen before.

The door shut behind them, and Sirana secured it with several locks. As she stood up from her task their eyes met. The anteroom was not large; they stood within two paces of one another. Sirana closed the gap between them. He could feel her breath on his face, smell the strong but not unpleasant odor of it, her haunting beauty close, just fingers away. Had he not been too full of suspicion, had it not been for Winter, and Cinzia—bloody Cinzia, too, for Canta's sake—he might have bent to kiss her then and there. But he didn't. For a moment there was pain in the bright green of her gaze. Then the look was gone, and she swept past him and into the next room.

Knot followed her, knowing the next room would be the sitting room. Beyond that, a dining room. The stairs to his left went both up and down; down to the kitchens and servants' quarters, and up to an office and a training room of sorts—with weapons, obstacles, and a sparring zone—and then up again to the bedrooms.

"Sit," Sirana said as she walked into the sitting room, toward a table at one end and a number of glass containers. "I'm sure you'll want a drink."

Knot recognized all of it, and yet none of it looked familiar. It was an impossible contradiction, one that almost made him nauseous. He took several deep breaths before he responded.

"Nothing to drink." He sat in one of the chairs, a large stuffed leather piece that was surprisingly comfortable. "Thank you," he added, for some reason feeling bad that it came as an afterthought.

Sirana sighed, pouring herself a drink anyway. "You don't drink, then?" she asked. "Or you just don't want to right now?"

"I avoid it," Knot said. Always had, at least since he awoke in Pranna. It clouded his senses, and he could not think of a single circumstance where he wanted such a thing.

"Let me guess," Sirana said, taking a sip of Cordonat. "It clouds your senses?"

Knot stared at her. It took effort to stop his eyes from widening.

"You used to say that all of the time," she said. "But, then again, it didn't stop you then. Things change, I suppose."

"You knew Lathe," Knot said.

Sirana laughed, but the sound was harrowing. She masked a great deal of pain.

"Yes," she said quietly, after a moment. "I knew Lathe."

They sat in silence for a moment. Knot figured it best to give this woman time; she did not seem to mean him harm, at least not yet. She had removed the threat of the dagger. Other threats might be lurking elsewhere, but Knot had not sensed any. As far as he could tell, the two of them were alone in the apartment.

"That was always your chair," Sirana said, nodding at the chair in which Knot had sat. She moved to another nearby. The two were angled toward one another. "This was mine. Do you remember that?"

Knot shook his head. "I..."

"You remembered the painting," Sirana said. "You sat in your chair."

"I remember some things, like the painting," Knot said. "And other things about this place. Physical, tangible, visual things. Other things are instinctual. Sitting in this chair might be one of them. Finding you at that inn—"

"We were regulars there," Sirana said.

"Those things are intuitive. Wouldn't garner meaning from them, if I were you."

Sirana took another sip, then put the glass down on a small table next to her chair. She leaned forward, peering at Knot's face.

"You wouldn't garner meaning from them, if you were me," she repeated.

Knot did not say anything, but let her look at him. She was having more and more of a difficult time hiding the pain in her eyes, on her face. The way she referred to him... the fact that they both had chairs in this room. The fact that Knot knew the upper bedroom contained only one large, comfortable bed told him what he needed to know.

After a moment, Sirana sat back, wiping her face with one sleeve.

"*Are you him?*"

Knot shook his head. Best get it over with quickly. "You know I'm not."

"You sure as Oblivion don't talk like him. But he's inside you, somewhere?"

It was more than that, Knot knew. Lathe had tried to take over his body again, months ago, in league with the Daemon Bazlamit. But, when Lathe realized what that meant, what it would mean being Bazlamit's thrall, he'd conceded his body back to Knot.

"In a way."

Sirana shook her head. She picked up her glass with one hand, while the other began to trace patterns on the arm of her chair.

"I could take you back to the Heart of the Void," Sirana said. "We would… help you. We could find a way to bring him back."

"You could do that," Knot said, the hairs rising on the back of his head. If Sirana was truly in the Triad, she was a powerful psimancer. The physical abilities she'd demonstrated at the entrance to the Swordpoint Inn—where, half-drunk, she had gotten the best of Knot—were only the beginning of her abilities. If she wanted to subdue him, she could. He might not be able to stop her.

No way in Oblivion he would go back there, though. Not like that. He had a distinct impression her use of the word "help" meant something more like "experiment on," or "Tinker with," and he had no interest in that.

"Relax," Sirana said, her eyes hooded. "I won't be doing that. You're too valuable as you are."

Knot frowned, but said nothing. Wyle had already taken the information they needed from him about what happened in Roden. Other than that, there were only two reasons Knot could fathom why the Nazaniin would find him valuable. The first, of course, was his connection with Jane and, to a lesser extent, Cinzia. If they had contact with him, they had contact with the leaders of the Church of Canta. While the Church was new, and clearly an enemy in the Denomination's eyes, they could prove valuable allies in certain circumstances.

The other was his wife, Danica Winter Cordier—if she really had become the leader he thought she had.

The Nazaniin might want to use Knot to get to the Chaos Queen. If that really was their plan, they might be in for a rude surprise. Knot was not sure Winter would want to see him at all.

"My hair is longer, you know," Sirana said, staring into her glass. "You would have noticed that if… if you were you. I always kept it short. The entire time you knew me."

Sirana clearly had other things on her mind than Winter and the Odenites. Knot struggled between a desire to find out more about Winter, and what, if anything, he might owe this woman.

"So we were together, before?" he prompted.

"Married."

Married. Of course. *Join the club,* he thought, though the humor of it was lost on him. His relationships were turning out to be more complicated than all nine sifts in his body combined.

"Five and a half years. Or at least it had been five and a half years the night I heard about your death. Now, I suppose it's been about eight."

"I'm not—"

"I know you're not, but you are for *me*, do you understand that? I can't look at you and see anyone but him. For Canta's sake, you *are* him. It's silly, he's in there somewhere, just out of my reach."

He's dead, Knot wanted to say. But he couldn't bring himself to say it. And it wasn't, technically, the truth.

"I'm sorry."

"We married late. I was twenty-seven, you were twenty-six. Far later than most people marry these days. Of course, in our line of work, marriages don't happen. We were an anomaly." Sirana chuckled, but this time the sound wasn't quite as sad. "People laughed at us. Other Nazaniin agents. Kosarin himself. They all thought we'd gone mad. But… we didn't care. It wasn't a normal life, but neither of us cared for normal. We just wanted to be together. That's it. And for a while, we were."

Knot tensed as Sirana's arm snapped up. She threw her glass across the room, and it burst into hundreds of pieces as it shattered against the far wall.

"And then we weren't."

She looked away from him. Knot remained silent and still. He felt pain, deep in his chest, for what had happened to this woman, and to Lathe, and he felt sorrow for his part in it. He wondered how much of those feelings were his own, and how much were echoes of someone else.

But he couldn't say anything like that, not here, not now. He knew instinctively, just as he knew the layout of Triah, that it would only make things worse.

After what seemed a long time, Sirana stood. Her face had returned to an expressionless mask. Her eyes were dry. Knot stood, and she finally met his eyes again.

"One of our agents will approach you soon," she said. "He's been tasked with befriending you. I was not joking when I said you were valuable, and we want to be connected to you. I suggest you let it happen. We have nothing planned that would harm you."

"And when those plans change?"

"Then you'll know."

"I have interests of my own," Knot said. "You said I'm valuable. I would trade information for my utility."

Sirana waved a hand, and turned back to the small table that contained the alcohol. She poured herself another drink.

"Work that out with our agent," she said. "You'll know when he contacts you."

That, at least, was progress.

Knot hesitated, not sure what to do next. He wanted to leave, but he did not want to leave this woman alone, either. Seeing her in pain hurt him, too. He wanted to help her.

"Our business is done here," Sirana said, without turning to look at him. "You know your way out."

Knot did and, silently, he took it.

5

The Void

KALI WAITED IN THE VOID, regarding without love the tiny, colorful, twinkling lights that speckled the darkness like stars in the night sky. Each sparkling light represented someone on the Sfaera, though most people lived their whole lives without being aware of this plane of existence. Psimancers like Kali and her old student Winter—and other, more sinister beings— knew better.

Kali waited in the Void, and then, finally, after what seemed like years but in reality had only been a few weeks, the Void changed.

Anticipation tugged at Kali's chest.

Winter's presence on this plane was different to any other. Instead of a tiny point of light, she was a great dark burning *absence*. She did not give off light, but rather drew it to her, consuming it. Kali had been trapped in the Void for almost a year and she still didn't understand it.

Canta's bloody bones, had it really been that long?

Slowly, the dark star shifted before her, becoming the outline of a young woman. Winter had changed since Kali first met her, in more ways than one. Where she had once been thin, her tiellan physique almost frail, she now had the lean, muscled body of a trained fighter. The tiellan had begun as Kali's student, but Kali could not help but wonder who was more powerful now. Psimantically, and physically. Kali yearned to pick up a sword and gauge the other's skill. But such things were impossible in the Void.

Winter's shade solidified into a woman with long black hair, one side of it braided tightly above one ear. Large black eyes. Her garments of black cloth and leather were expertly tailored to both fit well and allow for full range of movement. Kali wondered if the clothing existed in the physical plane, or if these were just what Winter would have liked to wear. There was such a thing as vanity in even the greatest psimancer, after all.

"You're here," Winter said.

Kali snorted. "You thought I'd be elsewhere?"

"I don't think of you at all anymore. What is it you want, Kali?"

It took every ounce of discipline Kali had to not let her rage at the barb show.

"You asked me to find your tiellan psimancers," Kali said. "The ones who stole your frost. I can tell you their location."

Winter showed no sign of surprise or eagerness, though Kali knew how much she wanted to catch Mazille. *Goddess, she's learning too much too quickly.*

"If you know," Winter said after a moment, "Then tell me."

Kali frowned. "Stop the act with me, girl. You may have learned a few things, moved up a bit in the Sfaera, but this is the Void. This is *me*. You won't get this for free."

Winter shrugged. "I have enough *faltira*, for now. If you want to share Mazille's location with me, do it. If not, I have more important matters to attend to."

More important matters? Who in Oblivion did this girl think she was?

"I didn't come into the Void for you," Winter said, "and

47

my other business can wait." The moment Winter's projection began to fade, Kali took an unthinking step forward.

"Wait," she said sharply, cursing how desperate she sounded. Winter had to be bluffing; Kali could not believe her addiction had been curbed enough that she didn't care about the stash of frost that had been stolen from her.

But Kali *was* desperate. She could not wait any longer.

"I'll tell you the location. I'll even help you get your frost back. But I need something from you."

Winter's form resolidified. "What do you want from me, Kali?"

Winter knew very well what Kali wanted, but apparently she was going to make her say it.

"I want to get out," Kali said. "I want to live again."

"And you think I can help you with this?"

"I know you can. You're the key to my freedom, Winter. In Izet—"

"In Izet you used me."

"And you attacked me," Kali snapped. "If you don't think that's how the Sfaera works, you have more learning to do."

"How exactly do you think I can help you leave the Sfaera, Kali? How do you expect me to help you 'live again'?"

Had she still held physical form, Kali would have taken a deep breath. She had thought this through time and time again.

"In Izet, I used one of your acumenic *tendra* to leave. In my previous attempts, acumenic *tendra* have always been key. But I've never had a lacuna prepared for me. So I'll need two things: I'll need your permission to interact with your acumenic *tendra*, and I'll need you to blot someone for me. Prepare them."

"You want me to kill someone for you."

"Oh please," Kali said, rolling her eyes. "You kill people all

48

the time. It would be a small matter to make one into a lacuna for me."

Winter did not respond, and for a moment Kali feared she would leave without another word. But then, Winter looked up, her black eyes meeting Kali's.

"I have been studying *rihnemin* lately. Every type of *rihnemin* I can get my hands on. Or my *tendra*, more accurately."

Kali blinked, unsure of the reason behind this change in subject. Winter had used a *rihnemin* in the battle Kali had shown to Knot. How, or to what end, she had no idea. She had very little way to contact or view the outside world, but she burned to know what connection the *rihnemin* might have with psimancy. Her fellow Nazaniin had guessed there might be a connection, but had found none in their experiments. How a talented but inexperienced psimancer like Winter had succeeded, Kali could not guess.

"I believe each *rihnemin* was created for a purpose. A firestone, an earthstone, a mindstone, and others. I think I have found a traveling stone, not too distant from Adimora. If it does what I think it does, I can use that to get to Mazille and her band as quickly as possible."

Kali stared at Winter, speechless and suspicious. What could Winter hope to gain by telling her this?

"You will tell me the thieves' location first," Winter said. "I will go there and destroy them, and you will help, if you can. We will reclaim my *faltira*. Afterward, I will attempt what you ask."

So Winter hadn't changed after all. Relief flooded through Kali, but she kept her feelings hidden. She had learned to do such a thing before Winter was born.

"I agree to your terms," she said, "but I must have your word that afterward you will help me."

Winter nodded, once. "You have my word, then. After I've killed Mazille and her band, and taken back my frost, with your help, I will provide what you need."

This time, Kali allowed herself a smile. "Good," she said. "Good. They are not so far from Adimora as I would have run, were I them. Fortunate for you."

"Show me," Winter said.

Together, they rushed through the Void to the small cluster of lights Kali had found.

Her salvation.

6

Adimora

THE SUN CREPT OVER the horizon as Winter rode out from Adimora. She traveled with those closest to her: Urstadt and Selldor, and Rorie, the clanswoman who had first brought them into Adimora, who still served as her advisor when it came to the unfamiliar laws and culture of the clans.

An autumn chill swept across the eastern plains, stirring a memory of her childhood village, Pranna, on the north coast. It had always been cold there, even on the warmest of summer days. As the river valley fell behind them, the flatness of the plains no longer disturbed her as they used to. She was beginning to feel at home in this strange land, even though she knew she was not, and would likely never be.

"You going to tell us where we're going yet, Your Majesty?" Selldor asked, pushing his horse alongside Winter's.

"I already have."

"To find Mazille, I gathered that much, but… what makes you think they are north of the city?"

"We're going north," Winter said, "To the travelstone."

"What's that?"

"You'll see when we get there."

Selldor glanced back at Urstadt and Rorie, who rode some way behind them, deep in conversation. "It's just us, Your Majesty. If you'll forgive me saying, ain't no need to be so cryptic."

He was right, of course. All three of them had proven their loyalty many times over.

"The travelstone is a *rihnemin*," she explained. "Like the one I used at the Battle of the Rihnemin; I believe you've heard me call that one the firestone." Since her use of the firestone, she had felt a draw toward every *rihnemin* she came within a certain proximity of, and had discovered the purpose of many of them, as she had told Kali.

The purpose of the immense *rihnemin* in Adimora itself still eluded her. No matter how many times she tried accessing it with her *tendra*, or in what combinations, the stone did not respond. The myriad runes she could touch lit up, but she could awake none of the power it must surely contain. Most of the stone was buried underground. Perhaps there were runes hidden by dirt, and without access to them it was defunct.

"Aye," Selldor said slowly, "so this one is for..."

"Traveling."

"In what way?"

"I'll show you," Winter said. Or she hoped she could show them. She'd only tried it once, on her last journey up here. Winter had ridden alone to visit the *rihnemin* she'd sensed, only to find herself back in her quarters in Adimora as soon as she'd accessed the power. The dangers of a wandering mind and a grumbling stomach, perhaps. Her euphoria at the swift journey had been tempered by the trouble she'd had maneuvering her indignant mare out of her cramped tent. But at least that proved she could bring more than just herself when she used the travelstone.

"And you're going to use this stone to... travel us all?" Rorie asked. Winter glanced round and was surprised to see she and Urstadt had ridden closer.

"To transport us all, yes," Winter said. *Hopefully*. It would be embarrassing if it didn't work, which was why she hadn't brought much of an audience. If it did work, the stone would take them to the place Kali had told her about: a forest outside the city of Darbon.

The return trip would take a week, unfortunately, unless Winter stumbled upon another travelstone near Darbon. She wasn't counting on it.

It took them less than an hour to get to the *rihnemin* Winter sought, a relic of the ancient tiellan civilization. The stones were scattered across the plains more commonly than the rest of Khale, it seemed to Winter. She had found a good half-dozen within a day's ride of Adimora alone. As the stone appeared in the distance, she took a *faltira* crystal. In moments, power flowed through her, as did the anticipation of what she was about to attempt.

The travelstone stood about as tall as she did when riding her horse; it was as wide as she could stretch out her arms.

"Ain't that impressive," Selldor muttered. He made to dismount, but Winter stopped him.

"I thought the same when I first saw it." She nudged her horse alongside the stone, drawing a dagger. "Stay close to me; Urstadt by my side, Selldor and Rorie directly behind us."

They did as she asked. Winter slid the blade lightly along her palm, refusing to wince at the pain. She placed her bloodied hand on the stone. "This might feel strange," she warned. She only needed to use about thirty *tendra* to access every rune on the stone, and did so quickly, each one drawn to a different rune, each rune subsequently glowing a slightly different color. When she had connected with them all, the myriad of colors shifted to become a single, faintly glowing violet. The glow of this *rihnemin* seemed softer, more subtle than that of the firestone.

Her conscious thoughts had not directed the fire on the day of the battle; she had never ordered it to attack the Outsider, and then the next, and so forth. It had just *happened*. Perhaps it had been powered by intention rather than thought.

She focused on the ache that arose within her whenever she thought of the stolen frost, and on the name of a city she had never been to: Darbon. The *rihnemin*'s violet glow pulsed, became a cloud that engulfed her and her horse and Urstadt and Selldor and Rorie and...

Winter blinked, the cloud fading. She stood in a very different place than the eastern plains. There was no *rihnemin* here, not that she could see.

But there was a city.

Winter moved as silently as she could between great trees that blocked the sun from view, leaves drifting lazily from the branches above in flakes of brown and orange.

"You are sure they are nearby?" Urstadt asked.

"I am sure."

You are sure they are nearby? Winter asked Kali.

Kali laughed. *I am sure.* Their ability to communicate while Kali was in the Void was improving; Winter did not know whether she liked that improvement. While it certainly made things easier, Winter could never be sure when Kali was there and when she wasn't, unless she cut Kali off completely.

Winter paid close attention to the ground beneath her, watching for unnatural disturbances in the leaves, broken branches and twigs from the smaller foliage, and other signs of recent passage. If she caught a trail, it would almost certainly be Mazille's. Assuming Kali was telling her the truth.

Don't forget your promise, Kali said.

I've given you my word. I'll get you what you need.

Winter crouched. "Here," she said quietly, pointing at broken and disturbed leaves. "People have passed through here recently."

This has to be them, Kali's voice echoed in Winter's head.

It bloody better be.

Winter held up one hand, and they all stopped. Voices came faintly to them on the breeze. They were in the right place.

Just the thought of regaining her *faltira* hoard thrilled her. The days of withdrawal she'd gone through after the theft, before she'd been able to procure more, had been almost unbearable.

The band crept through the leaves until they came upon a group in a clearing gathered around the remains of charred, extinguished fire. Mazille, a large tiellan woman, sat at the edge of the clearing, leaning against a tree trunk that was wider than Winter could reach with both arms outstretched. Her five fellow psimancers were still with her.

These are the six? Kali asked.

Yes. We've found them.

Suddenly, the youngest of the band—Vlak, hardly more than fifteen summers—stood sharply. He said something to the others, something Winter could not hear. Almost as one, the five moved toward Mazille at a word from her. Winter could hear the hysteria in their voices, high and tight.

Mazille was giving them frost. *Winter's* frost.

It was the last taste of *faltira* any of them would ever have.

One of them is a voyant.

Kali cursed in Winter's head. *You could have told me that earlier. If you're dealing with a voyant, you'll—*

I'll be fine.

Winter slipped another *faltira* crystal in her mouth and

almost immediately felt the drug's effects.

Their voyant has informed them we're here, Winter told Kali. *But I don't think he knows where we are, or what we're about to do.*

Be thankful for that. Means he isn't that powerful, or he hasn't learned to harness his power yet, at least. Apparently not all tiellans catch on as quickly as you do.

Winter motioned to her companions. They had agreed she would go in alone, first, and that they would only act as a backup, in case things went south for Winter.

She did not foresee that happening.

Kali's voice echoed in her head. *I hope you know what you're doing. You're my only ticket out of this place. If you die—*

Kali, Winter's thought was firm in her mind, and Kali stopped speaking. *If you really care about what happens to me, give me a moment of silence. Let me concentrate.*

Kali, blessedly, obeyed.

Winter stood from where she crouched in the foliage. One of the thieves spotted her almost immediately, shouting a warning to the others. Winter recognized him as Orsolya, one of the telenics. He and one of the others, Astasios, were siblings. She remembered their light brown, almost golden eyes.

Before the others could even turn to regard her, *tendra* burst from Winter. She sent ten *tendra* to each one of her enemies. Overkill—she needed only one or two for each person—but she would take no chances. And she wanted these people to witness her power.

She stripped them of their weapons first. The bows, then the daggers and swords in plain sight. They might have other weapons, and Winter would strip them of those as well, as the opportunities presented themselves. She sensed *tendra* moving toward her from each of the telenics: Mazille, Orsolya, and Astasios. The siblings attacked her with two each, while Mazille was able to summon more—seven that Winter could sense. Winter dedicated eleven of her own *tendra* exclusively to cutting off theirs at every turn, as Nash had taught her, breaking their hold on anything they came in contact with.

The acumens, Phares and Opal, attacked next. They were both older tiellans, Phares an old man with long silver hair, a stooped posture, and wrinkling skin; Opal stood at least a head taller than Winter, astoundingly tall for a tiellan woman, her limbs thin and wiry.

Winter felt the acumenic *tendra* slide toward her, nine in total, seeking to penetrate her mind.

Kali, Winter called.

I see them. I can handle nine tendra *from my end, no problem.* While telenic *tendra* had no manifestation in the Void, and both telenic and acumenic *tendra* were completely invisible in reality—Winter could sense where they were, but could not see them—acumenic *tendra* were visible in the Void. Winter could probably handle these *tendra* on her own, but she wanted to show as much strength as possible. The tiellan psimancers would likely not realize that someone else was helping Winter from the Void. They would think this was all her.

She wanted them to fear her as much as possible, before they died.

Do it, Winter ordered. *Your freedom depends on it, as you said.*

Winter lifted the psimancers from the ground, using their clothing to gain a hold. Telenic *tendra* could only interact with non-living objects, while acumenic *tendra* had the opposite limitation: they could only interact with the living.

She pinned each of her enemies against a tree.

For a moment, Winter's mind flashed back to Izet. She

had done something like this once before, on the orders of the Emperor Daval, then avatar of Azael. She had pinned a man against a wall, and had sent every weapon in the room at his vulnerable, helpless body.

Was she as much a monster as Daval ever was?

Winter shook the thought from her mind, and strode forward into the center of the clearing.

"Search the camp," she said. "Find my *faltira*." The moment she said it, Urstadt, Selldor, and Rorie slipped from their hiding places and moved past her to rummage in the belongings of the captives.

The psimancers struggled against Winter's *tendra*. The telenics tried to break her hold on them with their own, but Winter cut them off at every turn. It was as easy as swatting a child's hand away from a sweet roll before dinner.

"How did you find us?" Mazille asked, her voice strained. It could not be comfortable to be hanging by one's clothes.

No, Winter thought. *This will not do.* Not all of the tiellans could see her, so she moved several of them to different trees so they all were pinned within her field of vision. One of them, Vlak, cried out as he was violently moved through the air to a different tree.

That's better.

"Did you honestly think I wouldn't?" Winter asked.

She was met with silence. At least they weren't begging for their lives. That much was to their credit.

"No," Winter said slowly, answering her own question. "You always knew I would seek you out, eventually. You just didn't think I'd find you this quickly."

You have me to thank for that, Kali said softly.

If you want your freedom, you'll keep silent until this is through.

"You know what I want," Winter continued. "Where is the *faltira?*"

The captives said nothing.

Very well.

With one *tendra*, Winter took one of the daggers that she'd torn from a belt. Slowly, she sent it through the air until it hung, perfectly still, in front of one of young Vlak's eyes.

He reminds you of Lian.

Winter frowned. That voice was not Kali's. But she was not sure it was hers, either. But it was true; from the moment Winter had first seen Vlak in Adimora, she'd had that thought. The boy had light hair and light eyes, and a long, pensive face just like Lian.

It doesn't matter that he reminds me of Lian. I'll do what I have to do.

What are you talking about? Kali asked.

Winter ignored her. "Vlak will lose an eye, first. He'll lose more than that, the longer you refuse to speak to me. And when I'm through with him, I'll cut through the rest of you.

"The path you are on will not save the tiellan people," Mazille said.

Winter laughed. "I hardly think a thief cares about the tiellan plight."

"You think you are helping our people, but you are leading them to destruction."

The fake smile faded from Winter's face. "And why do you think this?"

"We *know* it," Vlak said. "I've seen the destruction of our people." He was staring wildly at the dagger, just a hair's breadth away from his eye. "At your hands."

Winter tutted. "You've 'seen' it? And I'm supposed to believe the word of a child?"

He reminds you of Lian.

"I'm a voyant," Vlak said.

"You've known you're a voyant for how long, now? At your age, it can't be more than a year. And you truly think you understand your powers, what your visions mean, at this stage?"

"That's all the time you've known you're a psimancer," Phares growled at her. His voice was low and rasping. "What makes you think you're any different than he?"

"I'm not," she said with a shrug. "I don't understand a hundredth of what I can do. But I understand enough to defeat the six of you, and that seems to settle a few things, in my mind. I'm the best hope our people have had in centuries at regaining some of their power."

"If you're our best hope, then we're doomed," Mazille said.

Winter was losing her patience, the stolen *faltira* still on her mind. And yet…

"Tell me your vision," Winter said. "We can confront it together."

"He'll only tell you if you promise to spare us," Mazille said, a mite too quickly.

Winter smiled. So that was it.

"That's your bargaining chip, then? This 'vision' you've seen?"

Mazille shifted in the *tendra* net. "If you really want to know how you can save our people, you'll spare us."

Urstadt approached Winter, a leather satchel in one hand. "Your Majesty."

Winter peered inside to see the satchel's contents. A few dozen *faltira* crystals. Each crystal was roughly the size of the last joint of a man's thumb, ranging in color from clear to crystal blue.

That was not enough. Not *nearly* enough.

"Your Majesty?" Mazille laughed. "So the rumors are true. The tiellans have made you their queen. Queen of *Chaos*. They'll have only themselves to blame."

Winter looked at Urstadt. "That's all you found?"

"That's all, Your Majesty."

Winter turned her gaze back to Mazille, eyes hooded. "Where is my *faltira*, Mazille?"

"That isn't it," she said, nodding at the satchel Urstadt held. "That's what we've procured for ourselves, separate from yours. We'll give the rest back to you, all of it that's left, but only if you let us go."

Winter's anger flared. "All of it that's *left*?"

"We've been using it, of course. Combined with what we've procured there, it might be close to what we took from you—"

"What you *stole*."

"Yes, what we stole from you. But you can't possibly have expected us not to use any of it."

Winter glared at Mazille. "Then you cannot possibly expect me not to take it back. If I can't have *faltira*, I'll settle for blood."

"If you—"

"Where is it?" Winter asked.

"If you let one of us go first, I'll—"

Winter wrenched the dagger away from Vlak. If the boy truly had seen something, it might be worth sparing his life. Everyone else, however, was expendable. She moved the dagger slowly until it hovered before Opal.

"You told me," Winter said, "when we first met in Adimora, that Opal had been with you the longest. She will be the first to go, unless you tell me where my *faltira* is. *Now*."

Mazille's eyes were wide and wild, now. "If you'd just—"

Winter did not have time for that. She shoved the dagger

straight into Opal's eye. The psimancers screamed as one.

Winter was aware of Urstadt shifting uncomfortably beside her, but she paid her general no mind.

"The location of my *faltira*," Winter said. She was already picking up another weapon, a sword, with a *tendra* and sending it toward the still-moaning Opal. "If I'm honest with you, I'm not sure she'll live," Winter said. "I can kill her now, quickly, if you like. Or let her die slowly. The choice is yours. Of course, either way, if you don't tell me where my *faltira* is, I'll just move on to the next one of you."

"Winter, *please*, let us go first," Mazille begged. *Begged*.

Winter shifted the sword over to Orsolya. She plunged the sword into the man's gut, and he writhed in pain.

What are you doing? Mazille will tell you where the faltira *is if you just let them go. You don't need this violence.*

Yes, you do, Kali responded. Winter cursed the woman again for being in her head. *They stole from you once. They will do it again, given the chance.*

So don't give them the chance.

"All right!" Mazille shouted, her head craned at an odd angle as she watched Orsolya in horror. "I'll tell you. I'll tell you where it is, but please don't hurt us any more."

"Give me a location, now," Winter said, as she lifted an arrow shaft with another *tendra* and left it hovering in front of Phares.

"It's buried," Mazille blurted, tears streaming down her face. "Not far from here. I can show you, I can—"

"You'll describe the exact location to us, and Urstadt will dig it up. When she comes back, and we know whether or not you're lying—"

"I'm not, bloody bones, I'm not!"

"—then we will decide our next course of action. Now, the location."

Mazille described, in panicked, choppy sentences, an area southwest of the hill on which they'd camped, near a boulder, by a particular tree. When Mazille had finished, Winter looked to Urstadt.

"That enough for you?"

"Yes, Your Majesty."

"Then go. Selldor, you may as well stay with me. I know you'll insist on it. Rorie, accompany Urstadt."

Selldor nodded, while Rorie followed Urstadt. The two picked up shovels from the camp on their way to the spot Mazille had described.

Winter turned back to the psimancers, still hanging by her *tendra*. Her *faltira* would wear out soon.

She looked at Vlak. They were probably lying about this vision the lad had experienced, but Winter needed to know for herself. She sent an acumenic *tendron* into the boy's mind.

The boy has no protection?

No, Kali replied. *An oversight on their part.*

Winter had learned the art of weaving protective webs around the minds of those she did not want delved by acumen spies. It was a complicated matter, involving creating a network of *tendra* around a person's sift in the Void. When dissolved, the ghost of what was left behind was enough to protect against all but the most powerful and direct acumenic onslaughts. Winter had practiced the skill until she became proficient.

Why had Opal or Phares not taken measures to protect Vlak?

* * *

She—Vlak—was alone, in a tent. Snow covered the ground and whipped through the open tent flap. Slowly, Vlak stood, and walked out into the cold.

The morning sun was low on the horizon, the sky clear, almost white. His tent was one of hundreds. Outside each one were the frozen bodies of tiellans, their skin mottled and frosted over. The oldest bodies had been picked over by scavengers before the cold set in. An eye missing here, a chunk of flesh from the cheek there, an arm ending in a mess of old brown blood and protruding bone somewhere else. Many of the corpses were far too small: children, babies, even. Others were old, crippled and shriveled long before the cold got a hold of them. Vlak's gaze didn't linger.

Bundled in furs, Vlak walked out of the camp. But the frozen graveyard did not end there.

Human and tiellan corpses, young soldiers both male and female, littered the snow-swept plain. These corpses, too, were frozen solid, just like the ones in the huge camp. Among the human and tiellan bodies were other carcasses, some Winter recognized—the Outsiders she had seen enter the Sfaera in Izet—and others she did not. Vlak looked on in horror at the monstrous bodies, twisted and frozen in the cold.

At this point, the vision shifted, swirling inward on itself and then exploding into a different scene.

Adimora. Or, it *was once* Adimora. Winter would not have recognized it if it weren't for the surrounding plains, the River Setso, the Eastmaw Mountains in the distance, and most of all the Spear of the Gods: the massive *rihnemin* at the very center. The city itself was gone. In its place was a massive crater, blackened death and smoking ruin, where the great underground city had once been. Only the Spear of the Gods remained, although it was no longer buried, but an obelisk the size of a mountain jutting up from the nadir of the crater.

Adimora, last stronghold of the tiellans, was gone.

Between the thousands of tiellan bodies at the frozen camp, and now the desolation that had once been Adimora, the tiellan race was no more.

And there was only one being alive who could bring this disaster about: Only the Chaos Queen could lead the entire tiellan race into such a battle as the first; and only the Chaos Queen could summon enough power to use a *rihnemin* with such destructive force.

Like the recoil of a whip, Winter snapped back into her own mind.

7

"THIS LOOKS LIKE THE PLACE." Rorie jammed her shovel into the ground.

Urstadt looked around silently. There was the tree the old woman had described, and the mid-sized boulder.

"Not sure we should've left her. You think she'll be all right?"

"The queen can handle herself," Urstadt said. *A little too well, perhaps.* Urstadt was not one to condemn the methods Winter had used in the clearing. She had hurt a lot of people in her lifetime, but the more she lived, the more she wondered how much of that, if any of it, had been necessary. The more she wondered what such acts had done to her, and more importantly to the people she'd hurt, that could not be undone.

"And Selldor is with her," Rorie said as she cleared the area of fallen leaves and dead branches and twigs. Urstadt had noticed that she talked to herself when apprehensive. "He's a strong fighter. The queen will be safe."

Selldor will not be able to help Winter if something goes wrong. Urstadt did not think any of them could, even herself. A single warrior could only do so much against a psimancer, and a group of them...

Winter knew what she was doing. Urstadt had to trust her queen.

Urstadt dug her shovel into the dirt next to Rorie's. "We'd

best find what we were sent here to get," she said. "So we can get back to the queen." Urstadt knew Winter's frost only lasted a quarter of an hour or so—its effects might have already faded. She could always take more, of course, but taking multiple doses consecutively was a risk.

A risk Winter never seemed to mind, but a risk nonetheless.

"Aye," Rorie said, pouring a shovelful of dirt out in a slowly growing pile. "Suppose you're right."

Together they dug until, not quite two rods down, Rorie's shovel struck something hard and hollow.

"Finally," she said.

Together they dug around what became clear was a wooden box, until they could lift it and set it on the ground near the pile of dirt. The box was light, but *faltira* was not a heavy substance. A brass lock hung from the latch.

Rorie growled, the sound low in her throat. "Bitch didn't say anything about a key."

Urstadt grabbed one of the shovels, and slammed the blade down onto the lock. It snapped off, and Urstadt crouched to lift the lid.

The box was empty.

Rorie swore again. "That ain't good."

Urstadt was already up, hefting her glaive.

"We're going back," Urstadt said. "Quietly. We don't know what we'll face."

Urstadt rushed back up the hill, as quietly as she could. For once, she was grateful she wasn't wearing her rose-gold armor.

People approaching, Kali whispered in Winter's head. *A few dozen, at least. You need to be ready.*

I will be, Winter replied.

Winter, they are almost here.

She had bound Mazille and the others, who were still alive, and had continued delving Vlak, revisiting his terrible vision again and again. But now Kali had brought her back to consciousness, she saw Vlak's eyes were blank. She tried reaching her acumenic *tendron* into the boy's mind again, but there was nothing there.

She'd blotted him; wiped his mind clean, erased everything that made him who he was and how he thought. Vlak was gone.

He reminded me so much of Lian.

Kali spoke. *Some of the approaching people are Nazaniin, Winter.*

Of course they were. *You waited long enough to tell me.*

I'm sorry, I wanted to be sure.

Winter swore. She reached for the *faltira* pouch at her belt. She would need—

The pouch was gone.

Winter looked down frantically, but it was nowhere to be seen. She looked back at Selldor.

"Where's—"

Selldor's lifeless body stared up at Winter, eyes wide in shock.

"Selldor, no," Winter whispered, crouching by the man who had been her friend, her first Ranger captain. Winter must have been so caught up in Vlak's vision, she had not noticed Mazille use her own tendra to take her frost—or murder her friend.

Behind her, Winter heard a laugh.

Slowly, she turned to face Mazille. "You wanted mercy for you and your group," Winter said. "It was something I might have given you, had you turned my frost over to me. But now—"

"You ain't in no position to make demands, my dear," Mazille interrupted. "It pains me that I've lost two, maybe three—Goddess knows what you've done to Vlak—people to get to this point, but here we are."

Winter, I can help you.

"What have you done?" Winter asked Mazille.

"We always knew you'd come after us, just as you said. The moment Vlak told us you were close, we sent word to the Nazaniin *cotir* in Darbon with the voidstone they gave us. We've already agreed to turn you over to them if they help us. We never wanted anything to do with the Nazaniin, but it'll be worth it to destroy you. You're no good, Winter. You've seen Vlak's vision. Ain't sure how you did it, but I can tell. You'll only bring death and destruction, my dear. We're just doing what's best for our people."

They're here, Winter. I can help you, but...

I have a lacuna for you. But you're not going to like it.

The tiellan *boy? I'm not going into a tiellan body, Winter. I—*

If you want this to happen, Winter said, *it has to happen now.*

Kali's eyes snapped open.

The sky was cloudy above, the air was cold, leaves fell to the ground around her, and she was bound to a tree. Kali looked down at herself. She now inhabited a thin, sinewy body, still ensconced in the smooth exterior of youth.

Winter stood before her, eyeing her critically—she looked every bit as she had in the Void, dressed in dark leathers, her black hair braided against both sides of her skull, while the top flowed out freely behind her in a much looser braid. And behind Winter, the Nazaniin *cotir* and their company were just cresting the hill.

What do you want me to do? Kali asked.

Find a way out of those bonds, first of all, Winter said. Their

69

acumenic connection was still there, despite Kali's recent transition. It was the same sort of connection she had had with Nash, what felt like an eternity ago.

Vlak, are you all right? Are you there?

Kali frowned. That voice was not hers, nor Winter's. Kali turned her head. Winter had already killed one of the acumens, but the other, the old man, was bound to a tree not far from her. He was looking at her, his eyes wide.

Vlak!

Yes, Kali responded. Best for the tiellans to think she was still the lad, if possible. Her voice would sound different, now—it was her voice, her *true* voice, that spoke from her sift, not the boy's—but she might be able to pass for a young tiellan lad. The connection she shared with the old tiellan acumen was different than the one she had with Winter; they would not be able to hear one another, and Kali could still effectively keep her communication with them separate. Kali's acumenic *tendra* connected her with Winter, while the tiellan's *tendra* connected him to Kali's body. The channels were different, but she still needed to be careful. The old man would be able to sense Kali's unguarded thoughts. Kali's decades of training as an acumen enabled her to keep the area of her sift the old tiellan acumancer occupied. But it would take effort.

I was in a dark place, Kali told the tiellan man. *I thought it was Oblivion. What is going on?*

She tried to keep her communication short. The less they heard from her, the better.

The cotir *has just arrived,* the old man said. *But our work is not done. We must subdue Winter, and Mazille thinks that may still be a challenge.*

Even with the cotir*'s help?*

70

The response was solemn. *You've seen her power, the destruction she'll bring to our people. We must stop her.*

The *cotir* approached Winter cautiously. Their soldiers hung back, weapons drawn and readied. She recognized Krasten, tall and thickset, despite his age, at the center of the three psimancers. His brown hair had turned gray, his dark brown face worn and weathered, but otherwise he was as Kali remembered him.

The two other psimancers who walked along either side of him were much younger, in their mid-twenties at the oldest: a woman, short with dark hair and a round, scarred face, and a young man, blonde, tall, and strong.

The soldiers behind them did not wear insignia of any kind—just leather armor, breastplates, and helmets, much of it lacquered black. The *cotir* had asked for a contingent of Nazaniin soldiers, then. Mercenaries paid for by the Nazaniin when a situation required more manpower than a *cotir* could reasonably offer. It was rare for them to be sent anywhere, let alone a location as remote as this.

Can you compel one of the soldiers to loose us from our bonds? Kali asked the old acumen. It was what she wanted to do, but she wanted to give this man the chance if there was any way she could still keep up the ruse of being on their side.

He hesitated before responding, and Kali knew she had made a mistake.

You know we don't compel people to do anything, the man said. *What has gotten into you, Vlak?*

Kali attempted a cover. *I'm afraid for my life*, she said. *What do you ex—?*

"Danica Winter Cordier, I presume," Krasten said, stopping a few rods away from Winter.

71

Winter's face was defiant. Krasten towered above Winter, head and shoulders and then some.

"You know me better as the Chaos Queen," Winter said. "Why don't you kneel?"

Kali could not help but feel a spike of pride at Winter's composure. As much rivalry as their relationship had contained, their connection was strong.

Krasten sniffed. "Kneeling is an archaic practice for the less civilized."

Kali barely stopped herself from scoffing. Krasten had always been pretentious, but this was ridiculous.

Krasten looked to Mazille. "You have her *faltira?*"

"I have it," Mazille said. "Both what we took from her, and what she brought today."

"Good," Krasten said. "We'll be taking that with us, along with her."

Mazille frowned. "That wasn't part of the deal. You said—"

"The deal has changed," Krasten said sharply. "I suggest you accept it."

"Then free us, at least," Mazille said. "My people need help."

Krasten glanced disdainfully at the dead acumen and telenic. Was this what she had looked like when she put on the airs of the typical Nazaniin agent? Kali made a mental note to be done with such theatrics. This level of arrogance did not become anyone.

"I think you can wait another few moments," Krasten said, "as we assess the situation."

Kali sighed. She had hoped she would not have to reveal her power just yet, but it seemed there was no choice. Krasten would surely sense her, but she had to take action.

As quickly as she could, Kali reached out an acumenic

tendron. She would need to make it happen quickly.

Winter's thoughts reached out. *Kali*, she called. *I did not put you in that body to do nothing. I need your help.* Now.

Working on it, Kali responded.

Krasten's head snapped around to stare at Kali—Kali, in Vlak's body.

"I thought you told me the young one was a voyant," he growled.

"He is," Mazille spluttered.

Kali broke into the mind of the young soldier that stood closest to them almost instantly. With acumency, there were a number of ways to go about convincing someone else to do something, from subtle methods to outright compulsion.

Kali had no time for subtlety.

Cut the ropes that tie me, Kali commanded.

Immediately, the man walked toward her.

Hurry, Kali urged.

He sprinted, drawing a knife. Kali could not say she felt completely confident, seeing this large soldier charge her, blade drawn. It had been more than a year since she had influenced anyone's mind in any real way with her psimancy. She half-wondered whether it would work.

"Soldier," Krasten said sharply. "Stand down."

Kali sensed Krasten's *tendron* snaking out to the fighter she'd snagged, but she cut it off immediately. She exhaled with relief as he slipped the dagger up through the ropes that held her, and sliced them effortlessly.

The old tiellan psimancer reached out to Kali. *Vlak, what is going on?*

Kali ignored him, focusing her attention on the soldier she had just compelled.

Thank you, Kali said to the soldier. *Now, protect me.* This much raw compulsion would soon obliterate his sift. He turned, raising his dagger between her and the *cotir*.

"Mazille," Krasten hissed. "What is this?"

Mazille blubbered a response, but she was clearly as confused as Krasten was.

Well done, Winter said. *What now?*

The male psimancer at Krasten's left unhooked two circular blades from his belt. He tossed them into the air in front of him, and the two blades dipped for a moment before being picked up by the man's *tendra*. Both flew directly toward Mazille.

The *cotir* would have their own connection through which Krasten relayed orders. That was one of the benefits of fighting with fellow psimancers; communication was usually clandestine and instantaneous. But that meant that Kali could not be sure what the telenic's orders actually were.

The female psimancer stepped toward Winter wielding a long curved Nazaniin blade. Krasten's eyes bored right into Kali.

"Release your hold on the soldier," Krasten said, "or we'll kill this excuse for a psimancer you call your leader."

Kali laughed on the inside. Krasten thought she was still with Mazille. That was good. She kept her face—Vlak's old face—scowling.

But Krasten, while pompous, was anything but a fool. Some of his pride, at least, was deserved. He looked from Kali, to Mazille, then to Winter.

"Canta's bloody bones. I'm too old for this shit. Kill them all."

Fear coursed through Kali's newfound veins. She had just found this body. She would not abandon it so easily.

But, then again, she had been trapped in the Void for the better part of a year, without senses, without psimancy.

She was itching for a good fight.

* * *

The moment the tall man ordered his people to "kill them all," Urstadt motioned for Rorie to follow her. She'd drawn her dagger in addition to her glaive; the smaller blade came in handy for close quarter combat.

Silently, she and Rorie slipped up behind the soldiers that stood at the back of the formation. Urstadt sliced the throat of the man directly in front of her with her dagger, then stabbed the one next to him just as he turned to see his companion fall, blood spurting from his neck.

As the soldiers whirled in alarm, Urstadt threw her dagger at the neck of one, then followed up by impaling the man on her glaive. She stepped back, withdrawing her weapon, and the man slid to the ground.

She had taken out three of the men; Rorie had taken two with her sword. That left sixteen.

Urstadt gripped her glaive, and charged.

She had been in more skirmishes than she could remember, and even more mock fights than that. She had rarely faced worse odds. She only hoped the distraction she and Rorie provided would give Winter the time necessary to take care of the real threats.

The wind whipped her braid behind her as she sprinted. She hefted her glaive and thrust it directly at the heart of the man closest to her. The sword screeched off his breastplate, but Urstadt anticipated his movement, and flipped her glaive around to slam the butt end into the man's face with enough force to take him down.

She twirled her glaive and attacked another. He parried one strike, but took the second in the leg. A blow to his face split his nose guard.

Rorie grunted behind her. Urstadt yanked her weapon out

of the dead man's face in time to turn and see Rorie taking on three soldiers at once. The clanswoman was both strong and quick, but her footwork was not always perfect, her strikes not always as efficient as they could be.

Urstadt swung her glaive, slashing the calf of one of Rorie's opponents. She felt a soft *thud* in her shoulder, and looked down to see a long, thick arrow shaft protruding from the soft point of skin where her arm met her torso. The pain came after the sound and sensation, searing beneath her skin.

Another soldier rushed in, halberd leveled at Urstadt. At such close quarters, it was risky for the soldiers to fire arrows. She needed to stay engaged, then, to make sure they couldn't get another off.

Urstadt parried and dodged. Pain grated down her arm and side with every movement. She rammed the butt of her glaive into the soldier's gut, and he doubled over. Urstadt slammed her elbow down on his back with all her weight and force and he collapsed to the ground.

She was doing well enough against the soldiers, but they were not the greater threat. She could guess who the three people that stood before Winter were. Their presence here, and their ability to keep not only Winter but Mazille and her band cowed as well, made it obvious they were Nazaniin.

Only Winter could turn the tide of the battle.

"Come with us, Winter," the psimancer said. An acumen; Winter had sensed his acumenic *tendra* reaching out to Vlak-Kali.

Kali, Winter reached out, *what do you know about clairvoyance?*

This isn't the time for lessons, Winter. I'm trying to find your faltira. *Just give me a moment—*

Sure enough, Winter noticed the mercenary Kali had

gained control over had started looking around.

I'm not sure I need it, Winter said. *Yet.* To say she did not need frost would never be accurate.

Winter sensed Kali's hesitation before she responded. *You think you can access clairvoyance as well?*

Vlak's vision was familiar to me.

How so? The mercenary Kali controlled still continued to search as surreptitiously as possible, while Mazille and the acumen shouted at one another.

I've seen visions like that before. On the battlefield, a few months ago. In Izet. Even what she'd seen outside of Cineste, when she first took *faltira,* what seemed like an eternity ago. The sensation she'd gotten while experiencing Vlak's vision was the same she'd felt then.

Clairvoyants are not usually useful in a fight, Kali said hesitantly.

But some are?

Some are, yes. If they close their eyes, concentrating on their clairvoyant tendron, *they can see things before they happen. Even if it's just a moment before, if they can fight, they can have the advantage in any fight, no matter their opponent. But only very few voyants can do this, Winter, and it takes practice…*

Winter continued to listen as best she could, but she was already looking for a clairvoyant *tendron.*

You said tendron, Winter thought, *singular. Does that mean—*

Voyants can only access one tendron, *period. They call it their aspect. Even Rune can only access one, and he is the most powerful voyant on record.*

What happens when two voyants fight one another? she asked, looking at the Nazaniin speculatively. The voyant must be the woman, since she could sense the other two were acumen and telenic already.

Winter, my man is about to find the faltira *Mazille stole from you, so why don't you just—*

There. Winter had found her aspect, she was sure. Different from her telenic *tendra*, invisible tendrils that emanated from her chest. Different from acumenic *tendra*, wisps of strange smoke that connected her with the Void, surging forth from her mind.

This is different. It's a good tendron; *it still has that wavy, ethereal quality, but instead of coming from my mind or chest, this is a projection of myself.*

I can see why they call it an aspect.

As soon as my aspect projects, the Nazaniin voyant looks up at me sharply.

Kali, *my mind whispers urgently*, what happens when two voyants fight?

The Nazaniin closes her eyes. I can hear Kali's explanation in my head. If they close their eyes, they can see things before they happen.

The woman takes a step toward me, her curved sword—so much like the one Knot carried, once—held ready. I draw the sword I wear at my side.

Then I, too, close my eyes.

The aspect I saw before me while my eyes were open, a mirror image of myself made of light and inseparably connected with me, bursts into fragments of light the moment my eyes shut. For a moment I think I'm in the Void, twinkling star-lights glowing all around me. But, quickly, these lights coalesce into other forms. Mazille, Kali, the Nazaniin cotir and mercenaries, still fighting Urstadt and Rorie. I see all of these figures, and yet they are all frozen in time, bright shadows of themselves unmoving in my mind.

All frozen except for one. The Nazaniin voyant continues to approach me. We mirror each other, our swords raised, angled inward, almost touching. Our feet step in time, crossing and pacing. We circle one another.

She lunges, sword slicing toward me. Our blades meet soundlessly. A bright flash illuminates the strange space in my mind as our swords touch. She strikes again, her movements something resembling the bu-kaido forms. Not quite the same, but similar enough that I can enter bu-shir, then bu-endo, and finally bu-du to counter them. Each time I parry, bright flashes light up the dark as our swords meet without sound.

She disengages, moving a few paces away from me. I hold my sword ready, in bu-hai stance—one of the safest, most stable stances I know. In this stance I feel strong, ready to take on whatever attack this woman might bring to me. In the background, blurred around us as my focus remains on the voyant, the other psimancers, mercenaries, and Urstadt and Rorie remain completely still.

She rushes at me again. Wordless, soundless, just a figment of light. As she moves, I realize why I feel so strong. While my body has conditioned itself to move with the forms, it always makes my muscles burn and strain when I do not hold back. I can keep them up for some time now, thanks to Urstadt's training and conditioning, but my muscles always smolder during and ache afterward. It's a dull pain I've come to enjoy, I realize now, because I'm suddenly without it.

There is no ache, no strain. My body moves effortlessly, exactly as I direct.

The moment I realize this, as the voyant charges me, I shift from bu-hai to bu-gin, a much more strenuous stance that I can only pull off on my strongest of days. It requires the most strength, balance, and dexterity of all the initiatory stances, but it allows me to shift direction and momentum on the smallest of axes.

The woman reaches me, moving with enough force to bring down a tree. I cannot parry such a strike, but in bu-gin all I have to do is shift my weight and bend my knees, leaning backwards; my torso flattens so

I'm parallel with the ground as her sword cuts directly above me. The moment she's past, I snap back up, twisting around to meet her.

Her momentum carries her past me, and she missteps as she turns. I dart forward, trying to penetrate her moment of vulnerability, but she recovers in time to dance around my blade. I envy her agility and grace; I do not think I've ever looked that good when I've dodged an attack.

But I'm still alive, and that's what matters.

Her blade snaps out as she twists around me, and I barely shift my own to parry. Light flashes at the contact.

We separate once more, the others a light-mural of stillness around us. My opponent's eyes are calm. What in Oblivion am I doing facing off against a Nazaniin assassin? I'm a simple tiellan woman from a village no one cares about in the north. I have no business doing this.

But I've made it my business. I'm not going to stop now.

I take up bu-gin once more, balancing lightly, the form not taking any effort whatsoever. The woman's eyes narrow, and then she mirrors me. This time her form isn't a facsimile of bu-gin, but the exact form itself. She expects me to make the next move, but I remain still. We both stare at each other, perfectly balanced opposites, blades pointed at one another. I'm drawn, for the briefest moment, to the slight curve of the woman's blade. I snap out of it just in time to see her break form and sprint toward me.

Our blades clash in another soundless flash of light. She kicks and connects, forcing me backwards, but I feel no pain. Nothing at all other than a pressure moving me back. I recover but she's already raining down blow after blow, and I barely have time to parry. I sweep my leg in her direction, tripping her up, and vault back onto my feet. There's surprise on her light-mural face, and for the briefest moment I wonder if I looked as good as she did. But the moment passes because the opening is there, and just as she regains her balance I slip my sword between her ribs, up into her lungs and heart. Light engulfs us, and I open my eyes.

* * *

Winter opened her eyes. Time unfroze. Urstadt's halberd jutted up into the neck of one of the mercenaries. The acumen screamed at Mazille. The telenic raised a circular blade and flung it toward Kali.

And, in front of Winter, the voyant still stood with sword raised. Winter, too, had hers raised, the two blades angled toward one another, tips nearly touching. The voyant looked at Winter, surprise in her eyes, and coughed violently, blood bubbling from her lips. Then she fell to the ground.

That, Kali's voice echoed in Winter's mind, *is what happens when two voyants fight one another.*

The Nazaniin acumen, face red from shouting, turned in time to see his voyant fall to the ground. He paled as his eyes rose to meet Winter's. Movement blurred behind the acumen, and something sailed through the air toward her.

"You're a voyant," he whispered. Winter could barely hear it above the chaos around her.

"I'm a queen," she said as she caught her *faltira* pouch in one hand, and immediately took a crystal.

Winter made quick work of the remaining members of the cotir. Deep inside Kali, horror writhed. Winter was a psimancer in every sense of the term; she could use all three of the art forms, with power and precision; her telenic power had been present from the start, and her acumenic force had awed Kali the moment she'd first encountered Winter's strange dark-light in the Void.

Now, Winter had discovered her aspect and defeated a very talented voyant in a matter of moments.

When the Nazaniin force—*cotir* and mercenaries—were

defeated, Urstadt and Rorie standing bloody before Winter, Kali motioned for them to speak alone. Winter inclined her head, and the two took a few steps away.

"I assume you're going to do what you need to do to them, to get your *faltira* back," Kali said, nodding at Mazille and the remaining captives, still bound to the trees.

"You assume correctly."

"Would you mind if I went for a walk?" Kali asked. "I'd rather not spend my first few moments back in the Sfaera witnessing torture."

Winter scoffed. "A walk? Kali, if you think you can run, you—"

"I'm not going to run." She meant it.

"You know I'll be able to find you," Winter said.

"You won't need to." They held one another's gaze for what seemed like a very long time.

Winter nodded, then turned away.

Thank you, Kali said, reaching out to Winter but not sure she would hear, *my queen.*

8

Triah

CODE FEHRWAY WAITED IMPATIENTLY at the main gate in the Second Wall of Triah, green eyes scanning the crowds. The Odenites were making passage into and out of the city difficult. The fanatics had been banned from the city proper, but they still had access to the third major circle of the city, outside the Second Wall.

The Nazaniin didn't like the Odenite presence. Just seeing their vast camp of tents in the fields beyond the city filled him with nerves. And the whole city buzzed with that same apprehension. Everything seemed different.

He finally found who he sought. Triah had become a melting pot of different cultures over the past few decades, and those with the darker skin of people from Maven Kol, Andrinar, or the Island Coalition were commonplace, but Code recognized these two the moment his eyes locked on them. Dressed in dark brown cloaks, the man and woman were pushed right up against the city gates, trying to make their way through. They wouldn't be allowed in—thanks to the Odenites, the guards were turning away almost everyone, unless they had some form of documentation that demonstrated their business or residence in the city.

It wasn't every day you saw the former crown prince of Maven Kol being turned away from the gates of Triah. The kid's

83

decision to give up his crown had been a foolish one, but there was no helping it. Alain and Morayne had never been quite right in their heads, either of them.

That was part of why Code liked them so much.

Code made his way through the crowds and met them a dozen paces in front of the gate. He relaxed a little when Morayne smiled at him. She was in one of her better moods today. That was good.

"Code!" Alain exclaimed. "I did not expect you to meet us at the gate."

Code wrapped his arms around Alain in a bear hug. "Last time we talked, there wasn't a brand-new religion knocking on the gates of the city, mate."

The lad looked behind him at the fields occupied by Odenite tents.

"A new religion?" he asked. "Like the communities?"

"No, no, that's all different, lad. The communities are an offshoot of the Denomination. The folk out there, they're not part of the Denomination at all."

"So they don't worship Canta?" Morayne asked. The chirp in her voice gave away her excitement.

"Erm... no, actually they do worship Canta," Code muttered. "Just a different type of Canta, I think."

"If they worship Canta, how are they a new religion?"

Code shrugged. "Oblivion, I know no more about them than the next person." That wasn't exactly true; as a Nazaniin, he'd been briefed in detail about the Odenites, their beliefs, who led them, and more. But the existing religion was bad enough; he wasn't about to waste his breath describing a brand-new one. "Best to forget about them. Much more important to get you two out of this press and into the city, right?"

"That's the idea," Alain said.

It wasn't exactly an orderly queue. Traders pushed brusquely past worried-looking villagers and youthful novices in Cantic gowns, trying to return to the seminary, no doubt; chickens squawked indignantly from wicker baskets; and at one point everybody had to jump out of the way of a herd of excitable heifers being brought to market. Code had slipped out easily enough, but getting back in was obviously the more difficult task. Four grim-faced guards stood abreast at the open gate, weapons ready. A dozen others would be stationed in close proximity to the gate, with a half-dozen more monitoring the crowd from the wall, crossbows ready. In front of the gate, two further guards were checking papers, asking questions of those trying to get into the city.

But the gates were open, at least. Triah would not close itself off unless the situation was truly dire.

"How's Maven Kol?" Code asked.

"The transition has been difficult," Morayne said, her eyes locked on Alain, "but it is what Maven Kol needed."

"The Denizens are still in power?" Code knew the answer. The Nazaniin had kept close tabs on the situation in Maven Kol; a monarch choosing to give up his crown and tip the scale of power in the people's favor had happened only twice in history. A hundred and seventy-three years ago, a king had abdicated; and a few months ago, Alain had refused coronation and given up all claim in favor of a people's movement called the Denizens.

"A group of nobles are contesting their rule, but the Denizens will prevail."

Of course Morayne would say that. She'd been a Denizen herself. At that moment, the family in front of them were hustled through the gate, and it was their turn.

"The three of you together?" the nearest gate guard asked. "We're not letting in any Odenites."

"We're not Odenites," Alain said. "We're—"

"Who are you, then, and what's your business in Triah?"

Code stepped forward. He hadn't realized the guard would be so bloody aggressive, or he'd have done it earlier.

The Nazaniin did not officially have a symbol or an identifying mark; as an organization of assassins and spies, they worked in the shadows. But, by now, they were well known enough that they'd needed to come up with something. So Code reached into his pocket and withdrew a gilded warsquares piece—his was the dragon, a particularly fearsome depiction, with gaping maw and claws extended—with a simple, blocky N etched into the base. The figure was smaller than the average warsquares piece, despite the fact that the dragon was traditionally the largest of any set. Kosarin had commissioned a set especially for the Nazaniin, with each piece of equal size, smaller in height than Code's palm. The pieces were nothing more than a novelty outside of Triah, but within the city, the dragon piece could get him just about anywhere, without question.

A few years ago, after Kosarin had first distributed the pieces, counterfeits began popping up here and there; a few began using the symbol to get into restricted areas or coerce others to do their bidding.

Kosarin had systematically killed anyone even rumored to have done such a thing. He then killed any goldsmith even rumored to have contemplated making such a set, or even a single figurine.

Quickly, the counterfeits had stopped circulation.

Code pressed the dragon piece into the guard's palm, keeping it hidden from other eyes around them.

"Ah," the guard said, his voice a dry rasp. His eyes drifted slowly from the warsquares piece to Code's face.

Code cleared his throat.

Immediately the guard handed the piece back to Code. "Very well, very well. You may all go through, of course. Please." The guard stepped aside, allowing Code, Alain, and Morayne to walk past him. He signaled the four guards standing at the gate. Code recognized the signal to mean something along the lines of "These people are important, don't question them."

Bloody right.

Morayne glanced back at the gate once they were clear of it. "That was easy enough."

"Almost too easy, if you ask me," Alain muttered.

Code laughed. "Take it from me, mate. You learn one thing in life, it's to take the easy things as they come. Life is full enough of the shit." He flashed them both a smile. "Not to mention you've got me with you. Things in Triah will always be smooth as silk if you stick with me."

Later, after Code had settled them into the Blessed Storm— one of the nicest inns in all of Triah; Code had set them up there with little expense, given his connections—he gave them a tour of the city. Or the Trinacrya at the center of the city, at least. Touring the entire city, even the entire Goddess-damned Center Circle, would take days.

But the Trinacrya and the surrounding locales they could manage in a few hours.

He took them to the Citadel first, of course. It was a second home to him by now, and though it didn't have the majesty of Canta's Fane or the significance of the House of Aldermen, it had *history*.

"This used to be a palace for your king?" Morayne asked as they approached the Citadel.

"Aye," Code said. "Almost two hundred years ago. You'll see when we get inside, but many of the decorations are originals from the Age of Revival. Some of Khale's kings and queens were on the creative side, and their work still remains."

"That is all very interesting," Morayne said, clearly not interested, "but what can you tell me about that?" She pointed to the northwest.

Code followed her gaze, to the tower that jutted so far up into the sky above Triah that it was practically on a level with the Cliffs of Litori themselves.

"That's God's Eye," Code said. "You want to go there?"

"We want to go there," Morayne said.

It wasn't a terribly long walk to the Eye from the Trinacrya, just under half an hour. In Triah, one got used to walking.

"God's Eye is much more than a single tower," Code explained when they arrived. "It is actually a network of them, and God's Eye is simply the tallest. This," Code said, indicating the tower and the surrounding area, "is Sky Plaza. You see God's Eye at the center there, of course, and then we have the Four Pillars." While God's Eye was easily the tallest tower in the city, the Four Pillars stood directly adjacent to the monolith on four sides, each one rising between ten and twenty stories, with bridges that connected it to the central tower. A large plaza opened at the base of the towers, with manicured grass and trees weaving in and out of the base of the five buildings, like children playing at the feet of giants.

"How tall is God's Eye?" Alain asked, shielding his eyes as he looked up at the massive building.

"Fifty stories, give or take a few," Code said with a hint of pride. There was nothing else like God's Eye in the Sfaera.

"Give or take? What is that supposed to mean?"

"Well," Code said, looking over his shoulder for dramatic effect, "This is some inside information, but I'll tell it to just the two of you." It wasn't insider information; anyone who cared enough to ask one of the Eye's operators would get this answer from them, but still. Never hurt to add a little drama. "They say it's only fifty floors, but that isn't exactly true. It's more like seventy. There are secret floors; levels they don't want the public to know about."

The truth was, he had no idea how many floors there were exactly; various rumors floated around the Nazaniin, but Code had never really cared to ask after specifics. Growing up near the Eye, he'd more or less taken it for granted.

Morayne rolled her eyes, and Code knew he wasn't going to get far with this audience. "Secret floors? Really? Who in Oblivion would even care about such a thing?"

"You'd be surprised," Code said, half-defensively. "Some people find that sort of thing *quite* interesting."

"And the apparatus... harnesses the power of the sun or something?" Alain asked.

Code shrugged. "Rumor has it, yes, but Triah hasn't had a need to use God's Eye in decades. No one has dared attack us in a very long time."

Like many apartments near the city center, Code's was a three-story structure with steps leading up to the entrance. It was roomy, and bloody expensive, but the Nazaniin paid their operatives handsomely. And Code had done well as a Nazaniin since he'd joined almost a decade ago; he had one of the most successful operation records in the organization.

He was valued, even if he wasn't particularly liked.

Alain and Morayne marveled at his place, but Code couldn't help but wonder if they really thought it was that impressive. Alain had grown up in a palace, after all, and even Morayne, as the daughter of a lesser noble house, would have had a mansion significantly larger than Code's apartment. But he showed them into the first-floor parlor, and Alain and Morayne settled happily enough on a large stuffed couch, with Code sitting across from them in a matching armchair.

Code had no sooner sat down than he bolted upright once more, and headed to the liquor table at one end of the room. "Almost forgot the most important thing," he said with a grin. "Drinks. What can I get for both of you?"

"Wine for both of us," Morayne said.

Code grunted. "Not into the stronger stuff, I take it?" He poured himself a glass of brandy and brought the drinks to them.

"You don't have a servant to do this for you?" Morayne asked, watching Code curiously.

Code laughed. "That's one difference between Maven Kol and Triah you'll note. Servants aren't as common. I do have a butler, Darion, but he only works specific hours for me. He usually is present when I have company, but I wanted to speak to the two of you alone, first. Besides, there's something to be said about doing work for yourself, you know?"

Alain and Morayne exchanged a look that Code could not decipher.

"Would've thought you two would be used to that, anyway, now that you're both free folk, as it were. Not nobles, not peasants, just... folk. Am I correct?"

"It will take some time for Maven Kol to catch up with Khale when it comes to that way of thinking, I'm afraid," Alain said, taking a sip of his wine.

Code decided it was long past time to change the subject. "And how goes the business of... er... what is it you do again?"

Alain hesitated, but Morayne spoke quickly.

"We help people," she said.

"You mean people like you?" Code asked. Alain had told him something of his plans before Code had left Mavenil, the capital city of Maven Kol, but that was some months ago, and Code had had a bit to drink since then.

"People like us?" Morayne asked, cocking her head to one side.

Code rolled his eyes. She couldn't possibly *not* know what he was referring to. "People that got caught in the Madness," he said. "Triggers."

The reason Code had been summoned to Mavenil in the first place had been to investigate and stop the madness epidemic that had plagued Khale's sister-nation over recent months. Based on Code's other experiences on Arro Isle in Alizia, and the information the Triad had shared with him, he'd suspected one of the Nine Daemons had been behind it.

He'd been right.

With Alain and Morayne's help, he'd defeated the Daemon Nadir (very well, it was more like he'd helped *them* defeat the Daemon), and the Madness had stopped, but those affected by it had not been saved. There were still hundreds of people in Maven Kol suffering from madness of various sorts.

Such a thing wouldn't be so out of the ordinary, of course, if these particular forms of madness didn't come with the ability to manipulate air, earth, water, or fire, often uncontrollably. Alain and Morayne were both affected by this madness, but had found ways to harness it. Part of the reason Alain had rejected the crown had been to help others recover from this madness, and live as normal a life as possible.

"I've heard good things about the movement you've established down there," Code said.

"We didn't establish anything," Alain said quietly. "The communities were already around before we began to help others. We've only changed the dynamic somewhat."

"We've changed it into something that works," Morayne added.

"So you're helping people, then?" Code asked. "With the madness?"

"We're sharing our experience," Alain said, "and what we know. Sometimes it helps, sometimes it doesn't."

Code knew that was a modest response; the Nazaniin intelligence sources had been astounded at the reports of recovery among those suffering from the Madness in Maven Kol.

"And how goes that fight for both of you?"

Alain and Morayne smiled at one another.

"It was never a fight to begin with."

Code didn't much care for their philosophy. Something about surrender being the only path to true victory. Whatever it was, Code was glad it worked for them. But he'd be damned if he'd ever give up a fight.

"The two of you seem to be getting on well enough, at least," Code said.

"Aye," Alain said quietly, his smile lingering. "At least we have that."

Code nodded, sitting back in his chair. At least one thing on the Sfaera was going right.

"Well, mates, we've had enough small talk to last us a while. I think it's time we get down to business."

"Indeed, Code. It is high time you told us why you summoned us to your great city."

Code nearly choked on his drink.

"Code, are you all right?" Morayne asked.

Once he got his coughing under control, Code nodded. "My apologies. I thought I heard you ask why *I* had summoned you to Triah."

Morayne and Alain both stared at him, and they did not have to speak for Code to understand. *Oblivion.* His heart began to race. "I hate to break it to you both, but I've done no such thing."

"But your message implored us to seek you out in Triah," Morayne said. "It said you needed our help."

Code took a deep breath. "I sent no such message. By the look on your faces, I can assume you did not send a message to me informing me of your imminent arrival in Triah, seeking *my* help?"

Alain and Morayne both shook their heads, mirroring their actions like an old couple that had been together for ages.

"No," Alain said. "We sent no such message."

Code swore. "Then we've got a problem, haven't we?"

"But who would want us to come to Triah, if not you?" Morayne asked.

"Haven't the slightest," Code muttered. He drained his glass and stood to refill it. "But there are not many candidates. Do you have that first communication from me?"

"I do," Alain said, with a glance at Morayne.

Morayne rolled her eyes. "You were right, I was wrong, there you have it. Show him the letter, would you?"

Alain reached into his satchel and pulled out a slim stack of letters with a ribbon tied around them.

Code scanned through the letters in the stack. "Most of those look familiar," he said. "And I'm sure you'll recognize the letters I have from you, save for one. Let's have a look at the letter that brought you here, and get to the bottom of this."

Alain slipped one letter free of the rest, still in its envelope.

Code inspected the broken seal: a single arrow, diagonal within an ornate square on black wax.

"That's the seal of the Nazaniin," he said. At least, it was *one* of the seals of the Nazaniin. The organization had a number of seals they used, for various purposes and some simply at random.

"Someone sent us a letter and counterfeited the seal of the Nazaniin?" Alain asked, eyes wide.

"It's possible. But forging Nazaniin seals is punishable by death. I haven't heard of a counterfeit in years. It's more likely the letter truly did come from within the Nazaniin." Code pursed his lips. "Just not from me."

"Who would do that?" Alain asked. "And why?"

"In theory, it could be anyone in the Nazaniin," Code said. "Or possibly a Citadel student."

"And… how many people is that?" Morayne asked.

Code opened the envelope and pulled out the letter. "Almost a thousand."

"That doesn't sound good."

"It isn't." Code unfolded the letter and scanned the contents. It was a simple note.

Alain,
  Please excuse the abruptness of this note, but what we dealt with in Maven Kol has resurfaced in Triah. I need your help, and Morayne's, too, if she can come with you. I hope to see you soon.

                                        Code

"The handwriting is very close to my own," Code said. "Almost an exact copy."

"Then the writing gives you no clue as to who it could have been," Alain said, slumping back into the couch.

"On the contrary," Code said, eyes running over the words, "I write much of my correspondence in a false hand—different than what I use at the Citadel, for example. Or on any official Nazaniin documents. So whoever wrote this knows my true hand." He glanced up at Alain. "And yours, as well. I did not notice anything different about the handwriting in that letter, either.

Morayne sat forward. "Does that narrow it down for us, or not?"

"Not by much."

Alain shook his head. "Why are we even here, then? We travelled all this way, left the work we were doing behind, for nothing."

Code cleared his throat. "Just because I didn't ask for help doesn't mean I don't need it. I didn't write that note, but the contents aren't wrong. There's a war brewing here, and I think it'll converge on Triah. We could use all the help we can get."

"We aren't going to help you fight that religious group," Morayne said, eyes narrowing. "Or in a war against Roden." It was common knowledge that Roden, the disintegrating empire to the north of the Khalic republic, had finally declared war— hoping to increase its territories while Khale was distracted by the tiellan uprising. For now, Khalic–Rodenese aggression had been limited to skirmishes on the border and a few fishing crews exchanging blows in the Gulf of Nahl.

"You know that isn't the war I'm talking about," Code said.

"You're referring to another being like the one we defeated in Maven Kol?" Alain asked.

Code nodded. "Daemons, mate. Best call a problem by its name. Doesn't do any good to ignore them."

Morayne placed her goblet back on the table. She had been holding it, frozen on its way to her lips, for moments now. "One of them is in Triah?"

"More than one," Code said. He paused. What he was about to say was confidential Nazaniin intelligence.

But he trusted these two. And, hopefully, they could actually be of some help.

"Some of our sources are saying all of the Daemons are converging on Triah."

Alain choked on the wine he'd just drunk.

Morayne's eyes widened. "*All* of them?" she repeated. "Nadir alone killed so many in that last battle."

"It's a possibility," Code said. "One we'd rather be prepared for than not. I'm glad the two of you are here."

"But we still don't know who summoned us here, or who sent you to meet us."

Code took a deep draught of his brandy. "We've got to figure that out, haven't we?"

9

Outside of Triah

CINZIA MADE HER WAY out of the Odenite camp quickly, her dark hood pulled down over her face. More than a year ago she had worn Cantic robes and cloaks, brilliant whites and crimsons, unmistakable and recognized throughout the nation.

Now, her cloak was nondescript, plain, dark. She would never wear Cantic regalia again.

You have many secrets, Luceraf whispered in her mind. *I like it. You're becoming more fit to be my avatar than I'd ever imagined.*

Cinzia continued walking, refusing to respond.

You cannot ignore me forever, you know.

Cinzia was willing to prove the Daemon wrong. She had enough on her mind to distract her. She'd lost the one thing that had made her unique. Translating had not only made her special, it had made her powerful.

Now, she was without that power.

I wouldn't exactly say that, Luceraf whispered. *You may have lost that ability, but you have me. And I can give you more power than translating ever could.*

"Your power is nothing but a mockery," Cinzia said, aware she was posturing but not wanting to give the Daemon any ground.

Luceraf laughed softly. *One day you will understand how wrong you are. And you never know... my strength might help you one day, my dear.*

Cinzia approached the outskirts of the Beldam's camp, not bothering to reply. The smaller group of pilgrims—once Odenites themselves, but now merely haunting the tracks of the larger group—had made camp in a rocky, sparsely forested area inland from Triah's main gate and the Odenite camp. By the looks of the camp, Cinzia would be surprised if the Beldam had gathered three hundred people to her cause.

Whatever cause that was. The Beldam and her followers had all been drawn to Jane just as the other Odenites had been, but they had left the larger group when Jane had refused to cast out tiellans from their number.

Two large men spotted her as soon as she came within sight of the first tent. Both carried bludgeons.

"Who goes there?" one of the men asked.

"That's the priestess," the other muttered.

Cinzia kept her head held high. "Cinzia Oden, to see the Beldam."

"Didn't think we'd see you back here, not after what happened before," said the taller of the two men, whose beard was so thick it hid his mouth. He twirled his bludgeon in one hand. "Come for another beating, have you?"

"No," Cinzia said, fear splintering in her chest. What in Oblivion had she been thinking, coming here alone again? "I just want to speak with her."

"We'll take you to her," the other man said, stepping forward as well. He, too, had his club drawn. "But not before we remind you why you shouldn't come back."

"Wait," Cinzia said, taking a step back. In her anger at not being able to translate, she had made an incredibly stupid decision. And now she was going to pay for it. "I am a servant of Canta. You cannot—"

The bearded man raised his club, and though Cinzia wanted to turn and run, something held her there. She raised her hands to protect her face.

I'll expect a thank you for this later, Luceraf whispered in her mind.

The bludgeon fell. Cinzia opened her eyes to find one of her upraised hands holding the weapon tightly. It had been as simple as catching a stick someone had tossed toward her.

"What in Oblivion—"

Before the attacker could say anything more, Cinzia wrenched the bludgeon from his hand. Once, she had protected Jane from an assassination attempt, and had been granted speed and strength to do so by a power beyond herself. The strength and power coursing through her was similar, but it was also different. Here, something primal drove her. A dark instinct, deep within.

Cinzia raised the bludgeon, and brought it down on her attacker before he had time to recover from his surprise. She kicked the bearded man and he flew several rods, sliding to a stop in the grass.

The other shouted in alarm and brought his own bludgeon down on her shoulder. Cinzia barely felt it. She raised her club to bring it down on his skull, then stopped.

Kill this man. It will teach these people a lesson, Luceraf hissed, her voice filled with lust.

We have taught them lesson enough. It took some effort, but Cinzia lowered the bludgeon.

"I'll do anything you ask," the guard whimpered. "Please, don't hurt me."

"Take me to the Beldam," Cinzia said. "That's all I came here for."

People from the nearby tents had started to emerge at the

sound of the commotion. A few rushed to help the injured man. He coughed violently, blood spurting from his mouth.

Will he be all right?

What do you care? Luceraf responded. *You ought to be thanking me, not worrying about the people I just protected you from.*

Luceraf was right. Cinzia would not have been able to defend herself in that situation, not without help. And Canta was certainly not helping her at the moment.

Thank you.

The Daemon didn't reply immediately, and when it did speak, it sounded a little surprised. *You are welcome. Just pay more attention next time. Yours is not the only life at stake when you're in danger.*

The cowed guard led Cinzia toward the center of camp where a couple of hundred of the Beldam's followers had gathered around a small wooden box. On it stood the Beldam, preaching. The guard attempted to slip away, but Cinzia blocked his path with the bludgeon. "Stay here until I speak with her."

The Beldam's voice carried well, though it quivered with age. "The time has come for us all to choose a side," she said, "and the choices are clear." She extended an arm, palm up. "On the one hand, we have light. Canta is the light, as are her doctrines and her teachings, and her creations as well. Life is light. The Sfaera, humans… we are all beings of the light."

The Beldam extended her other arm, palm facing down this time. "On the other hand, of course, there is the dark. The Nine Daemons, and all they represent. Fear, rage, death, pride, gluttony, lust, madness, deceit, and envy, these are all of the dark. The domain of the Daemons and their creations, their progeny—the tiellans—are of the dark as well. We all know this. The Prophetess has not seen this truth yet, but she will, just as each of you have seen it. Just as I have."

Cinzia gripped the bludgeon until her knuckles turned white. This was precisely the reason she and Jane had denounced the Beldam; her teachings were racist and divisive, in a time when they were trying to promote equality and unity.

But clearly the woman still had an audience.

"One day soon, the line will be drawn. Humans will fight for Canta, and tiellans for the Daemons. The conflict will decide the fate of the Sfaera. My hope and prayer is that each of you choose the right side. For though the conflict will be fierce, and there will be many casualties, we already know the victor. Canta will always succeed against the Daemons. She has done it before, and she will do it again. I stand as a testament of her power and glory, and each of you can, too. *Imass.*"

She has done it before, and she will do it again?

Luceraf laughed sadly. *You need to study up on your history, my dear.*

The Beldam descended from her box. Her followers flocked around her, but she caught Cinzia's eye, and made straight for her.

"Come, Disciple Cinzia," she said. "Let us speak somewhere more private."

The Beldam shooed her followers away from her tent, until she seemed sure they were alone.

"You are not the Cinzia I knew before." The Beldam's eyes glittered with malice. "You've chosen your side, and it isn't mine."

"That's why I've come to speak with you," Cinzia said, not minding at all that she wasn't on the Beldam's side. "I need help, and I—"

"You have a Daemon inside of you, Cinzia," the Beldam quavered. Cinzia caught the briefest flash of compassion in the woman's eyes. "There is no coming back from that, I'm afraid."

"That cannot be true." There was no conviction behind Cinzia's words. She was asking the *Beldam* for help, for Canta's sake. She must truly be out of options.

"Besides," the Beldam continued, any trace of compassion evaporating, "you are compromised, now. You and I can never be on the same side, Cinzia. It was difficult enough before; it is impossible now."

"How do you *know* it is irreversible?" Cinzia asked. If there was not a solution, perhaps she could at least discover the reason behind what had happened to her.

"The same way I know anything about the Daemons," the Beldam said.

Cinzia stared at the Beldam. "You learned about the Nine Daemons when you were a high priestess."

The Beldam frowned. "Of course I did. But—"

"Where?" Cinzia asked, a tiny seed of hope nestling inside her.

"In Canta's Fane, of course."

"The sacred texts? There is a partial translation of the Nine Scriptures there, is there not? What else?"

The Beldam held Cinzia's gaze for what seemed a long time.

"The Denomination will not let you access them," the Beldam finally said. "They must have excommunicated you by now. You will never see the sacred texts. Where are you going?"

Cinzia paused, already halfway out of the tent. "You have given me just what I need, Beldam. Our business here is done. For now."

"Our business is *done*? We still—"

"You have made your choice." She left the tent and the Beldam, speechless, behind her.

What is it you think you're going to do, my dear? Luceraf hissed.

Cinzia smiled for the first time in a long time. *You will just have to wait and see.*

10

Adimora

WHEN WINTER MADE IT to her chambers in the underground city, her back, feet, and legs felt as if they were on fire on the inside. She, Urstadt, Rorie, and Kali—still in Vlak's body—had ridden hard for the last few days, hardly sleeping, purchasing extra horses along the way. Winter was looking forward to a warm bath and a hot meal before she announced her intention to attack Triah.

She had just closed the door and was removing her boots when a knock echoed throughout her chambers.

Winter swore. What was the point of being queen if she could not have a quiet moment to herself?

One of her guards, Dreya, a Ranger who had been with her since Cineste, waited on the other side of her door.

"My apologies for intruding, Your Majesty. Ghian desires to speak with you. He says it is urgent. I would not have let him through, but he insisted."

"Fine," Winter said, looking over the guard's shoulder to see Ghian standing sheepishly in the torchlit stone hallway. Goddess, what time was it? The torches were a sad reminder of the real sun that shone above ground.

"Let him in," Winter said.

"Would you like me to stay—"

"That will not be necessary. Thank you, Dreya." She waved the guard away.

"Thank you for agreeing to see me, my queen," Ghian said, hovering just inside the door to her hut. Despite the tiellans making her their queen, she had not yet had the time or will to change her living situation. What was the point, when she would be leaving again so soon?

"Make this quick, Ghian."

"Of course, Your Majesty, of course." Ghian looked over his shoulder. "Your guard… what was her name? Dreya? She is rather protective of you. Said she would make my face bloody if this wasn't something important."

Winter collapsed onto a large chair. "My guard is protective of me, yes, thank you for the insight. Was that what you came here to say?"

"I came here to discuss two things."

"The first?"

"The first is Triah."

"I will march on Triah soon."

"And you're just taking Rangers? No one else?"

A brief flash of the vision Winter had seen through Vlak burst into her mind. Thousands of tiellan bodies on a cold, snow-swept plain of death. Adimora itself destroyed and gone. She was suddenly grateful Galce was still in Cineste; she'd thought about recalling him, lately, Chaos' direction be damned, but in Cineste he might be spared should these visions come to pass.

"Just Rangers." Two thousand fighters for the campaign, and a thousand to defend Adimora, but she had no intention of discussing specific tactics with Ghian. "And the second thing?"

"You have a question for me."

Winter swore. She did have a question for Ghian. As much as she despised what he had done and what now influenced him, that very influence was a source of valuable information.

"What happens next?" she asked.

"Eventually the Daemons are going to take their physical forms," Ghian said. "It is inevitable."

"And when that happens, you'll cease to exist, won't you?" Ghian hesitated.

"The Daemon will take its true form through your body. It will tear right through you as it enters this world; I saw Mefiston do it at the firestone. The body he'd possessed did not survive."

For a moment the confidence that had made Ghian's eyes bright since he'd joined with Azael snuffed out; they were all fear.

"You didn't know? You thought you would... what? Coexist with him when he took his true form?"

Ghian's mouth worked, but no sound came out.

"Bloody bones," Winter muttered. "You poor bastard."

As quickly as the moment of vulnerability had befallen him, Ghian straightened, the confidence back in his eyes. He spoke, but the voice did not belong to him. Winter could sense, ever so faintly, a deep, rolling tone, like the rush of fire, beneath Ghian's normally high, reedy voice.

"Ghian will serve me faithfully, and he will be rewarded," Azael said.

Winter rolled her eyes. "He'll be rewarded with a timely death."

"While Ghian's body will be destroyed, there are other options for him, if he chooses to continue to serve the Nine."

"The Nine?" Winter asked, sitting up. "Don't you mean the Eight? What happened to Mefiston, anyway?"

Azael—she could almost see the blackened skull through Ghian's face—frowned. "As far as I am concerned, you killed him. Be thankful I am not more vengeful about it."

"Seems a bit unfair. He died because some of you failed,

clearly. I opposed him, but I didn't kill him."Winter cocked her head to one side. "Can any of you even take physical form if one of you is dead?"

"We can, and we will,"Azael said. "Mefiston's death is a part of the cycle.You of all people should know that."

"What do you mean, me of all people?"

"You are the Harbinger, are you not? Inevitability is your watchword."

Winter stared at Azael for a moment. Kali had once told her that the Triad, the group who ran the Nazaniin, thought she was "The Harbinger"—though Kali said the Nazaniin didn't know enough about their own prophecies to agree on whether the Harbinger would usher in the Rising of the Nine Daemons, or simply bring death to the Sfaera, or perhaps do nothing at all—and she had heard whispers in the Void that called her both harbinger and murderer.

"What is the Harbinger?"Winter asked. "Will you tell me?"

The black skull's natural grin broadened. "The Harbinger is a herald of Canta. Its relationship with the Nine is only tangential. Insomuch as we are tied to Canta, the Harbinger also is loosely tied to us."

"A herald of… Canta?" Winter did not like the sound of that, but could it be much worse than being a harbinger for the Nine Daemons? She had given up any semblance of faith in Canta long ago; Winter had lost everything she loved in life, and as far as she was concerned, Canta was as much to blame as anyone else.Why would she be a harbinger of a goddess she did not care for, let alone believe in?

"*The* Harbinger, of Canta's Last Advent, I believe they used to call it. Or the Harbinger of Canta's Destruction, sometimes."

"Canta's Destruction? Canta will die?" That was slightly

better. If she was a herald to the destruction of the old hag that dominated the Sfaera, so be it. She'd accept *that* role gladly.

"Oh yes, She will die," Azael said. "Just not in the way She thinks. The Destruction will not happen, because we will take power. We will remake the Sfaera in our image, and Canta will become nothing but an old, dusty mortal. Her death will be as meaningless as that of the tiniest insect."

"What does that mean?"

"You will learn more when we reach Triah. We will all find answers there."

11

The Citadel, Triah

SUNLIGHT BURST IN THROUGH windows all along the twisted passageways of the Citadel, and Code hated it. There was a time for sunlight, and that time was summer. Code walked quickly, too preoccupied to acknowledge the dozens of students that greeted him as he passed.

He had too much on his mind. Who had sent Alain and Morayne to Triah? He'd asked them to lie low and not stray too far from the Blessed Storm until he could find out. It must have been someone in the Citadel, but without suspects he couldn't accuse anyone.

And he had his own troubles. He had not long returned from his most recent mission, which had been to aid King Gainil Destrinar-Kol with the Daemon situation in Mavenil. The Triad had not been happy at the unexpected death of the monarch, who had been a graduate of the Citadel and thus something of a puppet for the Nazaniin. The even more unexpected shift from monarchy to democracy had angered Triadin Kosarin even more. But despite the mixed results of Code's mission, he was due some down time. He'd accepted his assignment in Mavenil directly after returning from Arro Isle, and Oblivion knew they had both been harrowing experiences.

The Triad had recently awarded Code tenure at the Citadel—which, in Nazaniin speak, meant he was now in the upper echelon of psimancers in the organization, the small group of a dozen or so agents the Triad sent out on their most important missions. Sometimes these psimancers traveled in *cotirs*, or groups consisting of one member of each of the three psimantic arts: telesis, acumency, and clairvoyance. Other times, they were given leave to travel alone. Beneath the tenured were the Citadel associates: psimancers who had great potential, but were still learning, splitting their time between teaching at the Citadel and taking smaller missions.

And beyond the walls of the Citadel, scattered across the Sfaera, were the lesser Nazaniin *cotirs*—groups of field officers that comprised one acumen, one telenic, and one voyant where possible—though voyants were so rare nowadays that often *cotirs* were made up of only two psimancers.

The Nazaniin had claimed the Citadel after the King Who Gave Up His Crown vacated the palace. It still retained much of its former layout and style. The great hall was now the assembly hall, where the Citadel's five hundred students met for meals. Much of the original artwork from the Age of Revival monarchs remained in the palace; tapestries, sculptures, and paintings lined the corridors and halls. Suits of armor in all styles, from all ages and nations and parts of the Sfaera, lined the assembly hall, backed by tapestries depicting the history of the Sfaera. The many large bedroom chambers had been converted to classrooms, with dozens of chairs, desks, chalk and chalk-panels set up in each. Servants' quarters had become quarters for lower level students who were too young to live on their own out in the city. The Citadel prided itself in not employing any servants directly; the younger students divided their time between their studies and assigned chores and tasks, cleaning and serving as needed. It was quite the sight, sometimes, to see a foreign prince or princess or local noble on garderobe duty.

Code made his way through the students' quarters now. While the initial structure and setup of the palace had more or less been kept intact, the Nazaniin had made other additions that outsiders, and even most of their own students, knew nothing about: a half-dozen subterranean levels had been added to the Citadel, and these basement levels constituted the true headquarters of the Nazaniin, including the lowest level, the Heart of the Void.

Code's route wasn't the only way to access the lower levels, but it was the fastest for him. He sidestepped a flock of students, and then pushed through the entrance of a little-used stairwell, shutting the door behind him.

The stairwell spiraled downward one level, ending at a blank wall. He gently placed his hands on two of the stones in the wall, and pushed. The stones grated inward, and the entire wall began to move. When the way was open, he went below into the darkness, pressing another button-stone to close the passage door behind him.

The dark only inhabited the first anteroom, as it did with every entrance into the lower levels of the Citadel. Through another door, he was greeted by torchlight.

The austere halls of the Nazaniin headquarters did not remotely compare to the grandeur of the Citadel. Many Nazaniin agents despised the absence of art and light below, but Code welcomed it. There was a certain neatness to it all, down below, a feeling of equality. No hall was greater than any other, no chamber more grand. They were all the same, and they all maintained the same precise lines. But, more than the clarity, Code loved the dark. He found himself growing angry, more often than not, at the seemingly constant sunlight that bombarded the city of Triah—more recently than ever before, it seemed. He had never loved the sun; he preferred the clouds, and the gray, and the dark. He did his best thinking in such conditions. The lower levels of the Citadel offered his only refuge when the sun refused to hide itself.

The corridors below the Citadel were not as crowded as those above, but they were not empty, either. Code recognized almost all of the agents that crossed his path, some on missions, some with messages, some working in the library, and others on patrol, looking out for curious students.

The Heart of the Void was at the very bottom of the basement levels, six stories below the Citadel.

A Nazaniin guard waited for him outside the iron double doors that served as the main entrance to the chamber. The door on the left was lacquered black, while the one on the right lacquered white, and the stone arch surrounding them both was painted a deep crimson.

Kosarin's taste was more than a little brash.

Code was sure Sirana and Rune, the other two members of the Triad, had little to no input in the matter. Kosarin, the acumen, still acted as point of the triangle, while Sirana and Rune formed the base, as telenic and voyant, respectively.

The guard who greeted Code was one of the newer recruits, recently graduated from the Citadel. Farnid was a variant telenic, just like Code, which meant he needed to use the drug *faltira* to access his abilities. From what Code had seen, the lad's power was not anything special, but he seemed dedicated enough.

"The Triad is expecting me, Farnid."

"Of course. I was informed of your meeting with them." Farnid opened the white door and moved aside.

Code strode through the entrance into yet another antechamber. Doors to his left and to his right led to the corridor that encircled the central room, but Code went straight to the large red door that led into the central chamber, and stepped into the Heart of the Void.

Kosarin's tastes were no less ostentatious in the Heart of the Void itself. Alternating white, red, and black marble tiles spanned the floor, and the same colors trimmed the walls and furniture. Torches, lamps, and a large chandelier at the center of the chamber illuminated the space brightly. Cabinets, and shelves full of books lined the walls. This was not the Nazaniin's official library; it was the Triad's private collection.

Waiting for him in the Heart of the Void, seated around the great map table at the center of the room beneath the chandelier, were Kosarin, Sirana, and Rune.

Code saluted, arm diagonal across his chest, and then flashed a smile, despite his hackles rising. "A summons, so soon after my return. To what do I owe the pleasure?" Code seated himself opposite the Triad at the large circular table. The map, a relief model of the Sfaera, rose between them. "It's rare I get to see the three of you all in one place."

"We have a mission for you, Code," Kosarin said. He was twenty years Code's senior, at least. His spectacles and freshly shaved head reflected the chandelier's light. A white, impeccably trimmed circle beard was the only hair on his head. Seated as he was, he looked more like a particularly prim librarian than the Venerato of the Citadel and *Triadin* of the Nazaniin. But Kosarin was far more powerful, physically, than he let on. And psimantically speaking... well, there was a reason he was the leader of the Nazaniin. As he spoke, he peered over his spectacles at Code, for all the world like a stern father. Kosarin twirled a small figurine in one hand, close to the surface of the map table.

The word "mission" hit Code like a punch in the gut. "How can I serve, *Triadin?*" Code asked, hiding his surprise.

"This is a mission of a different sort." Sirana's hands were folded on the table. Her red hair, impeccably bound in a single ponytail, was longer than it used to be. Sirana had gone through a period of... oddness, after Lathe's disappearance. Hair unkempt, clothing disheveled. Highly unusual for someone of her stature, and even *more* unusual for Sirana herself. There had even been talk of her stepping down from the Triad. But now, she looked as elegant as ever. "Different than what you are used to, at least. But we needed our best agent."

Code resisted the urge to raise one eyebrow. There was usually only one reason the Triad requested Code's services specifically. He did not have a *cotir* of his own—not since Andrinar. If they needed a one-man job, he was the psimancer to do it.

Rune cleared his throat. Of the three members of the Triad, Rune had always been the odd man out. He was younger even than Code, perhaps twenty-six summers. His clothing was poorly tailored, and his long brown hair unkempt, strands always falling in his face. But Code knew better than to underestimate the voyant. He had only seen Rune's psimantic abilities in action a handful of times, but between what he had seen and the rumors he had heard, there was no psimancer of the Sfaera more powerful than this man. Kosarin was more experienced, Sirana more nuanced and tactical, but when it came to raw power, no one could match Rune.

That is, until the rumors of the tiellan psimancer from the north. The Chaos Queen might be able to challenge the entire Triad.

"Are you sure you want to send me away from Triah?" Code asked, masking his anxiety. "With the Odenite group at our gates and the tiellans on the move, I could—"

"Your next mission will keep you in Triah." Rune spoke over Code. "You are to befriend the psimancer previously known as Lathe. Gain his confidence. His services may prove valuable to us soon."

"You want me to *befriend* Lathe Tallon?"

"He is no longer Lathe Tallon," Sirana said, her voice hard and flat. "He is someone else entirely. Whatever rivalry existed between the two of you is over."

"Lathe is really gone, then?" Code asked.

"For our purposes, we must consider it so," Rune said.

The answer was cryptic as Oblivion, but then again, half the things Rune said made no sense whatsoever.

"The man wearing Lathe's body calls himself Knot, now," Kosarin said. "He is valuable to us. Not only does he act as a general and guard captain for the Odenites, but it is rumored he is married to the tiellan woman, Danica Winter Cordier. If we can exploit one of those relationships, good. If we can exploit both, all the better. You need to gain his trust, Code. Sirana will brief you further on your target. She has already had some… interaction with him."

Sirana returned Code's questioning glance with a cold and empty stare. He wondered why Sirana hadn't nominated herself to gain the target's trust, why she had left it to somebody like Code, who had never got on with Lathe.

Code almost asked the Triad if they knew about Alain and Morayne's arrival in the city, or about the note that had led them here. But something stopped him. Had they been behind the note, they weren't going to tell him now if they hadn't already.

Goddess, he hated these games. Give him an enemy to fight, that was one thing. But intrigue had never suited him.

The Triad stood, and Code stood with them. He saluted Kosarin and Rune as they left the table, and then he was left staring across the map of the Sfaera at Sirana, mountains and cities rising between them.

"Have a seat," Sirana said. "And let me tell you about my husband, and what he has become."

12

Somewhere beneath Triah

ASTRID AWOKE IN DARKNESS. It was true darkness, unilluminated by the green glow of her eyes, which meant it was daytime outside. How long had it been since Cabral had taken her?

The damp air clung to her skin and clothes, and it *smelled* wet; mildew and mold, and ancient rainwater and seawater both. The ground beneath her was dirt and rock, grimy and uneven, jagged edges of stone that jabbed her as she felt her way around. The only sound she could hear besides her own scuffling was a slow, irregular, *DRIP drip-DRIP* of water.

None of this helped her. But then, that would be Cabral's intention, to imprison her somewhere completely disorienting. The bastard was lucky she'd woken up during the day; if she'd awoken at night, she'd have more strength to escape.

She'd been Cabral's captive before. She had *escaped* him before.

Because of Trave, both times, said a small voice inside her.

The chamber was narrow, and the only egress a large wood-and-iron door in the middle of one bowing wall. The length of the chamber, however, baffled her. She'd walked away from the door, trailing her hand on the wall at her side for half an hour before she turned and made her way back to the door. The whole length she'd walked—the tunnel, as it seemed— remained roughly six rods wide, but continued, at a slight

116

downhill slope, for some time. The syncopated *DRIP drip-DRIP* of water came from further down the tunnel, away from the door, but how far she could not guess. No light reached her no matter where she walked in the tunnel; it was always darker than midnight.

Astrid yearned for night to fall so she could finally *see* something, even if it was just bare, grimy dirt and stone. When that happened, she'd explore the tunnel as far as she could. She could not imagine the place held any sort of real exit—Cabral would never make escape easy for her—but she could not help but hope.

So she waited at the wooden door. She waited for her retractable claws to sprout, half again the length of her child-fingers. She waited for her teeth to elongate and sharpen into fangs, for her bones, muscle, and skin to strengthen and harden.

She would try to burst through the door with brute force once night fell. The wood was damp, almost rotten, and while it was reinforced with iron Astrid could smell the rust when she put her nose close, could feel the corrosion. She could bend iron, perhaps even break it if it was already weakened.

But why would Cabral allow it?

Astrid did not have to wait long to find out why.

A small green glow soon began to illuminate her surroundings. As the sun set, her eyes grew brighter, until they were two tiny burning green suns.

The tunnel extended as far as her eyes could discern. The roof of the tunnel was much higher than she'd expected. But the more Astrid looked around, the more she wasn't sure she could call the place either a cave *or* a tunnel. The floor was dirt and rock, certainly, but the walls were cut stone blocks and mortar, manmade. Above her, a complex network of wooden rafters supported the stone ceiling.

Astrid shivered. The structure seemed stable enough, but certainly not impervious to collapse. Perhaps that was Cabral's intention: to bury her alive in an impenetrable tomb of crumbled stone, wood, and grime. He would leave her to rot and desiccate for the rest of eternity.

All the more reason to get out while she still could.

The door had no handle or opening mechanism that she could see, but the hinges faced her. That was odd. If she were in a cell of some kind, the hinges ought to be on the other side, out of her reach. Hinges were invariably the weakest part of any door; remove the hinge mechanism, and breaking the lock was just a matter of applying enough force.

It was easy enough to dig into the rusting hinges with her claws, and pry them apart. Soon, three iron bolts had fallen to the floor.

Astrid moved to face the door head-on, the wood and metal lit in an eerie green light by her own eyes. She tried not to let the stab of hope she felt at removing the hinges affect her.

This will not turn out the way you think, she told herself. *Cabral will have planned plot after plot around every eventuality of your escape.*

But was that really true? Was Cabral as brilliant as he professed? She had always thought he was, and yet she'd escaped his clutches twice now.

Astrid knocked sharply three times. *Thunp, thunp, thunp.*

It wasn't hollow, but it wasn't a continuous single block of wood, either. Instead, planks roughly the width of Astrid's stretched hand were stacked side by side, and three metal bands, corresponding with the hinge placements, wrapped horizontally around them.

But the dull *thunp* sound the door had made when she rapped on it was the best news. It was damp, certainly, perhaps all the way through. She guessed at least one lock would be placed around the middle of the door, near the central iron band.

Astrid planted her feet firmly. Then she kicked the middle band close to where it met the stone wall with all of the strength she could muster. The door quivered. Astrid kicked again, and again and again, and while the door did not burst outward as she hoped, it did continue to shudder clammily in its frame.

Astrid looked more closely at the door. While it had hardly budged, she did notice something else promising. The metal band she had struck repeatedly with her foot had pressed into the wood behind it so far that the wood swelled outward above and below the iron.

Progress was progress. Astrid planted her feet at an angle to the door, clenched her fist, and drove her hand into the wood above the metal band where it bulged outward. With her enhanced strength and hardened skin, muscles, and bone, it was like hitting it with a hammer the size of a child's fist, and hers plunged satisfyingly into the wood, damp splinters jutting out around her hand.

For the first time since waking up in her strange cell, Astrid allowed herself a smile.

She had not punctured all the way through the wood, but her fist had sunk half its length into the swell. Astrid pulled back again, and hammered her fist into the door. Again. Again.

THUNF. THUNF. THUNF.

Then, with a *THFOOK*, she burst through. Warm air greeted her fist as it penetrated the door, much warmer than the air on her side of the portal. She had not realized it was so cold in her prison.

She searched for a locking mechanism, and found one—a

sturdy slide bolt, easy enough to manipulate once she slipped her arm through up to her bicep. With a slide and a clank, the bolt slipped free.

She kicked the door again. It quivered significantly more this time, but still did not move from its frame.

Astrid went to work on the bottom lock, punching her way through the wood near the bottom band. She moved quickly, the sweet smell of hope sharp in her nostrils, and soon had the bottom lock unbolted as well.

She took a step back. The top metal band was higher than she could reach, and it would be significantly more difficult to break through up there. She could climb, bracing herself on the hole in the middle she had already made, but she would not be able to leverage enough force in that position. Best not to bother. She hoped there was only one lock remaining, and that the damage she'd done to the door had weakened it enough for her to break her way through.

If it hadn't, now that she knew the integrity of the door (or lack thereof), she could always punch her way through as a last resort. Her hand ached, despite her enhancements, but the pain would be worth her freedom.

Fortunately, she did not have to resort to that. With three firm kicks, punching her foot downward at the bottom band of the door, it swung open enough for her to push her way through and into the chamber beyond.

But, as Astrid looked around at her new surroundings, the hope she'd felt turned to a horrible, sickening pain.

She was in a circular stone chamber, with no ceiling above her. Instead, the walls of the chamber jutted upward, up and up, and in the distance she could see a hint of the night sky above, the indifferent stars twinkling. For a moment, as she gazed up at them, Astrid had the most unreasonable reaction to the lights above her.

She feared them. She feared them like she'd never feared anything else before, anything in her life. She could not explain it, other than a great dread that overtook her, that pierced her hardened skin and toughened muscle and bone, penetrating her and surrounding her all at once. She wanted to cower against the ground, to run back into the dark tunnel from whence she'd sprung.

But she couldn't. She couldn't because of who lay here in the chamber, dead on the dirt floor.

How had Cabral done this? How had he taken all of them, or even *known* who to take?

Two bodies lay in the center of the chamber.

Knot and Cinzia.

Dead, because of her.

Cinzia had been beaten to death with the sort of viciousness that only a vampire could manage; two bloody, gaping holes stared from where her beautiful eyes had once been. Astrid would not have recognized her, except for her autumn-colored hair and the Trinacrya she wore around her neck. Two corners of the golden triangle were clean and pure, one reflecting the starlight above, but the third corner was dark, and as Astrid looked more closely, she saw it was crusted in blood.

Astrid reached out and caressed her friend's skin. Something inside her swelled, building and building, threatening to burst.

She turned to Knot.

The feeling of dread compounded, increased without limit. As she approached, she understood why.

Knot had a ragged wound on his neck. A wooden stake impaled each limb. There was a lot less blood than there should

121

have been. Almost none, in fact; just a dribble, crusted around Knot's lips.

Astrid clutched her chest, where she felt the greatest pain she had ever felt in the long life she could remember boring into her, hollowing her out, carving away until she was nothing but a husk of vampiric intent.

Knot's eyes snapped open, emitting a bright red light of their own. The color burst into Astrid's world, conflicting sharply with the green light her own eyes emitted. Knot's mouth opened.

You did this to me, she imagined him saying. *This is your fault, you little bitch—I wish I had never met you—*

But he made no sound.

The stars looked down indifferently on the dead and undead alike, and Astrid feared them.

With a sob mixed with a scream of despair, anger, and horror, Astrid turned and burst back through the door she'd broken through, leaving the terrible starlit chamber, and sprinted down the tunnel, down, down, deep into the Sfaera, away from her friends and away from the dead as quickly as her feet would take her.

She ran until her muscles ached and cried out. The tunnel went on and on, and she began to wonder if she was running through the exact same stretch of stone, dirt, and wood over and over again.

She ran until, finally, the tortuous loop of the tunnel widened into a larger torchlit chamber, the ceiling twice as high. Astrid stumbled to a stop, her breath ragged and halting.

Two vampires stood in the center of the hall. One was a woman, young, dark-skinned, muscular and beautiful, long braided hair tied in a large knot at the top of her head. Colorful flowing robes elongated her already tall, majestic frame. Astrid stared in shock. The woman's eyes glowed yellow. Every other vampire on the Sfaera she had encountered had red eyes, as did the other vampire standing with this woman.

The other vampire was Olin Cabral.

"It took you longer than I had hoped, but here you are," Cabral said, smiling. "We've been waiting for you."

If Cabral was here, this was real. What Astrid had witnessed in the starlit cave—

"Was not real," the female vampire said.

"You could have kept up the ruse a *bit* longer," Cabral muttered. The creases around his red glowing eyes, still locked on Astrid, bespoke nothing but amusement.

"Your friends are not dead," the woman said, ignoring Cabral. No one treated Cabral this way—as if he were inconsequential. Even more surprising was the fact that he didn't seem to care. The Cabral Astrid knew would have made an example of—and then killed—anyone who treated him like that.

"Who are you?" Astrid asked, staring at the woman unabashedly.

"You may call me Elegance. The vision you experienced was of my own making."

A vision. Was Elegance a psimancer of some kind? Astrid had never heard of psimantic abilities surviving the transition from human to vampire.

"I owed Cabral a favor. That debt is now paid."

Cabral's smile faded. He knelt before the woman. "I thank you for it, Elegance," he said.

Astrid blinked, her weariness and the horrors she had just seen almost—*almost*, as Knot's wide eyes bored into her, burning red, his mouth moving—forgotten. Cabral, the most powerful vampire she had ever met, had just knelt to another. And her friends...

"My friends are not dead?" Astrid asked.

"It was not real," Cabral said, rising. "But I want you to understand something, my dear." His eyes flashed, a surge of red light brightening the room. "It was not real, *but it could be*. I could do that to you. I *will* do that to you."

Astrid stared dumbly at him. Relief siphoned through the stark grief that had consumed her on her hectic, wild run through the tunnel. Relief, and with it, the slightest hint of confidence.

Astrid did not hesitate in showing it off.

"You have me, Cabral," Astrid said. "But you cannot hurt my friends. They are more powerful than you know."

"The ex-Nazaniin?" Cabral asked with a smirk. "His psi-mantic power is spent, and he is nothing without it."

What Cabral said was true, but Knot's power wasn't what Astrid had had in mind. Cabral might be able to best Knot, but not Cinzia and Jane when the power of Canta settled upon them.

"Do not underestimate my power and patience, little girl. I will take away everything you love. The vision you saw was just a hint of what is to come."

Laughter bubbled up from deep inside of Astrid, and she took pleasure in Cabral's puzzled look. It had just dawned on her that she should have known better: Knot and Cinzia dwarfed Cabral; their destinies went beyond the squabbles of vampire lords. And Cinzia and Jane's ability to avoid assassination was truly uncanny.

"You cannot touch my friends," Astrid said. She did not say it as a challenge, or even as a warning, but a simple statement of fact. "You have me, but you can do nothing to them."

Cabral's red eyes bored into her. "You misunderstand me,

my dear," he said. "I've looked into hurting these human friends of yours, and believe it or not, I've come to the same conclusion as you have. They are untouchable."

Cabral took a step toward her, and an involuntary tremor worked its way down Astrid's spine.

"But you said it yourself. I have *you*, my dear. And to take your ridiculous friends away, you are all I need."

Astrid did not respond. Cabral knew exactly how to find the source of her hope and pierce a hole straight through it.

"I can see you do not understand. You've always been a step behind, haven't you, so allow me to explain it to you.

"Now that I have you, things will be different. You will not be a part of the new Fangs I form, not for many years at least. You will not be a servant, either. No, Astrid, I will take no more chances with you. You will be my prisoner. You will remain confined for quite some time—I don't know, a half-dozen decades at least, perhaps a hundred years or more depending on your attitude—but certainly long enough for your friends, for everyone you know and love today, to die."

Cabral glanced at Elegance.

"That is, unless I'm granted another option first."

Astrid felt the hope drain away completely. Cabral could keep her here forever if he wanted to. Even if he died, she would remain here. He could take away everything she loved, and he didn't even have to harm them to do it. While Knot, Cinzia, and the others could protect themselves from physical harm, there was one thing all mortals were vulnerable to.

Time.

Astrid's legs collapsed beneath her, and she crumpled to the ground.

13

INSIDE THE BLACKGUARD INN, near central Triah, Knot took a draught from a large mug of ale. He didn't know if it was his encounter with Sirana the other night, the fact he hadn't seen Astrid in a few days, or something else altogether, but there was enough on his mind that he actually wanted to dull his senses for a spell.

The atmosphere of the Blackguard Inn was exasperatingly jovial this evening. A lutist had struck up a tune as he'd walked in, and musician after musician had joined in until what seemed an entire bloody orchestra was playing. A few of the patrons had taken to dancing in the open space in the middle of the common room. Spirits were high, and laughter the most common sound.

For Knot, it was intolerable. The Blackguard was the seventh inn he'd been to that day, and still he hadn't had any luck. He'd been asking after rumors of the shamans, who Astrid had said might be able to help Winter, but no one seemed to know anything about such people.

And Astrid hadn't shown herself for three days. He'd begun to worry the first night she hadn't returned to their tent in the Odenite camp. He told himself again that Astrid could take care of herself. She'd disappeared a time or two, and had always come back. But he was afraid for her this time, more than he'd ever been before.

"You look like you need another drink, mate."

Knot didn't raise his eyes. He'd made note of this particular man the moment he walked into the inn: blond, average height, broad-shouldered. A dagger at his belt. His gait and mannerisms were strikingly familiar; it had taken Knot a few moments to realize they reminded him of himself. But he knew this man anyway.

Knot had seen him in his dreams.

"You're Nazaniin," Knot muttered.

"Canta's bloody bones. She told you I'd be coming, didn't she?"

"Sirana might have mentioned something," Knot said, "but I'd have recognized you anyway."

"She could have done me the same favor."

For the first time, their eyes met.

"You're too pretty to be a fighter," Knot grunted.

The man chuckled at that. "Aye, so they tell me. The old you would know why."

Just as Knot kept his appearance as nondescript and unremarkable as possible, the other man's attractiveness was a sort of camouflage. Knot felt his own unobtrusiveness was far superior to the ostentatious look of this Nazaniin.

"What do you mean 'you'd have recognized me anyway'? Do you know who I am?"

"No. Just seen you in my dreams."

Silence stretched between them.

"My name is Code," the other finally said. When Knot shrugged, Code added, "That doesn't mean anything to you? Jog something in the memory?"

"It doesn't." Knot took another swig of his ale. "That hurt your feelings?"

Code's mouth flattened. "If you're a completely different person, you could've done us all a favor and left his attitude behind."

"Don't take it personally," Knot muttered. "Just having a bad day."

Code signaled the innkeeper, and asked the man for another mug of ale.

Knot could buy his own drinks. He shook his head, about to say as much, but Code cut him off.

"It's for me, mate. Don't get your knickers in a squeeze."

Knot almost chuckled at that, but stopped himself just in time.

"So we knew each other before?"

"Aye, we did. Had sort of a rivalry going on, actually."

Knot snorted. "I imagine that was all in your mind, lad. I ain't the type to have rivals."

"You're right, you weren't." Code grinned. "Not until you met me."

"And you were a real challenge for me, then? Easy to say when I have no memory of it."

"I'm in your dreams," Code said. "How many people have you dreamt about, from before? I can't imagine it's many."

Knot frowned. "A lot of people have come through my dreams," he said. "More than you could imagine." He'd killed hundreds in his dreams, and seen many more besides.

But the lad was right. Only a few had graced his dreams more than once, let alone on a recurring basis. This man, Code, was one of the few. Sirana one of the others.

"You remember me for a reason. I never liked you, La—" Code stopped himself. "Knot. I never liked the man you were before. Lathe and I did not get along. But I respected him, and he—"

"You think just because the person who inhabited this body—"

Code shot him a meaningful glance, and Knot caught it immediately. He and Code had been speaking in hushed tones, but Knot had begun to raise his voice. He hadn't really caught the attention of anyone else in the inn yet, but he certainly would if he started shouting about swapping bodies and sifts and the like.

Knot took a deep breath, then spoke again, more quietly. "Just because the person who lived in this house before me respected you, don't mean I will."

"He *tolerated* me," Code said. "I learned a lot from him, whether he liked it or not."

"I'm not the psimancer he was. If you think you'll—"

"Will you stop? I know you're not him."

"Then why are you here?" Knot asked.

"If Sirana already mentioned we'd approach you, you know why."

Knot exhaled. Sirana hadn't mentioned specifically why, only that someone would approach him, and that Knot should let it happen. Knot had no illusions that he could trust her, or Code.

"I must be a valuable connection to you," Knot said. "But why should I let you have that connection? What allegiance do I owe the Nazaniin?"

"None," Code said quickly. "But if you let me… Goddess, I don't even care about being your friend. If you just share information with me, keep me updated—"

Knot chuckled, though the sound was completely humorless. "I won't spy on the Odenites for you. If your leader thinks that's what I'm going to do for him, he can shove his head up his own ass."

"We could help you, should you need it."

"You sent a *cotir* to kill Jane Oden," Knot said. "I think you've *helped* us enough, don't you?"

"We won't do that again," Code said. "You have my word on that, and you have Kosarin's as well."

"Forgive me if I don't put much stock in Nazaniin honor."

Code sighed. "We can use one another as a resource. This could help the Odenite cause."

Truth was, Knot didn't care for Jane's vision of Canta's Church more than any other—but she did want to stop the Nine Daemons, and he cared about protecting the Odens and their followers while they did that.

The Nazaniin might help that cause. Their knowledge and information network could prove invaluable.

Knot leaned closer to Code, lowering his voice. "What of the Nine?" he asked. "What do you know of them?"

The blood drained from Code's face. "If you want to talk about that, we should go somewhere else," Code said. "I've tangled with the Nine more than once. They need to be stopped."

Knot nodded slowly. If they had that goal in common, at least, perhaps there was some business they could do together.

"One more thing," Code added. "I'm a variant psimancer. I take *faltira* to access my abilities. I've gotten to a place where I can use *faltira* without suffering the addictive consequences."

Knot narrowed his eyes. "You know of the shamans who say they can control it?"

Code nodded. "I do, and I know what helps and what doesn't. I heard you've been looking for a solution for this particular problem—and I've also heard who it is you're trying to aid. If rumors of that woman's power are even fractionally true, we need to keep her as sane as possible. Without help, *faltira* will consume her, sooner or later."

Knot chewed his cheek. It would not have been difficult for the Nazaniin to tail Knot from inn to inn, and gather what information he sought and infer why he sought it. Code could be saying this just to pacify him, to get him to comply.

But if there was hope for Winter, Knot wanted her to have it. He owed it to her.

14

Wyndric Ocean

"FOG ON THE OCEAN. A bad omen."

Cova, empress of Roden, had known Garen Strongst was a superstitious man when she'd made him admiral. She hated to see it surface now.

He was right about the fog. From the *Crown Conquest*, the flagship of the Rodenese Navy, vision was limited. They were somewhere just south of the Roden–Khale border, about forty radials from the coast. The fog had come in with the sunset, and deepened through the night. Now, when the sun should be rising, Cova could see nothing but gray mist in all directions. Standing on the bow of the *Crown* and looking back, she could not even see the stern of her own ship, let alone the fleet following them. The scene was made eerier still by the awful silence that accompanied the fog. Other than the lapping of water against the ship, and the occasional order carried across the waves from her crew, there was no sound whatsoever.

The signal-officer, his flags useless in the mist, shouted instructions and coordinates to the ship next in the line.

Cova frowned. "Is that necessary? Should we not lie-to and wait for the fog to clear?"

"If you'll forgive me, Your Grace—" The admiral's condescending answer was interrupted by the arrival of a tall young man, who arrived with a salute. "What is it, Brakston?"

"The eyes in the nest above think they've seen masts," the sailor reported. "Not our own. Both to port and starboard."

"They *think* they've seen masts?" Strongst asked. "Have they or haven't they?"

"It's difficult to tell in the fog, sir, but—"

"Of course it's difficult to tell in the fog. Until they've confirmed that these sightings of theirs are real, we do not deviate. We stay the course, Brakston."

The signal-officer shouted again, and a distant shout from the ship behind them came in response.

Cova swore. "Shut that officer up! Caution is the order, Admiral. I'd prefer not to have my fleet ambushed."

"Your Grace, I assure you—"

"If you're not going to respect my office, you can stop calling me 'Your Grace,' Admiral."

"I..."

Cova turned to Brakston. "Find the captain," she said. "If Admiral Strongst will not do as I command, I'll relieve him of his office and give it to someone else."

Brakston saluted her, then rushed down the ladder to the main deck.

The admiral laughed nervously. "I assure you, Your Grace, that will not be necessary. I am happy to—"

"I don't have time to argue with you, Strongst." No more "Admiral." She'd already made the decision. "We must be more careful—"

The ship shuddered beneath them, and a crash of splintering wood split the fog's silence. The *Crown Conquest* swayed, leaning to starboard, and Cova gripped the rail to keep from losing her balance.

A smaller ship Cova did not recognize had rammed them.

All she could make out in the fog were its crimson sails, and while Cova couldn't see the ship figurehead, she could guess it was carved in the shape of a human skull.

Pirates.

Cova swore. It would be foolish to attack Cova's entire fleet—she did not think all of the pirates in the Wyndric Ocean would amount to enough ships to take on her navy—but the fog provided them cover enough, and the Rodenese Navy enough confusion, that they could cause some damage.

"Tensen," Cova shouted to her Reaper captain, "don't let them board!"

A series of smaller shudders made the deck beneath her tremble once more. Grappling hooks.

Tensen, a tall, sinewy man nearby, began to relay orders to his Reapers—Roden's elite fighters.

"First and second squad," he shouted, "cut the grappling ropes! Don't let them swarm us! Third squad, form an archery line, keep them down!"

But the ropes were not cut in time. A roar erupted from the side of the ship where the grapples had fallen; the sound of running feet and combat told her that, somewhere in the fog, a horde of wild, bloodthirsty men had streamed from the pirate ship onto the deck of the *Crown Conquest*. Her Reapers were there to meet them, and the two forces collided with the sounds of crashing metal, shuffling feet on wood, guttural grunts and shouts, and the screams of the dying.

Goddess, how can anyone be dying yet? Cova wondered, feeling cold. The soldiers had only just joined in battle, and already she heard screams that could mean nothing else.

A form barreled up to her out of the mist, and every muscle in Cova's body tensed. She took a step back, hand moving to the sword at her hip. She was proficient with the weapon, but no expert. And she had never been in a real battle before.

"Your Grace." As the shape became clearer, she recognized the ship's captain, Rakkar. "The ram hit us above the waterline. If we can pull away, we can salvage the ship."

At least someone is competent on this vessel. "Thank you, Captain," Cova said.

Rakkar saluted, and turned back to the deck, shouting orders at his sailors.

The mist had started to clear, and now Cova saw her initial fear at Rakkar's approach had been unfounded. Her two Reaper guards, Flok and Grost, stood on either side of her still. They and a pair of two other guards took shifts following her everywhere she went on the ship, and stood guard outside her chambers at night. She had been annoyed by the practice at first, wondering why on earth she needed protection on her own ship full of her own soldiers, but now she was grateful for their presence.

Both men had weapons drawn, their dark blue tunics damp from the fog. Beneath that, their gray plate armor reflected a soft orange glow.

Cova turned immediately to see more pirates boarding the *Crown Conquest*, torches and weapons in hand.

"Third squad!" Tensen screamed over the battle sounds. "Focus on the torch-bearers!"

By now General Horas had joined her on the upper deck at the bow of the ship. Tensen commanded her Reapers, but Horas commanded her entire army. "Your Grace," Horas said, breathless. "I've mobilized the forces belowdecks. Our numbers will soon overwhelm them, if nothing else."

Cova nodded, still wary of the battle. She trusted her generals—more so than she trusted her ex-admiral, at least—

but a thrill of simultaneous excitement and terror reverberated in her bones, unwilling to fade.

Another squad of Rodenese soldiers, in light blue tunics and bright mail, had already formed up and were firing on the pirates, but now turned their attention to the men carrying torches. They fired a volley, and half a dozen torch-bearers fell, many of them into the water.

The *Crown Conquest* lurched to starboard, trying to get away from the attacking ship, but the ram and harpoons held it too tightly.

Over her shoulder, Cova sensed a shadow moving. She turned to see another ship, much larger than the one that had rammed the *Crown*, pulling up alongside them.

"Tensen—"

"I see it, Your Grace." Tensen shouted at his Reapers to split, and half of the elite force moved to starboard. Fortunately, the Reapers were not called elite for nothing; with the cover fire from the archer squad, they were holding off the pirates from the first ramming ship well enough.

To starboard, three huge planks crashed through the fog and onto the *Crown Conquest*'s decks, one of them smashing into the upper deck where Cova stood with her guards and captains. Two massive steel claws on the end clamped into the deck boards. It would not be easily moved.

Immediately, more pirates wielding torches and weapons rushed across the ramp, eyes alight with fire and violence.

Cova drew her sword. Her guards and the soldiers nearby fanned out in formation to protect her, but she could not afford to stand by when they were so outnumbered. With any luck, some of the Reapers on the main deck would make their way up to where she stood to reinforce her position, but Cova could not rely on it.

They would have to make a stand on their own.

The ship that had lowered the gangplanks was a dark shadow in the fog, barely discernible, but the shadow seemed almost as large as the *Crown Conquest* itself.

This could not be happenstance. Her luck could not possibly be this bad. Khalic intelligence must have been tracking their movements, and Khale had hired these pirates to attack when her fleet was at its most vulnerable, blinded by the fog.

The pirates could not defeat her entire fleet, and the Khalic government likely knew that. But it would slow her navy down—and in attacking the flagship, with her on it, could cut off the head of the Rodenese Empire before the war even started.

Cova was not about to let that happen.

Pirates rushed across the plank that connected the two ships, screaming as they ran. Faces wild, eyes afire. She braced herself, planted her feet as she'd been taught, sword at the ready.

The pirates crashed into her small group with battle cries and the slick sound of blades cutting flesh. Her Reapers held strong, easily dispatching the pirates at the head of the charge, and behind them the other soldiers, Horas, and the disgraced Admiral Strongst waited for any who might break through. Cova stood last, tall in her gilded and blue-painted armor, sword ready.

Wave after wave of fighters crashed into the force before her, more and more slipping through the front line of her Reapers. One managed to break through, and Cova struck him down, her sword threading through his wild swings to pierce through his unarmored chest.

Not for the first time, Cova wondered whether she shouldn't have heeded the counsel of her advisors and stayed in Izet. It was traditional for the head of the empire to accompany

Roden's armies on any large-scale campaign, but her presence was needed at home, too. Izet needed rebuilding, and the political structure was fragile at best. She had left the mother of her dead husband, Hama Mandiat, to rebuild and rule in her absence. She'd brought Andia Luce with her, who was part of the Ruling Council of Roden, and, as the once-betrothed of the dead Emperor Grysole, was as close a thing to an heir as she had nowadays, but protocol insisted they travel in different ships, should the unthinkable happen to one of them. Many criticized her for the decision to bring Andia along; Andia Luce was the daughter of her father's most prominent political rival, and those closest to her suspected Andia might have ulterior motives. And that might be true; but Andia was a valuable ally, and had become Cova's friend.

Wherever Andia's ship was, Cova hoped it was not under attack as well.

Another wave of pirates crashed into her guard force, and a man broke through unscathed. She caught a glimpse of glittering piercings in his scarred face, and then he was bringing his broadsword down on her. She blocked the attack with her blade, her muscles straining and hand aching even from the single blow.

She could not last long against this man.

She leaned out of the way of another slash from her attacker. He was not particularly fast, but he was strong. Another strike, and Cova parried, deflecting his sword with a magnificent *ring* that pierced the air. Pain shot through her arms and hands.

"Protect the empress!" came a shout from the lower deck. But the glance she sent that way cost her a precious fraction of concentration, and when she turned fully back to her opponent, his sword was already coming down on her. She brought her own up to parry again, knowing it wouldn't be enough, and then an arrow shaft sprouted from the pirate's neck. His eyes bulged beneath pierced eyebrows, and his strike faltered just enough for Cova to knock it sideways and plunge her blade into his chest, piercing through leather and flesh.

The pirate slumped to the deck just as a loud, bellowing horn echoed through the fog.

Cova froze in fear as the blast echoed again, thinking the two blasts surely meant another ship would soon engage with them, but then the men in front of her turned and retreated across the plank that had buried itself in the upper deck, running back to the large ship, still shadowy in the fog alongside the *Crown Conquest*. Admiral Strongst made to follow them across—Goddess, he was the foolhardy sort of brave, and Cova wondered how in Oblivion the Council had ever suggested this man to lead her armada—but Cova shouted his name. Strongst turned to look at her, bloodlust in his eyes. Cova only shook her head. They may have won the battle on the *Crown Conquest*, barely, but there was no telling what awaited them if they followed the pirates onto their own ships.

Turning to the lower deck, she saw the pirates there had retreated, too.

A faint mechanical click echoed across the water, and then the large, shadowy pirate ship to starboard began to glide away into the fog, leaving behind the three wide, barbed planks embedded in the *Crown Conquest*'s decks. The pirates must have triggered some release mechanism at the hinges; the barbed ends of the planks would take time and great effort to remove.

The smaller ship that had rammed them to port disengaged, and the *Crown Conquest* shuddered again. Soon the *Crown Conquest* was alone in the clearing mist, crippled and listing to starboard.

A ragged cheer went up from the *Crown*'s three decks.

Cova did not share the sense of triumph. "Why are they retreating?" she asked. "If they'd pressed the attack a bit longer, they might've taken the *Crown*." *They might've taken* me, she thought.

"Look around you, Your Grace," Tensen said quietly. "The pirates suffered heavy losses."

Dozens of bodies littered the deck. Most of the wounded up here were pirates, left behind by their comrades. The ship's boys swarmed up the ladders to report, and Cova waited impatiently while they spoke to the captains.

"Give me your reports," she said, when they were finished.

General Horas was a broad man and, while not quite the tallest on the upper deck (that honor belonged to Flok and Grost), he was the oldest by a few years, nearly as old as Cova's father before he'd died. His usually smooth-shaven face was rough with stubble.

"Your Grace, our casualties are minimal," Horas said, his face and voice grim despite the news. "Less than ten dead, and roughly the same injured. Considering our odds, these are good numbers."

"And our attackers? What of their losses?"

"Significantly greater. Almost three dozen dead or wounded left behind on the *Crown*. No telling how many more fell into the sea, or back onto their own ships. We defeated them handily, Your Grace."

"I would not be so quick to label this a victory," the ship's captain said, overhearing the last of Horas's report as he arrived on the upper deck.

"Captain Rakkar," Cova said, "what is your assessment?"

"First of all, there is no telling what damage might have been done to the other ships in our fleet. Until the fog clears, I do not believe it prudent to attempt any audible communication.

We risk the pirates' return, perhaps in greater numbers, to finish what they started."

Strongst stepped forward with a frown. "Even if every pirate in the nine seas banded together, they could not stand a chance against our armada. We—"

Cova's sword, still drawn and bloody, moved to Strongst's neck.

"Garen Strongst," she hissed, "perhaps you have forgotten the words we had when this battle began—when you ignored my commands, and brought about this bloodbath through the shouts of the signal-officer. You have been demoted and have no say in these matters."

She glanced at her other commanders. "Gentlemen, *Admiral* Rakkar is now in charge of the fleet." She heard Rakkar's sharp intake of breath, but she was watching Strongst as she lowered her sword. He hung his head. "See to it that Strongst finds his way to the brig until I decide his fate." Strongst's neck was smeared with the blood from Cova's sword.

"Unless you would like to force me to decide now, Strongst?"

"No, Your Grace," he said meekly. If he had deigned to show such humility earlier, he might not have found himself in this position.

Rakkar gave the nod to two of his sailors, who escorted Strongst down the ladder to the brig. But, try as she might, Cova could not place the blame of this defeat into Strongst's hands. The Council may have suggested him, but she chose him. If there was any failing here, it was her own.

"Continue with your report, Rakkar."

"Beyond the potential damage to our fleet, beyond the fact that we cannot risk another attack, we must assess our own situation on the *Crown Conquest*. We are crippled, Your Grace.

We are not at immediate risk of sinking, that much is in our favor. The planks causing us to lean to starboard are keeping the battering ram's puncture above the waterline. We can gently steer her inland, Your Grace, but there is not much more we can do than that."

"Can we salvage her?"

"Your Grace," Rakkar said slowly, "The time it would take to bring the *Crown* ashore, get it repaired, and get back on course would delay us immeasurably."

"Khale ordered this attack," Cova said. "Would you all agree?"

"Aye, Your Grace," Rakkar said.

Tensen nodded. "They knew they would not stop us, Your Grace, but they must have hoped to slow us down. They hired these *pirates* to attack us, to attack *you*, Your Grace. A personal affront to the Azure Crown. They targeted your ship specifically. The best-case scenario for them would have been for the pirates to take this ship, take you, and end the war before it began."

Cova tried not to think about what the pirates would have done to her, had they taken her. She had never seen pirates with her own eyes before this day, but she had heard stories of their brutality, the atrocious acts they committed against the women and children they captured. Empress or not, Cova could not imagine she would have been exempt from their violent lust.

"Very well, we will send the *Crown* back to Roden for repair, with a skeleton crew." As much as she hated to lose her flagship, there was no other way. "These Khalic-hired pirates did not take me, and I'll be damned if they will slow us down.

"When the fog clears, we will assess our fleet's situation, repair the damage we can, take the resources from any ships we may need to send home or scuttle, and continue onward."

Her captains nodded, and she hoped to the Goddess that the looks they gave one another were positive. She was through with making mistakes.

The sick feeling in her stomach was just beginning to fade, and along with it, the fog. In the east, the outline of the sun could just be seen through the thinning mist.

"We will make it to Triah," Cova said, "and repay this attack a thousand fold."

15

Somewhere beneath Triah

WHEN ASTRID HEARD THE low clank of the lock turning on the door to her cell, she leapt into a crouch. She had already decided, in the days she had spent alone in her small prison cell, that she would not stop fighting him. Every opportunity she got, she would attempt to escape, she would attempt to fight, she would attempt to kill Cabral.

The significant word in each of those concepts was "attempt." She had no illusions that she might actually be successful; Cabral had already shown extreme caution when handling her thus far, and she could not imagine that would change anytime soon. But she could not give up hope.

So when the heavy iron door began to creak open, Astrid sprang through her pitch-black cell, barreling into the door itself and sending it flying into whoever was on the other side.

She did not wait to see who it was or how many others there were; instead, shielding her eyes from the bright torchlight, Astrid took off down the lit corridor—

—and slammed immediately into the tallest, largest vampire she had ever encountered.

The big man lifted her easily, slinging her over his impossibly broad shoulder. She blinked, stunned by the bright light and the sudden stop; she'd slammed into the vampire with a lot of force.

Astrid shifted her position, but the vampire's heavy arm

constricted around her. Turning her head, she could see the ceiling of the corridor, rock and dirt and occasional wooden rafters. If she had but one hand free, she could have easily reached up and brushed her fingers against it. And when a particularly low point in the ceiling came along, or a support beam, the huge vampire carrying her had to duck his head.

The floor rushed past, a dizzying distance beneath her. Three other vampires walked alongside the big one, but none of them even reached his shoulders.

Bloody bones, he was massive.

Cabral was not with them. Not surprising; he would think himself above the menial task of fetching prisoners. By the red glow emanating from the eyes of those escorting her, and the green of her own, Astrid could tell it was nighttime. She had been in that cell for at least a week, maybe more.

The vampire carrying her did not have the same red eyes as other vampires, but neither were they green like Astrid's. They were almost orange. That marked two sets of eyes Astrid had seen recently that were abnormal. She wished she had some inkling as to what that could mean.

"Where are you taking me?" Astrid asked.

None of them answered. The muscles of the big vampire were hard as steel, and that had nothing to do with the nighttime effects vampirism had on his skin. As big as this vampire was, he had very little fat and a great deal of muscle. Astrid repressed a sudden wave of fear at how strong this beast must be with vampiric strength added on to its natural muscle. All vampires were significantly stronger, faster, and tougher at night, when the sun was gone. But their enhanced strength was still based on their natural strength; even at her most powerful, Astrid was still comparatively a child to most other vampires. She was fast, she was quick, and she knew how to fight, but in a contest of strength she wouldn't stand a chance against a regular vampire, let alone this monster.

The tunnel forked a few times. Left, left again, then right, then a central fork of three, left again. Finally, it opened up into a much larger space, as her vampire escort passed through a low arch. Astrid's world turned on its head as the big vampire tossed her from his shoulder to the ground at the foot of a raised platform on which three thrones stood. Astrid tumbled into a heap onto a lavish, braided rug.

Unlike the austere tunnels and rooms Astrid had seen since Cabral had imprisoned her, this room was lined with tapestries, and in front of them stood pedestals on which sculptures, busts, and weapons rested. Even the sconces were highly decorative ironwork, the torches illuminating the room in a dim, flickering light.

Vampires crowded the room, Cabral among them.

She stood up, dusting herself off. It was a futile gesture; she'd been wearing the same faded dress and breeches for she didn't know how long.

The walls on either side angled inward, leading to a point directly across from the archway through which Astrid had just been carried. The ornate thrones were at the point of the room, their backs reaching high above the heads of the three vampires sitting on them. Astrid recognized the vampire on the left as Elegance.

Elegance's yellow eyes pierced the dim room like golden fire. Her hair, still in hundreds of tiny braids, was tied neatly into a topknot, secured by a bright gold band. She wore a yellow robe that complimented her dark skin tone, trimmed with gold. Yellow gemstones decorated her throne and much of her jewelry.

The vampire seated next to Elegance, on the throne in the middle, was another woman, tiellan, slightly younger and more slender in form than Elegance, her ears poking up out of very short, messily styled silver hair. Her eyes emitted a cool, deep blue glow. She wore a dress of dark blue; sapphires decorated her throne and jewelry.

"The color coordination is a bit garish in here, isn't it?" Astrid muttered.

If any of the vampires in the room heard her, they gave no sign of it.

The final vampire, seated on the right, was short and wiry, and wore robes that matched his glowing violet eyes, with lightly shaded amethysts and dark tourmalines bedazzling both his throne and the circlet on his head. His hair was speckled with gray, and creases pinched at the corners of his eyes. Astrid glanced over her shoulder. Cabral and his Fangs looked on grimly. Directly behind her was the big vampire, his frame even more imposing in the cavern, torchlight flickering on his face.

Every other vampire in the room, excepting the three on thrones, the big vampire who'd brought her here, and Astrid herself, had the typical crimson vampiric glow emanating from their eyes, adding a sinister shade to the room's already ominous flicker.

Astrid flashed her biggest, most charming smile up at the seated vampires. She clasped her hands together. "First of all I'd like to thank my escort, led by that outrageous piece of pure muscle, for guiding me safely here to be with you all." She looked over her shoulder again, winking at the big vampire. "I couldn't have done it without you.

"Secondly—" Astrid turned back to the platform "—let me just say what an honor it is to be in your polychromatic presence. Your fancy chairs are unmatched throughout the land, I'm sure."

The corner of Elegance's mouth twitched in a smile. But just as quickly as it came, it went. The vampire in the purple robe frowned down at Astrid. Behind her, Astrid heard a few of the vampires murmuring.

But she wasn't deterred. Instead, she turned to face Cabral.

"And finally," she said, opening her arms wide, "I'd like to thank the great Olin Cabral for making my presence here possible today. I can say, quite confidently, that there is no one in—or below—the city of Triah with a face that so closely resembles that of a mangy, abused hound."

The murmurs behind her grew louder; somebody guffawed.

"Or that hound's ass, for that matter," she added for good measure. Astrid focused on Cabral's creasing scowl, and the deep pleasure it brought her.

"And," Astrid said, her smile broadening, "no one on the Sfaera with a mind so exquisitely, excruciatingly dull."

She raised her hands placatingly at his angry Fangs. "Peace, cheese-cods. Let me finish." She must have sounded authoritative, because the Fangs actually did stop edging toward her.

"I'd even go so far as to say," Astrid continued, looking directly through the bleeding crimson light into Cabral's eyes, "That there has never been—and perhaps never will exist, ever—anyone in history who is quite the consummate plague sore that you are, Cabral. You—"

"*Enough.*"

The vampire did not shout, but somehow Astrid *felt* the voice resonate in her bones, rippling over her skin. She looked up at the platform to see the violet vampire standing, a scowl on his face.

Elegance smiled again, fully this time. That sight gave Astrid some confidence.

"Why," Violet said, pointing one long, sinewy claw at Astrid, "has this one been brought before the Coven?"

"This is Astrid," Cabral said, "a young vampire who——"

"She is not in our records," Violet said. "Has she passed the threshold?"

"No," Cabral said, bowing his head, "I have brought her here under special circumstances to request an audience with you."

Elegance leaned forward, looking at the violet vampire. "We have already agreed to hear this case, Equity."

The vampire took his seat once more. The moment he did, the tiellan woman sitting in the middle rose from her seat, levitating up from her throne. She floated down from the platform until she stopped, cross-legged and still suspended in the air, directly in front of Astrid.

"What in Oblivion is this?" blurted Astrid.

The tiellan vampire said nothing—nothing audible, at least—but instead Astrid heard a voice echo in her mind.

You are unfamiliar with the Coven. The voice, melodious and calm, resonated in her mind like harp strings plucked in an empty, dusty room. *That is not surprising. You would not have come to know of our existence for another one hundred and sixty-three years, had circumstances been normal. But Olin Cabral has brought you to our attention.*

"Eldritch, what are you saying to her?" Equity demanded. Astrid's vision clouded; the voice resonating in her mind consumed her.

"Fine, but be quick about it," Equity muttered, sitting back down on his throne.

When a vampire has been turned for five hundred years, they have

149

passed the threshold of requirement to be introduced into our presence, Eldritch went on.

"Who are you?" Astrid asked.

We are the Coven. The three of us have been around since the beginning of time.

"You are vampires, too?"

We are, but we have grown beyond what you could possibly comprehend.

"Your... powers?"

You witnessed Elegance's abilities the other night, albeit the circumstances were unfortunate and somewhat uncalled for. You are experiencing some of my own powers right now.

"I don't understand."

That is to be expected. You will, in time. I was against hearing your case at all, but Elegance insisted, and I have never been one to deny Elegance.

For now, we will hear what Cabral has to say, and then we will make our judgment.

Then the voice was out of Astrid's head, and Eldritch floated back up to her platform and settled herself gently back down on her sapphire throne.

"Very well, she is up to speed," Equity said. "Let us begin."

"Wait," Astrid said quickly, "saying I'm 'up to speed' is an understatement, don't you think? I don't understand what is happening here. Some sort of trial? How can I plead my case here if I don't even know—"

"You have misunderstood, child," Elegance said. It was the first time she had spoken since Astrid had entered the throne room. "You will not have a say here. We have convened to hear Cabral's case against you. As one of the Uninitiated, you have not yet earned your rights or voice in our presence."

"But—"

"Be silent," Elegance said, a hard edge to her voice, "or I will silence you myself."

So much for living up to your stupid name, Astrid thought.

But Astrid obeyed. She was completely outmatched if it came to a fight. Just the presence of the big vampire behind her was enough to make her twitchy, let alone whatever in Oblivion the throned rainbow triplets before her were all about.

Equity cleared his throat. "Very good. Olin Cabral, please step forward."

Cabral obeyed, not even bothering to look in Astrid's direction, and then knelt before the Coven. Astrid had never seen Cabral show such deference in her life. Not once.

"Rise," Equity said, "and state your case."

Cabral obeyed. "Eminent Ones," he began, "I have come here to ask for your assistance in punishing this vampire, Astrid, for the wrongs she has committed against me and my domain."

"What are the charges?" Equity asked, looking rather bored. He rested his chin on one hand, his elbow on the arm of his throne.

"She attacked my tower-house in Turandel," Cabral said. "She took my slaves, and killed the vampires and the infected who followed me."

"I didn't *take* your slaves," Astrid said, unable to contain herself. "I *freed* them."

Other than a burning yellow glare from Elegance, no one else acknowledged Astrid had said anything. Cabral continued speaking as if the interruption had never happened.

"She ruined the domain I had built up for myself," Cabral said. "The domain *you* had granted me. I demand she be punished."

Though the Coven did not say anything aloud, Astrid had the distinct impression that they were discussing Cabral's case together, via whatever power Eldritch wielded.

"This girl destroyed everything in your jurisdiction?" Equity eventually asked, raising one eyebrow.

Astrid smiled at the vampire's tone. If she'd destroyed everything Cabral had built, perhaps he didn't deserve to have anything in the first place.

She might even win this case without having to say anything.

"She had help," Cabral snapped. "Another of my former Fangs. Trave Tamlin helped her."

"Trave is one of the initiated," Elegance said, mildly surprised. "He should know better."

"He should, Your Eminence," Cabral said, head bowed, "but he is not here. The girl is the only one we could procure, for now. When I find Trave, I will bring him here for your judgment as well."

"Seems to me you want to punish this girl to satisfy your own rage," Elegance said thoughtfully. "Is that true, Cabral?"

Cabral frowned, and opened his mouth to speak, but Equity cut him off.

"Enough prattle. I have better things to do with my time. Do you have a punishment in mind, Cabral?"

"I do, Eminent Ones," Cabral said. Finally, for the first time since Astrid's insulting tirade when she'd first entered the room, Cabral turned to look at her. "I demand her sift be altered to be completely loyal to me. Take out any memory of the life she has now. Make her utterly dependent on me. She destroyed everything that was mine, and I demand she now *become* mine."

Alter her *sift*? Cabral was no psimancer. No vampire was.

But, then again, Elegance had shown her visions of her friends, dead and gone. If the Coven were as powerful as everyone around here seemed to think, perhaps Elegance, or one of the others, *did* have the power.

Astrid fought the growing panic in her chest.

"What's the matter, my dear?" Cabral asked, grinning widely. "No snarky remarks? No insults?"

"No," Astrid said quietly. "Just hatred. Hatred that will never go away, no matter how much time passes, no matter what this ridiculous hearing might do to me. That hatred will always be here, inside of me, Cabral. One day you'll face it, without anything else to help you."

Cabral held her gaze. The two stared at one another, until finally Equity spoke.

"We have made our decision," he said.

Cabral's smile returned. "What is your ruling, Eminent Ones?"

"Despite our misgivings over your failings as an overlord, Cabral," Equity said, glaring down at the vampire, "we acknowledge the crimes that have been done against you. As our chosen initiate, crimes against you are crimes against us, and that is a thing we do not tolerate."

"Of course, Eminent Ones," Cabral said, bowing his head.

Astrid shook her head, opening her mouth to protest, but no sound came out.

"That being said," Equity continued, "we do not accept your terms of punishment. This girl shows promise. Her eyes tell us that much. We would hate to disrupt that promise by altering her sift. You may keep her in your custody, and condition her as you wish in whatever way you think will be effective. But we will take no part in it."

"Eminent Ones, if you're allowing me to condition her, would it not be just as prudent for you to step in and—"

"We have made our decision, Cabral," Equity said, his voice hard. "Respect it."

Cabral bowed his head. "Of course, Eminent Ones."

"What right do you have to judge me?" Astrid demanded, fear crushing her chest. "What right do you have to turn me over to his *care?*" she spat.

"Our power gives us that right, child." Equity narrowed his eyes at her. "You began learning that lesson today; I suspect you will learn it again when you cross the threshold and officially join our order."

Astrid shook her head. "I'll never join you. Anyone who would choose *Cabral* as an associate doesn't deserve my allegiance. I don't care how old you are or what you can do."

"Watch your tongue, girl," Equity snapped. "You've already been told you have no voice here. That remains true. Nothing you say matters. We will not consider you, think of you, until you've crossed the threshold. Assuming you survive that long."

"You don't care about me now, fine," Astrid said, glaring up at Equity, "but you'll change your mind when I burn this place down around you, with each of you screaming inside it."

A heavy silence descended on the hall, the weight of it pressing her down into the floor. Every vampiric eye in the hall held her captive. She had crossed a line, she was sure. She had said what she'd said in anger, in terror, already sure of her defeat. Now she regretted it.

Then, as quickly as the silence fell, it evaporated as Equity and Elegance erupted in simultaneous, roaring laughter.

Soon every other vampire in the room was laughing, raucously and uncontrollably, at Astrid. Astrid heard a big booming chuckle from behind her that could only have come from the big vampire. Equity's loud guffaws and Elegance's ringing, musical laughter echoed above them all. Only Eldritch seemed unmoved, immutably calm.

Astrid let their derision wash over her, standing tall, her chin held high, her mouth firm and eyes dry.

When the sound quieted, Equity waved disdainfully in Astrid's direction. "Take her away, Igar. If we're lucky, she won't even make it past the threshold anyway." The big vampire scooped her up roughly once again.

She kept herself together all through the journey back to her cell. Only when the door had shut, and the footsteps had faded, and Astrid was alone in the dark with nothing but herself did she finally begin to cry.

PART II

THE AGONY OF BELIEF

16

Legion Barracks, Triah

NONE OF THE REPORTS on Riccan Carrieri's desk mattered to him except the one on top, detailing the rout of the pirates he'd hired to attack the Rodenese fleet. Roden had lost two or three ships, and at least three hundred people. Such losses weren't to be sniffed at, but Khale had hoped for more. The attack had barely made a dent in Empress Cova Amok's navy. And when he read how close the mercenaries had come to capturing the empress herself... it made him sick to think of the missed opportunity.

A knock at his door.

Carrieri leaned back in his chair, stretching his neck. The wooden paneling of his ceiling stared back at him dispassionately. His visitor knocked again, and Carrieri swore quietly under his breath.

When he opened the door to see Karina Vestri, Consular of the Khalic government.

"This is the second time in six months you've come to my door without first requesting my presence," Carrieri said flatly. "Not really fitting for your station, is it?"

"This is the second time in the year we've suffered a catastrophic military defeat," Karina snapped. "Is that really fitting for yours?"

Carrieri moved aside, and Karina stormed into the room.

"'Catastrophic' isn't the word I would use to describe it," he said. "I'm disappointed we didn't turn the navy back, but the attack was not a failure. And, need I remind you, I was against paying *pirates* from the beginning. Your own parliament overruled me."

"So you're saying that this disaster wasn't your fault?" Karina asked, her eyes bright with anger. "Khale's Grand Marshal?"

Carrieri's frown deepened. It was not like him to shirk responsibility, or make excuses. But it was *her* holding him responsible, and when it was her...

Karina sighed, collapsing into a chair in his open study, just a few paces away from the doorway to his chambers.

"Goddess, we're in a mess, aren't we?"

"Aye," Carrieri muttered, the muscles in his chest still tense despite Karina's clear resort to informality—or perhaps because of it.

"You defeated Roden in a war once before." Her eyes pleaded with him.

"Nothing is certain."

"Canta's bloody bones, you cannot say something comforting, just once? Even if it means lying?"

Carrieri hesitated. A part of him wanted to comfort Karina. Instead, he said, "I've always been a soldier first, and you a politician."

"I know," Karina said quietly. "That's why we've never worked." She leaned her head back against the chair, one palm pressed against her forehead. Her dark hair, streaked with gray, fanned out behind her.

Carrieri stood motionless by the door to his quarters, unsure of what to do. He did not want to say anything to make her leave. If they could not be together, at least they could be alone in the same room.

"The Denomination refuses to let up pressure about the Odenites," Karina muttered after some time. Something in her voice somehow gave him permission to move once more. He walked toward a cabinet that held several glasses and several more containers of liquid.

"Water?" he asked.

"Of course," Karina said. She continued. "They haven't said this in any official meeting with me, but some of my spies say that there are those within the Denomination—within the High Camarilla itself—that are calling for the execution of all Odenites."

Carrieri nearly dropped the water container. "You're sure about that?"

"Sure enough."

"It is my duty to protect the people of Khale," Carrieri said. "The Odenites may have struck out against the Denomination, but they are still Khalic. I will not allow genocide in my own country."

But, even as he said it, his words felt hollow. Wasn't an attack on Khalic tiellans—the murder of tiellans en masse as they left the city of Cineste—exactly what had started the war with the Chaos Queen? That had surely been genocide, by anyone's definition, and now he was waging a war against the survivors.

"I know you won't," Karina said, "and neither will I. But that doesn't change the fact that someone may attempt it. And with the Rodenese fleet bearing down on us from the north, we may not have the capacity to—"

"The Rodenese fleet bearing down on us from the north, and the tiellans from the west," Carrieri added.

Karina swore. "There's been movement?"

Since Carrieri had abandoned Winter and her forces at the Battle of the *Rihnemin*, the tiellans had more or less retreated to the western plains. What skirmishes they had fought since then were little more than banditry.

"I had a feeling after the most recent failed attempt by the Nazaniin to capture their leader, Winter Cordier, that we would see more of them," Carrieri said. "But I had nothing to qualify that feeling until I received word not an hour ago. A tiellan army moves westward, toward Triah." It was a force of just over two thousand strong, according to his scouts. He did not relish the idea of what the tiellans could do with two thousand of their Rangers, and the Chaos Queen at their head.

Karina paled. "We cannot fight wars on two fronts. Not after the losses we suffered over the past year."

Carrieri had gone through the scenario a thousand times in his head. If the tiellans besieged the city from land, and the Rodenese fleet blockaded them from the sea, Triah would be cut off from any source of food. The city's stores would run low. There was little chance of survival, let alone victory. And if the two forces coordinated their attacks, the city would be caught in a vise. Such a thing was unlikely—Roden had systematically murdered and exiled all tiellans decades ago—but Carrieri needed to prepare for any possibility.

"We have God's Eye," Karina said, a hint of hope in her voice. "We can keep the Rodenese fleet at bay with God's Eye, and our legionaries outnumber the tiellans."

Carrieri grimaced. God's Eye could be powerful, but it only worked during the day, and even then it took great effort and coordination to use the weapon. "Do not put all your hope in that. We have not used God's Eye in anger for decades," he said. "We should not rely on it now."

With a sigh, he met Karina's eyes. "But we are preparing war engines, strategically placed around the city and the harbor. If luck is on our side, and God's Eye is functional, we can perhaps keep the Rodenese at bay long enough to deal with the tiellans." It was one of the few scenarios that had a slim chance of working in their favor.

"Can you defeat the tiellan woman?"

Carrieri hesitated. Winter was a gifted field general, even though she was inexperienced, but he was not sure she could besiege Triah with only two thousand troops. Not against his ten thousand.

But Winter herself was one of the most powerful psimancers on the Sfaera, worth a thousand soldiers. Perhaps more. There was no telling what she might do to turn the tide of any battle.

"I'll need the full cooperation of the Nazaniin," Carrieri said. "Without them, I do not think it matters how many troops we have. She will crush them on her own."

"Is she that powerful?" Karina asked.

Carrieri sat down in the chair next to Karina and massaged his forehead.

"I can still hear the screams," he said, eyes closed. "The screams of my own men by the *rihnemin*, as daemons ripped through the fabric of existence, and then tore my men to pieces." Kyfer's screams, as he became a towering, wrathful terror, still echoed in his mind.

"I left that battlefield knowing no force on the Sfaera could stand up to such daemonic strength. I left knowing that, in doing so, I would eradicate one enemy, but have to deal with those daemons. But I also left because I could not see *how* to defeat such an army. I ran, Karina. I ran because I had no hope of defeating my foe."

Carrieri met Karina's eyes. "Winter Cordier somehow defeated hundreds of daemons, including *one of the Nine*. If she could do that——" Carrieri stopped as a thought came to him.

"The *rihnemin*," he said.

Karina raised an eyebrow. "Yes," she said slowly, "what about it?"

"We must destroy, or at least remove, every last *rihnemin* in or around Triah."

Karina's face scrunched together as she spread her palms wide. "Remove the *rihnemin*? Why in Oblivion——"

"Winter used the *rihnemin* at the battle to defeat Mefiston and the other daemons," Carrieri said quickly. "Somehow, whether through psimancy or some other means, she accessed whatever power was dormant in the stone, and defeated the monster in a rain of blue fire. Some of our soldiers witnessed it——those unable to retreat with the main body. Most didn't escape the tiellans and the daemons, but one did; I heard his report with my own ears. We cannot let her do the same to Triah."

"No," Karina whispered, "we cannot." Then the color returned to her cheeks. "We will do what we can about the *rihnemin*."

Carrieri shook his head. "Doing what you can is not enough. Take some of my forces if you need the manpower. We must remove them from the surrounding countryside. Uproot them, crush them, whatever it takes. And then... bloody bones, we throw them into the harbor for all I care. We must keep them out of her reach."

The two sat in silence for some time, contemplating the fate of their city. Karina finally broke it.

"Roden to the north, tiellans to the west. The Denomination out for Odenite blood. We still cannot broach the subject in the Parliament, as most of the senators do not believe the reports, but... Daemons lurk outside our doors, Riccan. I fear none of these conflicts will matter in short time."

Carrieri nodded, a hollow feeling growing in his chest. It had festered within him since he had fled the Battle of the *Rihnemin*. "I'm afraid you're right. But Khale cannot diffuse centuries of conflict with Roden any more than it can atone for centuries of tiellan slavery. We've dug ourselves into this hole."

He'd decided one thing, though. One thing in all of this. If it came down to the tiellan woman's life—no matter what was at stake—he needed to let her live. She destroyed Mefiston, when Carrieri did not think anything on this Sfaera could.

She might be their only hope against the coming darkness.

17

Odenite Camp, outside Triah

CINZIA HESITATED BEFORE KNOCKING gently on Knot's tent post. There was no response.

With a frown, Cinzia peeked through a small gap in the tent flaps. Two empty cots, with random belongings and an abundant supply of weapons strewn about inside, but nothing else.

"Sorry I'm late."

Cinzia jumped, whirling around to find Knot at her side.

"Didn't mean to scare you," he muttered, and swept past her.

"Knot?" Cinzia followed him into his tent, where he was already stuffing belongings into a pack. "What's wrong?"

"Astrid's gone. Haven't seen her for days."

Cinzia had heard the girl had been scarce. "She goes off on her own sometimes, does she not?"

"She did when she had the Black Matron to report to," Knot said. "But that's over. She wouldn't just leave. Not without telling me."

"What could have happened to her?" Fear awoke within Cinzia's breast, and shame with it. She had not noticed Astrid's absence. And her next thought was for the plan she had formed after meeting with the Beldam. Without Astrid, it would be almost impossible.

"Don't know," Knot said. "But I think she's in trouble. A feeling, that's all I got. No evidence. Just a feeling."

Cinzia had learned to trust Knot's instincts. She stood awkwardly watching as Knot sat on his cot rapidly stuffing things into his bag. She could not bear to see him so out of sorts. "Astrid is tough... I do not know of anyone tougher." Cinzia did not understand a fraction of what Astrid had been through, and yet of what she *did* know, she could not believe the girl had survived.

Knot stood up. Because of the constricted space in the tent—there was only room for both of them to stand at the very center, between the beds—they stood very close to one another. His breath was on her face, his body close to hers.

"Don't know why I didn't think to go after her sooner. Should've sensed something was wrong that first night she didn't come back."

"I care about her, too," Cinzia said. "But I know she is special to you." "Special" was putting it lightly; while she suspected neither Knot nor Astrid would ever admit it, he was like a father to the girl. "We will find her, Knot."

A knock sounded on the tentpole, shaking the fabric. Knot stood and pulled aside the tent flap, Cinzia peering over his shoulder.

Cinzia gasped. She recognized the vampire immediately— his scarred face, a ragged gray eyepatch concealing one eye— from that first day the Odenites had arrived at Triah. She remembered thinking how odd it was that he wore such a heavy cloak in the warm sunlight.

Now that it was dark, she would have expected his one good eye to be glowing. Instead, it stared back at her dully, devoid of any light whatsoever.

"I need to speak with you both," the visitor said. His voice came out in a low rasp.

"Who are you?" Knot asked.

"A friend of Astrid's."

Cinzia murmured in Knot's ear. "I have seen him before, Knot, speaking with Astrid when we arrived in Triah."

Knot stiffened as she spoke. "You a vampire?" Knot asked the visitor.

The man hesitated, then nodded.

"But your eyes," Cinzia said. "How...?"

"Glamour." The word sounded strange in his gruff voice.

"A power inherent in most vampires," Knot explained. "They can change their appearance, to a limited extent."

Cinzia's father had once shown her a lizard that changed the color of its skin, camouflaging itself and lying in wait for its prey. Until now, the telltale signs of a vampire—long claws and glowing eyes at night—had been a comfort to her. "Glamour" seemed more than unfair. She stared at the vampire's good eye, straining to find some sort of glow, some sort of hint of what was behind the glamour.

"Come in," Knot said. "Tell us what you know."

Cinzia did not like the idea of inviting a vampire into the tent with them. As skilled a fighter as Knot was, even he stood little chance against a vampire at full strength.

He might not, Luceraf's voice echoed, *but you would.*

It was the first time Cinzia had heard the Daemon's voice in a while.

I was beginning to think you had actually left me alone, she responded.

I'll never leave you, Cinzia.

Cinzia shivered involuntarily.

The vampire entered the cramped space. Cinzia sat on the edge of Astrid's cot, as far from him as she could get.

Knot motioned for the visitor to sit on the other cot, while he himself remained standing by the entrance. Cinzia wished he would sit down, too. She would feel more comfortable with him at her side.

The single eye in the vampire's scarred, pockmarked face stared back at her.

"My name is Trave," the vampire said. "Astrid and I have known each other for some time."

"Trave," Knot said. "Astrid told me about you."

The vampire looked up at Knot, something very like fear burning in his single eye. "I helped her escape from Olin Cabral in Turandel. She invited me to come with her, after that."

"Come with her?" Knot asked.

"Tag along after your group," Trave said. "She didn't want to introduce me to you until she knew I was trustworthy."

"And now she is gone," Cinzia said, "and you are here. It would seem she was right to have reservations about you."

"You worked for the vampire who enslaved her," Knot said. His eyes were cold, emotionless voids fixated on Trave. "He tortured her."

"Aye," Trave's head bowed. "And I did my fair share of torturing, too. If she didn't tell you about that, I will. I don't like what I did, but that doesn't change the fact I did it."

"And now... what? You are here to make amends?" Cinzia didn't keep the skepticism from her voice.

"I can never do that," Trave said quietly. "But I want to help her now. You've realized she's missing?" In response to Knot's nod, he added, "I think I know who took her."

"Her former master," Knot said.

"Cabral," Trave agreed, the name scraping from between his lips.

"Thought the two of you took care of him after we moved south."

Cinzia looked at Knot sharply. She had heard no such thing. But, then again, why would Astrid tell her anything about it? She wished the girl had told her anyway.

"We freed the humans he had enslaved," Trave rasped, "and killed the Fangs he'd left behind. But he was not there. I'm afraid we only stoked the fire with that attack."

Knot swore.

"Cabral is one of the oldest, most powerful vampires in existence," Trave said. "His power may only be eclipsed by the vampires of the Coven."

"What is the Coven?"

Trave shrugged. "How does one explain the movement of the stars? The Coven are vampires that have always been, and always will be. They have existed since the dawn of time, and will always exist."

"Surely they are like any vampires," Cinzia said. "They can be killed?"

Trave laughed—or, at least, Cinzia assumed the awful scraping sound that came from his throat was a laugh. She could not imagine what else it might be.

"No," Trave said, "They are not like other vampires."

I think they can die, though.

Cinzia's brow wrinkled. *What do you mean?* What knowledge could Luceraf possibly have about Coven vampires?

Because I'm quite sure I killed one, once.

Knot's empty eyes locked on Trave.

"I don't know where Cabral would have taken Astrid," Trave said, "but I know his lairs. If he is in Triah, I know who he would contact, and where he would stay." His hand strayed to the patch that covered one eye, touching it gently. "I owe her a debt, one I can never repay. But I'll spend the rest of my life trying."

"Then let's get started," Knot said.

18

Somewhere beneath Triah

THE LOCK CLICKED, AND Astrid bolted upright, ready to make another attempt at fighting her way out. But just before the door began to creak open, a voice echoed in her mind, calm and sonorous.

It is just me, child. Do not try to escape. You would stand a better chance against Igar and every other vampire beneath Triah combined than you would against me.

Astrid relaxed, although she had the fleeting thought that Eldritch might have something to do with causing her to relax, and didn't particularly relish the idea.

The door to her cell opened, and Eldritch entered. Instinctively, Astrid took a step back. The tiellan vampire was levitating, but this time instead of floating in a seated position, she was upright, one leg slightly bent beneath her. She did not wear the dress she had worn in the throne room. Instead, she wore simple, loose-fitting trousers and a pristine white blouse. Her feet were bare, her short silvery hair spiky around her pointed ears.

The door to Astrid's cell closed, and they were alone.

"What are you doing here?" Astrid asked. She still felt unnaturally calm, but she had not survived for a couple hundred years without learning to recognize danger in just about any circumstance. Tranquility and danger could coexist, and they certainly did here.

You have piqued my interest, and I wanted to have a discussion with you, if you'll allow it.

"Is it really my choice?" Astrid asked.

Of course it is. Eldritch's tone was surprised. *I will not force anything on you, child. I am nowhere near the stickler that Equity is about thresholds and what have you. You were not allowed a voice during the hearing, and I was willing to respect that rule. But there is no reason to ignore such an interesting specimen just because she is not yet old enough.*

Specimen. Well, at least Astrid knew where she stood with Eldritch.

"Can you tell me more about all this?" Astrid asked.

What would you like to know?

"Where am I?"

Beneath Triah. A series of ancient tunnels and chambers exist beneath the city, and our order has taken them over. For the most part. We had to give up some of our jurisdiction years ago when the Nazaniin dug out their ridiculous underground lair, but that was a price we were willing to pay for privacy.

Astrid thought about that for a moment. She had run for radials through these tunnels, and Igar had carried her for almost that distance, too. She wondered whether the tunnel network webbed beneath the entire city, or just certain parts.

"Who are you?"

Eldritch's blue eyes glowed even brighter, though she remained otherwise unsettlingly motionless, only the slightest shift in air rippling her clothing or through her hair. *I am the eldest member of the Coven,* she said. *I have existed since the dawn of time, and will exist until its end.*

A lofty claim, but Astrid wondered whether it was remotely true. "You've existed since the dawn of time, and you still look like *that*?" Astrid asked.

Eldritch's smile broadened, but she did not answer the question. *You are astute, child. I like that. When you do cross the threshold, I might even think of taking you on as my personal ward. Clearly it would be something of a battle with Cabral, but I believe he would see things my way in the end. I only hope he doesn't ruin you before then.*

"Were you always a vampire? If you are the eldest, you must have been the first. Were you ever a tiellan? How did you become a vampire?"

Eldritch's smile faded, and her eyes dimmed a little. *That is a very sad story, for another time, perhaps.*

"Can you at least tell me how you are doing what you are doing?" Astrid asked. "Speaking in my mind, and... levitating?"

Eldritch's eyes brightened again; the sadness left her face. *I suppose there is no harm in telling you now. Your threshold is not that far, after all.*

"I thought you did not care for this concept of a threshold," Astrid said.

I never said that, child. But I do find it overly strict at times. And, being who I am, I can bend the rules when I see a good reason for it.

What is your good reason here? Astrid wanted to ask, but she kept the question to herself. This woman said she was intrigued by Astrid, but Astrid had decided she could take nothing this woman said at face value.

Each member of the Coven has developed abilities, over time, Eldritch said. *While Equity rarely has reason to demonstrate his, he has generated control over certain elements. And, of course, you have already seen what Elegance can do.*

"She can make people see things," Astrid said. "Alter their minds... and their sifts? Is what Cabral asked you to do to me possible?"

There is very little that is not possible between the three of us. Eldritch spoke without hubris. *Had we agreed with Cabral's punishment, we could have done as he asked.*

Astrid suppressed an involuntary shiver. They would have altered her mind. They would have invaded and changed everything that made her *her*. The anger she had felt in the throne room returned, a slow-burning smolder.

The Black Matron had messed with her mind enough. She would die before she let anyone do that to her again.

"You and Elegance have the same powers, then?" Astrid asked.

No, child. Our abilities could not be more different, though they might seem similar to the uneducated. Elegance has mastered the art of illusion. She can make anyone see what she wants them to see, and for that person, the illusion Elegance gives them is reality. They would never know the difference, unless Elegance chose to show it to them.

I, on the other hand, deal in the art of perception. I can discern people's thoughts. I can create psychic links with them, speak to their minds.

"You're an acumen?" Astrid asked.

Eldritch's laughter chimed in Astrid's mind, though the woman's face remained unchangingly calm.

Of course not, child. I am infinitely beyond even the most powerful acumen you could imagine.

Astrid pursed her lips. "You can float, too," she said eventually. "I don't know many acumens that can do that."

Do you know any *that can float?*

"A figure of speech. I'm just saying that you're right, you can float and acumens can't. Um… speaking of floating, though. How?"

Perception goes far deeper than discerning thoughts and feelings. I can observe the sky and air and tell you what temperature it will be and exactly what weather we will have ten years from now. I can discern the same patterns in human behavior, and tell you quite accurately which nation will lead the Sfaera a hundred years from now, or a thousand. And I can look into the qualities that make the earth and the air what they are, and manipulate them to do my bidding.

Surely this was more posturing. Surely Eldritch could not *actually* do the things she claimed. And yet, unlike the sprout of suspicion she'd felt when Eldritch had told her her age, Astrid felt none of that now.

Now, she only felt awe.

"These powers," Astrid said slowly, "where did they come from? How did you get them?"

Being a vampire is about more than blood and strength, child, although precious few of our kind ever realize this truth. Any vampire, given enough time and will, can develop powers such as mine. Some manifest them earlier than others, but they all develop them, and those powers increase over time.

In a few hundred years, I am afraid Cabral is right, child. You will have forgotten all about the friends you have now, all the connections you have made. None of that will matter. You will be just beginning to understand what it means to be immortal.

If you survive that long, and with the right tutelage, in a few thousand years you will begin to experience what it means to have true power. You will begin to learn what it means to be a goddess.

"You're saying I could have powers like you?" Astrid asked.

Or Elegance, or Equity. Or Igar. All you need—

"Wait," Astrid said. "Igar has powers, too? The big vampire?" There was a connection there, something she was missing.

Of course he does, child. You cannot possibly think that a person that exquisitely muscular could exist without supernatural aid.

"Canta's bloody bones," Astrid muttered, "how strong *is* he?"

Eldritch's laugh rippled again through Astrid's mind. *Stronger than you could imagine. Igar is one of the youngest to manifest powers, at only nine hundred years old. He grows stronger by the decade.*

Astrid finally gained the courage to ask the question she had been dreading. "And... what about Cabral? What powers does he have?"

Cabral has yet to manifest any powers. That is not atypical for one of his age, however. Cabral is around fifteen hundred years old, if I remember correctly. If a vampire begins to manifest an ability, it usually happens closer to their two thousandth year. Igar is unusual.

"Have I met any other vampires with abilities?" Astrid asked.

Eldritch's blue eyes smoldered as she looked at Astrid for a moment. Astrid had the uncomfortable sensation that whatever Eldritch claimed to do with the weather and with civilizations she was now doing with Astrid, but on an individual level.

No, Eldritch said after a moment. *You have not met any other vampires who have manifested abilities.*

Realization clicked in Astrid's mind. The connection she'd missed suddenly appeared.

"Your eyes," she said. Blue, yellow, and violet in the Coven. Igar's orange tint. "There's a connection between power and eye color, isn't there?"

There is a correlation, child. We do not know much beyond that, but yes. There is something there.

"Then... what does that mean for me?"

Eldritch's smile broadened, and her eyes lit so brightly that Astrid's entire cell took on a brilliant blue hue. Long shadows cast by chunks of stone and mounds of dirt stretched away from Eldritch's presence.

I have no idea. That is precisely why you interest me so. Most vampires experience a change in eye shade after many hundreds of years.

It is… unusual for one as young as you—speaking of your actual age, of course, and not the age of your body when it turned—to have eyes that are not red.

"So you think I might manifest some kind of power?"

I think it sensible to speculate that the Sfaera has great things planned for you.

Astrid crushed the glint of excitement that sparked within her. She was no one special. She had proven her inadequacy time and time again. She had nothing to offer the Sfaera. And her friends lived in the here and now; even if Eldritch was right, even if there was a possibility that, thousands of years in the future, Astrid could manifest some wondrous ability, what did it matter?

All that mattered was what she did now.

Which brought her to her next question. "What do you know of the Nine Daemons?"

Eldritch's smile faltered. *What do you care about the Nine Daemons? Bedtime stories, told to scare children into obeying their parents.*

Astrid laughed out loud at that. "Please, Eldritch. Don't play me for a fool. If you really can do what you say, you'll be aware the Nine have infiltrated the Sfaera, that they are attempting to return in their full forms."

I may have felt some disturbances.

Astrid scoffed. "Disturbances. And that means nothing to you?"

I have my reasons for waiting.

"Please don't tell me you think they'll actually ally with you," Astrid said. "You cannot possibly be that stupid."

Do not try my patience. If my anger eclipses my curiosity, you will not last long.

"None of us will be long for this world if the Nine get what they want."

I have outlasted dynasties, religions, and the Khalic Novennium.

I will survive this, too.

"You might," Astrid said. "But the rest of the world won't. What good will the Sfaera be to you when everything else is gone?"

You think you can convince me to fight the Nine Daemons? I will adapt and change, as I always do. You would do well to learn from me, child. You could live long enough to see things my way, if you chose to do so. I see that strength in you.

You fear the Nine Daemons, and for good reason. But… history is not at all clear on their purpose. Things are not always as they seem.

"I'm sure I have a great deal to learn from you," Astrid said. "But I don't care about being around long enough to learn it. Not if everything else is gone."

Very well. The cell door behind Eldritch opened, and she floated gently out of the cell.

A moment of panic struck Astrid, and she rushed forward. "Wait!" she cried, but the heavy door closed in her face, leaving her once again in darkness.

19

Cliffs of Litori, North of Triah

SAY WHAT YOU WILL about tiellans, but these Rangers know how to travel, Kali thought as she leaned forward and patted her horse. She'd named the animal Garex, after nothing in particular, but she remembered how Nash always hated to not give an animal a name, and that thought had dug into her and wouldn't come out. And Garex wasn't half bad a horse, it turned out. He'd brought her all the way from Adimora to Triah, and much faster than she had expected.

Their group emerged from the wooded forest atop the Cliffs of Litori. They had taken a longer road at the end of their journey, directing their steeds to this vantage point rather than approaching directly from the east. The small settlement of Litori stood less than a radial to the north of them.

Kali dismounted and left Garex to content himself with a nosebag. She passed a group of the tiellan engineers Winter had recruited from Adimora. The majority of their force were Rangers, those skilled in battle, but before leaving Winter had sent out a call for any tiellans with skill in carpentry and engineering. And, just moments ago when the tiellans had arrived at Litori, Winter had ordered the engineers to begin procuring wood from the nearby forest and any other materials they needed. It was clear Winter intended to make war machines with which to besiege Triah. Kali did not see the point; first of all, the cliffs were far enough away from the city that no conceivable siege engine could damage anything important; they might be able to bombard the outer circle with a few well-made trebuchets, but the Legion would care little for such attacks. A trebuchet would have to be truly massive to reach any important targets, and the trajectory from up here would make it impossible to hit anything with any accuracy.

Walking to the cliff edge, Kali finally got a full view of Triah, far below her. She breathed it in, but even that act left a bitter taste in her mouth. She breathed in through tiellan lips and throat; she looked on her city with tiellan eyes.

"How does it feel?"

For all the talk of her being a queen, Winter looked more like a warlord. Kali had played her part there—thank the goddess the girl didn't wear those silly tiellan dresses anymore.

"It feels like shit," Kali muttered.

"Are you still upset about that body? I thought you'd do just about anything to get out of the Void."

"I would," Kali said quickly, "and I did, but that doesn't mean I'm content. I could still... improve my situation, if you would just—"

"No," Winter said flatly. She had expressly forbidden Kali from procuring a new lacuna to inhabit.

Kali had once held the power in their relationship; she had held the knowledge, she had held the *faltira*, and the experience and skill with acumency. Her student's acumency skills now exceeded her own. And Winter had plenty of *faltira*, too, after reclaiming Mazille's stolen stash. She wasn't remotely dependent on Kali any longer. If it had just been a battle of acumency, Kali might be able to stand toe to toe with Winter, but Winter also had access to telesis *and* clairvoyance. If it came to a fight, it would be short and with a foregone conclusion.

"I could at least find a woman," Kali said. She was sick of being a man. One too many dangling parts.

But Winter wasn't listening. Her gaze was on the city below them.

"I never thought Triah would be like this." Her voice was almost reverent.

"It is an impressive sight. Once you get down there, you find out it's a stinking, overpopulated shithole run by a pseudo-noble class that pretends to champion the interests of the people, but the city itself—"

"It's something special."

"It is that."

"Do you want to go down there?"

Kali stood very still. "Are you serious?"

"I am," Winter said. "You'd be in a tiellan body, so I don't know how easy things would be for you down there, but if you wanted to visit Triah, I would allow it."

The excitement welling up within her faded. "And what is the catch?" she asked. "You want me to do something for you down there?"

"I do. So you can choose whether it's worth it to you or not, but… I need to know about *rihnemin* in the area."

Kali nodded in understanding. The few *rihnemin* landmarks she was used to seeing near Triah had been removed—she imagined the Legion or the Nazaniin, or perhaps both, were behind that move. They certainly didn't want the Chaos Queen to have a *rihnemin* readily available with which to assault their city.

"I'll go," she said. "I'll find out what I can." Her old contacts might know what had happened to the local *rihnemin*. If those didn't work, there was an old Nazaniin rumor that might be worth following up on.

And, most importantly, she wasn't about to pass up an opportunity to revisit her city.

"Good." Winter handed something to her.

A Voidstone.

Not just any Voidstone, Kali realized, but... this was the companion to the Voidstone she and Nash had given Winter, so long ago.

"How did you—"

"The emperor's Reapers took what you and Nash left behind back in Roden, when you..." Winter didn't finish the sentence.

When I killed Nash, Kali remembered, *and when Lathe—Knot—killed me.*

"Before I left Izet," Winter went on, "I asked for your things. I figured this might be of use. I never thought I would give it back to you."

Kali ran her thumb over the rune.

"Keep in touch with me through that," Winter said. "Don't linger too long in the city. It may not be safe for you."

It may not be safe for me, or it may not be safe for anyone? Kali wondered. But Winter had given her enough.

She was finally going home.

20

Triah

CINZIA DID NOT LIKE HIDING while Knot checked out the dilapidated building at the edge of the city, but it was what she had agreed to do, like it or not. The building looked more or less the way Trave had described it; splintered and stubby rafters, charred from a fire years ago, hung down over crumbling, blackened stone. Dawn had just broken, though the sun hid behind a ceiling of gray clouds, and looked like it would stay that way for the rest of the morning at least. Cinzia began to feel the first drops of rain patter against the hood she wore drawn over her face.

Trave walked with them, wearing a large greatsword on his back, and a dark hooded cloak concealing his features.

As long as the sun was up, any vampires would be at their weakest, and vulnerable to sunlight. The weakest vampire was still stronger than almost any human, but Cinzia hoped the element of surprise, along with her enhanced abilities and a few other tricks Knot claimed to have up his sleeve, would help them.

I could choose not to help you, you know, Luceraf whispered in her mind. *I could leave you defenseless when you most need my help.*

If you did that, you would lose your precious avatar.

"Cinzia Oden, I presume?"

Cinzia jumped in surprise and spun around. A blond man with a topknot, dressed in black, inclined his head. As he raised his head, she saw his eyes were a light green, with a tinge of gray that matched the cloud cover above. He had high cheekbones, and a few days' stubble.

Handsome, Luceraf said, almost teasingly.

Cinzia cleared her throat, embarrassed at having been startled.

"Yes," Cinzia whispered. "You are Code?"

The man nodded, extending his hand. "I'm glad to finally meet you, Cinzia. I have heard—"

Cinzia folded her arms. "I am sure you have heard a great deal about me, Code. Knot told me all about your objectives in befriending him. Including your orders to get closer to me, and my sister. I am telling you now, that will not happen. I am grateful for your help today, but I do not care to become your puppet, let alone your informant."

"I've gone over the parameters with him," Knot said from behind her, making her jump again. She was getting tired of these Nazaniin sneaking up on her. "He knows this is a test, and he knows he's got to do well if he wants this deal to work out between the two of us. And it'll be *just* between the two of us, ain't that right, Code?"

"Absolutely," Code said, his smile broad on his face.

Goddess, he is *handsome*, Luceraf said. *Look, even if you don't care for him, you could at least get closer to him for my sake. It has been so long since I—*

Cinzia did her best to tune the Daemon out.

"What's the deal with him?" Code asked, nodding over Cinzia's shoulder, where Trave stood some distance away. Cinzia frowned. He'd been at their side only moments before.

"Your associate is loaded with enough nightsbane to take down a vampire army," Trave rasped. "I'll keep my distance, if you don't mind. Who is he, anyway?"

"Help," Knot said. "Figured we'd need it."

185

Trave nodded, but he didn't come closer. "You figured right, though I don't know what good another human will do. We'll still be lucky to get out of there alive."

"Code is a psimancer. A powerful telenic."

"Better than nothing." Trave locked eyes with Code. "But I've killed my fair share of telenics, and I'm nothing compared to what we might face down there."

Code didn't flinch from the vampire's stare. Instead, he smiled.

Cinzia let out an exasperated sigh. "We don't have time for a pissing contest. Let's get moving."

Code, still eyeing Trave, nodded. "Aye, of course." He slid his pack to the ground, and opened it.

Cinzia peeked inside and saw dozens of sharpened wooden stakes, as well as a few sprigs of a plant that Cinzia recognized.

She had seen nightsbane's effects once; just the presence of the herb had completely incapacitated Astrid in Navone. She understood why Trave kept back.

"Fortunately, we have nightsbane in decent supply," Code said. "That'll be our first line of offense."

"How do I use it?" Cinzia asked.

Code took a sprig from the bag. "Pin this on your dress. Near your shoulder."

She took it from him nervously and fastened it on as he'd told her. "Is that... all?"

"That should deter most vampires from getting too close to you—" he nodded again to Trave "—but that means our friend there can't be too close to us, either."

"I'll be scouting ahead," Trave said. "I'll be close, though you may not see me. If I run into any trouble, I'll let you know."

The herb she had pinned to her dress was nothing special; just a series of tiny green leaves stemming from a dark stalk.

She had studied most herbs at the seminary, for their healing properties, and remembered now that it only rarely bloomed. When pressed directly on a wound or, more effectively, when its leaves were boiled and made into a poultice, it could stem bleeding. When she'd been studying her herb books, she couldn't have possibly imagined that she'd one day be about to crawl into a den of vampires, nightsbane pinned to her dress.

Not just any vampires, but some of the oldest, most dangerous vampires in the world.

"What if the nightsbane doesn't work?" Cinzia asked.

Code crouched back down and pulled a wooden stake out of his bag.

"That's what these are for," he said.

Cinzia stared at the stake, one eyebrow raised.

"Wood weakens a vampire when it pierces their skin," Code explained. "'Pierce' being the important word—it has no effect unless it has actually penetrated them. The closer the spike is to their heart, the better. And if you manage to puncture the heart itself, that is the first step toward killing one of them."

"The first step?" Cinzia asked. She glanced at Knot, who had remained quiet throughout Code's tutorial. She wondered if all of this—hearing the different ways Astrid could be hurt, or even killed—was difficult for him.

He's also hearing how he can kill the people who've captured her, Luceraf whispered. *If it were me, I'd be soaking it all up, absorbing every drop. Looks like that's exactly what he's doing.*

"There is some debate on what can actually kill a vampire," Code said, "other than prolonged exposure to sunlight. That seems to work without fail, but it is, unfortunately, a resource we cannot rely on given the cloud cover, and the fact that we'll probably be underground the whole time."

"So, other than sunlight?" Cinzia asked.

"A wooden stake through the heart has been rumored to be enough to kill some vampires," Code said, "but not all sources agree. Some insist you must decapitate the vampire after staking it. Others suggest you go further, and burn the staked body and severed head in separate fires."

They all stopped talking as Trave's low, rasping laugh reached them.

"You've never killed a vampire," Trave said, more amused than anything.

Code took a long, deep breath before answering. "I've killed my share of the undead," he said. "Enough for more than one lifetime. But no, I've never killed a vampire."

Cinzia was about to inquire what Code meant by killing the undead, but his hollow, expressionless face stopped her. She realized *this* was the dispassionate Nazaniin agent she had expected.

Trave nodded, and an unseen understanding seemed to pass between the two. Whatever animosity existed between them was gone. "Then let me be clear," Trave said. "Toss me a stake. *Carefully*."

Code did so, the wooden spike arcing between the two. Trave caught it, and held the point to his chest.

"Always go for the heart," he said. "If you hit them there, or close enough, it should immobilize them completely. Decapitation works as well, but I doubt we'll have time to go around staking, decapitating, and then burning every vampire we come across. We should rely on nightsbane and staking as much as we can."

Cinzia glanced at Knot. He rested a hand on the strange sword he carried, a daemon etched in stone on the handle. Code, too, had a similar sword at his hip.

"What about me?" Cinzia asked. "I'll need a weapon for that, should it become… absolutely necessary."

Code cocked his head to one side. "You… want a sword?"

Cinzia huffed. "You do not want to give me one because I am a woman?"

"I know many women who are better with a sword than I am," Code said. "I don't want to give you a sword because you don't strike me as someone who has had much training in that area. Am I wrong?"

Cinzia frowned. "You are not wrong."

"But she needs a weapon," Knot said.

Code sighed, then offered his own sword to Cinzia. "Take this."

Cinzia reached out a hand hesitantly. "What will you use?"

"I've got an axe in the bag, that'll do the trick well enough."

"Can I use the axe?" Cinzia blurted.

Good choice, Luceraf whispered.

Code looked at her quizzically. "An axe requires a lot more strength than a sword, so—"

"I want the axe."

"She wants the axe," Knot said.

Code shrugged. "Fine. I prefer my own sword anyway." He reclaimed his blade, and then reached into the bottom of his bag to pull out a long wooden handle, a long metal spike at one end, and a large single axe-blade on the other, with a hooked spike balancing it out.

Yes, Luceraf whispered, *that will do just fine.*

Code offered the weapon to Cinzia. "It's a bit heavy, but—"

Cinzia snatched the weapon, and hefted it. She took a few practice swings. She was no expert with an axe, that much was certain, but after hours of chopping wood at Harmoth, and thanks to Luceraf's enhanced strength, it felt right in her hands.

"...but I think you'll be able to make it work," Code finished, eyes wide.

Trave chuckled wryly, but she ignored him.

Code divided the wooden stakes, giving Cinzia, Knot, and Trave belts that held almost a dozen stakes each. As they strapped the belts around their waists, Code withdrew a small crossbow from his bag, and checked the winding mechanism. He slung a quiver of crossbow bolts around his shoulder. Cinzia eyed the bolts as Code inspected them. Each was a wooden shaft with feathered fletching, and a sharp steel barb at the point.

"Will that still work?" Cinzia asked. "With a steel tip like that?"

"It'll work well enough," Trave said, answering for him. He nodded at the spike at the base of Cinzia's axe. "Speaking of which, that might come in handy as a stake, too. Keep it in mind."

Cinzia inspected the long steel spike. What in Oblivion was she doing, carrying an axe and a belt of wooden stakes?

You are about to wreak havoc. Pleasure bubbled in Luceraf's voice.

"We need to move," Knot said. He looked at Code. "Anything else?"

Code shook his head.

"Good."

The dull patter of the rain increased to a roar as Trave led the way into the dilapidated building.

Code waited for Knot and Cinzia to climb down the ladder, then dropped down quickly after them. His boots splashed in a shallow puddle as he landed.

The three of them huddled together to light torches, and then Knot and Cinzia began to walk down the tunnel, Code following behind.

"Trave said there would not be a guard," Knot said over

his shoulder, "but that ain't an assumption I'm ready to make. Keep your eyes open." The vampire had already scouted ahead of them, out of sight, but had relayed instructions to Knot.

Code resisted the urge to roll his eyes. Of course he was on the lookout; Goddess, that was just like something Lathe would say. There was little need to post a guard down here; the entrance had not exactly been easy to find. Even with this Trave fellow's directions, it had taken the three of them the better part of an hour to locate the switch that opened the secret door that led to the secret room, and then find another switch which led to the trap door they had just come through. And, Code suspected anyone who actually *did* find their way down here would very soon find themselves the main course of a meal for a host of deadly vampires.

Code shivered despite himself. Not his preferred way to go, certainly.

After a few minutes of walking, Knot held up a hand. They had reached a fork in the tunnel. Code and Cinzia stopped, and Knot nodded at one of the forks, putting a finger to his lips.

Code strained his ears, but all he heard were crackling torches and a faint, distant dripping sound.

Lathe's reputation among the Nazaniin had been infamous for a few reasons. He'd had outstanding instincts, first of all, better than any fighter Code had ever seen. He also seemed to have particularly acute, almost inhuman senses. Knot seemed to have the same qualities.

"Where in Oblivion is Trave?" Code whispered, but Knot just held up a hand to silence him. Code frowned, his jaw set. If the vampire had betrayed them, Code would make him pay for it. Assuming he lived long enough.

Then Code heard it, too. Footsteps echoing in the tunnel,

approaching from the left fork. The faint echo reverberated off the walls, until Code realized it wasn't just a reverberation but multiple footfalls. Three, maybe four vampires were walking toward them.

The rocky walls were smooth, without ingress; there was nowhere to hide, other than down the right fork—and hope the vampires didn't catch them up. Knot had the same idea, and moved quickly a few rods up the right fork of the tunnel; but then he stopped and pressed himself against the rock wall. Apparently Trave's instructions indicated they take the left fork here. Otherwise Code assumed Knot would have led them away from the danger.

Wait it was, then. Wait, and then fight. Code suppressed a shiver, but a smile crept to his lips. It was true what he had told Cinzia about not delighting in fighting more undead, but it was also true what he'd said about being curious. And, honestly, he'd never fought a vampire before. He wanted to see how he held up against the creatures of legend.

Fighting three or four vampires at once was something else entirely, of course, but he'd take the bad with the good.

Code's hand drifted to the pouch at his belt. He only carried three crystals with him—two was the largest number of *faltira* crystals he could take without harming himself, but it was always good to carry a reserve—and each crystal would last him roughly twenty minutes, close to a half-hour if he was lucky. That was, at best, an hour and a half of psimancy at his disposal, assuming he had some time in between doses. There was no telling how long they'd be down here; it might be twenty minutes, but it could also be hours. Best to rely on their other methods of dealing with the vampires unless things became truly precarious. He willed his hand away from his *faltira* pouch, instead glancing at the sprig of nightsbane pinned to his jacket.

This will work, he told himself. *You aren't going to die in the tunnels beneath Triah fighting a den of vampires. That would be ridiculous.*

Beside him, Cinzia raised a stake in one hand, the axe he had given her in the other. She was tenacious, Code would give her that. And, apparently, far stronger than she appeared.

The footsteps grew louder, and Code could hear voices whispering now, too. He deliberately slowed his breathing, and wished he could do the same to his heart as it thumped heavily in his chest. He had heard that, in perfect silence, a vampire could hear a human's blood pumping from thirty rods away.

"Stop," one of the vampires said sharply, and very close now, probably just around the corner. "Do you feel that?"

"Aye," another responded. The first had clearly been a male, but this one Code could not quite place. Could be male or female, young or old.

Knot signaled for Code and Cinzia to follow behind him at a distance, and he crept quietly toward the fork.

"Nightsbane," said a third voice, although this was more of a growl.

Knot sprang around the corner, stake in one hand, Nazaniin sword in the other.

"Alert the Coven," one of the vampires hissed. "We'll take care of this one."

Code swung wide around the corner in time to see one of the vampires running back down the tunnel, while the other two—a man and a woman—backed slowly away from Knot.

Code raised his crossbow, aiming at the fleeing form, and pulled the trigger. The bolt connected with his target, who stumbled, then fell to the ground. Code was already winding his crossbow again, another bolt at the ready.

"There's more of them," the woman said, as Cinzia rounded the corner too.

"Then we'll kill them all," the man said. Both drew their longswords.

But their words did not match their actions; Knot continued advancing on them, and the two retreated as he did.

Code reloaded. The fleeing figure had stumbled to its feet, but it moved noticeably slower. Code took aim, exhaled, and fired. This time the bolt missed, ricocheting off into the tunnel. The figure continued running, until a shadow pounced out of nowhere, tackling the vampire to the ground.

Code squinted. That had to be Trave. Perhaps he wouldn't have to make the vampire pay, after all.

The female vampire looked back at her fallen comrade, then at Knot, Cinzia, and Code advancing on her.

"We cannot get close to them, Vladek," she hissed.

Code hooked the crossbow on his belt. He raised both hands in peace.

"Vladek, is it?" he asked. Knot eyed him, but he didn't care. "A bit obvious for a vampire name, don't you think?"

"You don't know what you've walked into," Vladek growled.

Code shrugged. "Nightsbane. Wooden stakes. Use your observational powers, mate; I think we know pretty well what we've walked into. We just want one thing, really. We're looking for a little girl, a vampire like yourself. Any idea where we could find her?"

Vladek sneered. "You won't. You'll be dead long before you do."

If the vampire moved quickly, he could strike Code with his longsword in a lunge—if he could withstand the nightsbane for long enough. Code thought he could reach his own sword in time to parry a strike. Probably.

Code nodded at the vampire who'd collapsed in the tunnel, pierced by his crossbow bolt. "That one doesn't seem to agree with you. If you tell us where the girl is, we probably won't kill you. How does that sound?"

Vladek shook his head. "You really don't know where you are or what you're doing. Nightsbane might work on me, but it won't work on others down here. You've stumbled on something more powerful than you can imagine. Take my advice, and leave while you can."

Code took another step forward.

This time, Vladek took a step back, and that told Code all he needed to know.

With his right hand Code slipped from its sheath a wooden stake that he'd hidden on a wristband beneath his sleeve, while he drew his sword with his left. He lunged as Vladek's eyes widened, and the vampire took another step back, but it was not enough. Code plunged the stake into the vampire's shoulder, missing the heart by a good margin, while deflecting a wild blow from Vladek's longsword with his own Nazaniin blade. Vladek grunted, clearly in pain from the nightsbane less than a rod away from him and from the wood now embedded in his shoulder.

Knot clashed with the female vampire while Code parried another wild blow from Vladek. He drew another stake from his belt with the intention to seek this one into the vampire's heart, but Vladek recovered far more quickly than Code anticipated. He'd hoped, during the day, at least, with his training and skill, he'd be able to overpower Vladek quickly enough to end things without much of a fight.

But despite his first two wild blows, the nightsbane, and the wooden stake protruding from his shoulder, Code barely got his sword up in time to parry Vladek's next strike. The longsword clashed into Code's sword with a sharp *clang* that sent a tremor up Code's arms.

Code danced around Vladek, but the vampire stayed with him step for step. Code's training with the sword was formidable; hours a day every day for two decades. But, as the vampire's footwork matched his own impeccably, and as the vampire matched Code blow for blow despite his clearly weakened and pained state, Code began to understand for the first time what he was up against. He had trained for decades; the vampire had trained for centuries.

Disengaging after another flurry of blows, Code threw the stake at Vladek's chest. The vampire deflected the stake midair, but Code followed it quickly, now holding his sword with a two-handed grip.

Cinzia flanked the vampire. He tried to catch her eye, shaking his head as subtly as he could—Vladek would undoubtedly sense her approach, and could kill her with a single stroke—but Cinzia paid him no mind.

Code increased the power and speed of his attack, keeping Vladek on the defensive and his attention away from Cinzia. But then something changed in Vladek's eyes, nothing more than a flicker but enough to tell Code the vampire knew where Cinzia was and what she was doing. Vladek deflected another strike from Code's blade and *twisted*, simultaneously kicking Code in the stomach, sending him stumbling back, and lashing out at Cinzia with his sword.

Code watched in horror as the sword cut toward Cinzia's unarmored, completely unprotected shoulder.

His horror turned to confused awe when Cinzia caught the blade, bare-handed, stopping it mid-arc.

Vladek seemed just as surprised as Code for a fraction of a second, before tearing the sword from Cinzia's grasp. Not, however, before Cinzia buried a stake in the vampire's heart. Vladek choked out a gasp, then fell to the ground, clawing ineffectively at the stake in his chest.

Code did not waste time; he brought his sword down on the vampire's neck. It took three strikes to sever Vladek's head, but when it was done Code kicked it across the tunnel, away from the body.

"What," Code gasped, catching his breath as he glared at Cinzia, "in the mother of all Oblivion was *that*?"

Cinzia didn't answer. She was spattered in blood from the decapitated corpse.

Code glanced back to see the female vampire lying prone, three stakes piercing her chest. Her head, too, had been removed from her body, now a healthy distance away. Their bodies leaked blood onto the dirt and rock, almost black in the dim, flickering torchlight.

"Did you know about this?" Code asked Knot, pointing at Cinzia.

"Knew enough," Knot said, but he, too, watched Cinzia warily.

"Not now," Cinzia said. "We have a mission to focus on."

Code glanced up the tunnel at the third vampire to make sure it hadn't moved: it was still motionless on the ground. Trave stood in the distance, waiting for them. But Code wasn't done. "This isn't something you just shrug off. I've seen a lot of crazy shit recently, but an ex-Cantic priestess stopping a vampire's sword swing with her bare hand might actually..."

Code trailed off, something clicking in his mind.

He *had* seen this before. He had seen this exact behavior before, both on Arro with the Daemon Hade, and in Maven Kol with the Daemon Nadir. The avatars they had both claimed, whatever they had been before, gained superior strength, speed, and durability.

"You're all right?" Knot asked Cinzia.

"Yes," she said. "I will tell you more, I can tell you everything, when we have Astrid back."

Knot shrugged, and began walking up the tunnel. Cinzia followed.

"Wait a second, mate," Code said, walking quickly after them. He opened his mouth, but then closed it almost immediately.

Now was not the time. If Cinzia was the avatar of a Daemon, the deed was already done. There was nothing they could do about it. And, truth was, they could use someone with her strength. Code had thought Cinzia a liability until now.

They reached the third vampire; his head had been severed messily from his body. Trave was already walking ahead of them, wiping off his greatsword. He beckoned for them to follow.

"I trust Cinzia," Knot told Code, kicking the vampire's head down the tunnel, toward the other two bodies. Dark blood spattered as the head rolled away in the dark. "You will, too, if you want anything to do with me."

They continued walking for the better part of an hour, Trave keeping just ahead of the rest of them. Knot hated the formation—it put them completely at Trave's mercy—but if Astrid had trusted the man... well, Knot sure as Oblivion wouldn't trust Trave under normal circumstances, but when Astrid's life was at stake—when they had no other options, he certainly would.

They had not encountered anyone else since they'd killed the three vampires. Knot glanced over at Cinzia. She'd been silent since their encounter with the three vampires, and Knot worried about her. He knew she'd become the avatar of a Daemon to help him. He wanted to help her, but he was at a complete loss.

Finally, Trave stopped ahead of them. A door, large and banded with metal, stood tall to one side. Knot culled the sprout of hope blooming in his chest. Didn't want to get his hopes up. Not yet.

"About bloody time," Code said. "We're burning valuable daylight."

That was true, but they still had a good six hours of daylight left at least. Unless they ran into real trouble, they should be able to make it out before sunset.

"I've seen dozens of doors that look like they might hold prisoners," Knot said as they approached Trave and the door. "What makes you think she wasn't in one of those?"

"They'd be— Keep your distance, for Canta's sake."

Knot, Code, and Cinzia stopped. They each still carried nightsbane on them.

"They'd be keeping her in the Deep Cells," Trave said. "And this is the deepest of them. That's why it took so long to get here."

Knot glanced around. No other vampires in sight; Trave had said the cells were typically not guarded. Vampires knew exactly what would imprison one of their own kind and what would not.

Trave moved in a wide circle around the others, with an eye out for anyone that might intrude on their little prison break, while they approached the door. Knot and Code squatted to lift the huge wooden plank, held in place by two iron arms bolted into the rock on either side of the door. Knot *wanted* Astrid to be here. He didn't know what he would do if she wasn't. So he focused on the task at hand, his muscles straining, but he and Code barely lifted the plank.

"Bloody bones," Code grunted beside him when they'd finally lifted the beam free of the metal catches. They set the beam on the rock floor with a loud thump. "Did not expect the thing to be that heavy."

"For Canta's sake," Cinzia said, stepping forward.

"Should've anticipated this," Knot said. "A vampire at full strength could probably lift it…"

Cinzia lifted the middle beam free of its catches and leaned it up against the tunnel wall next to the door, then did the same thing with the lower beam.

"…alone," Knot finished, unable to take his eyes off Cinzia.

Cinzia had told him what had happened, but Knot had no idea it meant she would become like this. Goddess, if he didn't know she was imbued with a Daemon's power, if he didn't know she hated every moment of it, it'd be hard to find the negative aspects of such power.

Code said nothing, his eyes slightly narrowed as he stared at Cinzia. Trave remained where he was, keeping watch.

"You two were taking too long," Cinzia said, wiping her hands on her dress. She nodded at the door, now unobstructed. "Shall we see if she is really inside?"

Code hefted his crossbow while Knot approached the door, unlocking the simple bolt mechanisms that still held it in place, praying to whoever was listening that Astrid would be inside.

The moment Astrid's door opened, she bolted into it, knocking it wide open and barreling through the figures beyond until a burst of pain racked through her entire body, and a sick feeling overcame her. She stumbled to the ground, confused.

She was close to nightsbane.

Astrid raised her head to see dim shapes standing above her. As her eyes focused, she recognized Knot.

Leaping to her feet with a growl, Astrid dashed at the figure. But the moment she got close, nightsbane took effect as pain cracked through her body. She wanted to vomit, but she persisted, pressing forward.

This was an illusion. One of Elegance's tricks.

"Astrid, it's me," the illusion said, throwing the nightsbane that had been pinned to its clothing away.

"You're not real," Astrid growled, pouncing as the figure moved away from where it had thrown the nightsbane.

The illusion grunted as Astrid collided with it. "I'm real, Astrid."

Astrid fought, despite her weakness from the nightsbane still in relatively close proximity to her, despite having gone so long without blood and trapped in that wretched cell, despite the horrible feeling she could not quell inside of her that told her that Knot was not here, that he couldn't be, that she was alone and always would be, and her loneliness would never end.

She fought, kicking and clawing and biting, but the illusion kept with her, move for move, never attacking, always defending.

That is just what Knot would do if he were here. Of course, Elegance would make the illusion as real as possible.

Astrid disengaged from the illusion only to fall to the ground. She lifted herself up to a seated position and shouted into the dim corridor, "*Where are you, Elegance?*"

She looked around, vision blurry. An illusion of Cinzia stood back from Knot, a few paces to his left. Of course Elegance would make one of Cinzia. But, as Astrid looked at the other two figures, the light brightened again.

One was Trave. There was a chance that they would send

an illusion of him to toy with her—Cabral had told the Coven of Trave's betrayal—but why? And this one was not threatening her. Why send her an illusion of Trave if not to torture her?

The fourth figure perplexed Astrid even more than Trave. It was a man she had never seen before; handsome, with a strong jaw and long blonde hair tied in a bun atop his head.

"You're not real," Astrid whispered, but allowing herself the tiniest sliver of doubt as she said it.

Why would Elegance form an illusion of someone Astrid did not even know? To play an even deeper game with her? Astrid could see Cabral doing such a thing, but the Coven had not seemed so petty.

The figure that looked like Knot approached her again, slowly. "Astrid, it's me. We're going to get you out of here."

The illusion's hands reached for her, and Astrid backed away, but then stopped herself.

Chances were, this *was* an illusion. But Astrid had a choice. She could choose to believe, or choose to not.

If she chose not to believe, she could run, or hide, only to be inevitably taken and thrown back into her cell. If she chose to believe, she would likely end up the same way.

But at least in that case, she might have a moment of happiness.

"You're an idiot," Astrid said.

A slow smile spread across Knot's face. "Aye," he said, "so you've told me, many times."

"You could've at least brought something that would make me certain it was you," she said. "This could all be an illusion. I could live a lifetime of this, only to wake up back in that cell, only a few hours having passed."

Knot knelt down. "That doesn't sound pleasant."

Astrid looked up at him, really *looked* at him. Before she

knew what she was doing, she touched the scruffy stubble that he hadn't shaved in at least a week.

"I'd say don't worry about being an idiot because you have your looks, but, well... your face isn't much to write home about either, nomad."

The feel of his face as the laugh escaped his lips seemed to crackle down her arm and into her body.

She knew this face.

Then Knot was hugging her, and Astrid was letting herself be hugged, and apparently Cinzia couldn't help herself either because suddenly there she was, too—squeezing far harder than she had any right—and Astrid found herself in the middle of the two of them.

The stranger cleared his throat. "Hate to interrupt the reunion," he said, "and I hate to point out the obvious even more, but when it clearly isn't obvious to you, I can't help myself..."

Knot let go, smiling down at Astrid. "I know, Code. Let's get moving."

"Who is he, anyway?" Astrid asked, nodding at the blonde man.

"I'm the help."

Astrid raised an eyebrow. "The help? Have you done much helping, then?"

Code laughed. "Hey, I'm doing this job for free, little girl. My motivation isn't particularly high at the moment."

"You *are* getting paid for this gig," Knot told him.

"Oh I am? In what currency, exactly?"

"My friendship."

"Fine, mate. Your friendship is a fine treasure, indeed, but as I was saying earlier, about the escaping..."

It took a moment for them to find the best arrangement for them to walk, considering the three humans still carried nightsbane and the two vampires couldn't abide it. They settled on the vampires taking the lead, since Trave knew the layout of the place fairly well, while the humans followed a healthy distance behind.

Astrid was about to say something to Trave about how she appreciated his help—she couldn't imagine Knot and Cinzia finding their way down here on their own, so Trave's part in this must've been healthy, indeed—when Trave stopped, hand up.

Voices ahead of them.

"Let us take the lead," Knot said from behind them. In the event that they ran into other vampires, having the humans with nightsbane as the first line of defense would be the advantageous position, to be sure.

"Shit." Astrid moved against the tunnel wall, the effect of the herb making her queasy as the humans passed her.

"Be careful," she told them. "Mainly Knot and Cinzia. Code, I don't much care about you."

Code looked back at her and winked. "You sound like my mother." She also noticed Code slip something from the pouch at his belt into his mouth. She'd seen Winter use a similar pouch. Code was a psimancer.

Astrid rolled her eyes at his comment, but her gut was doing twists and his light-heartedness helped.

Knot stopped, indicating they all do the same, but it was too late. Around the corner of the tunnel walked a dozen vampires, Cabral leading them, a sneer on his face.

But, worse than that, Elegance, Equity, and Eldritch stood—or, in Eldritch's case, levitated—at the back of the cadre.

Against Cabral and his Fangs, they might stand a chance. But even with nightsbane, she knew the Coven outmatched them.

"Well, well, I thought I'd have to isolate you and make

you outlive all of your friends, but here they are. Lambs to the slaughter, isn't that what they say?" As he spoke, Cabral stepped forward, then stopped, frowning.

Astrid sneered at him. "Yes, they've got nightsbane, you bastard. Go ahead and come closer, if you dare."

Cabral glared at her, then looked over his shoulder.

"A little help?" he said.

"We are not your parents, Cabral," Equity said.

Cabral's eyes still smoldered on Astrid. "I'll kill your friends while you watch, girl."

Knot lunged, and there was a scuffle. Astrid's heart contracted.

"What are you doing, nomad?" she whispered. She did not know how she'd be able to join the fight when nightsbane was in play.

Knot had impaled Cabral with two wooden stakes, both in the chest. He gripped Cabral by the collar of his shirt, his sword raised high. Cabral struggled weakly; the stakes must not have actually pierced his heart, otherwise he'd be completely immobile.

A ray of hope sliced through the oppressing fear that weighed down on Astrid's chest.

"Back off," Knot said, glaring at the other vampires, "or I'm taking his head."

Cabral's struggling intensified. Even pierced by two stakes, his will to live empowered him.

The Coven remained where they were, observing silently. A few of Cabral's Fangs looked at one another.

Several things happened at once in a flurry of movement. Two of the Fangs charged Knot. Trave threw himself at Cabral, but was intercepted by more Fangs. Code tossed three wooden stakes into the air in front of him, and all three of them immediately shot forward.

The Coven hung back, watching dispassionately as Cabral coughed up blood on the ground, his face contorted in rage.

The nightsbane hindered the attacking Fangs long enough for Knot, Code, and—Goddess, *Cinzia?*—to make quick work of them. Knot and Code both staked the vampires, wielding swords that Astrid realized were nearly identical.

Cinzia, however, was a different force entirely.

She overpowered each vampire she encountered with brute force, punching stakes into their bodies, only to decapitate them with the axe she carried—as if it didn't weigh anything at all. While Knot and Code dodged and parried vampire attacks, Cinzia simply blocked each vampire's strike with an upheld arm.

"Let us go," Astrid called to the Coven. They stood back a little, observing the fight, along with three other vampires who seemed to be part of their personal entourage rather than Cabral's Fangs.

"Astrid…"

The voice was Cinzia's, but there was an underlying, wavering current of horror that compelled Astrid to turn. She followed Cinzia's gaze to see Cabral had somehow removed the stakes from his torso, and now stood behind Knot, holding a dagger to his throat.

Cabral's remaining Fangs moved quickly to his side, swords held ready.

"Cabral," Astrid said slowly, "This is over. Let him go. He isn't the one you want, anyway."

Cabral laughed, the sound of it wet and hacking. "On the contrary, my dear. I think he is exactly who I want. If I want to hurt you the most, I—"

"That's enough, Cabral."

A low growl issued forth from Cabral's throat as he stared at Equity. "I'll have my revenge. I'll—"

"We have come to a new decision. Let the human go, Cabral. We will take this back to our audience chambers for a trial by combat."

"I'll be damned if I—" Cabral stumbled back as if he'd been struck, though no one but Knot stood within a rod of him.

Knot turned to face the Coven. "We're leaving, like the girl said."

No, you are not.

Astrid recognized Eldritch's voice. The others seemed to have heard it, too, as Knot, Cinzia, and Code all looked around for the source.

Knot leapt toward Cabral, but stopped in midair, as if held by an invisible hand. Code tossed another three stakes in front of him, but they, too, stopped in place. Cinzia thundered forward, axe held high, but the axe disintegrated in her hands.

*You have invaded our home. You will abide by our rules. We will not harm you—*yet*— but you must accompany us to the trial, and stand as witnesses.*

Astrid opened her mouth to speak, but found she could not.

They all had no choice but to follow the Coven, and do as they suggested.

21

ASTRID ONCE AGAIN FOUND herself in the Coven's strange hall in the vampire tunnels, tapestries and statues and suits of armor all looking down at her. The Coven sat in their thrones, Eldritch cross-legged among her sapphires between the other two, waiting patiently. Cabral's three remaining Fangs stood with him at one end of the hall, to the Coven's right. Astrid and her rescuers stood to the Coven's left. Knot, Cinzia, and Code had been stripped of their nightsbane—apparently it had no effect on the Coven, anyway—and their wooden stakes, though they had been allowed to keep their other weapons. Opposite the Coven stood Igar, towering over everyone else in the room, and a half-dozen other vampires that Astrid assumed were part of the Coven's inner circle.

"This is bullshit," Knot muttered. He could not tear his eyes away from Cabral; every few moments Cabral noticed, and would send a smirk Knot's way, which only seemed to make him more angry. "They can't make you do this."

"They can, and they are," Astrid said. She had resigned herself to the fight that awaited her. Goddess, the Coven almost looked *bored*. "Cabral and the rest of them be damned. You don't understand how powerful those three are." I *don't even understand how powerful they are.*

"I'm more worried about that bloke," Code said, nodding

at Igar. The beast of a vampire stood expressionless with his arms folded across his massive chest. The vampires around him barely rose to his hips, and he had to be at least three times their girth, thick with muscle.

"I don't think he's the worst of them," Astrid muttered, her eyes locked on Eldritch.

The mood in the room shifted, and Astrid realized it was because the sun had set. Eyes began glowing around the room, mostly red, but Astrid noticed the yellow, blue, and violet of the Coven, as well as Igar's orange, and a few more colors near him.

"And here I was thinking all vampires had red eyes," Code said quietly. "How closed-minded of me."

Before anyone else could say anything, Equity stood from his amethyst throne.

"This trial by combat will begin when I finish speaking," he said, his reedy voice ringing out through the hall. "The rules are as follows. Astrid and Cabral only will fight; neither will use any weapons not already granted them by their abilities, and they will receive no help. The fight will last until the death of one of the participants. Anyone who attempts to interfere will be killed on the spot, without warning." Equity's eyes roamed to Knot. Astrid gripped his hand.

"You need to listen to him, nomad. Promise me."

Knot, jaw clenched, finally nodded. That would be the best she would get out of him.

"The stakes," Equity continued, "are as follows. If Astrid wins, she and her friends go free. An atypical allowance, considering it has been a millennium or so since a human has visited our lair and lived, but my sisters have outvoted me." His annoyance was palpable. "If Cabral is victorious, he can do what he pleases with Astrid's companions, considering she will already be dead."

"Oblivion," Code muttered. "The price of your friendship grows higher by the moment, Knot." He looked down at Astrid. "Hope you know what you're doing, girl."

Astrid wanted to say something snarky in response, wanted to ease the fluttering in her chest and stomach, but she couldn't form the words.

"If both participants are ready," Equity said, seating himself and not bothering to look at either Astrid or Cabral, "you may begin."

Cabral's Fangs immediately backed away from him, distancing themselves from the fight. Astrid motioned for her friends to do the same, and she heard the scrape of their feet on the stone as they stepped back.

Only she and Cabral remained, facing one another.

Cabral grinned at her, his red eyes glowing with delight. Beneath the facade, a barely controlled rage festered and boiled.

"This isn't how I envisioned our final confrontation, my dear," he said as they began to circle one another, "but I suppose it will do. I would've loved to have you watch as I kill your friends. I'll do it slowly, of course. Might even take a few months, if the Coven allows it. It's a shame you'll have to die first, but I can at least tell you some of what I'll do to them." Then Cabral sprang forward, claws outstretched.

Astrid rolled to the side, her speed saving her. She had fought adult vampires before. She had killed a few.

But this was Olin Cabral. Fifteen hundred years old; one of the most skilled fighters she had ever seen. He had taught her a great deal himself, and she had no idea how she was going to defeat him.

So, for now, her tactic was to avoid him as much as possible.

Cabral sprang at her again, but anticipated her dodge this

time, and managed to gouge a long, shallow cut down her back.

"Aren't you going to put up a fight?" Cabral asked, that stupid grin still plastered on his face.

Astrid said nothing. He charged again, and she managed to swipe one claw away while slipping around him, escaping his attack unscathed.

Cabral growled. "This is supposed to be combat, not a game of cat-and-mouse. You'd better fight me, girl." His grin returned. "Besides," he said, "I've taught you better than that, haven't I?"

He was right. She couldn't keep going like this; it was only prolonging the inevitable. She had to seize initiative, catch him by surprise, do *something*. But the more they circled one another, the more the fear inside of her grew. It grew and it grew and it grew, until it seemed all she could feel, all she could see or understand. She was just a girl, fighting a full-grown man. She did not stand a chance.

Again and again he came after her, getting more and more angry, and finally, as Astrid dodged, trying to skid around him, Cabral anticipated the momentum and direction and caught her by the arm. He snapped her toward him—she did not weigh any more than a child her size would—and gripped her by the neck, then slammed her into the floor. Stone crumbled beneath her.

"*Finally*," Cabral said, grinning down at her. He straddled her, one hand still pressing into her neck. It wouldn't hinder her breathing—she didn't even need to breathe—but she suspected he did it out of habit. She'd seen him do the same to countless slaves, and even his own Fangs.

Cabral punched her with his free hand, hard, sending ringing pain through her skull. Her vision blurred; before her were two realities: one of Cabral, laughing maniacally on top of her, and the other of herself, on a ship, sailing toward a sunrise.

He really was going to prolong her death, Astrid realized. He really was—

Then she heard it. Through Cabral's laughter as he hit her, through the otherwise silence of the room, she heard weeping. She knew it was Cinzia, knew from the tone and the catch in the throat and the sound of her breath on the air, and then she heard Knot whisper something. A name, but not hers...

"*Trave*..."

Astrid heard a roar, and craned her neck just in time to see Trave leaping toward Cabral. *No*, she wanted to tell him, *don't*, but before her mind could think the words Trave flinched even as he moved. Then he burst into a cloud of dust and ash.

In that moment Astrid came out of a stupor she hadn't even realized she'd been in.

Trave, despite all he had done to her in the past, had gone to his death trying to make amends. If her life was all that was at stake, she would gladly die rather than face a life of torture, or even pursuit from Cabral. But it wasn't. Trave had died, but Knot was still here, and Cinzia. Even the Nazaniin, who didn't know her at all, had agreed to come here to rescue her. They would die horribly if she did nothing.

Astrid slipped her head to the side, and Cabral's fist slammed into the stone. He growled in pain. She jammed her claw into Cabral's left eye—she had done the same to Trave, years ago. The wound would heal eventually, she knew, as she had no fire around to cauterize it, but she hoped it would at least distract him enough for her to get out from under him.

Cabral's free hand snapped up to his face where his eye had been and he screamed, but through it Astrid gripped the hand that held her neck with both of hers and *squeezed*, squeezed with every last bit of her strength, squeezed through his hardened skin and muscle until she reached the bone and felt a hard *crunch*.

Cabral's thighs still gripped her tightly, but his grip on her neck loosened, and Astrid shoved with all her might, throwing him off her. He rolled away, moaning, nursing both his eye and his arm.

Glancing at the mess of ash on the ground where Trave had once been, Astrid's eyes moved to Cinzia, and then Knot. She had no time to read their expressions, because then Cabral was up and coming at her again.

Astrid blocked his first blow with her forearm, his claw wide open and ready to slash; the next she dodged. Then she punched him in his kidney, and followed with a left hook to his ribs. She landed a flurry of blows before he managed to turn on her, gripping her bodily with both hands—Goddess, how that must have hurt his crushed forearm—and then Astrid flew through the air, everything tumbling end over end until it was all black, just for a moment, before she focused enough to see Cabral bearing down on her, red eyes glowing, smile gone, claws extended.

Every part of her ached, but especially her face and her neck. She tried to stand but stumbled and fell. His smile returned, widening through blood dripping down from a temporarily ruined eye, and suddenly Astrid was back in Cabral's tower-house in Turandel. Cabral had beaten her to the ground many times in that tower-house. Trave had done it, too, as had other Fangs when she was a slave there. The Black Matron had done the same, perhaps not with her fists, but with Astrid's own tortured, misshapen memories. And another memory, from long ago, before Astrid ever turned, lurked among these, too. Someone else had done this to her, forcing her to sit in that chair in that cabin so long ago, a child of only nine summers waiting to be beaten and abused.

She imagined everyone else those people might have hurt,

everyone else they might have knocked to the ground. A great heat burned within her, so hot she thought she might catch fire, so hot she would have believed the sun had somehow broken through the night and the layers of dirt and rock to pierce the Coven's hall and engulf her in flames. The heat of the sun on her face, as she sailed toward the rosy dawn.

Astrid did what she did not have the strength to do those many, many times, as she lay broken and bleeding on the floor. She did what all the slaves, the women and children and other vampires Cabral had beaten and raped and killed, could not do. She did it for herself, and she did it for them.

Astrid rose to her feet, and faced Olin Cabral.

Time slowed, and she observed the look on Cabral's face as he strode toward her. A cocksure grin, blood dripping down his face on one side, smearing his lips, cheek, and chin red. But as she stood, the grin faded. Cabral's stalking steps slowed, and he stared at Astrid, his grin morphing into an open-mouthed look of pure shock.

Every single other being in the room had the same look on their faces as they stared at her, eyes wide.

Astrid looked down. This was her body, her feet and legs and arms and hands, standing strong and facing Cabral, and in one hand...

Astrid blinked.

In one hand she held a colossal, burning sword.

Canta's bones, she thought, *no wonder they're all staring*.

But she wasn't one to look a gift horse in the mouth. The sword was so huge—longer than Cabral was tall, thicker around than his torso—that when she lunged it burst through Cabral's chest easily, ripping a vertical hole in him from neck to navel. The weapon was so light, as if Astrid hardly wielded anything at all. The blade itself seemed a golden color, but the bright orange flames made it difficult to tell.

Am I dreaming? Astrid wondered. If she was, she didn't know what to do about it, and if she wasn't, she didn't want to waste time, so she yanked the sword upward, cleaving Cabral's torso in two from the inside out. His entire body went up in an inferno as he screamed in agony.

You are not dreaming, child, a voice spoke in Astrid's mind. Eldritch. *This is just you, as the Sfaera meant you to be. As you must be, for what is to come.*

Cabral's screams did not last long. When killed with fire, vampires did not burn like a regular person might, leaving charred skin and bone. Instead, they burned completely, like a log in a raging bonfire but far more quickly, until there was nothing left but ash and smoke. The strange burning blade that had appeared in Astrid's hand was gone, without a trace it had ever been there.

Knot and Cinzia rushed to her, embracing her. She stared down at the dust and ash that had once been Olin Cabral. She would notice, quite some time later, that tears rolled down her face in almost a constant stream for hours afterward, but they were tears of relief.

They emerged from the tunnel into a starry night sky. The Coven had been true to their bargain. But as she stood under the stars, Astrid suddenly felt a tug, a *pull* on her mind. Not unlike the pull she used to feel when the Black Matron would voke her. Astrid turned. A pair of bright blue eyes stared at her from within the tunnel.

The others stopped. She felt Cinzia's hand on her shoulder, but shrugged it off.

"It's all right," Astrid said. "I'll only be a moment."

She moved back into the tunnel, the green glow of her eyes illuminating Eldritch, who waited, levitating, at the tunnel mouth.

Well done, my child, Eldritch said, a soft smile on her face.

Astrid was not exactly grateful. Despite the outcome, she had not forgotten that the Coven had orchestrated that entire scenario to begin with, even if Eldritch and Elegance had supposedly bargained for her friends' lives. And Trave was dead, never to return.

I understand your anger. But all things are as they must be.

Astrid could not help but roll her eyes.

"I get enough of these crypticisms from Jane. I'd prefer not to hear them from you, too."

Eldritch's smile twitched, and Astrid got the distinct impression that constituted a laugh for the woman.

"That sword," Astrid said, remembering the feel of it, the warmth of it she seemed to have felt through her entire body, "That was… real?"

It was very real.

"Is that my power, then?"

Nothing is certain, Eldritch said, but before Astrid could complain about more crypticisms, she continued. *But if I were to hazard a wild guess… yes. I absolutely think that is your power.*

"A burning sword? What kind of power is that?"

I'm not one to make assumptions, but it seemed the exact power you needed in the moment. Whether that means your power will always manifest this way, or whether it might be something different in the future, I do not know. As many powers do, I imagine this ability will augment and change with age and experience.

Astrid looked down at her hand. She tried to summon the blade again, but nothing happened.

"How am I supposed to use it?" she asked.

That is something you will have to learn. It is also, if my experience is anything to go by, something no one else will be able to teach you.

Astrid swore. "Some use that's going to be, then. What if it doesn't come when I need it?"

It might not. That is a possibility for which you will have to prepare.

Astrid sighed. "You aren't much help."

I never said I would be.

"But…" Astrid looked back at her friends, waiting for her outside the tunnel. "Will I see you again?"

Nothing is certain, Eldritch said, and again her mouth twitched up in a smile. *But I sincerely hope we meet again, Astrid. You have grown beyond a mere curiosity for me, at this point.*

As she turned to leave, Astrid felt that pull once more on her mind.

Any good sword needs a name, child.

Astrid looked over her shoulder at Eldritch, levitating there, her blue eyes glowing. She remembered the warmth of the sword, the heat swelling within her.

"Radiance," she said, without hesitation. Then she walked back to meet her friends.

22

Wyndric Ocean, near Triah

COVA SAW THE SPIRE of God's Eye long before she saw anything else in the city of Triah. The tower stabbed upward, straining to pierce the sky itself. From a distance, the stone appeared a mottled gray color, but as Cova's fleet drew closer, she realized the various blocks of stone were all different colors, mostly grays intermixed with pink, brown, black, and even a few bluish hues.

Atop the structure, even from a distance, Cova could make out some details of the Eye's war apparatus through her spyglass. A series of huge brass rings housed circles of glass and mirrors of varying sizes; the diameter of the largest had to exceed the entire length of her new capital ship, the Reckoner, while the smallest must have been no taller than a man.

She was glad they had arrived on a relatively cloudy day. According to legend, God's Eye could harness the power of the sun itself, redirecting it toward Triah's enemies. But her fleet was still far away; it should be safe even if the stories of God's Eye's destructive power were true.

For now, Cova intended to blockade Triah's harbor rather than attack the city. That would give her time to make contact with an old captain of her father's in Litori—and that meeting, she hoped, could change the course of the war. Her fleet could stay out of reach of the weapon for the time being.

And yet, as she looked at the Eye, she thought she could discern some of the mechanism moving, shifting around.

"Make sure we are all prepared to move," Cova told Admiral Rakkar.

"Good idea." Rakkar, too, watched the Eye warily.

Terris Clayborna, chief Eye operator, strode about the top floor of God's Eye, ordering the other operators about with a nervous confidence. They all wore brass operator's goggles to protect them from the high winds atop the Eye, and the traditional brown overcoats of their station. The Eye's war apparatus, at the very top of the tower, was completely open to the elements.

"Swing the mainframe about," he called, pointing at the largest circle of brass and glass, attached to a massive metal arm that, in turn, crooked down and into the top level of God's Eye. The mainframe, the largest circle in the apparatus, held a giant mirror, and always had to be positioned first; it dictated the efficacy of the rest of the apparatus, and had to be exactly correct. "Point it in a west-northwesterly direction, about..." Terris looked to his assistant, Hindra, who held a great tome full of handwritten calculations open before her.

"Two hundred and eighty-nine degrees," she said immediately, her finger stopping on a single line.

Terris grunted. "Two hundred and eighty-nine degrees," he said. Hindra's mind was far quicker than his own. She would take over his position as chief operator one day, and likely do a far better job of it.

A dozen operators rushed to do as he ordered. The mainframe lens loomed around and caught the full reflection of the sun's rays.

Down below, the steely ring of warning bells sounded

throughout the city. The Rodenese fleet remained stationary in the bay, not quite a radial from the coast.

"Halo Three, in position!" Terris shouted, his eyes scanning the apparatus. Two dozen halos in total, twenty-five counting the mainframe, each one of slightly varying size and housing either a lens of convex glass, or a concave mirror, and each mounted on a swinging, swiveling metal arm.

"You are sure the Eye's beam will reach them from here?"

Terris turned to Grand Marshal Riccan Carrieri, a smile on his face. "A good question, Grand Marshal. What do you think, Hindra?"

Hindra looked up from her tome. "We could reach them if they were yet another half-radial out. Striking them where they are now will be a simple matter of getting the angle and trajectory right."

"And you will be able to do damage with this?" Carrieri asked, looking up at the cloudy sky.

Terris could understand the Grand Marshal's skepticism. The Eye's power had not been demonstrated in decades, and no one had seen it used at full capacity for even longer. Part of that was purposeful: Triah did not want others to know the full strength of the weapon they held so close to their heart, but at the same time was also so visible to the world.

"The Eye requires but little sunlight to work, Grand Marshal—the merest beam; and the clouds are moving swiftly today. We will send a message Roden will never forget," Terris said.

It took a few moments to get the rest of the apparatus in position. Terris did not need every halo for this attack, but he did require the use of eighteen of them. When all of them except one were ready, Terris turned to the Grand Marshal, sucking air through his teeth.

"We are ready, sir. At your command, we will take down those ships."

The Grand Marshal hesitated, as if considering, and for a moment Terris feared the man would go back on his decision to use the Eye. But then the Grand Marshal nodded.

"Do it."

"Halo Two, in position!" Terris shouted. Prompting the Eye's mechanism was less majestic than firing a weapon of any other sort: it had no physical trigger, but only needed every piece to be moved into an exact location. With each of the other halos prepped and ready, Halo Two slid into position. As if by his command, the sun slipped out again from behind the clouds, and the bright reflection that issued forth from the mainframe lens distorted, instantly reflected and refined through the series of eighteen halos until it burst forth in a fine bar of golden light, jutting west-northwest, toward the ships in the harbor.

The beam of light came in an instant, and silently, and Cova hardly noticed it in the distance. It almost seemed a particularly bright glint of the sun on the water, until it struck out toward them at a speed that took her breath away, and the seawater the beam moved along began to sizzle and pop. Cova followed the beam back up from whence it came. Not the sun, she realized, but the top of God's Eye.

The beam of golden light curved toward them and before Cova could react, it reached the next ship over, slicing the craft cleanly in an uneven diagonal, leaving two burning, charred masses that steamed in the ocean.

We're too close, Cova thought, far too late. Only luck saved her; instead of continuing north toward the *Reckoner,* the beam curved west and then south, and then arced east again, cleaving three more ships down the line. The beam had cracked four of Cova's ships like eggs, each one already taking on water as her men panicked, many of them already abandoning their ships, in the space of time it took Cova to take just a few breaths.

"*Come about!*" Cova screamed—and then realized that her captain was already giving orders. The *Reckoner* tacked, and the other undamaged ships followed suit. The Eye's beam arced swiftly along the water, mocking them as they fled.

"Get out of range!" Cova shouted, having no idea how far that actually was but knowing the weapon had to have *some* range, because holy Goddess, something simply could not be that powerful.

23

Canta's Fane, Triah

CINZIA APPROACHED CANTA'S FANE, her hair whipping in the wind. It had been almost two years since she stepped foot in the most holy place in the Denomination, but she felt she had been gone for decades.

An aching sense of loss had lingered in the back of her mind ever since receiving her papers of excommunication, and now that feeling only grew. This temple had once been the nexus of her faith, her religion, and her everyday life.

Now, it had nothing to do with her, or so the Denomination claimed.

Canta's Fane rose high and wide, two tiers of great pillars, capped by a massive dome rising up above everything around the Center Circle, including the House of Aldermen and the Citadel. With the destruction of the imperial dome in Izet, Cinzia mused, the dome of Canta's Fane was now likely the largest on the Sfaera. The Fane's entrance faced directly east. In contrast, the House of Aldermen faced northwest, while the Citadel faced southwest, forming the three corners of the Trinacrya's triangle.

Standing atop the Fane's first tier of pillars and in between the pillars of the second were huge statues of each of the Nine Disciples, carved from bright white stone—almost twice the height of a woman. Each Disciple had been sculpted into a specific pose and carried an artifact: Lucia knelt, eyes cast upward in pious prayer, hands clasped around an ornate scepter, capped with the image of a blazing sun; Danica stood straight and tall, her hair and dress flowing behind her, holding a sword in one hand and a shield emblazoned with the Trinacrya in the other; Arcana looked down at the pages of a great tome, held open in her hands. The Disciple Cinzia's artifact was a tiny egg-shaped stone, which was paneled with geometric shapes, like some kind of rare gem.

The statues—and the sheer size of the temple—were impressive, but from the exterior, Canta's Fane was not particularly ornate, at least not compared to other cathedrals. The spires of Ocrestia's cathedral in Cineste were certainly a sight to behold, and Valeria's cathedral in Cornasa had taken the statue theme to the extreme, with hundreds of statues of the Nine Disciples, other important figures in the Denomination's history, and one of Canta Herself at the apex that dwarfed all the others.

But Cinzia loved Canta's Fane. Something felt right about the balance between simplicity and artistry. It felt an appropriate homage to the Goddess and all she had done for the Sfaera.

Two arched double doors, four times Cinzia's own height, constituted the main entrance to the Fane, but as usual they were closed. They were incredibly difficult to operate, even with the system of chains and pulleys that had been integrated into them a couple hundred years ago, and the Denomination only opened the great doors two or three days per year, for holy days or particularly special occasions. One door displayed a silver circle, and the other a golden triangle.

On either side of the great doors were two smaller, simpler sets of doors. Even these were twice Cinzia's height, and would have been impressive on any structure save for this, where they were dwarfed by the Fane's central gate.

The doors on either side were always open, at any hour of the night or day. All Cantic chapels used to follow this rule, keeping their doors open at all hours, until thievery became too much of a problem. Most now locked their doors at night. Only those that could afford to commission Sons of Canta to guard them through the night kept them open. The Fane's open doors were a formality, however; only members of the Denomination's ministry were allowed in after hours, and a whole platoon of Sons kept watch.

But it was daylight now, and Cinzia entered unquestioned; she wore a large cloak with hood up to keep her face in shadow. Excommunicated, she was no longer allowed in Cantic places of worship.

All three of the entrances at the front of the building led into a wide corridor that ran perpendicular to the doors. Huge marble tiles, cream-colored and accented with red, gold, and silver, inscribed and engraved with aspects of Cantic lore and doctrine, covered the floor. Cinzia walked past the row of wide columns at the other side of the corridor, her footsteps echoing on the tiles, and into the main worship space of the Fane.

Hundreds of wooden pews lined the cavernous interior. Canta's Fane was the largest Cantic cathedral in existence, and could accommodate over forty thousand people when occasion called for it. At the moment, it seemed that hundreds of worshippers occupied the pews—not uncommon for a midday recitation in the middle of the week—and many more benches could be brought in when the Fane expected larger audiences. Right now, there was a fair amount of open space. Beneath the center of the massive dome at the back of the Fane rose a large circular silver altar, and above that an ornate, great golden canopy on three twisting columns of bright, polished gold.

Only high priestesses ministered in Canta's Fane, and one now stood at the altar beneath the canopy, reciting Cantic history as a large choir of men and woman chanted and hummed behind her.

Cinzia sat down on a pew. The sights and sounds of it all overwhelmed her. The woman in crimson and ivory robes, her voice carrying loud and clear throughout the Fane, the familiar tones of the choir's singing, the silver altar and golden canopy that formed a Trinacrya when seen from above, the people looking up to the high priestess expectantly, hopefully, or even with boredom, an expression Cinzia had seen more than once herself while she recited these same passages, an expression that she'd thought was inevitable in any religious sermon until she saw her sister preach...

The high priestess had just reached the Zenith, the part of the recitation where she spoke of Canta's birth on the Sfaera, her ministry, and her death. Cinzia realized how different the history recited by the high priestess was from the history she and Jane had translated from the Codex of Elwene. She had recognized the differences as they had translated the Nine Scriptures, but she had never been fully aware of the disparity until now, as she heard a high priestess reciting what Cinzia herself had recited so many times before.

"While Canta was born in the spirit eons ago, we know she came to us in the flesh during a very special time. At the midpoint of the Age of Reification—indeed, at the midpoint of our entire history—Canta condescended to be born among us. We do not know the circumstances of Her birth, but they must have been humble. Her mother was but a servant to a high house of the time, and her father hardly more than a beggar. She was born in the wilderness, but became the greatest among us."

Cinzia shook her head. That had been one of the most shocking revelations of Elwene's Codex: In the book of Arcana, Cinzia and Jane had learned that the Goddess's mother had been a prostitute, of all things, and Her father a cruel nobleman who had tried to have the prostitute killed when he found out about her pregnancy. The woman had escaped, and borne her child amidst a circle of ancient standing stones in the wilderness, with only wild animals to keep her company—the only thing the Denomination seemed to get right. Cinzia could imagine why the Denomination would lie about such a thing—to say the Goddess their entire religion worshiped had been birthed by a prostitute wasn't exactly good publicity.

But, according to Cinzia and Jane's translation, it was the truth.

"She was born with neither privilege nor advantage," the high priestess continued, "but she grew in wisdom and compassion. The baby soon became a young girl, instructing the very priests and priestesses that taught of gods from which Canta herself had sprung. That girl became a woman, and that woman changed the Sfaera."

Cinzia found her lips moving with the high priestess's with the next section of the recitation.

"When we sought wrath, she taught patience. When we ran from death, she taught the beauty of life. When we valued pride, she taught fear. When we grew greedy, she taught temperance. When we lusted, she taught love. When we could not bear the madness of the Sfaera any longer, she taught serenity. When we deceived one another, she taught integrity. When we coveted, she taught compersion. And when fear overcame us, she taught hope."

The subtle references to the Nine Daemons were not lost on Cinzia. She was surprised Luceraf had nothing to say; the Daemon seemed to be in and out of Cinzia's head lately, her presence unpredictable.

If the attributes of the Nine Daemons were everything wrong with the world, weren't these the antidotes? Was Canta not the cure?

But if Canta was the cure, where did Cinzia, an excommunicate, stand? She had consorted with a Daemon, and was not even sure she was still worthy to be one of Jane's disciples. And, more than that, Cinzia could not help but wonder whether both administrations of the cure were flawed. Both the Denomination and Canta's Church had accomplished great things—even miraculous things—but both had also been responsible, inadvertently or otherwise, for great suffering.

The choir's chanting became more melodious, splitting into harmony and rising in intensity with the high priestess's words. Cinzia continued to mouth the recitation.

"She taught us in word, but also in deed. She led the people of the Sfaera against a great darkness, a darkness we have not known since and will likely not know again. She led us against the darkness, and saved us all. Only she could have done it. No other has done so much for the Sfaera. Her life did not begin that night in the wilderness, nor did it end that day as she fought the battle that none of us could fight. She lived before us, and she will continue to live after all of us have passed.

"She is the bride, and Her Denomination the groom. She is the mother, and we Her children. She created our souls, and she will reap them when the time is ready. One day we will all see Her again, and know her as She is, and be one with her, breaking the bonds of Oblivion. Her path is the way to happiness in this life and joy in that which is to come. Canta be thanked for her incomparable gift to us."

The high priestess's last words echoed through the Fane, with the last tones of the choir's harmony. Cinzia wiped the tears from her cheeks. She cried because she felt nothing, and she was not entirely sure it was because of the Daemon inside of her.

A matron and her priestesses administered to the congregation with water and oil. When one priestess approached Cinzia, she shook her head, hood still drawn over her face, and the priestess continued on through the crowd. Cinzia breathed a sigh of relief. There were hundreds of priestesses in the Denomination, but Cinzia had at least been able to recognize most of the ones in Triah. She was sure most of them could say the same about her, especially now.

Afterward, the high priestess offered some closing words, and then the crowd dispersed.

Cinzia had arrived at the Fane during a recitation for this reason. She hoped the departing crowd would mask who she was and where she was actually going.

Instead of following the majority of the crowd back to the Fane's entrance, she joined a smaller group moving west, and then north, toward the offices of the Ministry. There were always a few dozen laymen that made their way through the offices after a recitation, usually to speak with a particular member of the Ministry or to observe the Cantic artifacts visible on the main floor of the offices.

Those artifacts were hardly what the Denomination claimed them to be. Most of them were replicas of the real artifacts held in the Denomination's security chambers below—the basement and higher levels of the Fane were strictly reserved for those with the rank of priestess or higher.

But the artifacts, real or not, were not what interested Cinzia today. The stairwells leading up to the restricted offices were not under constant guard; she just needed to slip into one without looking too conspicuous.

A few of the people who had entered the office corridor with her had gone straight to their destinations, whatever they were. A half dozen more lingered about, without any clear purpose. Cinzia remained with that group for a few moments. There were no Goddessguards in the room, and the members of the clergy present—a matron and two priestesses—were otherwise occupied.

Cinzia slipped away from the group she stood among and up the spiral steps, keeping her footsteps as light as possible. She passed the entrance to the first-floor offices, reserved entirely for priestesses. She wondered if the two women with whom she had once shared an office here still remained. Surely by now they had found someone to take her place.

She was halfway to the second level of offices when she heard two voices in conversation. Cinzia froze.

"The movement will eventually disperse, as will the followers," one woman said. "This will amount to nothing, as these things always do."

"'These things?'" asked a second woman. "I should not have to remind you that something like this has *never* happened before, not in the history of the Denomination. You cannot possibly speak to what might happen here, sister."

At first, Cinzia had been unable to tell whether the voices came from above or below her, but now it was clear they came from above. She paused for a moment longer, the voices growing louder, before she finally leapt to action and moved back down the stairwell as quickly as she could. She slipped out onto the first-floor corridor—still blessedly empty—and hid herself in a small alcove. A wall now separated her from the stairwell.

The women's voices grew louder, and Cinzia hoped they would continue downward to the ground floor, but instead two women—two matrons—made their way onto the first floor, passing not one rod from where Cinzia stood. She could have touched the hem of one of their garments if she had desired.

Fortunately, the two were still engrossed in conversation, and did not yet notice her. Making sure neither were looking back, Cinzia slipped back out of the corridor and padded her way back up the stairwell.

"Did you hear something?" one of the women asked, her voice growing faint below. Cinzia did not stop to see what came of the question, and made her way upward.

The second-floor offices were reserved for matrons, and the third for diviners, but she had no business there, either. When she finally reached the fourth floor, she peeked around the corner into the corridor. Empty, thankfully. There were three floors above this: one for the high priestesses, another of meeting rooms for the High Camarilla, and the top floor reserved explicitly for the Triunity—the Oracle, the Holy Examiner, and the First Priestess. The Essera's quarters were somewhere else in the Fane, their location unknown to the general public and the lower offices of the priesthood.

But the fourth floor was what drew Cinzia today. The Holy Crucibles of the Arm of Inquisition made their offices on the fourth floor, and there was one specific Crucible that Cinzia hoped to find.

She made her way down the corridor, passing rows of doors on either side. The offices on this level were noticeably nicer than those on the previous two floors. The wood was darker, stained and polished, and same with the flooring. There were twenty-seven Holy Crucibles in total, and while their seniority among one another was determined by how long each had held the position, there was no rhyme or reason to how the offices themselves were arranged. Shiny bronze nameplates declared to which Crucible each office belonged. Cinzia recognized most of the names—Crucibles, like high priestesses, were known to just about everyone in the ministry.

Finally, she stopped in front of the name she sought, engraved into one of the many brass nameplates.

Nayome Hinek.

Cinzia rapped sharply on the dark wood doorframe. The faint sound of a clearing throat reached Cinzia's ears, and a rush of relief came with it. If Nayome had not been in her office, Cinzia would have had to make another attempt another time—and soon—and the more time she spent near the Fane and the Ministry, the more chance she had of being caught.

"Enter," a woman's voice, high and melodious, called out from inside the office.

Slowly, Cinzia pushed open the large wooden door, and entered the Crucible's chamber. A Crucible's office was much larger than the one Cinzia had shared when she was a part of the Ministry.

Thinking of her involvement with the Denomination in past tense still stung, and she fought back threatening tears as she took in the room. A large window extended almost the full length of the wall directly opposite the door from which Cinzia had entered. Daylight filled the room. To Cinzia's left, a series of paintings hung from the wall above a set of large stuffed chairs. The floor was polished hardwood, and a large plain rug sat in the middle of the chamber.

To Cinzia's right was a wooden desk, two empty wooden chairs on one side of the structure, with another, much larger chair on the other side, on which the Holy Crucible Nayome Hinek sat, her tiny stature dwarfed by the chair's tall back.

"Hello, Your Grace," Cinzia said, removing her hood and bowing her head. A part of her was still nervous, but she was surprised at how energized she felt at the same time. She was finally here, in front of Nayome, and was ready to speak her piece. She might not last long—Nayome might call immediately for the nearest Goddessguard—but at least she was here.

Nayome stood. She was a small woman, even shorter than Cinzia. Her blonde hair was pulled up neatly into a tight bun atop her head.

"*Miss* Oden," Nayome said, inclining her head only slightly. "Ironic that now you refer to me in the correct terms, but you yourself are no longer a part of the Ministry. It took that long to…"

A deep frown creased Nayome's face, and her eyes narrowed.

She senses me, Luceraf hissed in Cinzia's head. *Your mission, whatever it is, is thwarted.*

Cinzia did not respond, but an inward thrill moved through her. While she was never happy to hear the Daemon rummaging around in her mind, this time it was part of her plan. She had counted on Nayome sensing the Daemon's presence within her. It was Nayome's job, after all, as a Holy Crucible to seek out and destroy any potential threats to the Ministry.

There was no threat greater than a Daemon.

Nayome's legs almost buckled beneath her, and she steadied herself with an iron grip on the tall chair by which she stood.

"Cinzia, what has happened to you?"

"Do you not know, Nayome? Can you not sense it?"

"I..."

Slowly, Nayome closed her eyes.

Is she a psimancer? Luceraf asked, the surprise clear in her voice.

The Crucible's eyes snapped open, and she took a step back from Cinzia, one hand still gripping the chair behind her desk, knuckles pale.

"Out," Nayome hissed. "The High Camarilla were right. Excommunication was too light a sentence for you. I testified on your behalf, but this is worse than I could have imagined. We should have brought you in for execution, as we should have executed your sister in Navone."

Cinzia hesitated. Nayome had testified on her behalf? Why would the Crucible have done such a thing? They had been friends once, but that had been long ago. Before Cinzia had betrayed Nayome, and the Denomination itself, in Navone.

"I need your help, Nayome," Cinzia said. It was the only card she had to play, and Nayome's admission, whether inadvertent or intentional, only made it more valuable.

"I cannot help you. You are not the Cinzia I knew."

"I am."

Luceraf laughed. *She will never believe you.*

You're right, Cinzia thought, *she will never believe me.*

Then why are you here? Such foolishness. You're only putting us both in danger.

If it puts you in danger, then nothing could be more important.

There is more at stake here than your life or mine.

Cinzia faltered. There it was again. There was something about the way Luceraf spoke at times, infrequently and unpredictably, when Cinzia could have sworn the Daemon was actually making an attempt at sincerity.

But, just as quickly as the sincerity came, it passed, and Luceraf was full of rage once more. *Idiot girl,* the Daemon whispered, *your life will not be yours for much longer. When we have united, I will force you out, banish you to Oblivion, and that will be the end of it.*

It had almost happened that day on the Coastal Road; she'd felt Luceraf pushing her out, felt her very *self,* everything that made her *her,* begin to disintegrate, and she never wanted that, not ever—but, at the same time, this was exactly what she wanted Luceraf to say.

She will never believe me, Cinzia repeated. *But my hope,* she said, her eyes meeting Nayome's, pleading, but still speaking to Luceraf, *is that she will believe* you.

Nayome's eyes widened.

Luceraf growled. *You will not get away with this betrayal.*

This isn't a betrayal, Cinzia said. *I don't want you in my head.*

And then Luceraf was gone again.

"Cinzia, what was that?" Nayome asked. She had backed up all the way against the stone wall behind her, both hands pressed back against it, palms flat.

"That was Luceraf," Cinzia said. "One of the Nine Daemons."

"And she has possessed you against your will?"

"Possess is a strong word," Cinzia nodded, "but she and I are now in a... relationship, of sorts." She refrained from responding to Nayome's inquiry about will. The truth was, Luceraf had needed Cinzia's consent to possess her. Cinzia had allowed it, in order to save Knot. Now that Knot was safe, she wanted nothing more than to be rid of the Daemon, but Luceraf had only needed her consent once.

"Nayome," Cinzia said, looking the woman in the eye, "The Daemon has temporarily left my mind, for now, but I do not know what she is up to. She could return at any moment, or worse, we could face other challenges."

"We are in the offices of the Denomination," Nayome said, "what could she do to harm us?" The caution in her voice belied the confidence the words implied.

"That is why I have come to speak with you," Cinzia said. "I need your help with something. With getting rid of this Daemon, and all of the Nine Daemons, once and for all."

Nayome scoffed. "The Denomination have sought ways to do this for centuries. What makes you think you have actually found a method?"

Cinzia pointed to her head. "I have come to know one more intimately than I would like," she said. "And I know someone who thinks we might find answers in the Denomination." Cinzia doubted Nayome would recognize the Beldam by that title, and she did not know the woman's actual name.

"Did your sister send you here, then?"

"No. I came here without her knowledge. She is not aware of my arrangement with Luceraf."

"She is not also possessed by one of the Daemons?" Nayome asked. Cinzia could hear the incredulity in her voice.

"No," Cinzia said sharply. "My sister's movement is in opposition to the Nine Daemons. She works against them, more even than the Denomination."

Nayome raised an eyebrow at that, but she seemed to consider all of this. "I see." Cinzia wondered how Nayome could take it all in so calmly. If someone possessed by one of the Nine Daemons had come to her for help, she did not think she would be so accommodating. Let alone calm. "What is it you would ask of me, Cinzia?"

Cinzia did not hide her relief. Though tentative, Nayome's

response gave her hope.

"I need access to something called the Vault, in the Fane," Cinzia said.

Nayome snorted. "The *Vault*? How do you even…" She shook her head. "Even if I wanted to get you there, it would be impossible."

"I am assembling something of a team to help with that," Cinzia said.

"If you think you can smash your way into—"

"No one will get hurt," Cinzia said, hoping her promise was true. "Nothing will be damaged. I just need to get into the Vault. I need some time there to compare notes."

"Compare notes? Cinzia, what information do you need? I can likely get whatever it is to you in a much simpler way than helping you break into the Vault."

Cinzia shook her head. "It needs to be me. I need to see what the Denomination has, the core texts."

"Impossible."

Cinzia took a deep breath. She had one more card to play. "I have something else to tell you, Nayome."

"In exchange for this favor?"

"You need to know it whether you help me or not. A Crucible's duty is to root out corruption and heresy, is it not?"

"Of course. Currently, your sister's movement—of which you are a disciple, my dear, do not think we don't have that information—is the center of our investigation, though it's proved maddeningly difficult to infiltrate, let alone confront and eliminate."

"'Look to the inward vessel before extending your arm of judgment,'" Cinzia quoted. The phrase came from the writings of the Cantic scholar Nazira; her work was so influential in the

Denomination that Nayome could not but recognize it.

The Crucible's face darkened. "What are you suggesting?"

"I am not suggesting anything," Cinzia said, "only telling you what I know. We crossed paths with a matron from the Denomination in Turandel. She called herself the Black Matron. She served the Nine Daemons. Having now encountered her and seen what she was capable of, I believe the Cult is real, and she was one of its leaders."

Cinzia regarded Nayome carefully. Nayome had clearly changed since becoming a Crucible, and Cinzia would never forget what had happened between them in Navone, but this woman was Cinzia's best hope.

And yet one of her concerns in approaching Nayome had been the fear that Nayome herself might actually be a part of the Cult—a group of Cantic priestesses who served the Nine Daemons. Until she had encountered the Black Matron, Cinzia had thought the Cult was nothing more than a story novice priestesses told to scare one another.

But surely Luceraf's anger at her meeting with Nayome showed that the Crucible was not part of the conspiracy.

Nayome's face was so motionless and hard it could have been sculpted from marble.

"*Was* capable of?" the Crucible finally asked.

Cinzia cleared her throat. "The Black Matron perished on the Coastal Road." *I killed her. I nearly snapped her neck off of her body.* The image, and the sickening crunch, still haunted her. It was not, however, the first time she had taken a life, and that thought made her unendingly sad.

Nayome nodded slowly, her jaw set as she eyed Cinzia. Likely discerning Cinzia's thoughts at that very moment.

So be it. Let Nayome see what Cinzia had done. That did

not mean Cinzia had to say it out loud.

"So you have no proof the Cult exists, then?" Nayome said. "How do you know it did not die with this woman… the Black Matron… on the Coastal Road?"

"Do you really think it would be limited to one matron and a few priestesses?" Cinzia took Nayome's silence as agreement. "I do not know who you can trust," Cinzia said. "I do not know how far up members of the Cult may have infiltrated the Denomination. I do not know for how long they have festered in our… in your ranks. But someone needs to do something about all of it. It is past time."

Cinzia had said her piece. She had no other cards to play. She could actually hear the other woman's teeth grinding.

"I'll need to know more about what you are planning," Nayome said. "Much more. And I'll have to approve it all, as well as the people involved."

Cinzia swallowed. That might be a difficult task, considering half of them were people Nayome had captured in Navone, but it would not be impossible.

"I agree to that," Cinzia said.

"Good. Send a message to me when you know the time and place, and I will meet you. It is not safe here, especially in light of what you have just told me."

Cinzia hesitated, not sure what else to do.

"You may go," Nayome said, sitting back down at her desk and studying a document, as if nothing had passed between them.

Cinzia, her head bowed, put her hood back over her head and left.

24

Litori

URSTADT HAD BEEN WAITING for the better part of an hour when Cova arrived.

The empress was not late, but Urstadt had wanted to survey the meeting space first. The Eagle's Roost was one of the few commercial establishments in Litori. The inn seemed a popular destination for the wealthy, even in such troublesome times. With the Odenites camped outside the city, tiellan Rangers atop the cliffs, and Roden's fleet blockading the bay, cavorting in some inn so far away from the protection of the city seemed an odd choice. The wealthy, perhaps, did not understand the dire situation in which Triah found itself. Either that, or they simply did not care.

Urstadt ran her hand along the polished blackbark table at which she sat, marveling that the inn had the capital to use so much of the fine wood, and for such a mundane purpose. The tables, chairs, and thin columns spread evenly throughout the room were all made of the same treated, polished blackbark, intricate patterns carved in their surfaces, emphasized with gold paint.

The patrons of the Eagle's Roost were no less ostentatious. Nobles in fine jewelry and wealthy merchants with cloth-of-gold sewn into their silks populated the common room. A quiet, intricate melody permeated the inn, played by a small professional orchestra on a raised dais. The low conversational hum would occasionally lull as the music crescendoed, and at the end of every piece the audience would offer polite, but enthusiastic applause.

Urstadt wrinkled her nose. The place smelled of freshly oiled wood and a menagerie of exotic perfumes and colognes—floral scents, oils, and distilled fruity smells most prominent among them—some so strong they made Urstadt's nose twitch and want to sneeze. Such scents might have been welcome individually, and conservatively, but their cacophonous combination was too much for Urstadt's sensibilities. If anything, she preferred the musk of a strong body after a training session. Such a scent was at least honest.

Cova entered the inn, flanked by two Reaper guards. The three new arrivals wore nothing that marked them as Rodenese citizens—let alone the empress of the Azure Empire and her escort—but an astute citizen, well versed in culture and history, would surely notice their taller frames and light hair. In her simple, dark blue dress and soft brown leather overcoat, Cova seemed dressed down for the space, if anything, given the glittering nobles and merchants all around her. Urstadt would not have expected anything less. Cova had never been a fool, and parading wealth was a fool's errand.

Cova caught Urstadt's eye, and her lips twitched with the hint of a smile. While Urstadt's face remained stone still, she felt the echo of a similar sentiment in her chest. She missed her people, Cova first and foremost among them.

Urstadt stood as Cova and her guards approached. She recognized Flok and Grost Erstand, veteran Reapers, brothers, and two of the best warriors Urstadt had ever known.

She could not very well bow or curtsy in the Eagle's Roost;

such an act would draw far too much attention to Cova. Besides, Urstadt's loyalties lay with a different monarch, now. While she loved Cova, and the woman would always be an empress in Urstadt's eyes, she was bonded to her queen.

Urstadt inclined her head, showing as much deference as she dared. "I am pleased you have come to meet me, my Lady," she said. When she looked up, she nodded to Flok and Grost as well, who both inclined their heads in return.

"The pleasure is mine." Cova met her eyes with a smile. Addressing each other by name would be folly—Carrieri surely had informants, even in places like this.

Flok pulled out a blackbark chair at Urstadt's table, and Cova seated herself. Urstadt returned to her seat opposite the empress, while Flok and Grost moved to locations where they could both survey the room and keep Cova safe at a moment's notice. The Eagle's Roost was lined with many such people, bodyguards of the nobles present, though some seemed hardly vigilant.

Urstadt could not imagine the two Reapers were the only guards Cova had brought. If it had been Urstadt planning the meeting, she would have sent a few men in disguise to the inn ahead of time, to scout the location and remain there until after the meeting ended, should extra help be necessary. She'd also have a contingent of Reapers stationed nearby, within signaling distance, should real violence break out. There was no doubt in Urstadt's mind that Cova had taken the same precautions, with Flok and Grost's counsel. She had already flagged a few patrons in the inn who were likely Cova's undercover Reapers.

"The north is weaker for your absence," Cova said quietly, her eyes still locked on Urstadt's.

Urstadt inclined her head once more in gratitude. "Thank you, my lady. The north will always be my home."

"But you do not miss it."

Urstadt understood the statement was not a question, and sighed with a slow shrug. "We all have our paths," she said. "Mine has led me south, for a time."

"And into interesting company."

Urstadt nodded slowly. "Interesting, indeed, my lady. And I have heard your journey south has been... interesting, too." Even if she'd had cloth ears, it would have been hard to miss the news of the devastation God's Eye had wrought on Cova's fleet—the clientele of the Eagle's Roost spoke of nothing else.

"We have a common enemy," Urstadt said.

"What do you propose we do about that?"

Urstadt frowned, glancing around the room. She knew what Winter's carpenters were constructing at the edge of the cliffs nearest Triah, but she could not very well explain it to Cova at the moment. She leaned in, lowering her voice.

"God's Eye cut through your first attack on the city," she said. Cova leaned toward her as well, and strands of the woman's long blonde hair drifted down, wavering close to Urstadt's face.

"A fluke of the weather," Cova said, though her hard tone conveyed her frustration well enough.

"Perhaps. But can you risk leaving the rest of your fleet open to the Eye's desolation?"

Cova's lips pursed together tightly.

"If the Eye weren't functional, could you continue your offensive?" Urstadt asked.

"The Eye is all that keeps us at bay. If it were... rendered ineffective, we would be free to attack the city outright. But... how could you do such a thing?" Cova's voice was barely a whisper.

Urstadt shook her head slightly. "How we deal with the Eye is our business, my Lady. All you need to know is that we can."

Cova's eyes remained on Urstadt, boring deep into her. For the briefest moment, Urstadt was reminded of Cova's father, Daval. Before he became what destroyed him, in the end. Daval's gaze was piercing, intense, and had always made Urstadt slightly uncomfortable, even before his body was hijacked by a Daemon.

Cova had inherited that quality from her father.

"Very well," Cova finally said, her eyes never leaving Urstadt's. Urstadt was beginning to feel the proximity of Cova's face to hers, the closeness of their eyes, their mouths, the strands of Cova's hair waving gently. "But even if you can do as you claim," she continued, "what is in it for you? Or, to be more precise, what is in it for your *companions?*"

What is in it for the tiellans, she meant.

"With the Eye incapacitated, you will attack the city?" Urstadt had to be sure.

"Unless something else stops us."

"Then that is what is in it for us," Urstadt said.

"I've brought many ships here," Cova said. "Such an offensive is expensive." Another way of saying Cova wanted to make sure she retained her share of plunder and land, when this was all over.

"You will get your share," Urstadt said. "I've made sure of it." Or as sure as she could be, anyway. She had proposed such an option to her queen. Winter was not easily influenced, but if Cova helped them accomplish their goal, Urstadt was confident Winter would be fair.

Cova sat back, nodding. This could not have been new information to her; it was the basis on which this whole meeting had been predicated.

The sudden distance Cova put between them jarred Urstadt, but she kept her composure.

"I must say," Cova said, her demeanor relaxing somewhat,

"I am disappointed she did not come herself. I would have liked to see her again."

"She sends her regards," Urstadt said. Winter had indeed told her as much—and expressed her own disappointment at not being able to attend. But as a queen mounting her own offensive—and now tackling the problem of the Eye—Winter had enough business occupying her time.

And she was far more conspicuous than Urstadt. Rumors abounded of the Chaos Queen's appearance—some claimed she was as tall as a tree, her hair a halo of fire around her head or other such nonsense, but most descriptions were relatively accurate. If a short tiellan woman with jet-black hair and eyes showed up anywhere, Urstadt imagined Carrieri's staff would be notified immediately.

"Has she become everything they say?" Cova asked, unable to keep a hint of awe from her voice.

Urstadt hesitated a moment before responding. "In most ways she is not much different than the woman you knew in Roden, however briefly," she said slowly. "And yet, in many other ways, she is not the same person at all."

Cova waited a moment, obviously expecting Urstadt to say more, but Urstadt did not know what more there was to say—at least nothing that was any business of the empress of Roden.

"I have one more question for you, old friend," Cova finally said.

Urstadt inclined her head. "Of course, my Lady."

"Say we defeat our common enemy," Cova whispered. "And both your group and mine are left standing. What then?"

Urstadt's slow nodding stopped. She knew this question would come, and yet it still caught her off guard. Winter had not given a direct answer when she'd brought it up, but it was the heart of the whole alliance.

"We have a history with your companions, after all," Cova said. "If the city falls, and we remain, how do I know your friend will not turn her powers on me?"

Urstadt took a deep breath. Roden had not been kind to the tiellan people. Decades ago, the empire had banned tiellans from entering Roden at all—the penalty for any caught in the empire had been imprisonment, and sometimes death, until recently.

"They accept *me*," she said slowly, "knowing my background and where I am from. There is good reason to believe they will accept you, too. You had no personal involvement in what happened to their people."

"Only because we'd banned them from our empire completely," Cova muttered. "And I'd wager most of the citizens of Triah did not have much to do with what happened to the tiellans of Cineste, but something tells me your Chaos Queen will not spare them."

Urstadt looked around at that, hoping no one else had heard the reference. Truth be told, it probably wouldn't be that uncommon for the Chaos Queen to come up in conversation pretty much anywhere these days, but she didn't like taking the chance. When it seemed no one heard—or cared whether they heard, at least—Urstadt turned back to Cova.

"You also implemented the law allowing tiellans back into Roden, revoking centuries of expulsion. They'll surely give you credit for that."

Cova snorted. "Some good that's done. The tiellans are just *flocking* to my home, aren't they?"

Urstadt said nothing at that. Of course Cova couldn't expect tiellans to immigrate to the empire so soon, especially when most were caught up in what people were now deeming the Tiellan War.

"Can you guarantee that Winter will not turn on me, when all of this is over?" Cova asked.

Urstadt pursed her lips, meeting Cova's eyes, and shook her head ever so slightly.

"Even if we draw up an agreement in writing?"

"She claims that humans have never kept their word in dealing with tiellans, so there is no reason to disadvantage her people any further by keeping to hers, my Lady. I am sorry."

Cova swore. "I thought as much. But as things stand, it seems I must attempt an alliance anyway, or return where I came from. Wouldn't you agree?"

"I would, my Lady."

Cova nodded. "Very well. Do whatever it is you have planned for the Eye. We will watch, and wait. Send us a signal when you've disabled it and we will make our move."

Urstadt cleared her throat. "I... do not think a signal will be necessary, my Lady. You will know when the time comes."

Cova frowned at that. "I do not like such vagaries, but I understand the necessity for them. Very well, my friend. Do we have a deal?"

Urstadt nodded, extending her arm across the table. Cova took it, and they gripped one another's forearm.

Goddess, Urstadt pleaded, *I hope we do not end up enemies.*

Urstadt approached Winter in the chill rain. Had she been in Roden, the snows would have started at least a month ago, perhaps two if the winter was particularly bad. She was beginning to miss the snow.

"My queen." Urstadt bowed her head and dropped to one knee. When she looked up, Winter's smile had faded, replaced by a distracted frown.

"Up, Urstadt," Winter mumbled.

Urstadt stood, looking down at Winter.

"You have news for me?" Winter asked.

"I do," Urstadt said. "The empress has allied with us, for now. When we disable the Eye, she will make her move, and we will destroy Triah together."

Winter's gaze left Urstadt, and moved to the great beams of wood the tiellan carpenters were working on at a breakneck pace. Urstadt was sick of the sight of the siege-engines. Mostly trebuchets, but a few catapults and ballistae as well, and something else, something massive that Winter so far refused to explain. Shifts of men and women worked on the long planks of wood, knotted rope, and great gears day and night: when she woke up early to train with Winter; when she retired late after strategy meetings with Winter, Rorie, and Nardo. Even when she stumbled from her tent in the middle of the night to relieve herself, she couldn't avoid the sight of it lit up by the workers' lanterns.

"When will this all be finished?" Urstadt asked.

"In the next day or so."

"And..." Urstadt hesitated, looking around. Nobody else was near. "You are sure this is what you want to do?"

"We have no other options," Winter responded.

Urstadt resisted the urge to sigh. This was not the first time they had had this discussion, and not the first time Winter had insisted it was the only option that remained to them. Urstadt had tried to make her see other choices, but Winter discounted them, whether logically or with some internal reasoning that she refused to share with Urstadt.

"I understand, my queen. One last time, if you'll allow it, let me emphasize the destruction this attack will cause. Not only will many people die—civilians, the old and the infirm as well as children—but it will open the door for the city to be attacked by Cova's forces, where even more perish."

"More humans," Winter said.

"I… I'm sorry, Your Grace?"

"Not just people, Urstadt. *Humans* will die."

A chill worked its way up Urstadt's spine. She had never heard Winter speak like this before about the conflict between tiellans and humans. Until now, the tiellan battles had always been in self-defense. This was the first time Winter had alluded to the idea that killing humans—no matter who they might be—was a good thing.

I, too, am a human, Your Majesty, Urstadt wanted to say. If Winter caught the unease behind the emotionless mask Urstadt forced her face to display, she did not show it.

The two of them stood, both silent, watching the workers carve and shape and hammer. The sound of work echoed up toward them, the muffled metallic ring of hammers striking nails and the dull thud of pounding wood. The grating and grinding of saws, and the sharp *tak-tak-tak* of chisels. The scent of the wood reminded Urstadt of the strong oiled blackbark from the Eagle's Roost. This wood was cheaper, easier to work with—pine and oak and ash, as far as Urstadt could tell—but the smell permeated the entire tiellan camp. It was a smell Urstadt had appreciated at first, but now it almost made her sick as she thought about what the work was for.

"I have killed a great many people, Urstadt."

Winter was gazing out at the workers, her eyes hooded. She wore her hair braided tightly along both sides of her head, as she did almost all of the time now, with the top and back looser, her black locks flowing. Despite the suggestions of those close to her—and to the consternation of some—Winter's wardrobe had not changed at all since her ascension. She wore no crown, no great flowing cloaks or bright colors. She only wore her black leathers, now accompanied by a long black overcoat to protect her from the cold rain.

"Many of them I've killed in battle. You can understand this. I've killed others, too, for one reason or another. Hirman Luce. The two Kamite men in Pranna. The humans in Cineste who violently interrupted the Druid meeting." Winter hesitated, and when she continued her voice was so soft Urstadt could hardly hear her above the din of the workers.

"There was one time, before I came to Roden, when I... I was still learning about psimancy, and I could hardly control myself—and I saw the man I'd been looking for, my husband, Knot, about to be executed on the Holy Crucible's orders. I took frost to save him. No one knew the power I could wield back then. I certainly didn't. If Kali and Nash, my mentors, had known my potential, they would have taken greater precautions. I wish they had."

Winter laughed softly, the sound cold and mirthless. "Thinking about the *tendra* I wielded then is strange. I am so much more powerful, now, so much more in control. And yet... I've never again felt as powerful as I did then." Her eyes were unfocused. "I lost control completely. I killed men, women, children. Soldiers, Sons of Canta, families. All I saw was my objective, all I knew was I had to reach Knot. I did anything to close that gap. Anything my abilities would allow.

"I've killed a lot of people," Winter repeated. "But I've forgotten most of them. What I haven't forgotten is that day. It's there, all of that destruction and death, whenever I close my eyes. The blood, the mayhem, the chaos. It's all there, and it hasn't left me. It hasn't faded. I don't believe it ever will."

Winter turned, her eyes finally focusing to meet Urstadt's. "I understand the weight of death, Urstadt. I understand what I am doing here, and what the consequences are. Do you believe me when I tell you this?"

Urstadt blinked. "Yes."

"Then believe me when I tell you that what I am choosing to do here," she said, gesturing toward the workers, "is necessary. I understand what will happen. I understand the consequences." She looked back at the construction site. "Sacrifices must be made."

To destroy, I must first know love, Urstadt thought.

"I understand," she said instead.

"I am not sure you do," Winter said with a sigh. "But perhaps you will, one day. I have chosen my path, Urstadt. I will do what I must."

"Yes, my queen."

Her hand flexed, tightening around her glaive. Winter had chosen her path. Urstadt had a strong feeling that, someday soon, she would have to choose hers as well.

25

Triah

CINZIA, KNOT, AND ASTRID arrived at the apartment in Triah's inner city just as the sun began to dip into the ocean on the horizon. God's Eye stood tall in the distance, distinct against the Triahn skyline. The mood in the city was one of confidence and levity since the Eye had so soundly rebuffed the Rodenese fleet; the people of Triah were actually prone to a smile or two, which in Cinzia's experience was incredibly rare.

The three of them wore loose disguises—or, at least, something very different from their typical clothing. Cinzia wore pants—a new fashion for middle- and upper-class women in the city, and one she found oddly restricting. A dress seemed so much more practical, all things considered; these pants hugged her hips and thighs far too tightly. They were not quite as tight as the breeches she remembered Winter wearing, but she could not imagine they left much to the imagination of anyone remotely willing to ogle her as she walked by. She'd covered up somewhat by wearing a long gray overcoat and simple brown leather boots. She had to admit, as they walked the streets together, that she fit in rather well. She could have easily been a merchant-class woman, or a lower noblewoman, out with her family for a night in the city.

Her family being Knot and Astrid, who were both dressed to match despite their protestations. Astrid wore a simple brown dress and a bonnet that she'd complained about vociferously when Cinzia had handed it to her.

"It is for the sun," Cinzia had said, a wide grin on her face. What she had said had been half true, at least—the bonnet would protect Astrid from the sun. She had not mentioned she also thought it would look hilarious on the vampire.

"It's for children," Astrid had muttered in response. But she had taken the bonnet anyway, and it was what most girls her age wore around the city.

Knot, too, seemed truly uncomfortable in his light gray trousers and long brown overcoat. Cinzia had even insisted on combing his hair, brushing it back and away from his face. It had been growing for some time, now, and was long enough for her to tie it in a small, tight ponytail at the base of his skull.

When they'd seen the full look, Cinzia and Astrid had both burst out laughing. He'd scowled at them, pointing at Astrid. "Least I'm not wearing a bloody bonnet," he had muttered.

"At least she looks comfortable in her disguise," Cinzia had said, stifling a giggle. Knot was completely out of his element. He walked away from them as if he had spent too long on a horse, his legs bowed beneath him, and he couldn't stop scratching his head.

Cinzia rushed up to him, taking his hand in her own. "Stop that," she scolded, "you'll unsettle your ponytail."

"So what if I do," he muttered, apparently unable to meet her eyes. "It only took you a moment to put together."

Her smile faded as she realized she still held Knot's hand in her own, and he was holding hers in return. She slipped her hand out of his, and walked with purpose toward the city.

"Come now," she said, "we have an appointment to keep."

They looked for all the world like a small merchant-class family. Cinzia and Knot strolled arm in arm, without awkwardness, and Astrid scampered along at their side. Cinzia could easily have forgotten how the girl was one of the most deadly creatures she had ever known.

"I know this area," Knot said, looking up at the building Code had directed them to. "Came here weeks ago, when I was first seeking out the Nazaniin. Must be a number of these buildings around here."

"This was when you met Sirana?" Cinzia asked. She had been jealous of the meeting when Knot had first told her about it, but quickly realized how silly such an emotion was. Knot was not married to Sirana; Lathe was. And Lathe, for all intents and purposes, was now gone.

And Knot, for that matter, was married to Winter. A tangled mess of marriages, indeed.

"Aye," Knot said.

"I am surprised they would house all of their operatives in the same quarter," Cinzia observed.

Knot glanced down the curving street. "Ain't all next to each other," he said, "at least not the ones I've seen. But they're all within the same few circles."

Before they could even knock, the door before them opened, and an old man stood in the doorway. He beckoned them, his fingers slender, his knuckles swollen.

"Please," he said slowly, "come in."

He led them through a sparse hall into a high-ceilinged sitting room. Standing at the top of a spiral staircase on a balcony overlooking the room stood Code, dressed in simple black clothing, his long blonde hair in a loose bun atop his head.

"Ah," he said, "welcome. And just on time. I suppose I have you to thank for that, Cinzia. The schedule I gave everyone will certainly attract the least amount of suspicion if followed closely."

"What do you mean, thank *me* for it?" Cinzia asked, narrowing her eyes up at him.

Code laughed, raising his hands defensively. "My apologies. I don't mean to offend. I've just heard you're all about being in control, and I figured as one such, you'd have a vested interest in making sure things ran smoothly and on time."

Cinzia huffed, glaring at Knot. His eyes widened and he shook his head, although a smile tugged at one corner of his mouth, too.

"Oh it wasn't him, my dear," Code said. "I'm a Nazaniin agent, remember. It's entirely possible I know more about you than you do about yourself."

He doesn't know about me, Luceraf whispered.

Cinzia grimaced. It had been so long since she had heard the Daemon's voice, she had almost forgotten she was inside her at all. And what Luceraf said was true; despite Code accompanying them to help Astrid, he was still quite unaware of Cinzia's status as an avatar. For now, she preferred to keep it that way. That said, she wondered where the Daemon had been—or if she had even truly been gone, at all. Cinzia was clearly plotting against Luceraf and the other Daemons, but as of yet, Luceraf had not done much to stop it. Cinzia did not like the silence. Luceraf had something up her sleeve, but Cinzia did not know what.

"Have the others arrived yet?" Cinzia asked, changing the subject.

"My friends from Maven Kol are here," Code said, "but we have yet to be visited by this Beldam, as you call her, or your contact from the Denomination."

Cinzia raised one eyebrow. "I am surprised you do not already know my contact's name," she said, "given all you know as a *Nazaniin agent*."

Code laughed out loud at that, motioning for them all to join him upstairs. "You've got me there, I admit it."

The stairs led not just to a second-level mezzanine, but also a corridor that led off into several different rooms. Cinzia was only passingly familiar with the apartments in this area of the city, but she knew that it was a well-to-do area.

"We'll be meeting in my decision room," Code said, opening the third door on the right as they walked down the corridor. "Right through here, if you please."

Cinzia, Knot, and Astrid walked through the doorway into a spacious room lined with shelves and cabinets. At the center of the room stood an oblong table, surrounded by chairs, and a massive blackboard covered the wall at one end.

At the opposite end of the table from the blackboard sat two people Cinzia had never seen before: a dark-skinned man and woman, both of them quite young.

"May I present Alain Destrinar-Kol and Morayne Wastrider, of Maven Kol," Code said.

Both Alain and Morayne stood and bowed. No, Cinzia realized, the woman—Morayne, she supposed—bowed, bending at the waist, but the man, Alain, barely inclined his head.

Destrinar-Kol. The name clicked in Cinzia's mind.

"Maven Kol's crown prince?" she blurted, eyes widening.

Alain glanced at Morayne, and Cinzia noticed him clenching and unclenching his fists repeatedly. A nervous man.

Morayne smiled encouragingly at him, and Alain took a deep breath and turned back to Cinzia. "*Former* crown prince," he said. "I am no longer involved in Maven Kol's political... situation."

"Don't be modest," Morayne said quietly. She met Cinzia's eyes. "He's actually the second king in history to give up a crown. The people hold the power in Maven Kol, now, just as they do here in Khale."

Cinzia pursed her lips. To say that "The people" held power in Khale would hardly be accurate, but that was a debate for another time.

"Alain and Morayne will be of some help to us, Cinzia," Code explained. "We're breaking into Canta's Fane, after all. Alain and Morayne both have… talents that might be useful."

Morayne moved over to Cinzia. "You do not believe you can trust us," she said, without a question in her tone.

Cinzia exhaled. "It is not so much that I do not believe I *can* trust you, but rather whether I can trust you *right now*, just after meeting you."

Morayne nodded. "I can say the same thing about you, of course. Or we could have faith in one another." *Faith,* Cinzia thought. *Where has faith gotten me lately?*

A knock echoed in the room, and the man who had let them in appeared in the doorway.

"Sire, an old woman has arrived. Should I tell her…?"

"By all means, let her in, Darion. Let her in."

The old man nodded, then shuffled back down the corridor.

"That'll be this Beldam woman, I take it," Code muttered.

Knot and Astrid were already whispering in a corner, thick as thieves. Alain and Morayne spoke in hushed tones together. Cinzia looked back at Code, taking in his handsome features again.

"I remember you, you know," she said, quietly.

Why would you bring this *up?* she asked herself. *Now, of all times.*

"I should hope so. We only last saw each other, what, a week ago? If you didn't remember me, I'd be offended. Or worried."

"No," Cinzia said, shaking her head. "I remember you

from… it was a few years ago, I think. Three or four. You came to see me, you came to confess at my chapel."

Code laughed. "Confess? Hate to disappoint you, but I don't confess. Seems an easy way for the Denomination to keep folk under its thumb."

Cinzia hesitated. *Was* it Code that Cinzia remembered? It could have just been another tall, attractive blonde man. Triah surely had no shortage of those.

But she remembered, above all, the man's eyes. She remembered how they seemed like the eyes of a corpse, blank and lifeless and completely uncaring. She remembered how Knot's eyes had appeared that way to her, at first. She no longer viewed him that way, but she was not sure whether that was because his countenance had actually changed, or her attitude toward him had. Knot was still a cold-blooded killer, when it came right down to it, even if she happened to be on his good side.

Cinzia peered into Code's eyes. She had thought he looked familiar from the moment she first saw him, and now she was sure. Despite his jovial attitude, his jokes and his laughs and his smiles, despite the vibrant green-gray of his eyes themselves, they were nothing more than terrifyingly empty, emotionless pits.

"Whoa there, sister. That kind of deep-eyed stare usually accompanies a relationship I'm not ready to commit to."

Cinzia tried to ignore the color rising in her face. "I *do* remember you," she said, matter-of-factly. "You came to my chapel, in the Cat District, I believe it was… four years ago? You came to confess, the eve of Penetensar."

Code opened his mouth as if to respond, then shut it almost immediately. He narrowed his eyes at Cinzia, opening his mouth again, but no words came out.

Cinzia could not help but smirk. "The garrulous Code,

speechless? I never thought to see such a sight." But she saw she had struck a deeper chord with Code—and she regretted her words as soon as she said them.

Why have I brought this up? she asked herself. A confession was supposed to be private. Had her hurt at her excommunication caused her to lash out? Or... A thread of panic ran through her. Was the Daemon inside her *becoming* her? Or, worse, was *she* becoming the Daemon?

"Penetensar," Code said quietly, his gaze fixed on the ground between them. Then he looked up. "Penetensar means I was drunk." The smile he gave her didn't ring true. "Whatever I said can't be taken seriously."

"Oh, I hardly remember what you said. I just remembered your face. Your eyes."

That was a lie. While Cinzia did not remember *everything* Code had told her that night, she remembered a few significant details. Things that had stayed with her since that night.

The mood in the room shifted, and when Cinzia looked at the door she saw the Beldam had entered. The old woman looked around at each of them, sighed, and then seated herself at one of the chairs around the table.

Code approached her. "Ah, you must be the—"

"Save it," the Beldam said, raising a hand. "I don't care for introductions. Making me walk all the way here was punishment enough, don't make it worse."

"We're just waiting on one more," Code said to the room, and as if on cue, the Holy Crucible Nayome Hinek entered the room.

Code's smile grew wider. "Ah," he said. "And here we have... a Holy Crucible, is it? Hinek, if I remember correctly?"

Nayome did not even bother looking at Code. She observed

the room, a deep frown on her face, her gaze finally resting on Knot and Astrid.

"The vampire," she practically hissed. "I should have known. And your loyal human companion, of course."

Both Knot and Astrid glared back at Nayome, animosity thick in their eyes. Cinzia had warned them that Nayome would be here; the woman had tortured Astrid and nearly hanged Knot in Navone. But she'd told them how important it was that they gain her help, and she was grateful to see them keeping their word not to harm the Crucible.

"Loyal human companion?" Knot and Astrid both said, almost in perfect unison.

Nayome's glare moved to Cinzia. "And you," she said. "I trust you are still in league with that… that…"

"That is a discussion for another time," Cinzia said quickly.

"You mean you haven't told everyone? Is that not the very reason you have gathered us here?"

Cinzia felt the Beldam's eyes boring into her. "Told everyone what?" the old woman asked.

"Nothing of any consequence," Cinzia said. She turned so she stood next to Code, facing the rest of the room. "Now that we are all here, we can begin discussing our course of action."

"Wait a moment, sister," Code said, glancing sideways at her. "I'd like to know whatever it is we aren't being told, too."

Cinzia cleared her throat, glaring at him. "If we're going to go into *that*," she spat at him, "my memory about a certain Penetensar night a few years ago might suddenly become *much* more clear."

Code frowned, but then cleared his throat. "Very well, then. Go ahead." He sat himself down on one of the chairs, propping his black boots up on the table.

"Care to enlighten us as to what we're all doing here, priestess?" the Beldam grumbled.

"She is *not* a priestess," Nayome snapped.

Not for the first time, Cinzia wondered whether getting all of these people under the same roof would prove a mistake. "As all of you know," she said, before the two women squabbled any further, "our world is under threat. The Nine Daemons threaten the Sfaera." She glanced at Alain and Morayne. "I realize some of you may not be aware of what that even means," she said, feeling her face begin to color. She did not realize Code had invited these two; she had not planned on explaining the whole situation to newcomers.

"Let me stop you right there, sister," Code said, raising one hand. "Those two have more experience actually fighting servants of the Nine Daemons than anyone here except me. They know what they're getting into."

"And what makes *you* think you've got the most experience?" Astrid asked.

Code grunted. "I don't have to prove myself to you, girl." He nodded to Cinzia. "Get on with it, then, and don't coddle us."

Astrid grumbled something in response, but Cinzia did want to get on with things. "We're here to see if we can strike a blow against the Nine Daemons," Cinzia said. "Perhaps even stop them completely."

She turned to the Beldam. "The Beldam here has knowledge to share with all of us. Beldam, I know we've had our differences, but surely you want to defeat the Nine more than you want to hurt me, don't you? Now is the time for a straight answer."

"Very well, very well," the Beldam said, after a moment. "We all grew up around the Denomination," she said, looking to Nayome as the two locked gazes for the first time. "We all know what they teach about Canta. We all know they don't say a word about the Nine. Well, the Denomination is full of secrets. Some of them are harmless, some are kept purely for political reasons. Others—"

"Excuse me," Nayome interrupted. Cinzia cursed inwardly. She had known a conflict between the two was inevitable, but she had hoped to avoid it until they had at least revealed more of their plan. "Who is this woman?" Nayome began, but then seemed to question why she was speaking to Cinzia instead of the offending party and turned to the Beldam herself. "Who are *you* to make such accusations? What could you possibly know of the Denomination? What secrets do you think we are keeping, madam?"

There was no hint of a smile on the Beldam's face, hardly any emotion at all, and yet Cinzia got the strangest sensation that the older woman was *enjoying* this.

"We're getting ahead of ourselves, dear," the Beldam said. "If you'll let me finish, I'll reveal exactly what it is I'm talking about."

Nayome opened her mouth to protest, but the Beldam continued speaking right over her. "We all know of the artifacts the Denomination holds," the Beldam said. "We know of the vaults and record rooms beneath the Fane. But what few people know of—" and here she looked directly at Nayome "—is the sacred vault at the top of the Fane."

Nayome opened her mouth to respond, but then her eyes widened in recognition. "Danica Fendi," Nayome said. Slowly, a smile spread across her face, and she began nodding. "Danica Fendi," she said again.

To Cinzia's surprise, the name actually penetrated the Beldam's usually unflappable demeanor. An angry shade of red spread from the woman's neck to her forehead, and she scowled at Nayome.

That must be her name, Cinzia realized. And yet she had never heard the name before in her life. She had hoped she would recognize the Beldam's true name if she ever found out what it was, but Danica Fendi did not sound familiar at all. She was aware of a few high priestesses who had left the Denomination for one reason or another in the organization's history, but they had all lived and died decades, even centuries ago. There was nothing about such a thing happening recently.

"You're the high priestess," Nayome said, "The one that left the Denomination."

"I suppose they still talk about me, then," the Beldam muttered. She glanced at Cinzia. "At least among the *upper* levels of the Denomination."

Nayome, too, turned to face Cinzia. "And this is who you've aligned yourself with?" the Holy Crucible scoffed. "I shouldn't be surprised. An ex-priestess with an ex-high priestess. Not surprised at all."

"You know why you are here, Nayome," Cinzia seethed. "Either shut up and listen, or get out."

Immediately she regretted the ultimatum; if Nayome chose to leave, she would surely inform the Denomination of Cinzia's agenda. Their operation would be over before it began.

But Nayome, chin raised, remained seated. "Fine. Have this traitor tell us what she *thinks* she knows about the Denomination. At that point, I suppose I shall have to make a decision."

Cinzia knew that would be the best she could hope for. She nodded to the Beldam to continue.

"Finally," the Beldam muttered. "Now, as I was saying before that particularly rude interruption, the Denomination has *many* secrets. The one that concerns us most is the Vault, atop the Fane.

"In that vault, there is a copy of Nazira's original writings.

In that document, we will find the truth of the Denomination, and a weapon to help us combat the Nine."

Astrid's voice piped up from the back. "We'll find all of that in one document?"

"Aye," the Beldam said. "More or less, anyway. Nazira's public work informs the basis of their doctrine, but she revealed far more than the Denomination tells us, as all high priestesses know. I assume her words are not freely read amongst the Arm of Inquisition?"

Nayome folded her arms. "No, of course not." Some of Nazira's writings were available to all in the priesthood, and even the general public. It had been a verse of Nazira's writings that had inspired Jane to seek out Canta in the first place. But apparently there was more to Nazira's work than what was readily available.

Nayome's face was red with anger. *Goddess, what was I thinking putting these two women in the same room together?*

"Please, Beldam," Cinzia encouraged, "Tell us more about this document."

"There is not much more to tell, my dear," the Beldam said, already moving to sit down. "You'll only truly understand once you read it, I'm afraid."

"And we're just supposed to... *believe* this woman?" Nayome asked, gesturing at the Beldam. "She hates the Denomination. Has done since she—"

"Since I read the document in question," the Beldam said, relaxing back into a chair, "and the Denomination chose to hate *me* for not liking what I read. Yes, my dear, I can't deny I've hated them since that point in time."

"I do not wish to read such a document," Nayome said. "I want nothing to do with it."

"*You* do not have to read it, Nayome," Cinzia said. "I will. No one else need even see it."

"*I'm* a bit curious," Astrid said, but Cinzia ignored her.

"We must remember our purpose here," Cinzia said. "We are trying to defeat the Nine. That is our common goal. Are we not all committed to that?"

When the rest of the room only stared at her, Cinzia sighed in frustration. "Are we not all *committed* to that?" she asked again, with more emphasis.

Slowly, each person seated around the table nodded, until only Nayome was left.

Nayome, who had come to Navone and nearly killed Jane, Knot, and tortured Astrid. Nayome, who knew Cinzia shared her mind with a Daemon.

"Are we *all* committed?" Cinzia asked, looking directly at Nayome, watching the muscles in her jaw clenching and unclenching repeatedly.

"We must stop the Nine," Nayome said. "I see nothing in the Denomination that says they are remotely working toward that. Not yet. So, if this will help, then yes. Yes, I am committed."

Cinzia nodded, a flood of relief rushing through her. "Good," she said. "Good. Now, as far as our plan is concerned..."

26

ALAIN AND MORAYNE STOOD in the Trinacrya at the center of
Triah, waiting for Cinzia's signal.

"You really think this will work?" Morayne asked.

Alain tried to stop his eyes from darting around nervously,
from looking over his shoulder every few moments, but it was
almost impossible. Bright red flames—imaginary, thankfully,
at least for now—crept at the edge of his mind. Living a life
of serenity was simple for other people, but complicated for
him. A year ago, he would have been out of his mind with
nervousness; today he felt relatively calm. Compared to a
normal person, he supposed he would seem quite anxious, but
for him it was a decent day.

That said, espionage had never been his specialty.

"Look at me," Morayne said.

It was midday, and a chilly breeze drifted across the open
Trinacrya area, despite the clear skies and the sun beating down
on them. Alain tightened his long, dark overcoat, grateful for
the chilly weather. He rarely took his coat off anyway, so he
might as well be in the cold.

The breeze brought with it the smell of the ocean. Not
the smell of fish, thank the goddess—one of the worst parts
of this city was the rancid smell near the docks. Fish were an
occasional meal in Mavenil, given its proximity to a river, but

there were not entire districts of the city devoted to the gutting and cleaning of fish of every type. Here, it was miserable.

Neither the chilly air nor the sea breeze, absent of fish smell, managed to calm Alain's nerves, however.

Alain looked down at Morayne as he popped each of his knuckles, one by one.

"We're all right," she said, her voice low and soothing. "We can do this. Together. Remember?"

Alain nodded, but he didn't feel any better. "You just asked whether this was going to work," he said.

"And I still have my doubts," she said flatly. "We don't know these people, and we don't know whether anything will come of this that will have any effect on the Nine," she said. "But we're *us*, Alain. You know what we've been through. You know what we can do."

Alain's breathing slowed, and the flames in his mind receded. She was right. No matter how much work he did on himself, no matter how much he helped others, he was still surprised at how easy it could be to fall back into his old self.

"You're right," he said. "We can do this." He held her face and kissed her.

"I like it when you do that."

Alain's heart quickened. "You seem in good spirits, at least," he said.

"I am," Morayne said, her voice calm. Alain was glad to see her this way. He loved all of her, whether she was happy and competent or depressed and all over the place, but it was good to see her erring on the side of the former, now of all times.

"But," Morayne said, "just because I'm feeling good at the moment doesn't mean I've forgotten our *disagreement*."

Alain swore.

"Don't you swear around me."

Alain was tempted to swear again, but let it go.

"I thought we'd taken care of that," Alain said.

Morayne scoffed. "If you think *that* was taking *care* of a conversation, you've got a lot to learn. We aren't even close to resolving that particular issue."

"Then how can you be in such a good mood?" She looked off into the distance, past the Fane and the House of Aldermen, and toward the ocean.

"You know me," she said.

True enough. Sometimes she struggled when there was nothing to struggle over, and other times she felt great, giddy even, despite the Sfaera crashing down around them.

"Also," she said, "just because we're having a disagreement doesn't mean *we* disagree."

Alain blinked. That was *exactly* what having a disagreement meant, wasn't it?

He was about to say as much when he noticed a little girl with a long red scarf running across the Trinacrya toward Canta's Fane.

That would be Astrid, rushing to meeting Cinzia and the others, and that would also be Morayne's signal.

"You see that?" Alain asked.

"I did," Morayne said. She looked so calm. Alain wished he could experience what it felt like to be so still, just once. His own foot tapped incessantly, while his fists clenched and unclenched repeatedly.

"Then here we go," Alain said.

"Here we go."

Then the earth beneath their feet began to move.

The motion was slow and subtle at first, as if something

deep underground was vibrating, momentarily and ever so slightly. It was more of a buzz, and felt more in the air than from the ground, really.

Three or four dozen people were walking through or sitting in the central area of the Trinacrya, while the edges were lined with many more, some selling wares, others just lounging, walking, or chatting with one another. Alain noticed a few heads perk up and look around, clearly wondering what the vibration was, but most simply continued to go about their business.

Alain wanted to ask if she was keeping calm, but he knew the question would probably compound the answer. Instead, he reached for her hand.

"Doing fine," she said, answering his unasked question anyway. She stared blankly out at nothing, her face tightening in concentration. "Just about to… pick it up a notch…"

Just as she said the words, the vibration gradually, almost imperceptibly grew in power until the ground beneath their feet was, quite unmistakably, trembling.

Everyone in the Trinacrya stopped what they were doing, looking about.

"Earthquake!" someone shouted. A few people began rushing, some away from the center of the Trinacrya, some toward it. Most remained in place; earthquakes were not altogether uncommon in Triah, and most, historically, were nothing to worry about.

"You still in control?" Alain asked.

"I'm never in control," Morayne said through gritted teeth.

Alain smiled at that, but he felt her hand tighten on his.

"You see an option?" he asked.

"I think so," she said, her eyes finally focusing. She nodded her head at a space in the Trinacrya, roughly fifteen rods away, where no people sat, ran, or walked.

"Then let's get this over with," Alain said, more for her benefit than anyone else's. He could not imagine the concentration and control Morayne had to muster to do what she was doing now. If Alain were to try to control fire on this scale, well... he'd burn himself and everything around him into ash in seconds, he was sure.

Morayne clenched her jaw, and then several things happened at once. The trembling earth beneath their feet intensified, for the briefest moment. Cries of shock, fear, and confusion sounded throughout the courtyard as people either began running or started, planting their feet firmly in place, looking around frantically. Above the cries, a loud *crack* sounded throughout the Trinacrya. And, in the space where Morayne now stared, her brow slick with perspiration, a long, jagged fissure appeared in the stone.

The opening widened until it was about an arm's length, and then the shaking stopped.

Morayne stumbled, and Alain steadied her. Exhausted, she let her weight fall into his arms. It wasn't long before she regained her strength and could once again stand on her own feet.

The shrieks and cries from the people in the Trinacrya had faded, but most still looked around in fear. While tremors were always a startling thing, a moment of peace was not necessarily the end. Sometimes aftershocks swept through after a quake, and on occasion the tremors were only a warning of much larger quakes to come.

As Alain glanced toward the Fane, he was pleased to see Sons of Canta already pouring out of the building. Their objective in creating a distraction, of course, had chiefly been to vacate as many security forces from the Fane as possible.

"Did it work?" Morayne asked.

More Sons continued to pour out of the Fane, with priestesses and matrons following, trying to calm the crowd.

"I think so," Alain said.

Now, it was up to the others.

Cinzia, Knot, Astrid, and the Beldam stood in a small alleyway alongside one edge of Canta's Fane, staring into the Trinacrya courtyard.

"Holy shit," Astrid whispered.

The shaking of the earth had finally stopped, but Cinzia still gripped Knot's hand tightly, her other palm pressing firmly into the wall of Canta's Fane beside her.

The group stared into the courtyard. Even Knot seemed surprised at the display. While they had formulated their plan, Alain and Morayne had tried to explain the nature of the powers—powers that apparently stemmed from the Daemon Nadir that had infested Mavenil. Cinzia had not quite understood the details of it all, something about madness being the cause of it, and Alain and Morayne helping other people to control their powers, and how Alain could manipulate fire and Morayne earth. Cinzia *did* have other things on her mind, so it had been difficult to absorb all of the details, but now she wished she had listened more closely.

When Morayne had said she could cause a distraction with her power, Cinzia had *certainly* not expected whatever in Oblivion it was she had just seen.

Code was not surprised at all. He was smiling.

"Well, I'm glad they're our friends," Knot said. "Hate to see what they do to their enemies."

The Beldam, however, frowned. "Their power comes from one of the Nine. They cannot be trusted."

"They seem trustworthy enough so far," Cinzia said. "They have done what we asked of them. Now it is our turn for action. Come."

Cinzia turned and led the others down the alleyway toward the entrance Nayome had indicated.

"You are sure this woman will help us enter the Fane?" the Beldam whispered, her breath warming Cinzia's ear.

"She will help us," Cinzia said, "I am sure of it." She was not sure of it. Far from sure. But they had no other option.

"If she doesn't, we can always bust our way in," Astrid said. "I'm itching for a good fight."

Well, there was that option, too, Cinzia supposed. Not that it was a realistic one, but there it was nonetheless.

"It has been hardly a week since your other adventure."

"Don't physicians recommend at least one good fight a week?" Astrid asked. "I'm due another."

"I think that's scripture, actually," Code said. "'Thou shalt brawl with one another at least once each holy set of days, and no less. More is fine, though.' Something along those lines, eh?"

Cinzia whirled on them both. "Our goal is not to harm anyone tonight. *Anyone*. Do you both understand?"

Astrid rolled her eyes. "I get it, Cinzi, all right? No killing." She raised both hands. "Fine by me."

Cinzia glared at Code, who cocked his head toward Astrid. "What she said."

"Unless it's necessary," Knot grunted. They were some of the first words Cinzia could remember him saying since they had started this particular mission.

Cinzia rapped four times on the small door in the alleyway. This one was very different from the Fane's main entrance. Even the side doors that faced into the Trinacrya on either side of the main doors were large; this one was just large enough for a single person to walk though. Cinzia had been aware of these side doors as a priestess, but they were rarely used.

Before Cinzia finished knocking, she heard the latch on the other side lift. Inside, Nayome waited for them, a small oil lamp held in one hand. In contrast to the bright daylight, the passageway looked perilously dark.

"And here I was worried—and hoping, let's be honest— you would not come," Nayome said, without a hint of a smile.

Cinzia took a deep breath. The levity she had felt out in the courtyard was completely gone now, replaced only by a fluttering anxiety in her chest. "We are here, Nayome. Now, please, lead the way."

Nayome nodded curtly, motioning them all inside.

Cinzia turned to Code. "Wait here, please," she said.

"Right, like I came all this way to..." Code's perpetual smile morphed into a frown. "You're serious."

"I am," Cinzia said. "We can't have too many people roaming about in there. We will attract enough attention as it is."

Code scoffed, but Cinzia held up her hand. "It is not that I do not trust you," she said. Although, being honest, that was part of it. "It is not that I do not appreciate your skill and talent." More true, that, but she appreciated those same skills and talents far more in others. "Your place is here, Code. With any luck, we will be coming back through this door soon, without any commotion whatsoever. Stay here, wait for us, and make sure our exit is safe."

And the last thing we need is someone encouraging Astrid's sense of humor.

Code sniffed. "Bloody guard duty, then," he said, shaking his head. "I'm a Nazaniin, you know that?"

This time it was Cinzia's turn to smile. "I know that, Code. And I have no doubt you are a big, strong, very talented Nazaniin at that. But your place is here."

Cinzia turned and followed the others into the dark corridor, leaving Code standing alone, outside in the sun.

Inside the small passageway, with the door closed, Nayome's lamp proved the only light. Cinzia's eyes took a few moments to adjust to the darkness after the daylight, and for a few moments all she could see was the dim light from the lamp Nayome carried as she led them.

Cinzia and the others remained silent. She had alerted them beforehand that only she was to communicate with Nayome, unless otherwise directed. She imagined Astrid had a difficult time keeping quiet, but everyone had obeyed the rule thus far.

Nayome and her lamplight turned at the end of the corridor, toward the offices of the Ministry. When they reached the office hall, she looked at the Beldam.

"I hope you know what you are talking about," she said. "And at the same time, I hope to the Goddess you do not."

Fortunately, Alain and Morayne's distraction seemed to have worked. They encountered almost no one—Goddessguard, Son, or clergy—and the few people they did see either seemed focused on the earthquake that had just happened outside, or their own business.

"Don't like how empty it is," Knot said quietly.

Cinzia looked at him. "Was that not the point of the little distraction we orchestrated?"

Knot grunted, but she knew he was right to be wary.

They continued up the stairs until they reached the sixth floor. The stairwells on either edge of the office halls stopped at this level, and the only option was to walk through the corridor that led to the offices of the High Camarilla. Cinzia had only been up here a handful of times when she was a priestess. Here, the decor was significantly more expensive than any of the previous levels. Gilded columns lined the hallway on either side between the doorways, and the marble floor was etched in gold and silver. Carved busts of important people in the Denomination's history lined one of the walls, and Cinzia recognized Joana Jars, the youngest woman to ever hold the office of Essera. Her face was thin, even for a woman so young—she was only nineteen when she ascended—and the sculptor had made her eyes strangely narrow, as if she were looking at someone with faint disapproval or suspicion.

She would be looking at you that way, if she had even a remote idea what you were about, Cinzia told herself. A part of her still could not believe what she was doing. Breaking in to Canta's Fane, the most sacred place in all of Canticism, the religion she had devoted her life to upholding and teaching. She imagined Nayome felt the same way, but even worse. At least Cinzia had the mask of heretic to hide behind, now.

Beside Joana was a bust of Lucia Wayright, the Essera in power when the last king of Khale gave up his crown. While she was by no means ancient, even in comparison with Joana, she was much fuller-faced, her cheeks round, her head resting on an ample neck and shoulders.

More busts lined the wall, but Nayome stopped them before a set of large double doors equidistant from either end of the otherwise empty corridor. A large gold and silver Trinacrya, the size of Cinzia's arms if she encircled them, was set into the wood where the doors met. A silver, ornate doorknob stood out on one door, while the other held a pyramidal, golden lock mechanism.

"That leads up to the Triunity's offices," Cinzia said quietly.

She had never been up that far. No priestess ever had. Typically, only the members of the Triunity—First Priestess, the Holy Examiner, and the Oracle—roamed above this level. On occasion, a high priestess or a Holy Crucible was allowed up under very special circumstances.

"Goddess, Cinzia, just *go*. We're all right behind you."

Cinzia glared at Astrid, but felt encouraged by the girl's words nonetheless.

She felt a strong grip on her arm, just above her wrist. She and Nayome locked eyes.

"Are you sure?" Nayome asked.

No, Cinzia wanted to say. *I am no longer sure of anything.*

"Yes," she said, with as much force and conviction as she could muster.

It seemed to be enough for Nayome. The Holy Crucible turned, pulling a keyring from her robe. She fumbled with it for a moment, and then selected a black iron key.

Cinzia had expected a more ornate key for such a fancy lock. But Nayome turned the key, and the mechanism *clicked,* and then Nayome swung one of the doors open wide. Along with it came the silver part of the Trinacrya embedded in the door, part of the circle jutting out, while part of the golden triangle remained in place, jutting out from the door that remained. A triangular open space remained on the swinging door.

"Doesn't seem the most secure of doors," Astrid mumbled.

"It usually doesn't have to be," Nayome said.

In front of them was another flight of stairs, leading upward. Nayome took one more glance back at Cinzia, then started up them. They all followed close behind.

"It has been a long time since I have been here," the Beldam said as they ascended the stairs.

"You're lucky to be returning at all," Nayome said.

At the top of the steps was another door, but this one was plain, iron-banded wood, with a single doorknob at its center—and no locking mechanism that Cinzia could see.

Nayome pushed the door inward and walked into the Triunity's chambers. Cinzia took a deep breath and followed, just as she heard a sharp gasp from Nayome.

Cinzia's heart froze. They had chosen the time of day that, according to Nayome, all three members of the Triunity should be caught up in meetings and other business, and were least likely to be in their chambers. But there was always the chance that they would walk right into one of the highest-ranking members of the Denomination. If that were to happen—Goddess, if that was what was happening *now*—Cinzia had still not decided what they should do.

When she entered the chamber, she realized she would not have to make that choice, at least not yet—but there was no relief. Instead, her gut tightened.

The Triunity's chambers were large, but not lavish. Simple rugs covered the floor, and tapestries more valuable for their content than for their artistry decorated the walls. The room itself was circular, and directly in front of Cinzia a large window looked out onto the Trinacrya square. Two other windows looked out at Triah at different angles: one toward the ocean and God's Eye, and the other inland, toward Khale itself. The room was well kept, a large desk stacked with papers and books and a few other chairs across from where she stood in the stairwell doorway. She would have liked to look around and see what else the room contained, but the seven figures at the center of the room occupied her full attention.

Three women from the Sect of Priesthood stood facing

them, accompanied by four Goddessguards, armed and in chain mail, two on either side of the women. At the center was the high priestess who had delivered her papers of excommunication, Garyne Hilamotha. Her long black hair hung in a braid down her back, and her dark eyes stared right past Nayome and bored into Cinzia. One of the other women was a matron, her Cantic robes trimmed in gold, and the other a simple priestess. Just as Cinzia once was.

And yet something about these women did not seem right to Cinzia. Why were they here, in the Triunity's quarters? None of them belonged here.

Did you really think I'd let you do this without opposition?

A shiver ran down Cinzia's spine as the voice echoed within the walls of her own mind.

Luceraf.

"Who are you?" Nayome asked the three, but Cinzia was too involved in the conversation in her own mind to hear how the women answered. And, after all, she already knew the answer, now. These women were part of the Cult.

You have been there all along? Cinzia asked.

Of course I have, my dear. You are too valuable to leave to your own devices.

I did know it, Cinzia thought. But she had let her guard down anyway.

She looked back at Knot and Astrid. Astrid was crouched, short swords drawn, ready to pounce, and Knot had drawn his Nazaniin sword.

"So many of our enemies here at once," High Priestess Garyne said with a smile. "How fortunate are we, ladies?"

The two women on either side of her did not share her amusement. A sheen of sweat slicked the priestess's forehead.

278

The matron appeared slightly more composed, but her face remained deadly serious.

We have a special treat for you, my dear. Luceraf's words were cold, devoid of the amusement usually so prominent in her speech.

"Who are these women?" the Beldam demanded, stepping forward. "You have no right to be here."

Garyne cocked her head to one side. "Is the famous heretic finally going senile? Or is that why you left the Denomination in the first place?"

The Beldam spluttered a response, but Garyne spoke over her, nodding to the Goddessguards.

"Seize them. Kill everyone but the vampire. Leave her to me; she owes us a debt."

Cinzia glanced back at Astrid to see fear in the girl's eyes. "You're part of the Cult," Astrid said, putting together what Cinzia already knew.

Garyne did not respond to Astrid's question directly, but the implication was clear. "You once served the Black Matron," the high priestess said. "She answered to me. An affront against my servant is an affront against me, dear girl. I cannot allow such things to go unpunished."

Anger bubbled up within Cinzia. She stepped purposefully between the high priestess and Astrid. "Leave her alone," Cinzia said.

The high priestess bared her teeth. "You can't tell me you've actually developed *feelings* for that little daemon?"

"Enough talk," Cinzia said. "Or is that all you can do?"

Garyne sighed. "All right, then. You heard the heretic. Enough talk, let's get at it, ladies." The matron and priestess looked at one another, faces pale, and then both drew daggers from their robes. The four Goddessguards stepped from the flanking position they held to stand between the three Cult members and Cinzia's party.

Cinzia heard muttered curses from Astrid and Knot simultaneously behind her, and the blood drained from her face.

The voices of the matron and priestess rose in unison, their words trembling.

"*My blood for the blood of Aratraxia,*" they both said.

Cinzia froze, even as Knot and Astrid both rushed past her. The Goddessguards moved to intercept them, and with a scream from Astrid they all clashed in a flurry of steel.

She had seen this before, heard these words before, when the young man had slit his own throat in front of her and Arven. Afterward, an Outsider—a great daemon from some faraway plane—had entered the Sfaera.

They had to stop these women.

"*My blood pays the price of passage, from their realm to ours,*" the two continued, their voices still in perfect unison.

Knot and Astrid would not get to either of the women in time. Both the matron and the priestess raised their daggers, dark steel toward the pale skin of their throats.

Cinzia bolted forward, past the Goddessguards, all of them distracted by Knot and Astrid, one of them already down. The priestess was closest to her. She could make it. She *had* to make it.

Cinzia noticed something *shift* in the air around her just as the wide oak desk that had been off to one side slid across the floor directly in front of Cinzia, blocking her path.

Psimancy. Someone in the room—Garyne?—was a telenic.

Cinzia leapt over the desk, but two of the wooden chairs nearby suddenly flew into the air, rushing directly toward Cinzia. She raised her arms to block them as best she could, but Cinzia felt two sharp, hard blows against her arms, chest, and stomach.

Above the sound of wood splintering, she heard the women's voices.

"*My blood for the blood of Aratraxia.*"

Cinzia plowed forward, ignoring the dull ache in both arms, and tackled the priestess to the ground. Both the priestess and Garyne shrieked, and the priestess's dagger clattered to the floor. The matron collapsed in a shower of blood.

The dagger moved slightly. Cinzia gripped the priestess— her right arm screamed in pain—and rolled just as the dagger twitched into the air and shot toward her, embedding itself in the priestess's back.

Garyne cursed, but then she seemed to relax. "Two would have been better," she said, panting, "but one will do."

A shadow moved over the chamber, and then a dark shimmer appeared, swirling in the air above where the matron now lay, face down in a pool of her own blood.

A man groaned, and Cinzia heard the soft, slick sound of a blade sliding through flesh. She pushed the priestess's body off of her, and turned to see the last Goddessguard fall to Knot's sword.

He and Astrid both turned to face the shape forming in the air.

"Are you mad?" Cinzia asked, looking at Garyne. "An Outsider in a space this small… it will destroy the Triunity's chambers. It might kill every one of us."

"And besides," Astrid said, "we've faced these before. We can handle one of them."

With a great *thump*, a dark shaped dropped to the floor of the Triunity's chambers with such force that it fell through it, stone crumbling and breaking beneath it. Cinzia heard the sharp crack of breaking glass, and the nearest window shattered into a hundred pieces at the impact.

"I'll just have to give it a head start."

The four weapons the Goddessguards had carried lifted into the air—three swords and a short stabbing spear. All four of them turned so they pointed toward Knot and Astrid.

"No," Cinzia said. Before she knew what she was doing— perhaps before she even spoke the word, Cinzia could not be sure—she found herself sprinting toward Garyne. The woman turned her head slightly as Cinzia charged, but there was nothing she could do. Cinzia crashed into the high priestess, and the two went flying toward the shattered window. In a panic, Cinzia realized she could not control their fall. The window was so tall and wide that the lip of it was less than a rod from the floor of the chambers. Cinzia and the high priestess barreled over the lower edge of the window, and out into the blue midday sky.

Astrid rolled to the side, the high priestess's blades narrowly missing her. One embedded itself in the rising, dark shape before her.

The Outsider thrashed, its tail flicking out. Nayome had hidden herself the moment fighting had broken out in the chambers. It was probably for the best. The Crucible had no fighting prowess that Astrid knew of, and would likely only get in the way. The Beldam she had lost track of, however. She hadn't left, of that much Astrid was sure, but she, too, must have hidden herself when the fighting broke out.

Astrid heard the faintest sound of scuffling, and a struggle outside the window. If her memory didn't fail her, there would be a large, gradually sloping roof directly outside of the window. With any luck, Cinzia had stopped herself from falling any farther, and the high priestess had toppled to a grizzly death. From the sound of things, that wasn't the case, and the two were engaged in a struggle on the roof outside the window.

At least, Astrid hoped, that meant Cinzia was still alive.

The hope gave her strength, and Astrid advanced on the Outsider, swords at the ready. She'd been confident earlier, but the last time she and Knot had faced an Outsider during the day, they'd at least had Eward's archers to back them up. Here, it was just the two of them, and in a complicated space, to say the least.

"How d'you want to handle this, nomad?" Astrid asked.

When Knot didn't respond, she snapped her head back to look at him.

He lay on the ground, perfectly still, the spear the high priestess had psimantically thrown embedded in his chest.

Astrid choked on the next breath she drew, her lungs contracting, throat tightening. She was aware of the fact that the Outsider now stood at its full height, its head almost touching the high ceiling of the chamber, a low growl rumbling with enough force that Astrid felt it in her chest. She was aware of the struggling outside the window, the faint voices. She was aware of Nayome, curled in a ball, beneath another large desk off to the side.

But most of all she was aware of Knot's stillness, and the length of wood sticking straight out from him.

Within this awareness an entire world seemed to exist, a world Astrid never knew was there until this moment, outside of time and space, because even as the Outsider's growl trembled around her and into her lungs, in this other world, this special world she had just become aware of, Astrid was without Knot, and that absence ached and echoed with an immediate pain that she could not ignore.

He can't be dead, she told herself, but she had no evidence one way or the other. He lay still on the ground, a spear in his chest. She knew what the chances of surviving such a blow were.

The tower shook as the Outsider took a step toward her.

Astrid didn't have time to wait for the creature to take the initiative. With a deep breath she sprang forward, hacking at the Outsider's nearest leg. She got a few good strikes in, but even with all her strength her blades hardly broke through the armored hide.

Goddess, what she wouldn't give for a bit of holy magic right now. Jane wasn't her favorite person, she had to admit, but she'd once completely vaporized an Outsider with a ray of light, and Astrid would do just about anything to end this as quickly as possible.

The Outsider looked down at Astrid, cocking its head to one side. With a strange sound somewhere between a bark and a scream, the monster kicked her, hard, full on in the chest, and Astrid flew backwards.

She crashed into the wall, chunks of stone falling around her. Astrid gasped but took in a mouthful of dust and began to cough violently. She struggled to stand, but as she prepared herself to meet the Outsider once more—not knowing how in Oblivion she could possibly take on the beast—she realized it wasn't striding toward her. It wasn't even *looking* at her. Instead, it was staring at the desk behind which she knew Nayome was hiding.

What in Oblivion...

Suddenly, Astrid remembered their battle against the Outsiders under the dome in Izet. The Outsiders had seemed particularly drawn to, almost enraged by, psimancers.

"Nayome," Astrid said, speaking as loudly as she could while still keeping her voice calm, "if you're a psimancer, the Outsider is going to target you. You need to do something about that."

Astrid took one step toward the desk under which Nayome hid, but so did the Outsider, which also glanced her way before refocusing on Nayome.

Astrid swore. She would barely be a distraction to it. If it wanted to kill Nayome, it would, and Astrid would not be able to stop it.

"Nayome," Astrid said, but before she could continue, Nayome stood up. She was shaking, her hair in a frazzled blonde halo around her face. She stared down the Outsider, and Astrid recognized the pure, white-hot rage radiating from her eyes.

"I," Nayome said, her voice wavering through gritted teeth, "am a Holy Crucible of the Cantic Denomination. I serve the Goddess and all she stands for. I root out heresy and abomination, and purify such things out of existence." Though her voice wavered and her body shook, Astrid felt the power radiating from her. Even without psimantic ability, she knew Nayome must be aiming a tremendous amount of acumenic pressure at the Outsider.

The Outsider met Nayome's gaze, huge black eyes clashing with her brown, and remained almost perfectly motionless. Astrid had never seen an Outsider so still, unless it was dead. Once they took form, they only seemed to care about thrashing, clawing, devouring, and destroying, with all the energy they had.

"And now," Nayome said, "it is time for your purification." Her body remained still, albeit trembling, but Astrid could sense even more power radiating from the woman, all of it directed straight toward the Outsider.

Nayome uttered a guttural moan, the sound escalating into

a scream, and then in a single, swift motion, the Outsider's head snapped back, and the beast collapsed, lifeless, to the stone floor.

Astrid coughed, waving her hand in front of her face to clear the newly formed dust cloud as best she could. She had seen an acumen do something similar to a person once before, in Izet, when Kali had killed Nash. Kali had sent a psionic blast directly into the man's mind, essentially bursting his brain inside his own skull.

Dark blood drained from the outsider's large black eyes, and she knew Nayome had done the same thing here. But, just for good measure, Astrid rammed a sword into one of the black, lifeless eyes, full on to the hilt.

There was much to be done.

First, she ran to the window where she'd last seen Cinzia and the high priestess topple out into the blue sky.

"Goddess, it took you long enough."

Cinzia lay on a disrupted patch of the clay tiles that lined the roof, limbs spread awkwardly to keep her from sliding toward the edge.

Astrid couldn't reach her, so she ducked inside to find the halberd one of the Goddessguards had been carrying.

"AstridwhereareyougoingIneedhelp—"

When Astrid returned, reaching the halberd handle out to her, she coughed, reaching for the weapon. "Ah. Thank you," she said.

"You got a good grip?" Astrid asked.

Cinzia nodded. Astrid pulled. Eventually, Cinzia made it close enough for Astrid to grab her and lift her back into the Triunity's chambers.

"The high priestess?" Astrid asked.

"She fell," Cinzia said, staring at the body of the Outsider.

"How in the Sfaera did you—"

"Wasn't me," Astrid said. She nodded at Nayome, who stood exactly where she'd left her, face pale. "It was her."

Then, she rushed back to Knot.

27

CINZIA WAS ABOUT TO say something pithy about Astrid rushing away from her, when she saw the body. Knot lay prone on the floor, unmoving, a spear in his chest.

"Oh Goddess," Cinzia whispered. Then she was right behind Astrid, moving to him.

"Is he—"

Knot lurched up, coughing.

"He's alive!" Astrid exclaimed.

Cinzia moved to him, her mind racing. A thrill of elation rushed through her; for a moment, she had thought he was dead. And, as she got closer, she realized the spear was less in his chest and more in his shoulder. She breathed a sigh of relief. A shoulder wound was relatively easy to treat compared to a punctured lung or heart.

Knot mumbled something, and a thrill of elation rushed through Cinzia.

"What was that, nomad?" Astrid asked.

"I said," Knot rasped, his voice hardly audible, "you're bloody right I'm alive. But I need you to get this spear out of me."

"Goddess, Knot, I want to hug you," Cinzia said, aware now of tears streaming down her cheeks. Instead, she took his hand, and felt Knot grip her own tightly.

They worked together to get the spear out of him. His

leather had stopped the barb from penetrating deep enough to get hooked into his flesh, and they could pull it out instead of having to push it all the way through. Cinzia heard the slick, wet, sliding sound of the spear moving, and felt Knot's grip tighten. She held his hand with both of her own, until she heard a clatter as Astrid flung the spear away.

Quickly, Cinzia and Astrid put pressure on the wound using some cloth from the nearest bed in the chambers. Blood seeped from the wound, but Cinzia knew Knot would be all right.

She told him as much, and Knot coughed, eventually nodding. He made an attempt to get to his feet, but Cinzia put a hand on his shoulder gently.

"Do not try to move until you have to," she said. She looked to Astrid. "Help him when he is ready."

"We need to get out of here sooner rather than later," Astrid said. "No telling when more of these bleeding Cultists will show up."

"You're right," Cinzia said. "You need to get Knot to safety."

"But not we?" Astrid asked.

Cinzia took a deep breath, and shook her head. "No," she said. "Not we. You."

"I can't leave you here alone—" Astrid said, but Cinzia cut her off.

"You must. I will be damned if I let all of this be for nothing," Cinzia said. "We came here for a reason. I can still accomplish that."

"What if there are more of them waiting for you in the Vault?" Knot rasped, pushing himself to his feet despite Cinzia's admonition. Bloody idiot. But she was glad to see him on his feet so soon, even if it was ill-advised.

Cinzia gave a small shrug in response. It was a chance they

would have to take. But she could not bring herself to say that to Knot.

"I did defeat their high priestess," Cinzia said. "What more could they send against me?"

Cinzia knew there were myriad answers to that question, but she hoped her bravado was enough to convince Knot.

"I can't leave you," he said again.

Cinzia gave him a look. "You are in no condition to remain, let alone protect me," she said. "Astrid will not be of any use to me either, not if she has to split her time between protecting both of us."

Knot looked back at Astrid, clearly torn.

Cinzia would not have that. As much as she liked Knot— Goddess, as much as she *loved* him—and as much as she wanted Knot with her, she wanted both him and Astrid safe.

And she had a feeling that, whatever she was about to face, she had to face it alone.

"You don't have a choice," Cinzia said. "I forbid you from following me."

Knot raised an eyebrow. "Forbid?"

Cinzia did not look away from him. "Forbid," she said.

The two held one another's gaze. Cinzia wanted to reach out for him—Goddess, she wanted to kiss him, to feel the roughness of his cheek on her own, his lips on hers as he held her close.

But she knew she could not. Mainly because she did not want to aggravate his shoulder wound, but there were other reasons, too.

Which was why she was so surprised when he pulled her in to him, wrapping her in a one-armed embrace with his uninjured arm. He held her tightly for a moment, and Cinzia let herself be held.

Then she pulled away from him.

"Go," she said, wiping the tears from her cheek, hopefully before he saw them.

To his credit, Knot actually did as she asked. Astrid moved to him quickly, helping him walk, and they descended down the stairs together.

Cinzia glanced at Nayome, still staring at the body of the Outsider before her, face pale, strands of hair loose and waving around her face.

"Where is the Beldam?" Cinzia asked, looking around the chambers.

No response.

Cinzia walked quickly around the circular room, searching for any sign of the woman. Goddess, if the Beldam had abandoned them—if she had *used* them, and gone on without her...

Then she noticed a small, limp form, crumpled against the outer wall of the chambers.

She approached the Beldam, and heard a low moan as she got closer. Cinzia was surprised at how small the Beldam looked. Her frame usually seemed much larger, more imposing, but now as she lay collapsed on the floor, her robes seemed uncharacteristically large, as if there were far too much fabric for such a slight person.

The Beldam's eyes were open wide.

"What happened?" Cinzia asked. The twisting in her gut she had felt at seeing Knot so severely injured was completely gone now. Knot would be all right. And try as Cinzia might, she could conjure very little compassion for this woman. She only felt a sense of urgency; the Beldam knew of this secret vault, while no one else did.

"Daemon..." the Beldam said, nodding at the outsider.

291

"Smacked me with its tail. Strong bugger. Sent me flying, and now I think… I think…"

The Beldam's eyes rolled up into her head, and a wave of panic washed over Cinzia.

"Beldam," Cinzia said, kneeling beside her. She reached out and touched the Beldam's shoulder gently. "I need you to stay with me. Can you move your legs?"

"I can't move anything," the Beldam wheezed.

Cinzia dared not transport the woman, especially if she claimed to be unable to move any of her limbs. The Outsider had likely broken her back.

"Beldam," Cinzia said, weighing her options. She could help this woman, or she could get what she needed from her, and move on.

Cinzia felt as if her heart were encased in stone. This woman had caused so many problems for the Odenites. She had caused so many problems for the *tiellans*.

"Can you tell me where the Vault is?"

"Vault…" the Beldam rasped.

"Yes," Cinzia said, the impatience rising inside of her. Along with the impatience, a hot shame burned within her. Shame for not caring about what happened to this woman. Shame for what she knew she would do if the Beldam gave her even a hint of the Vault's location. The Beldam's life was a life, and whatever else Cinzia believed, did she not view life itself as sacred?

But this was also the woman who had led hundreds of Odenites away—who had preached hate against the tiellans, and sowed discord throughout Jane's movement.

There is no fairness, no freedom, nothing of the sort. There is only truth and the inevitable pain that follows.

292

"Tell me where it is," Cinzia said, keeping her voice steady.

"Vault, yes…" the Beldam whispered between long, ragged breaths. "Vault… painting."

Painting? Cinzia looked around. At the opposite end of the chambers from which she knelt with the Beldam, a large painting hung on the wall between two of the large windows. If Cinzia had to guess, that wall faced the main body of the Fane—and, behind that section of the wall, a small ridge along the roof between the Ministry's quarters and the Fane that Cinzia had always thought decorative more than anything.

Cinzia stood.

"Wait—" the Beldam said, but Cinzia did not. The shame filled her, overflowing, but she could not care about that now. She could not hear what else the Beldam had to say.

If the Beldam was still there when Cinzia had found what she was looking for, then she could think about helping her.

She grabbed Nayome on the way to the painting, making the other yelp.

"Come on," Cinzia said, "we still have work to do."

"What about—"

"There are more important things," Cinzia said, the shame still hot inside of her. "She said the painting has something to do with the Vault. It's time we investigate it."

They approached the painting together, staring up at the huge frame.

It depicted the Triunity themselves: the First Priestess, the Holy Examiner, and the Oracle. The Oracle was seated in a simple wooden chair, while the First Priestess and Holy Examiner stood slightly behind her, each with a hand on the Oracle's shoulder. The painting seemed… tacky.

"We cannot just leave her there," Nayome said. "She will die."

293

"She is a heretic," Cinzia said. "Is that not her fate, according to your own law?"

"After a fair trial, yes," Nayome said. Definitely back to her normal self, then. "It is my duty to see to it that she receives such."

"A fair trial," Cinzia scoffed. "Like the one you gave my sister in Navone?"

"That…" Nayome blanched. "Those were unusual circumstances, Cinzia."

"It is an odd portrait, is it not?" Cinzia asked, reaching up to run one hand along the gilded frame.

"I…" Nayome blinked, took one last look back at the Beldam, then nodded. "Yes," she said. "The Triunity's pretentiousness has never been subtle."

Cinzia gripped the frame.

"Be careful," Nayome said, "I'm sure it is quite…"

With a gentle tug she removed the painting from the wall, and set it on its side on the ground.

"…heavy," Nayome finished, but her lips formed the word almost as an afterthought.

Cinzia looked up to where the painting had been, and saw what Nayome stared at so intently.

It was a door.

Cinzia was not sure why she was so surprised; the Beldam had informed them this was exactly what they were to expect. A vault implied an entrance of some kind or another.

The door, neither protruding nor set into the stone but exactly flush with the wall, seemed to be made of a single, solid piece of wood, with no hinges or locking mechanism that she could see.

"That's it, then?" Nayome asked.

"I... believe so," Cinzia said.

The two of them stood there for a moment, and then Cinzia stepped forward, and pressed on the door. It swung inward, revealing a stark, dimly lit corridor. Dust particles swam through the air in soft beams of light.

The corridor it revealed kindled a spark of excitement inside of her. This place, wherever it led, could hold the answer to what she had been looking for all along.

Cinzia took a step toward the portal. She peeked into the corridor, and saw in the distance another door at the end of the hallway. Cinzia stepped up through the door and into the corridor.

Nayome had not moved from where she stood.

"Are you coming?" Cinzia asked.

After a moment, Nayome shook her head. "No," she said, "I do not think so."

"We have come all this way. How can you stop here?"

"I can stop here," Nayome said slowly, "because I am comfortable in my faith. I am confident in it. Whatever is in there, whatever you're about to find, I don't need to know.

"I helped you because I think you are right: something must be done about the Nine Daemons. But if whatever you find in there has something to do with Canta, or the Denomination, I do not want to know about it."

Cinzia stared at Nayome for a moment, completely aghast. She had never considered Nayome would stop at the threshold of something so bizarre, so interesting, so potentially groundbreaking.

"Are you not the least bit curious?" Cinzia asked.

"No, Cinzia, I am not."

"Very well, then," Cinzia said. "Will you wait here?"

"For a time," Nayome said. "But if you take too long..."

Cinzia nodded. "I understand," she said. Which she did, and she also did not.

Did you actually think you were rekindling your friendship with this woman? Cinzia asked herself incredulously. Things were strained for them when Cinzia was actually a part of the ministry; to think that they could have a relationship now was preposterous.

She left the door open behind her. The corridor itself was long, and stuffy; small rectangular glass windows shone light into the hallway where the wall met the ceiling every few rods. Cinzia did not see much opportunity for ventilation in the hallway; the dust was everywhere, the air thick and musty.

The doorway at the other end seemed to be the twin of the one through which Cinzia had just walked: a solid piece of wood. This one, however, had visible hinges on her side, and a small latch. Both doors opened inward into the corridor that led from the Triunity's chambers to the Vault.

When Cinzia reached the door, she placed her hand on the small iron latch. With a deep breath, she pulled, and the door opened to reveal a surprisingly bright, clean room.

Daylight streamed in through bright stained-glass windows all around her. She estimated that the room must be directly above the Fane's chapel. Thick, round pillars interrupted her vision of the room, in roughly the same places where she knew thick, round columns rose up from the floor of the chapel. But the stained glass, the columns, even the strange objects on display throughout the room did not catch her attention.

There was a woman standing directly opposite her.

Cinzia did not recognize her at first; the woman was older than Cinzia, perhaps in her fortieth summer, with the faintest crinkles around her mouth and eyes, but otherwise her face and skin were dark and smooth. Her wiry jet-black hair formed a tight halo around her head. It was not until Cinzia took a few steps closer that she realized who it was she was actually facing. Instinctively, she knelt.

Cinzia knelt before Arcana Blackwood, Essera of the Cantic Denomination.

She forced herself to stand again, reminding herself she was no longer part of the Denomination.

"I almost did not recognize you without your robes, Essera."

Normally, the Essera wore her traditional robes in public and when conducting the necessary business of the Denomination: a large, thick, hooded affair, one half of which was cloth-of-silver, the other half cloth-of-gold, the line separating the two running straight down the middle of the robe. Crimson trimmed the sleeves and hem of the garment. It was unmistakable, even more remarkable than Arcana's personal appearance, as one of the few women in the upper ministry from Maven Kol.

But now, the Essera wore a simple white dress, light and loose, that cascaded around her slight form. The Essera inclined her head.

"Cinzia Oden. I wondered whether I might see you here."

"What are you doing here, Essera?" Cinzia asked, adding quickly, "If you will forgive me for asking."

The Essera's dark brown eyes met Cinzia's.

"You seem to have no trouble asking other questions," the woman said, her voice heavy with weariness. "Why would you not ask me that one?"

Cinzia did not know what to say. Questions raced through her mind—why was the Essera here, in the Vault, of all places? Had she known about Garyne? Did she know about the Cult in general? Did she know about the Nine Daemons?

The Essera represented everything Cinzia had left behind;

everything she had abandoned to follow her sister, and everything that had now abandoned her. The Essera was the literal mouthpiece of Canta, according to the Denomination's doctrine. She spoke for the Goddess; she was, for all intents and purposes, an avatar of the Goddess.

Cinzia wobbled on her feet, catching herself with both hands against the nearest pillar.

"Are you all right, my child?" the Essera asked, taking a single step toward Cinzia.

Looking into this woman's eyes was like looking into the sun for too long; Cinzia felt an intense discomfort, an almost incomprehensible desire to look away as quickly as she could.

"I am not all right," Cinzia said quietly.

"No, I do not imagine you are."

"Why did you excommunicate me?" Cinzia asked, the question ripping from her, accompanied by a sob of pain. She felt immediate embarrassment for the sob, for even asking the question in the first place, but she could not help it. The pain was too great and had been buried for too long, and she could not help but ask it in that moment.

"My child," the woman said, reaching out to touch Cinzia's face.

When the Essera's fingers made contact, an ethereal shock spread from Cinzia's cheek, through her face and down toward her toes. It was not painful, but rather a feeling of intense and sudden heat, and Cinzia found herself standing tall, face to face with the Essera. Or, as close to face to face as Cinzia could be; she was shorter than average, after all, and the Essera tall and elegant.

"You know why we did what we did," the Essera said, her voice warm, but sad. "You knew it was the only consequence of your choice to remain with your sister."

The Essera was right, of course. Cinzia had known she would be excommunicated the moment she chose to go against the Denomination—to go against *Nayome*—in Navone.

"Are you a part of the Cult?"

"No, Cinzia, I am not. I was warned they were coming to the Triunity's quarters, and I knew I had to get out of there. Garyne is perfectly willing to bend the knee to me in front of someone else, but I fear behind closed doors, with other goals in mind, she would not be so accommodating to my office."

"But you know *of* the Cult?" Cinzia asked.

"I know about everything in the Denomination."

"So you are... hiding?" Cinzia asked.

The Essera nodded, her hand still on Cinzia's cheek. The warmth continued to spread through her, from her face to the tips of her toes and fingers.

"And Canta told you to hide here?" Cinzia asked.

"My child," the Essera said, "you have been through a great deal. You may not believe me, but I am happy to see you. While we have our differences, I know you do not seek to harm me, at least. Or wrong the people of the Sfaera."

She did not answer my question.

With the warmth, Cinzia realized, was something else that permeated her body, and her mind. She felt emboldened, strangely, as if she could do anything she desired, but at the same time her head felt... fuzzy. Unclear.

Cinzia took a step back, breaking the contact with the Essera, and immediately shivered, as if a stiff, cool breeze had flurried through the chamber, and she no longer felt quite so bold. Instead, she felt just a little sadder, a little more inadequate than she had been just a moment ago.

But the fuzziness in her head was gone.

"What were you doing to me?"

The Essera cocked her head to one side. "What do you mean, Cinzia?"

"Your hand on my face, I felt something…"

The Essera's eyes widened, just for a moment, but then her face returned to the affectionate, understanding openness that Cinzia had noticed since she first recognized the woman.

"I am not sure what you—"

Cinzia shook her head, taking another step away from the Essera. "No," she said, "we are past that, I am afraid. You cannot lie to me as if I were a little girl, Essera. You cannot lie to me as if I were still one of your priestesses."

The Essera looked at Cinzia, the woman's face slowly morphing into something expressionless, something… dead. Goddess, for just a moment Cinzia recognized a flash of the same deadness she had seen in Knot's face, and in Code's so long ago.

The Essera sighed, her shoulders slumping.

"Call me Arcana," the Essera said. "And I shall just call you Cinzia. No more of this 'child' nonsense. We're both adults here, after all."

"Call you… Arcana?" Cinzia repeated. She had almost preferred it when the woman was playing the part of the Essera as she expected it; this new personality, whether the woman's true self or just an act, put Cinzia completely off her guard.

As, Cinzia imagined, it was meant to do.

"I'm lauded as the great Essera of the Cantic Denomination every day, all day long, and it will continue that way for the rest of my life, I think. A break is welcome." The Essera indicated the room they were in. "But you came here for something—not to meet me."

It felt like permission, of a kind. With the Essera at her side,

Cinzia began to slowly walk through the Vault, and *really* take it in for the first time.

It was not stocked full of documents and artifacts, as Cinzia had expected it to be. It took her only a moment to count nine pure white marble pedestals, each with an item of some kind on a platform at their top.

"Of course it is nine," Cinzia whispered.

"Numbers are significant," the Essera said, "more so than any of us realize. And the number nine, well, it is one of the most important."

"Just because it is repeated often in history," Cinzia said quietly, "does not make it something magical or divine."

"I would not be so sure," the Essera said. "There is power in repetition. There is power in what people think, and repetition can shape what they think—even what they believe."

"What are all of these things, then?" Cinzia asked, gazing around at each of the items: a large book, not unlike the Codex; a pile of pages, unbound and loose, yet stacked in perfect symmetry; a large dagger, perhaps the length of Cinzia's forearm, with a wide, dark gray blade, hilt wrapped in dark leather, and a bright blue jewel embedded in the pommel; a velvet box with a gold-and-silver Trinacrya embedded on the lid; a simple folded brown cloth; a Trinacrya larger than Cinzia's spread fingers that almost seemed to give off its own light; and, perhaps oddest of all, an entire dining set—plates, bowls, cutlery, cups, and a goblet, all carved from some strange dark stone, and set up atop the pedestal as if someone were about to sit down to eat there. Just as the Trinacrya seemed to give off its own light, this dining set also had the faintest of glows coming from it, if Cinzia looked at the thing sideways, anyway, although the colors emanating from the plates, forks, and so forth seemed multicolored in nature. Lastly, the pedestal closest to Cinzia held a blood-red jewel, oblong in shape; one moment it seemed no larger than the last joint of Cinzia's thumb, the next the size of an egg, and then the size of a human head, and in the blink of an eye it shifted back to the size of Cinzia's thumb.

The ninth pedestal was empty.

"Keepsakes," the Essera said. "Items of great value and worth. Illusions. There are even a few magical artifacts, if you could believe such a thing."

"You would be surprised what I…"

Cinzia stopped. The words felt wrong in her mouth as she formed them, and she trailed off.

Her personal beliefs, or lack thereof, aside, what Cinzia saw fascinated her. *I want to know about all of them,* she wanted to say. *Tell me their names. Tell me what they do, where they came from. Tell me their importance and significance.*

But she was here for a reason. Cinzia could not forget that.

"I need to fight the Nine Daemons," Cinzia said. "I need something that will help me combat them."

"Something to fight the Nine Daemons," the Essera said slowly. "I can't pretend I did not expect this, Cinzia, but… how can you be sure such a thing exists? Let alone in this room?"

Cinzia glared at the Essera. "It is here," she said. "I know it is. It *must* be here."

"You have faith that it is here, then?" the Essera asked.

Faith. That word again. A thing Cinzia had once had, as a priestess. Or thought she had possessed, at least. Then she had found her sister, at the head of something she could only believe was heretical… and yet she witnessed miracles from her sister, and herself, as well.

But then, she had realized many things about faith. That she could have faith, and give up her own right to control.

Why did she not feel that way now?

Perhaps because you no longer have any idea who, or what, you are supposed to have faith in anymore.

She remembered feeling love on the rooftops of Izet. She remembered that sense of innate worth, of acceptance. She had thought it had come from Canta at the time.

Was it possible the feelings had not?

"Why don't you ask the question you truly came here to ask?" the Essera said. "It is time you got this off your chest."

Cinzia frowned, frustrated.

"Is…" As the question formed in her mind, she immediately felt stupid for even asking such a thing, but she was too far into it now, the chance to have someone like the Essera answer it too tempting; the potential for an answer overtook any embarrassment she felt. "Is Canta real? Does she truly exist?"

Now there is a question worth answering, Luceraf said, her voice once again devoid of sarcasm or anger.

The Essera's shoulders rose and fell, either in a slow shrug or a long, deep breath.

"Of course she is real," the Essera said. "You have witnessed her miracles firsthand. You have felt her love, have you not?"

"Her miracles? You mean what we have done with the Codex?"

"That, and all the other things you, the other disciples, and your sister herself have done."

"Then we are not heretics?" Cinzia asked, unable to hide her confusion.

"Oh, you are certainly heretics. There can be no doubt about that. But that does not mean what you have done is not miraculous. That does not mean what you have done does not come from Canta. Or, at least, some version of her."

Some version of her?

"Whether she exists was not quite the right question, either, Cinzia. Think harder. Look deeper. There is something more."

Arcana's answers only produced more questions, but Cinzia felt a strange, momentary sense of peace as she settled on her final question.

"If Canta exists... does it matter?" Cinzia asked slowly.

Arcana nodded, although this time Cinzia knew, somehow, that it was not in answer to the question, but in affirmation of the question itself.

"There it is," Arcana said softly.

Cinzia looked around at each of the artifacts again. She thought of where she was—above Canta's Fane, one of the most impressive structures ever built, something that took decades to complete. She thought of the Denomination itself, the organization that had dictated how people had lived and loved and died for centuries. She thought of how she had jumped from the Denomination to Jane's movement, without so much as asking why.

She looked back up at Arcana, their eyes meeting once more.

"Does it?" she asked, repeating her question. "What is the answer?"

Of course it matters, a part of Cinzia wanted to scream. *It matters because if it does not, what has all of this been for? What has been the* purpose *of Jane's entire movement? What has been the purpose of the Denomination meddling in the lives of countless people throughout the ages? It* must *matter, because if it does not, then we are truly lost. It must matter, because if the evils the Denomination has brought upon the people of the Sfaera are simply... human evils, then it is not a world worth living in.*

And if those evils are from a deity, how is that better? a voice asked in her mind. Whether it was her own, or Luceraf's, Cinzia was not sure.

Arcana's lips formed a thin, flat line. "I do not offer answers, Cinzia. I am only here to help you ask the right questions."

"What in Oblivion is that supposed to mean?"

"What would you have me say? That yes, it *does* matter? Or that it should? Or would you rather I told you Canta's existence does not matter at all? Or should I answer your question with another question, and ask you why in Oblivion *my* opinion on all of it matters?"

"Your opinion on all of this matters," Cinzia said through gritted teeth, "because you are the Essera. You are supposed to be Canta's mouthpiece on the Sfaera. You are supposed to speak *for her.*"

"I do," Arcana said, "and I have. But not always. You know this. I speak for her, but I am not *her*, Cinzi."

Cinzia began pacing, still shaking her head. "Do not call me that," she said.

Arcana inclined her head, but her demeanor did not change.

"So I came all this way to not get an answer?" Cinzia asked.

"I think you came all this way," Arcana said slowly, "To learn the right question."

Cinzia's legs wobbled, and her knees suddenly felt very weak. She leaned her back against one of the columns, and before she knew it she slid down until she sat on the floor of the Vault, her head in her hands.

"This cannot be all there is," Cinzia said quietly. "Questions, and more questions. Only questions, and no answers."

"I never said there were no answers," Arcana said. "But there are fewer than we like to think. And between the two, the question is by far the more important."

Cinzia snorted.

"There are questions and answers, and there are questions and choices. We ask questions, and we rarely get answers... but we can always make choices."

"I did not come here for a life lesson," Cinzia said.

"And yet here you are, getting one, and for free, more or less." Arcana smiled, and Cinzia could have sworn the woman winked. "Canta be blessed."

Cinzia sighed in frustration. "As fascinating as this conversation is," she said, only meaning it sarcastically in part, "I do have important business to be about. As, I am sure, do you."

"Don't I always," Arcana muttered. "Very well. If you insist we move on to the business at hand, we shall. In so doing we will reach one of those aforementioned choices, Cinzia."

Steadying herself on the ground, Cinzia stood awkwardly, brushing dust from her dress. "And what choice is that?" Cinzia asked, looking around at each of the artifacts. "I need to take whatever will help me fight the Nine Daemons the best," she said. "It seems to me that there can only be one choice, given that information."

"That is what you *need*," Arcana said, "but you have yet to take into account what you *want*."

Cinzia threw up her hands. "Oblivion, enough with the games, Arcana! Just tell me what is going on."

"You can only take one item from this room," Arcana said.

Cinzia eyed each of the items warily. "What do you mean? There is some kind of curse on them, then? Or this room as a whole?"

Arcana laughed. "Nothing so mystical. I have told my closest aids of our situation. A group of Goddessguards and Sons, along with psimantically powerful priestesses, await the outcome. If anything should happen to me, or if you leave this room with more than one item, they will kill you. And your friends."

"My... friends," Cinzia asked.

"We apprehended the vampire and your friend Knot on their way out of the Fane," she said. "They are in our custody."

Cinzia's heart stopped. "Knot—"

"—is fine," Arcana said, "for now. As is the vampire. As long as you play by the rules, Cinzia."

"Why are you doing this?" Cinzia asked, all of her confidence deflating. After all of their planning, all of their sneaking around and organization, this was the result? "You could take all of us captive. You could *kill* us, if you wish. What is stopping you? Why allow me to just... walk out, with an artifact?"

"Believe it or not," Arcana said, "we are not completely at odds, you and I. Outward appearances dictate I respond in a certain way to you, your sister, and the so-called 'church' you've initiated. But that does not mean we are enemies, Cinzia."

"You are saying," Cinzia said, "you want to see the Nine Daemons defeated as much as I do."

"Of course," Arcana said. "Don't we all want that?"

Something about the way the woman said those words made Cinzia pause, but too many other thoughts overwhelmed her before she could continue down that path. "You are going to give us something to help us fight the Nine Daemons," Cinzia said slowly, "so that you do not have to?"

"More or less."

"You want to use us," Cinzia said, "as weapons to do the work that you do not wish to do?"

"You can think of it that way if you wish, but it is only a half-truth. We want you to be our weapons, yes, but we need you to do the work that we *cannot* do. It is not a matter of convenience or wish, Cinzia. It is a matter of ability. You and your group have abilities and freedoms that we in the Denomination do not have."

"You also have a corrupt Cult within your own organization," Cinzia said bitterly. "How can I trust that you are not in league with them? That you are not their leader, for Canta's sake?"

"I already told you," Arcana said patiently, "The only reason we find ourselves in this unique situation is that I came here to *hide* from the Cult. I knew I would be no match for Garyne, not alone. So I hid here."

"You set a trap for me."

"When I saw you coming, I knew I had an opportunity. I took advantage of it." Arcana said, with another demure shrug. "You have the question, Cinzia. Now, let me present you with the choice."

Cinzia took a deep breath. She had no other option if Knot and Astrid truly were in danger; she needed to do as asked. "Very well. I can choose one of the eight items, I suppose?" She walked to the nearest pedestal—the one holding the dark crimson jewel.

"You can choose one of two items, actually," Arcana said. "We know what you *need*, or what you think you need, at least. I have an idea of what you *want*, as well. Your choice will be between the two."

"And there are two items here that will satisfy each of those requirements?" Cinzia asked, incredulous.

"There are," Arcana said. "The first is that jewel, the one you are so close to touching."

Cinzia's hand was already halfway toward the jewel.

Don't be a fool, Cinzia. That was Luceraf, to be certain. This woman is insane. She has no idea what she is talking about.

Strange that you have been silent for so long, Cinzia responded thoughtfully. *I take it you have been listening to everything she says. You are the common enemy here. Should I not just do the opposite of whatever it is you want?*

You cannot be sure, Luceraf whispered. *I might be trying to trick you.*

Luceraf was right, of course, but the way the Daemon whined the words made Cinzia confident in her assessment. Luceraf's outburst just now had been one of self-preservation, and the Daemon was only trying to cover her response, now.

"I wouldn't recommend touching it, if I were you," Arcana said. "Not yet, at least. If the history behind that object is to be believed, it can have very *ugly* effects on those who are not worthy or ready to wield its power."

"This will help me combat the Nine Daemons?" Cinzia asked, taking a careful step back from the red jewel. The fact that Luceraf did not like the item made her confident, but she did not want to touch it until she was ready.

"That," Arcana said, "is Canta's Heart. It warns of the presence of any of the Nine, and when used with the correct sacrifice, it has the power to overcome them. To cast them out."

To cast them out.

A small, twinkling star of hope burst in Cinzia's soul.

I could be rid of you.

Do not be so sure, the Daemon said. *That does not work the way you think it does.*

But the Daemon sounded afraid, and that in and of itself gave Cinzia courage.

"I think," Arcana said, looking Cinzia up and down, "you might have particular need of such a thing."

Cinzia shot the woman a glance. "What do you know of that?"

"I know what possesses you," Arcana said simply. "Beyond that…" She shrugged. "But I do think this could help you, if you chose it."

Cinzia stared at the gem. It continued to shift sizes, though the longer Cinzia looked at it, the more stable it seemed to become. It now only fluctuated between the size of an egg and the size of a man's fist. While its deep red color shone brightly, Cinzia also noticed what appeared to be bursts of other colors. She was not sure whether it was a trick of the light, or reflections, or something else altogether, but the burst of color appeared to come from within the gem itself.

"And my other option?" Cinzia asked, still staring at the gem.

Arcana walked away from Cinzia, and with some effort she tore her gaze away from the gem so she could follow the Essera.

The woman led her to the two pedestals Cinzia had seen first; the two pedestals between which Arcana had stood when Cinzia had first entered the room. To the left, a pedestal held the book that looked so much like the Codex of Elwene. Cinzia wondered if, somehow, this actually *was* a copy of the Codex, exactly as she and Jane had been translating, until Cinzia had been robbed of that privilege.

The gem will help me gain that privilege back again, Cinzia thought.

But you would lose your strength, Luceraf whispered, *the speed with which I have blessed you.*

Cinzia allowed herself a smile. The Daemon, apparently, no longer cared whether Cinzia thought she was bluffing or not.

Arcana pointed one long, bony finger at the stack of papers on the other pedestal. "This," she said, "will tell you the truth. I cannot say for certain, but it may hold answers to some of the questions that seem to concern you so."

"Answers," Cinzia said quietly, walking toward the stack of papers. As she got closer, she looked up at Arcana. "Can I look at them? Or will something *ugly* happen to me if I touch these, too?"

"Go ahead, if you wish," Arcana said.

Immediately Cinzia picked up the top page. It was heavier than Cinzia had expected, but still seemed to be made out of paper of some kind, not stone, as it seemed, or thin metal like the Codex. The page was blank. No writing, runes, or anything of the sort. Keeping the page in one hand, she reached out with her other to retrieve the second. It, too, was blank.

"What—"

"You of course will not be able to read them," Arcana said, "until you make your choice. The contents of those papers... not many people know the truth of them. Not many people at all."

"Do they have a name?" Cinzia asked.

"The Veria," Arcana said. "That is all anyone has called them."

"And they are not bound because..."

"Because they cannot be," Arcana said. "If you choose to take them, you could try, and you would see. Such a thing is impossible."

Gently, Cinzia placed the two pages she had taken back on top of the pile. They settled into place as if an unseen force compelled them back to where they belonged.

Cinzia looked around at each of the pillars. These artifacts belonged to the Age of Marvels.

"The Denomination has kept these things secret for so long."

"We have," Arcana said, "and we do not apologize for it. Only the uppermost people in the Ministry know of this vault. Myself, the Triunity, and the occasional high priestess..."

Cinzia remembered the Beldam, lying broken on the stone floor of the Triunity's quarters. If Arcana knew about her, she gave no indication.

"The time has come to make your choice, Cinzia. What will it be? The gem, or the pages?"

Cinzia glanced back over her shoulder at the gem, once again shifting radically in size. "You said one of them I need, and one of them I want."

"That is what I said, yes."

Cinzia closed her eyes. The gem would help her fight the Nine Daemons; the pages would... give her some answers?

Take the pages, Luceraf whispered.

Of course you would want me to take the pages, Cinzia responded. *The other option would expel you from me.*

Allegedly. Even so, Cinzia, there is more at stake here than you or I.

Luceraf had said that to her before.

What do you mean, there is more at stake? Cinzia asked.

"I know it is a difficult choice, Cinzia, but we really do not have much time. Please, make your decision soon."

"Choices like this cannot be rushed," Cinzia muttered.

I cannot be specific, Luceraf responded, *but I can tell you all is not as it seems. This woman speaks to you of wants and needs. She thinks you want whatever answers lie in these pages, and need the gem to fight the Daemons—to fight me. I say she has it backwards. You would like me gone, I understand that. But you* need *to know the truth of all of this, Cinzia. You need to understand what we are doing.*

If I need to understand, why do you not just tell me?

I can't, Luceraf said, her voice rising in tone and tightness. Goddess, was the Daemon *panicking?*

"It is time, Cinzia."

Cinzia locked eyes with the Essera. She could feel Arcana's brown eyes scanning her, trying to see past her own into her soul, into the choice she had to make.

You think she is lying to me? she asked Luceraf.

I think she is telling you her version of the truth.

And you are telling me yours. How can you expect me to choose between the two of you?

When no response came, Cinzia grew worried. Would the Daemon truly have left her now, at such a crucial moment?

Luceraf?

You are right. I cannot expect you to do such a thing. I will leave you alone to make the choice yourself, then. But please, remember my words, Cinzia: All is not as it seems.

And then, at least for the moment, Luceraf was gone.

"You've been conversing with him, haven't you?" Arcana asked.

Cinzia took a few deep breaths, Luceraf's sudden departure making her somewhat dizzy. "I... With who?"

"With the Daemon inside you," Arcana said, her voice not without its own accusatory tone.

Cinzia finally broke the staring contest with the Essera, and looked instead at the pages. "It is a woman, actually," she mumbled, almost absent-mindedly.

"It's a... what?"

"The Daemon inside of me," Cinzia said. "It's one of the female Daemons. Not a 'him,' anyway."

Cinzia remembered Luceraf's words. *She is telling you her version of the truth.*

Then, she turned on her heel, and strode toward the red gem.

"You have made your—"

Before Arcana could finish her sentence, Cinzia had grasped the red gem in both hands, the size of the thing immediately stable—she could hold it comfortably in one hand. The red glow darkened the moment she picked it up, but so far the gem seemed to have no adverse effect on her.

"...choice," Arcana said, clearly surprised at Cinzia's resolve.

"I have," Cinzia said, feeling the weight of the gem in her palm—much heavier than she would have expected. Though its size had stabilized, it seemed far too heavy for something so small. She looked back at the Essera. "Has anything ugly happened to me yet?" Cinzia could not tell whether she asked the question in jest, or with sincere concern.

"No…" Arcana said slowly. "Very well then, Cinzia. You have made your choice."

"How does this work?" Cinzia asked. "You said something about sacrifice."

"I did, but I am afraid I do not know any specifics. The lore of that gemstone states that the user will come to understand it intuitively. It has not been used in many centuries."

The gemstone drew Cinzia's gaze back to it. Had she sacrificed potential knowledge for a shiny rock? She felt no different, having picked it up. Luceraf made no acknowledgement of Cinzia's choice. Other than the weight of it, and the strange appearance of the gem, there was nothing out of the ordinary.

"Very well, the choice is made. It is time for us to part ways. I will order my people to release yours. And, my dear Cinzia, I hope this does not end our relationship. I hope we can do business together again sometime." The woman made as if to move toward Cinzia, to embrace her or grasp hands, but seemed to think better of it. The Essera of the Cantic Denomination instead inclined her head toward Cinzia, and then swept out of the room, her white dress flowing behind her.

Cinzia stared after her. Was she supposed to follow the Essera? Or wait—

In a flash of red light, the Vault around her disappeared, and everything went dark.

28

NAYOME HINEK WATCHED FROM behind one of the great columns in the Vault as the Essera inclined her head toward Cinzia— an *ex*-priestess, for Canta's bloody sake—and swiftly removed herself from the room.

While Nayome had meant what she had said, about wanting to stay behind and leave whatever business Cinzia had in the Vault to her, she apparently had not been completely honest with herself. Not long after Cinzia walked through the painting door and into the corridor, Nayome had slipped after her. She had called for her personal Goddessguard to gather others and retrieve the Beldam, of course—if the woman had any life left in her, she would see to it that she paid for her heresy—and had thus stepped into the corridor behind Cinzia with a generally free conscience.

When she heard voices inside the room, Nayome had crept as silently as she could into the Vault, hiding herself behind one of the columns closest to the wall, and began to listen.

To say that she had been shocked to recognize the voice of the Essera, having a conversation with Cinzia, would have been the understatement of the Age. What the most powerful woman in the Sfaera was doing speaking to a lowly ex-priestess, Nayome could not begin to guess, and their conversation had only left her more confused. Bits about needs and wants had left Nayome intensely curious as to the Essera's intentions. She clearly did not seem party to the absolute heresy of the Cult within the Denomination, but the fact that she treated Cinzia with such *friendliness* made Nayome wonder.

Nayome could remember taking Cinzia under her wing at the seminary; the girl had been a year behind Nayome at the time, and Nayome had seen something of herself in the small, unusually pretty girl. Not the prettiness, of course, Nayome had never had any illusions about such things for herself, but in the girl's intellect and curiosity, certainly.

They had lost touch after Nayome moved on from the seminary, climbing the ranks of the Arm of Inquisition. She had almost forgotten about her friend until the day she was tasked with investigating the Oden family; in that moment, she had remembered Cinzia's name, and knew in her heart that the girl—the woman, at that point—would already be in Navone.

And now here that same woman was, no longer a priestess, no longer part of the Denomination at all, but nevertheless conversing with the Essera herself.

The jealousy bloomed in Nayome's chest, so powerful she could sense it clouding her vision.

But Nayome was nothing if not prudent; she waited patiently for the conversation to take its course, and then after the Essera had left, she prepared herself to confront Cinzia. But as she had rounded the pillar, she'd witnessed a strange flash of crimson light, and then Cinzia was gone.

Nayome was alone in the Vault.

"Oblivion," she muttered, staring at the place Cinzia had occupied not moments before. Where had she gone, and how?

Nayome's anger faded—somewhat—and she could not help but look in awe around her at the artifacts on each of the pedestals. She dared not pick any up—the Essera's warning to Cinzia before she had picked up Canta's Heart had been frightening enough. She could not imagine what unpleasant surprises the other artifacts might have for the poor soul that thought it a good idea to ignorantly pick one up.

That did not stop her, however, from admiring each of them.

She found herself particularly drawn to the strange dagger. The weapon appeared ageless; Nayome felt she could be looking at a dagger millennia old or one that had just been forged, and neither answer would surprise her. The bright blue jewel set in the pommel particularly caught her attention, and it was with some effort that she finally pulled herself away and sought the only other artifact in the room she knew anything about, based on Cinzia's conversation with the Essera.

The pages.

The Essera had said that these pages would tell Cinzia the truth—that they held the answers to the questions that Cinzia had been obsessing over. Cinzia was clearly having a crisis of faith, and not just a crisis in relation to the Denomination. Nayome recognized disillusionment and malcontent when she saw it; she had made it her life's business, after all.

And, now that Cinzia and the Essera were gone, and now that the Nine Daemons were on the rise and the Sfaera was falling apart all around her, Nayome walked up to the pedestal that held the document, reached for the first sheet with one hand, and began to read the words that immediately appeared on the page.

29

Cinzia was not sure whether she awoke from unconsciousness, or had been awake the entire time, but as she came to herself, traces of red mist surrounded her, and with it a deep-rooted, expansive emotion.

Fear.

As the red mist faded, darkness replaced it. Thick blackness inked over her body, so heavy she was not sure she could breathe. She could neither see nor feel her hands, feet, body, anything. It was all dark.

And yet it was not, because light surrounded her, too. Tiny pinpoints of light, a rainbow of stars twinkling in the horrible darkness, and even though Cinzia feared the darkness, she feared the stars more. The dark, while encompassing and suffocating, remained a knowable quantity. The stars, on the other hand, Cinzia could not know. Could never know. They were mysterious, the unknowable and something altogether apart from herself.

Cinzia did not know how long it took, or how long she simply drifted in the star-studded darkness, but eventually she realized what this place was.

She was in the Void.

Cinzia could remember Knot's description of the Void, and Wyle's. Like a moonless night sky, but with colorful stars. The

318

idea did not sound too bad, in theory, but Cinzia could remember the chill that ran up her spine when she heard of the place.

And now here she was.

She looked down at the gemstone in her hands, sure it must be there. Only darkness, and stars. That was strange; she could feel the weight of the stone, heavier than it should be, still in her hand, but still nothing there.

Don't...

The voice was so quiet, so subtle, that she almost could not understand what it said. But when it spoke to her again, Cinzia recognized the voice through the faintness.

Please, Luceraf whispered.

Cinzia's jaw set. *I am sorry*, she said, genuinely meaning it. Whatever Luceraf's intentions, Cinzia could tell the Daemon was terrified. *But I have work to do, and you stand in my way.*

Please—

Another voice echoed over Luceraf's. This voice was not whispered in Cinzia's head, but rather reverberated throughout the Void itself. Cinzia wondered whether every being here could hear such volume.

"Take the dagger," the voice said.

The dagger? Cinzia wondered. She had seen a dagger in the Vault, but she had not taken it, obviously. Did she need to return for the dagger, or was the voice referring to something else?

"Draw your own blood," the voice continued.

The fear never left Cinzia, and she began to wonder. Fear was a side effect of the Fear Lord Himself. One of the Nine Daemons. But why would he speak to her? Why would he tell her how to use the stone?

"Azael?" Cinzia called. But the voice continued, heedless of her call.

"Be rid of the shadow."

"Be rid of…" Cinzia looked around her. Nothing except colorful pinpoints of light.

Then the darkness around her *shifted*, and for a brief moment, Cinzia saw her body, the gemstone in her hand, her hand attached to her arm, her arm attached to her body, her body in… Goddess, was that her tent in the Odenite camp?

And, she realized, the gemstone was no longer a gemstone. It was a dagger, twin to the dagger with the gray blade and blue pommel she had seen in the Vault, but with a shimmering, golden blade, and a dark red jewel in the pommel.

"Take the dagger," the voice repeated.

Cinzia was back in the Void, darkness and stars all around her, but she could *feel* her body, feel it attached to her, feel the weight of Canta's Heart—the golden dagger—in her hand.

"Draw your own blood."

Cinzia hesitated. Blood did not seem the right thing here, somehow. Was blood not the tool of the Nine? She remembered the young man slitting his throat at the Odenite camp outside of Kirlan, blood spurting all over her and Arven. Blood had always been part of the rituals that brought in the Outsiders. Knot and Astrid had told her of that night in Izet, where Lian's bloody death had ushered in a whole host of them.

"Be rid of the shadow."

And yet, despite her misgivings about blood and daggers and the nature of the gemstone itself, a single idea drove her forward.

I could be free of Luceraf.

You will never be free of me, Cinzia.

Cinzia froze. She had not realized she had even been raising one hand, the hand that held the gemstone, or the dagger, or whatever it was, toward her other open palm, until she stopped. Luceraf's voice had been faint, barely an echo, but audible because the other voice that spoke to Cinzia, the one she did not recognize, was quiet in that moment.

Cinzia waited, silence ruling her both inside and out. For a moment, blessedly, no voices spoke to her; not Luceraf's, not the other's, and not even her own. For a moment, Cinzia feel genuine clarity.

Take the dagger. Draw your own blood. Be rid of the shadow.

The words were not spoken by any voice, her own or otherwise, but rather hung in the Void like the star-lights themselves, ominous and imposing, and simply *there*.

Cinzia held the stone close to the open palm of her other hand, felt the sharp edge of a blade, curiously warm against her skin.

With one slick movement, she pulled, and roaring pain erupted like fire on her skin; fire where the blade cut her, fire that dug deep and infested, roiling, into her blood and bones and every part of her. For a brief moment, or perhaps hours, or even days, Cinzia's entire body agonized, racked with an inferno of pain.

When she finally opened eyes she could not remember closing, she immediately covered them with her hands to protect them from the sudden bright burst of daylight. As her eyes slowly adjusted, she recognized the familiar pale canvas walls of her tent in the Odenite camp, sunlight streaming through the parted door flaps.

She had noticed an odd bulkiness on her left hand when she had raised her hands to cover her eyes, and squinted to see it wrapped in cloth. A treated wound. As she gently flexed the fingers of her left hand, a dull burning pain sprouted in her palm.

Cold sweat broke on her brow and the center of her

back. Had everything she'd recently seen, and done, actually happened? The Vault, the Void, all of it?

Luceraf? Cinzia whispered.

No response came. That would not be remarkable, not normally, as Luceraf had a tendency to depart for hours, sometimes days at a time.

And yet, this time, the empty darkness that only echoed in response was different. Luceraf had occupied a space within her that she had not even realized existed until now, as it gaped emptily inside.

You will never be free of me, Cinzia remembered hearing the Daemon say. And yet the memory of Luceraf's voice was already fading from Cinzia's mind.

"Look who's finally up."

Knot. Cinzia sat quickly, looking to the door of her tent. She could not make out his face; the daylight streaming in behind him was too bright, and she saw only shadowy features. But she did not need to make out the features to recognize who it was. The shape of his frame, the sound of his voice, even his presence was enough.

"You're all right?" she asked immediately.

"I'll be fine, darlin'. Back to my usual self in no time."

"Astrid?"

"Also fine, and still annoying as all Oblivion."

"How long have I been..." Cinzia hesitated. Asleep? Unconscious?

"Three days, if you can believe it," Knot said. "We've had medical folk monitoring you around the clock, and I've been in to check on you... more times than I can count, I guess." His face twisted up in a half-smile. "Glad I was the first one to see you awake, though."

322

Cinzia's face flushed. "Me too," she said.

The two remained there for a few moments, unmoving and silent. Cinzia reveled in the silence, the comfort that existed between them, but could not help but be conscious of the tension that underlined it all.

Then, still unsure of herself, Cinzia cleared her throat, looking down at her hand.

"How did I get here?" she asked.

"Some of the Odenites found you outside of the city, unconscious," Knot said. "We're lucky they found you, and not someone else like the Denomination. While they seem to have stopped their open hostility toward the Odenites, they sure as Oblivion ain't our friends. And the Beldam's people have been more hostile toward us, too, since…"

Since I left her for dead? Cinzia thought, unable to say the words out loud. Her face grew hot, this time from shame.

"They found you with a nasty wound on that hand," Knot said, inclining his head toward Cinzia's large bandage. "Don't suppose you remember how you got that?"

Cinzia looked at Knot, hesitating. But the hesitation only lasted for a moment. This was Knot. This was her Goddessguard. This was her friend, for Canta's bloody sake, the man she probably trusted most in the entire Sfaera.

As she opened her mouth to tell him everything, another thought skirted across her mind. Cinzia looked down at both hands once more, though she knew neither held the item she sought. The gemstone. Canta's Heart.

"Did they find anything with me?" Cinzia asked quickly. "A red stone. Or… perhaps a dagger?" Goddess, was her mind failing her? She could not remember whether she had brought a gemstone or a dagger from the Vault. She could have sworn it had been a stone, and yet she sliced the skin of her hand with *something*, banished Luceraf from her body with *something*…

"Was it that?" Knot asked, nodding at the makeshift table beside Cinzia's cot.

Cinzia followed his gaze to a plain wooden box.

"Look inside," Knot said.

Cinzia did, lifting the lid of the box.

"Had to keep it out of plain sight," Knot said, "due to its… properties."

A sigh of relief escaped Cinzia's lips as her eyes took in the crimson gemstone in the box, glowing darkly, its size shifting impossibly.

"I take it that has something to do with the cut on your hand?" Knot asked.

Cinzia nodded slowly. She closed the box, and turned her eyes back to Knot.

"It does," Cinzia said. "And… with any luck, I think it can help us defeat the Nine Daemons, once and for all."

Then she told him everything.

A TALE OF TEN MONARCHS

A tiellan folktale

ONCE, A LONG TIME AGO, the Nine Tiellan Kingdoms stretched across the face of the Sfaera. Tiellans were far more numerous, then, almost double the population of humans, and they directed everything from trade to technology to art and much more. Nine tiellan monarchs ruled these kingdoms, and each of them was beloved by their people; each did their best to rule fairly and justly.

Humans occupied a place in this world, too, but with a much smaller footprint than the great bloody boots with which they traipse the Sfaera now. An empress ruled the humans, with a fist and will of iron. She was not cruel, but had learned the best way to love her people was to keep order among them.

The human empire and the tiellan kingdoms lived in harmony for some time, until one day, quite suddenly, that harmony ceased. A war whose cause was forgotten by the legends we have forgotten today, broke out between the human empire and one of the tiellan kingdoms. Soon other tiellan kingdoms came to the aid of the one, and eventually the entire Sfaera was at war.

The nine tiellan kings and queens witnessed what this war did to their people, the pain and terror that violence wrought, and chose to treat with the human empress so they could finally end the war. The empress, too, witnessed the suffering of her people, and agreed to meet. But while the kings and queens prepared to compromise for peace, the empress had other plans.

When the ten rulers met at the Heart of the Sfaera, they quickly agreed on the horrors the violence between them had caused, and formed a pact of peace. Each of them walked away happy, satisfied the violence had ended and they could once again return to a life of harmony.

But, one by one, the tiellan kings and queens fell ill. The poison coursed through each of them, twisting their bodies, scarring their faces, changing them until they were no longer themselves. What these former kings and queens did not know, what they did not suspect until too late, was the poison the empress had placed in each of their goblets as they sat together, discussing peace.

When the tiellan kingdoms did not recognize their kings and queens, they fell into chaos, and the empress was quick to consolidate her power, assimilating each tiellan kingdom into her empire, creating the largest, greatest civilization the Sfaera had ever known. The tiellan kings and queens, now beggars and pariahs, were cast out, never to be seen or heard from again.

And, for many, many years, there was peace.

Eventually, the empress faded away, as if nothing but a dream in the minds of her people, and the humans and tiellans lived alongside one another. Left to their own devices, small wars and skirmishes broke out, and eventually the humans enslaved all tiellans, taking away their freedom and culture, robbing them of their power, and forcing them into submission. And so the wheel turned.

But as all things must, the Sfaera itself began to grow weary, and buckle, and break. The end of all things had come, and all people feared and trembled. Lightning fell from the sky like rain. Liquid fire burst forth from the mountains. The seas boiled, and all life seemed on the verge of one final, terrible death throe. The worst of all these disasters came in the form of nine terrible monsters, misshapen and ugly, and the people began to wonder whether they had been dead all along, whether this was just some torture dreamed up in Oblivion.

And then, in a burst of light, the empress returned to save her people, one final time. She fought the nine monsters, her light against theirs, but even with her great power and glory the nine matched her equally, and eventually the two sides destroyed one another completely. No trace remained of the empress, or the monsters she fought so valiantly to defend her people against.

And yet, when the empress took her last breath, evaporating into a beam of light, and the monsters sank into the earth in death, something changed.

The Sfaera began to heal.

The Sfaera began to heal, and the people with it. Tiellans and humans, for the first time since the dawn of time, lived as equals and accepted one another. The world knit itself back together, and while there was not always peace, there was, more often than not, love.

In the midst of the remade world, nine great trees grew forth from the Heart of the Sfaera, each one different, each one similar to the other, and each one blossoming and growing and offering shade for weary travelers for many, many ages to come.

PART III

UNREDEEMABLE TIME

30

The Fellhome Bar, Triah

CODE TOSSED BACK ANOTHER whiskey, hardly having time to taste the stuff as it burned its way down his throat.

"Another," he grunted, slapping the bar. The innkeeper grunted in return, reaching for the most accessible bottle, and poured another swig into Code's glass.

He had a lot to think about. This business with the vampires, first of all. Goddess be damned, he'd never thought the creatures had such a presence in Triah, let alone that their powers could be so... broad and terrifying and peculiar, all at once. He'd informed Kosarin about the details he'd gleaned of the Coven, of course, and he was sure the Nazaniin would investigate the presence further. Code just hoped he wouldn't be part of it.

Breaking into Canta's Fane had been exciting, until Cinzia had insisted he remain outside the bloody door. He hadn't even been able to go with them to the Triunity's quarters, let alone the Vault itself. And he'd been curious about it, too. Damn the ex-priestess for ordering him around, and damn himself for letting her do it.

He still had no evidence of who had brought Alain and Morayne to Triah, though he suspected one of the Triad members had a hand in it. Alain and Morayne had mostly stayed out of sight, thank the Goddess. It wouldn't do to have the former crown prince of Maven Kol strolling about Triah during

331

all this chaos. The two of them wanted to visit the Odenites, and the tiellans on the cliffs, of all things. Code would be damned if he let them go more than a few blocks away from their inn, let alone out of the city.

Then there was the business that had gotten him involved with these insane people to begin with: Knot and, ultimately, Winter. He still had yet to make contact with the tiellan woman—Oblivion, *Knot* had yet to make contact with her, and the two were married. Code had informed Knot of Winter's presence on the cliffs just the other day, but instead of going to see her, he'd remained in the Goddess-damned Odenite camp. There was no way Code could reach the infamous Chaos Queen until Knot did so.

Which, he was slowly beginning to realize, was fine by him. Kosarin's orders appealed to him less and less, lately. Other things appealed to him far more.

For that matter, there was the ex-priestess's claim that he had come to her, confessing his sins, some Penetensar years ago. That didn't make sense at all. He could remember doing something vaguely along those lines when drunk, once or twice, but he was sure he would have remembered Cinzia. Beauty aside, Cinzia had something about her…

Code shook his head, and knocked back the glass of whiskey that had been waiting for him, the burn calming him all the way down into his gut.

"Let me guess: you've had a long day."

"Long day isn't the half of it," Code muttered, slurring his speech slightly. He wasn't as drunk as he appeared, but he didn't want to have to pretend to care about whoever in Oblivion was talking to him any more than he had to. Hopefully his disoriented air would throw them off.

"I can help you with that, if you like."

A woman's hand on his wrist, then the fingertips slowly making their way up his arm toward his biceps. Code fought the urge to snap out of her grasp and twist her arm behind her body, incapacitating her. His mind knew she wasn't a threat, but his body didn't, and right now the two weren't having the best of times communicating.

"Mm-married," Code lied.

"I don't see a ring."

Goddess, there was no quality more annoying than persistence.

Code turned to get a good look at her, taking in her features. Round face, small nose. Alizian, almost certainly—come to think of it, he should have known by the slight lilt to her accent. Dark hair and dark, narrow eyes, with tanned skin. Something of an ageless visage; she could have seen twenty summers or forty, and Code would've believed either. Her simple dark dress, not modest but not particularly revealing, didn't scream harlot. The strong scent of perfume and painted face could have indicated anything from a noblewoman to a merchant experimenting with new beauty products. But the way the woman's fingertips grazed back along Code's forearm told him enough.

"Left it at home," Code said.

That brought a smile to her face. "Must be a reason for that." She sidled up onto the barstool next to him, one foot positioned strategically on one of the stool's crossbars, the leg nearest Code draped casually, the slit of her dress open nearly to the hip.

An exasperated sigh leaked out of him. "You're not giving up anytime soon, are you?"

"I know what I'm looking for." Her delicately laced boot grazed his foot.

Code almost left the bar right then. He had no interest, not at the moment. Too much on his mind. A few weeks ago something like this might've been a welcome distraction, but... he tried to envision himself with this woman, tried to see their bodies together. She was attractive, objectively speaking, but when he closed his eyes, it wasn't her he found himself tangling with.

"I don't have any money," Code said, his throat dry despite the drink he'd just gulped down. He nodded to the innkeeper. "Another."

"You've got enough money for all the whiskey you're downing. What's a few more silvers?"

Code cursed inwardly. His guard was down, just slightly, and he didn't know why. Just enough for him to make a stupid mistake by saying he didn't have any money and then ordering another whiskey in the same breath.

That little ex-priestess has got you all out of sorts.

"Look," Code said, finally meeting the woman's eyes, "I'm not interested. You're an attractive woman." He nodded around the room. "I'm sure you could have any bloke in here. No need to go after me."

"All the more reason," she said, a smolder in her eyes that almost made Code uncomfortable. One of her feet brushed up against his, and even after the touch was gone Code still felt the echo of it there, tingling against him. "These other men would treat me as an object. I've had my fill of that. You would treat me like a woman."

Code snorted.

"I've been at this a long time," she said. "I've had my share of... unfortunate encounters. We all do in this business." She

334

rolled her shoulders back, standing a little taller. "I choose my customers, now. And I sure as Oblivion won't be going back to what it was like before this."

"None of that means I'll be taking you home."

She seemed confused. "You really are different, aren't you?"

Code rolled his eyes.

The innkeeper, who'd been helping customers at the other end of the bar, finally made his way down to them, pouring Code another glass of whiskey. He nodded appreciatively, and slung it back, his throat and mouth burning.

"Goddess, you're a poor whiskey drinker. You can't even taste it like that."

"Don't care about tasting it," Code said. *I just want to get drunk, go home, and forget for a while.*

The innkeeper was already pouring him another glass.

But the woman didn't move away, and the silence began to bother him almost more than their conversation.

"Different how?" Code finally asked.

"Sorry?"

"No need for games with me," he said. "Goddess, it'd be refreshing to drop all the pretense for once."

It'd be nice to do that with Cinzia.

"That's how," the woman said, inclining her head toward him. "You speak plainly. No honeyed words."

"Every woman's dream, I'm sure," Code muttered.

"You'd be surprised."

"I'm not always this plain-spoken."

"I'm just that lucky?"

"Guess so."

Code swirled the glass of whiskey the innkeeper had most recently poured him. He'd reached his limit, but here it was in front of him, and he didn't fancy wasting a passable whisky. A conundrum for the ages.

"There's more than that, though, if you care to hear it," she said.

"I asked, didn't I?"

She gripped her stool with both hands and scooted it closer to Code. She looked decidedly unsexy while doing it. For some reason, Code appreciated that.

"I'll tell you a little something about fucking," she whispered.

Code spluttered into his glass. "Shouldn't we at least tell each other our names first?"

She smiled at him—was that the first time he'd actually seen her smile? *Really* smile, anyway, not the fake smile that so obviously came with her profession. With his profession too, for that matter.

It'd be nice to see Cinzia smile like that, wouldn't it?

Goddess, he was obsessed. If Cinzia knew he thought about her this often, she'd probably never speak to him again.

"Enura," she said, extending a narrow arm.

"Code." He took her forearm with his hand, and she did the same. He liked that, too. Not a greeting with a kiss on the cheek or a demure glance, but straightforward and to the point. Businesslike. Perhaps he could like this woman after all—although when he pictured it, once again it wasn't her body he saw himself moving with, pressing against.

This is what she does for a living, he reminded himself. *She discerns people's weaknesses, tells them what they want to hear.*

Goddess, that's what *he* did for a living—though he doubted her profession left the trail of dead bodies his did.

"You were saying?"

"Yes…" Enura cocked her head to one side. "What is it about, do you think?"

"What? You mean what you do for a living?"

"And what everyone else lives to do. What is the point of it, for you?"

The point of it. Oblivion, no one had ever asked him that before. "The point… would be fairly obvious, wouldn't it? To get you both… er, both parties involved, to… um…" Code blushed. He could not remember the last time he'd done that. The embarrassment itself was refreshing.

Enura's soft chuckling added to both his embarrassment and delight.

"What?" he asked, unable to stop one side of his mouth from creeping up in a half-smile. "I'm not the one that should be embarrassed, it's you who's asking the question."

Enura's laugh faded, but her smile remained. Her eyes left Code's, and moved from person to person around the bar. It was late, nearly midnight, but the Fellhome was busy, as it would be for another few hours. The bright fire burned merrily in the large hearth. A darts game in one corner, a card game at a large circular table near the center of the room.

"I'd be willing to bet," Enura said, "That each one of the people in this room would answer more or less the way you did. It's about finishing, isn't it? Climax. And that might actually be what some of them think. But, beneath that response, whether consciously or unconsciously, every single person in this room thinks that sex is about power."

Code, his eyes following hers as she gazed at the other punters, grunted in surprised agreement.

Enura's eyes returned to his. "You think I'm right?"

Code ground his teeth, leaning back. "Well, I don't think you're wrong, I'll say that much."

"And what do *you* think, Code? Is sex about power?"

Code's head was too fuzzy to come up with a good answer.

"I think that sounds right," he said slowly, "but I think it sounds wrong, as well."

Enura nodded. "Too many think sex is about power. One person's power over another—usually a man over a woman, let's be honest, but there are always exceptions. Perhaps someone doesn't feel fulfilled or in control of their job, their life, their relationship. They vent that feeling the only way they know how, one of the only ways they're taught. Selfishness is involved, too—they want to make sure they get off, and only then do they think of their partner, if at all. But power always takes center stage. Sex is the only way some think they can exert power in their lives, so they take every opportunity and advantage they can. For the already powerful, sex is the culmination of that power. The most personal, complete power a person can experience."

Code found himself nodding. Though his brain fuzzed against the inside of his skull, he felt what Enura said was true. "You can hardly call that sex, though," he said slowly.

"Indeed," Enura continued. "And yet that is all everyone in the Sfaera seems to think the act is about."

"So..." Code began, but shook his head. He took a few deep breaths, trying to sober up. "If it isn't about power..."

"Ideally? It's about forgiveness," Enura said.

"Forgiveness," Code repeated. His brow furrowed.

"Forgiveness. Yes. But what I'm talking about has nothing to do with gods or goddesses. It's just one person with another— or with a few others, what do I care—and choosing to accept that person for all their faults, their foibles. The flab on his belly. The way her breasts hang down. The failure to rise in society, past infidelities, harsh words said the night before... but here they are anyway, together and choosing one another. Never an obligation, always a choice, and all parties involved must make it. 'I accept you, I love you, and I want you, all of your flaws and imperfections aside.'"

Code found himself shaking his head. "Nobody does that."

"Not everyone," Enura said, her voice quiet. Her eyes bored into his. "Certainly not enough. But everyone *should*."

Forgiveness. The word echoed in Code's mind, and with it, the thought of Cinzia. All thoughts of Cinzia, and ultimately the fact that he could not imagine what he would have to forgive her of, and at the same time how impossible it was for someone to forgive him for all he had done.

Something interrupted his thoughts, then, a light tug at the back of his mind.

He was being voked.

He reached into the pouch at his belt, instinctively knowing which stone to grasp, and glanced down at it. A bright green rune inscribed on a dark blue stone.

Kosarin.

Code cursed under his breath.

"Are you all right?" Enura asked.

"I…" Code did not know what to say.

He stared down at the stone, and a realization struck him.

He felt confused about Cinzia, that much was certain. He liked her, but this bizarre conversation with Enura only emphasized the fact that there was no possible connection that could exist between them.

And his troubles went deeper than that. His orders from Kosarin were to befriend Knot, to infiltrate the Chaos Queen's inner circle and discover her plans, her plots. To use the people who had become his friends, and report all of the intelligence he gathered back to the Triad. But as far as he had seen, these people had no connection to the Chaos Queen anymore—she had left them long ago.

But Code had seen the Nine Daemons at work in Arro and Mavenil—both had been the scenes of terrible massacres. Kosarin's orders seemed to him counterproductive, if they were to prevent another such massacre—or a greater disaster, one that stretched across the entire Sfaera.

Code had seen such terrible deaths. He could not let that happen again.

And yet, this was Kosarin Lothgarde. He could not very well ignore the man, either. Not to mention the coin and prestige that came with being one of the Nazaniin.

"You sure you're all right?" Enura asked.

Code puffed out his cheeks. Then he stood, his last drink untouched.

"I thought about making a life-changing decision just now, to be honest with you," Code said. "But looks like that isn't in the stars for me." He tossed a small pouch of silvers down the bar toward the innkeeper, who swept up the payment in one hand and nodded to Code.

Code inclined his head toward Enura. "Thank you for the conversation. I appreciate what you've said, but I'm afraid duty calls. I hope you find…" He hesitated. He'd been about to say, "I hope you find forgiveness," but that sounded ridiculous, even to his fuzzy mind. "I hope you find something good," he finished lamely.

He left before she could respond, marching right out of the Fellhome and toward the Citadel to see what in Oblivion the *Triadin* wanted at this hour.

31

Cliffs of Litori

URSTADT PACED BACK AND forth as the final piece to the War Goddess rose into place.

A ragged cheer rose up from the tiellan engineers. Back when they'd first left Adimora, Urstadt had wondered why Winter had brought along so many engineers. The army of Rangers and Winter's own abilities were more than able to wreak havoc among the Triahn soldiers.

But, clearly, Winter intended to do far worse than wreak havoc.

At its full height, the War Goddess stood one hundred rods tall—a mountainous siege-engine. It was so large Urstadt wasn't sure it would work at all; the dynamics of hurling rocks seemed inapplicable at such a scale.

The gray light of early dawn was just beginning to appear on the horizon. The engineers had concealed the true nature of their project by building it in pieces, keeping those pieces hidden in brush and piles of wood, and only putting the parts together this evening. A half-dozen significantly smaller trebuchets stood at the base of the War Goddess, as well as a few ballistas, like children at the feet of a giant. They'd have to be moved to lower ground, and much closer to cause any real damage to the city within the walls. But they were for show, and nothing more. A distraction for the enemy. Urstadt doubted Winter intended to move the smaller war machines; the War

Goddess was the main attraction here. Whether Carrieri had fallen for the ruse, Urstadt could not say, but the War Goddess now stood completed, fully functional, and ready to make its first attack on the Circle City of Triah, the Center of the World.

All around them, the Rangers rose from their cots and bedrolls, heads craning back to take in the completed war machine before them.

Only Winter herself knew the full extent of what she planned; the queen shared less and less of her strategy with her captain. Urstadt had been most comfortable—Goddess, she had actually been enjoying herself—when she had been tutoring Winter, checking every decision the younger woman made, sparring with her daily. But the queen had grown into her position and closed herself off, and now Urstadt found herself feeling rather useless. She was nothing more than Winter's glorified sparring partner, now—even her normal task in battle, leading the tiellan infantry, hardly mattered anymore since they had brought almost exclusively cavalry to Triah. She could still take Winter easily in a one-on-one spar, but that was a small consolation.

But where had Winter gone? She had been standing at the base of the War Goddess moments ago; now she was nowhere to be seen. Urstadt frowned, walking toward the siege engine, looking around for the queen.

At the base of the War Goddess, a line of not quite a dozen boulders, somewhere between one and two rods in diameter, stood in the grass. Urstadt could not imagine the damage such a large projectile would do to a wall or building. Even more horrifying than the boulders were the three barrels, each as tall as Urstadt herself, lined up behind them. They contained a mixture of cotton, sulfur, saltpeter, and pitch.

Urstadt gripped her glaive tightly.

Why are you letting this happen? she asked herself, not for the first time. Had she not accompanied Winter to make sure the young tiellan did not become another Daval? Was this warmongering not worse than anything Daval had ever done?

To destroy, I must first know love. She had come to love Daval before she killed him. She had come to love Winter, too.

She was not ready to destroy Winter. Goddess, if such a thing was even possible. Urstadt outclassed Winter by far in physical combat, but she had nothing like psimancy, or the two thousand loyal, adoring Rangers at her back.

A few people in the gathering crowd pointed up, about midway to the top of the War Goddess. Urstadt looked and finally found Winter perched atop the pivot of the trebuchet, where the two massive triangular frames met at their peak, forming a fulcrum around which the huge arm swung.

"Tiellans!" Winter shouted, getting the attention of the entire crowd. By now, all of the engineers had gathered at the base of the trebuchet, along with most of the Rangers who were not on duty. Nearly two thousand people, gazing up at Winter, shading their eyes as the first rays of dawn began to peel out over the land.

"We have been through much to get to this point," Winter shouted. Urstadt wondered whether the tiellans on the edge of the crowd could even hear her; the wind threatened to carry away every other word.

"But now, we are here, and we have a purpose. We have a *weapon!*" Winter raised a fist in the air, and the tiellans erupted in an almost deafening cheer.

Urstadt glanced back toward Triah. Carrieri surely had eyes monitoring the tiellans on the cliffs, and the tiellans were making enough ruckus by now that they must have been noticed, spies or no spies—just like the massive war machine that had sprung up seemingly overnight. There was no sign of an incoming force yet, but she knew in her bones it was only a matter of time. Within the hour, surely.

"And we have a purpose," Winter said, as the crowd's cheers died down somewhat. "The humans outnumber us. They always have. You saw what the Eye did to the Rodenese fleet weeks ago, and it has kept them at bay ever since. But numbers and scare tactics have never mattered to us; you saw what we did to the Legion's forces when they met us in battle! Each of you were there, each of you helped us defeat forces two, three times our own number. You fought against the daemons when they rained from the sky. You saw what we can do *together*."

Winter smacked the wooden arm of the War Goddess. "Now, with this weapon, we will put a dagger in their heart, and pierce them through with fear.

"They will send soldiers to respond," she continued, "but we will be ready for them. And today, we will see humans suffer, and we will watch as they cower in fear."

Another ragged cheer rose up from the tiellans, although Urstadt couldn't help but think that this one seemed less enthusiastic. Whether that was true, or the spawn of her own misplaced hope, she could not say.

"For tiellans!" Winter cried, both arms jutting above her.

The tiellans below repeated the cry in a deafening roar, but the chant slowly shifted. "For tiellans, for tiellans," they chanted a few times, no more than half a dozen, before the words changed, and the overwhelming majority of the Rangers shouted, "For the *queen*, for the *queen*!"

Winter clambered down the War Goddess, landing on

the grass next to Urstadt with a flourish. "Prepare the War Goddess," she told the engineers. "It is time we attack, and show the Center of the World our *own* power."

"How many?"

Carrieri stormed down the halls of the Legion's barracks, a milieu of his generals, admirals, aides, and Nazaniin swarming around him. His chief aide, Ryven, spoke to him. Ryven was also the filter through which all intelligence passed through to him. "Not quite a dozen of them, Grand Marshal—"

"There's no way those engines could reach the city, even from atop the cliffs. What are they planning?"

"That is... generally true, Grand Marshal, but there is one engine that defies that assumption. They must have been building the parts in secret since they've been here, but it only started going up last night, and, well, it's assembled now, and it's—"

"It's *massive*, Grand Marshal." General Toggo Marshton, of the Sapphire Regiment, spoke. "We have no doubt such an engine can reach the city proper, perhaps even the Trinacrya. And the size of projectile it must be able to launch..."

"Let's not forget it was made by *tiellans*," Admiral Seto said. "While it might look imposing, its functionality remains in question."

Anger burned within Carrieri, chiefly toward himself. He had known of the tiellan presence in Litori for weeks, and had allowed them to remain on the clifftops unmolested, other than the occasional test of force. He'd successfully removed all the *rihnemin*, and thought it best not to pursue violence where violence wasn't needed. The tiellans were not besieging the city, after all, only biding their time atop the cliffs. He had thought the war engines they'd been constructing were nothing he could not handle—the creations of inexperienced fighters; distractions. The possible alliance between the tiellans and Roden worried him, and he had thought the tiellans might be trying to pull Triah's attention away from the war at sea. Winter was not above alliances of convenience, after all. She had proposed just an alliance to him, in the middle of a pitched battle, in order to defeat daemons.

But he had not expected a formidable weapon to appear on the cliffs above the city.

"We should get to the Eye," someone said.

"And do what? Watch while they bombard the city?" Carrieri's laugh was mirthless. "You know as well as I do that the Eye was not designed to fire at the cliffs." He stopped to consider. The barracks would likely be a target, if the tiellans had remotely good intelligence on Triahn geography. But so could any number of buildings, locations, and key areas of the city.

But, first things first.

"If we cannot take down the engine itself, we can reduce the numbers that guard it." Carrieri looked to his psimancer, Illaran. "What of the Hood Regiment? Are they in position?"

"They are, sir."

"The tiellans will surely ride to meet the Hood Regiment if we send them out; they have the advantage of higher ground. Tell the Hood Regiment to attack." The Hood Regiment, under command of General Arstan Gerundi, consisted of three thousand good soldiers; not his best, but quite nearly. The tiellans only numbered two thousand, but Carrieri had seen what they were capable of against forces twice their size. "Send the Orb Regiment out as reinforcements," he said in a snap decision. "We must be sure to put as much pressure on them as we can."

Aides scrambled to relay those orders as Carrieri continued speaking to Illaran.

"General Gerundi's orders are to distract, if he does not have the numbers to destroy," Carrieri said. "Tell him to be cautious—to distract the tiellans from using that thing, but not to risk his entire force. We can't afford to lose the Hood Regiment, not when our forces are already spread so thin." Even sending the Orb out to reinforce the Hood might prove folly if Roden chose to attack.

And that massive war engine could just be a distraction, to lure Triahn forces into a trap atop the cliffs.

But he had to take that chance. He couldn't just let them bombard the city from the cliffs without retribution.

"We move to the top of the Merchant's Tower," Carrieri said. It was farther south than the Trinacrya, and would be a very difficult target, even with a machine the size his lieutenants described. "Bring maps of the city and the cliffs. We monitor the situation from there." He thought for a moment, then looked to General Marshton, commander of the Sapphire Regiment. Marshton's troops were mostly the children of nobles and wealthy merchants, and rarely saw battle because of the sway their parents held in the Parliament, but Marshton himself had a knack for tactics and positioning. "Marshton, send orders to your regiment to be battle-ready, and confine them to the southern barracks for now, out of shot of the war machine; if the battle is long, the Hood and the Orb will need relief troops quickly. But in the meantime, go yourself to the Eye. Survey the situation as best you can from there, but keep eyes on the harbor, too. Make sure God's Eye is battle-ready. We can't risk an attack from the sea as well."

"Yes, sir." Marshton saluted, then turned on his heel and marched off, his pace quick.

"Admiral Seto, ready the fleet. We will not be caught unawares, and even with the power of God's Eye we want to be ready on the sea as well."

The admiral saluted, and then rushed away with his own aides.

Carrieri nodded. Looking around, his eyes rested on Illaran, the Nazaniin representative.

"One more thing, Illaran," Carrieri said, and the young man met Carrieri's eyes. "In private, if you please." He hoped the best for the Hood and Orb regiments, but he had a contingency plan, too.

Cinzia walked alongside Jane through the streets of Triah, the other eight chosen disciples trailing behind them. They had finally filled the last two disciple positions, unsurprisingly with the two remaining names the current Disciples had lacked from the original set of nine: Danica and Lucia. Together with Cinzia, Elessa, Ocrestia, Baetrissa, Arcana, Valeria, and Sirana, they made a quorum of nine disciples, mirroring the names of the original Nine Disciples that had followed Canta when she walked the Sfaera.

Cinzia was uncomfortable with the most recent appointments. Astrid's given name, she had recently found out, was Lucia, and Winter's was Danica. The knowledge rubbed her the wrong way—even though it was common for people to name their children after the Disciples. But when she looked at the disciples Jane had chosen—good, dedicated Odenites, both of them—it felt as if something was out of place.

The light of dawn broke over the eastern horizon, bathing the city in pale pink and orange light. It was a clear, crisp day, almost cloudless.

"It is a beautiful morning, Jane. Perhaps it is worth stopping, just to watch the sunrise?"

Jane looked over her shoulder toward the rising sun, and

for a moment Cinzia thought her sister would ignore her suggestion. But Jane stopped, turning fully to face the dawn with a smile on her face. She looked particularly beautiful in the early morning light, her cheeks rosy with the morning chill.

"You're right, sister. We should take in the beauty of Canta's creations when we can, of course."

They had left camp an hour ago. Jane had informed each of the disciples only last night that they would be journeying into Triah, for the first time, together. With the Denomination's ban on Odenites entering the city lifted after Cinzia's interaction with the Essera, Jane seemed to think it important that they enter the city immediately and "see what good needs doing."

Cinzia had originally been worried about all ten of them going into the city together, but Knot, her brother Eward, and a small contingent of the Prelates he led were following close behind. Cinzia could not help but feel they were all targets. Not so much from the Denomination—she actually believed the Essera when she said they wanted to use the Odenites as a tool—but the Essera's plans were not widely known. A typical Cantic faithful would not have much reason to treat the Odenite leadership cordially, and Cinzia had seen enough of that treatment in Tinska to suspect that Triah could not possibly be any better. At least, Cinzia mused, Jane had not settled on any insignias or symbols that would make them stand out.

And now here they were, traipsing about Triah, looking for whatever it was Jane thought they needed to accomplish here.

Cinzia had some ideas. There had been rumors of large groups of people in Triah who supported the Odenites, but could not leave their homes, families, or occupations to join the new Church outside of the city. The disciples had been discussing ways to connect with these people for a few weeks now.

But, in typical fashion, Jane refused to tell any of them where they were going, and they had to follow their prophetess blindly through the streets.

Cinzia had not heard a word from Luceraf since she had woken up in her tent after the ritual. Now that she was free of the Daemon, Cinzia felt more at home with the other disciples. She had yet to try her hand at translating; she feared that, although Luceraf was gone, Cinzia's connection with the Daemon would be unforgivable in Canta's eyes—and in Jane's eyes, too.

Cinzia wore the gemstone, Canta's Heart, in a pouch at her waist. She hoped eventually to tell Jane about it, and see if she could offer any insight into how to use it against the Nine when the time came, but she had felt more distant from Jane than ever, lately.

She caught Knot's face in the distance, looking at her quizzically. *Why have we stopped?* Cinzia nodded at the sunrise.

Knot looked over his shoulder, then back at Cinzia. He shrugged, and continued his vigil, eyes moving slowly all around the near-empty streets. The throngs that crowded Triah's streets would not be out for another hour or so—and Cinzia was enjoying having the streets to herself. Or, at least, to themselves. Sharing with the disciples would have to do.

As the sun's bright orb rose above the horizon, Knot walked quickly toward her and Jane. She had seen that look in his eye more times than she liked, now: at Jane's assassination attempt in Tinska; when they had been attacked by Kamites; when Outsiders had appeared in the Odenite camp outside Kirlan. The expression was all business, and reminded her of the impression he'd made on her when they'd first met: dead eyes, with nothing behind them at all.

"Move to the side," Knot said. Eward and the other Prelates

were already ushering the rest of the disciples away from the middle of the road.

Cinzia immediately did as asked, and was grateful to see Jane do the same. While Cinzia had learned to recognize the look, and Jane likely had as well, half the time Jane refused to listen to reason.

Just as Knot ushered Cinzia and Jane off the road, Cinzia heard it. A soft, rhythmic pounding, growing louder. The sound of many feet marching in unison. As she looked down the road, she saw, not far off, a group of soldiers marching toward them.

Her heart froze, and Cinzia gripped Knot's arm. Had the Essera betrayed them after all? Lured them into the city, only to have them captured? But that did not make sense; the armor, the gryphon insignias on their tabards and breastplates, the banners they carried with them did not belong to Sons of Canta. These were soldiers of the Khalic Legion.

The first soldiers approached, but none of them looked at Cinzia, Jane, or any of the disciples standing at the roadside. They marched directly past, rank after rank, heading out of the city. The line of soldiers stretched out of sight.

"What is this?" Cinzia asked Knot. She realized she still gripped his arm tightly, and forced herself to let go.

"They're going into battle," Knot murmured.

Cinzia followed his gaze, and realized he was looking to the cliffs. Worry creased his face, and Cinzia saw why. A trebuchet stood atop the cliffs, overlooking the city. Even from this distance it was immense. She wondered at how the tiellans could have built it seemingly overnight.

"Winter," Cinzia said softly. Knot had shared Winter's location, atop the cliffs with the other tiellans, with her shortly after he had found out. She had asked if he wanted to go to her, unable or unwilling to tell him to do so, and he had expressed uncertainty, to her surprise. But now, she knew she could not keep him any longer. She could not do that to him.

"Go to her," Cinzia said to him.

"I'm your Goddessguard," he said. "I've sworn to protect you."

"You are her husband," Cinzia said, each word grinding out a deep, painful hole within her. "That is more important."

For a moment Knot appeared to be frozen.

"*Go*," she told him. She could not hold it together much longer. "I will be safe here." The disingenuous nature of the comment struck her immediately. There was no telling what the massive war machine atop the cliffs could do, or how wide it could reach.

But Knot did not belong to her, or to anyone else. He needed to make his choice.

Finally, blessedly, Knot nodded, and she wanted to hate him for it but knew she could not.

"I'll find you soon," he said. Then, he turned and moved quickly away, avoiding the soldiers as he moved out of the city.

Only then did Cinzia's hand move to her mouth to prevent her sob from being heard by the others.

The soldiers continued to march past, and a slow, over-whelming fear built in Cinzia's chest.

32

TERRIS POLISHED ONE OF the Eye's mirrors at the very top of the Eye, thinking how this would be yet another work-filled but terribly uninteresting day, when he heard the ruckus below.

Terris looked to Hindra, one eyebrow raised.

"Were we expecting visitors this morning?"

Hindra, her long brown hair tied in loose ponytail, shook her head slowly. She had been inspecting the core of the Eye's apparatus, a large system of interlocking metal cylinders that punched through the top level of the Eye and continued down through the building below, all the way into the Eye's foundation, anchoring the apparatus as well as the tower itself. Hindra had been inspecting the large, rune-covered amber stone the core housed near the apparatus, but now she pushed her protective brass-rimmed goggles up onto her forehead.

Terris sighed. "I'd best go see what that is about, then." He couldn't help the excited fluttering in his chest. Perhaps Roden was attempting another attack on Triah; perhaps they would have the chance to use the Eye again. Terris had been cleaning, checking, testing, and retesting equipment for so long that until recently he had completely forgotten what it was like to actually operate the Eye at full power. His experience a few weeks ago as Roden attacked had felt like an awakening.

And it was a glaringly clear day—perfect conditions for the Eye.

Slowly, Terris stood, his tall frame hunching over to avoid smacking his head on the bottom of the brass frame suspended above him. He moved toward the stairwell as Hindra spoke.

"Do you think Roden is attacking again?" she asked.

Terris sucked air through his teeth. "It is possible," he said, "but I don't hear warning sirens, as of yet. It may be Carrieri has received some sort of advanced intel. Or, most likely, another group of bumbling bureaucrats."

Since the Eye's success at the Harbor Battle, as people were calling it, all manner of senators, high-ranking Denomination clergy, generals, and even nobles and wealthy merchants had somehow procured permission to ascend the Eye and see the weapon that had wrought such destruction.

Hindra sniffed at the thought, and Terris could not blame her. These people had not cared one whit for the Eye before; they had called it a relic, a gimmick, something better left to rot while resources were put toward more promising projects. Only Carrieri himself had kept Terris and Hindra's jobs—along with those of the other few dozen mechanics and operators—intact for the past few years, insisting they keep the Eye ready should need ever arise.

And, Oblivion, had need arisen.

Looking over the railing, Terris saw faint movement down the spiral staircase. The corkscrew pattern of the stairs curling around and around seemed infinite at times, and the view still made him dizzy, even after all these years. But the purposeful march of boots on stairs told him this was a military visit. Straining his ears, he could only make out a few words, but those words sent a chill through his spine.

The first was "Tiellans," and the second was "attack."

Terris sucked air through his teeth. Perhaps it would be an interesting day, after all.

"Khalic forces approaching, Your Majesty," Urstadt said.

Winter nodded. Both of them looked up at the War Goddess. The sound of straining wood and rope filled the air around them as two Ranger teams on either side pulled on the ropes attached to the trebuchet's arm. A system of pulleys made the task easier, but both Ranger teams—consisting of the strongest tiellans under Winter's command—were still hard-pressed to pull the arm down. As the huge beam slowly lowered, a colossal counterweight rose.

"We knew this would be their reaction," Winter said, her eyes still on the War Goddess. "How many?"

Urstadt glanced back at Triah. From where they stood, they could not quite see the force snaking east and then north toward the cliffs. "At last glance, at least twenty-five hundred soldiers," Urstadt said. "I'd estimate closer to three thousand, all things considered. Perhaps more coming up from the city, but it should be some time before they arrive."

"Rorie!" Winter called.

The tiellan rider approached quickly. "Yes, Your Majesty?"

"You and Urstadt will lead the defense of the War Goddess. Take fifteen hundred riders, find the best ground you can, and prepare for the battle. Defend our position."

"Yes, Commander." Rorie saluted.

Urstadt, however, remained behind.

"Is there something else, Urstadt?" Winter asked

The Ranger teams had fully lowered the beam, now, and secured the massive arm of wood. Another team placed one of the three-hundred-pound boulders into the sling.

Goddess, this is really going to happen.

"Your Majesty, I don't think the incoming regiment is Carrieri's only tactic. He'll send another team, much smaller, to take out the War Goddess itself, if they can. He might even send psimancers. I'd like to remain here, at your side, to protect you."

Winter's eyes finally met Urstadt's, and Urstadt resisted the immediate urge to look away.

"You want to protect me?" Winter asked.

Urstadt kept her face stone-like, with all the discipline she could muster.

The engineers cleared a space around the trebuchet, moving tiellan Rangers—those Rorie had not already called to move for their defense—out of the way in a wide arc around the weapon.

"Yes," Urstadt finally said. "I do not agree with what you are doing here. I have made that clear. But… I am still with you." *For now.* Those last two words, unsaid, nevertheless remained in the air between them, and Urstadt suspected Winter sensed them there, too.

Slowly, Winter nodded. "Very well. Stay here. Protect me, and the War Goddess, from whatever other attacks Carrieri might be sending our way. Thank you, Urstadt."

She turned back to the War Goddess. "Ready?" she asked.

Goddess, not so soon.

"Ready, Your Majesty," the chief engineer said.

"Fire," Winter said.

"Fire!" the chief engineer ordered.

A lone pin—the size of Urstadt's arm, but a lone pin nonetheless—held the trebuchet's beam down against the counterweight. Now a team pulled a rope attached to the pin, and the long metal trigger sprung out of the trebuchet's beam.

For a moment the trebuchet remained still, and Urstadt thought, with an overwhelming hope, that the entire project might have failed before it even began.

The feeling was short-lived. The counterweight dropped with aching slowness at first, then it picked up speed and swung low with a *whoomf*. A deep crack sounded above her, and the sling flung wide, hurling the missile as it *whooshed* through the air toward Triah.

Cinzia was surprised at how quickly Jane found Odenite sympathizers in Triah.

"You'd think she already knew exactly where she was going," Eward muttered.

"We should be used to such things by now, brother," Cinzia said, trying to push aside her fears for Knot, and of the towering weapon atop the cliffs. They stood within the walls of a merchant's estate. The grounds and mansion looked like they had once belonged to a family of noble birth, but the merchant had likely bought the estate a generation or two ago. It was an old-fashioned type of place to find in Triah; most nobles nowadays preferred tower-houses, building their wealth skywards rather than buying up large plots of land.

Jane had led them to a crossroads, where the Radial Road met the Twenty-Fifth Circle, and there a nervous young man had stood waiting for them. When Jane had introduced herself, the man's eyes lit up, and he led them excitedly to his family's estate, where Jane, her disciples and Prelates, and about two dozen followers now gathered.

The lad had told them that he had been inspired to wait on that street corner—he knew not what for at the time, but having found the famed Prophetess, the woman he and his family had already begun to venerate, he knew he'd been inspired by Canta.

Or so he said. Cinzia had a difficult time believing such things, even after all she'd seen. Odenites continued to join their cause outside the walls, so it made sense that they had a large following within the city, as well. The pilgrims who found them often came out with such strange stories, tales of the supernatural circumstances that led them to find the Odenite camp.

And yet she still could not believe them.

"You are one of the Prophetess's disciples?"

Cinzia turned to see a woman of about her own age approaching.

Smoothing her skirts, Cinzia nodded. The smile on her face felt fake, plastered there, as if it would crumble should she move it too much. "I am Disciple Cinzia," she said.

Priestess Cinzia, Disciple Cinzia. Is there even a difference?

Would it matter if there was?

The woman's eyes widened. "You are the Prophetess's sister! I am so happy to meet you. I cannot imagine what it must be like to be so close to the Prophetess. Is she this amazing all of the time, or just when in public?" The woman had said that last part in jest, Cinzia could tell, but it was difficult to actually take it that way.

"My sister is an incredible woman," Cinzia said, the smile on her face unmoving. Goddess, she could not keep this up for long.

"I am so sorry, where are my manners," the woman blustered. "I am Cinzia Grinatan. My husband, Garand, owns this estate."

Cinzia curtsied, bowing her head. "Well met, Cinzia. I do like your name, wherever did you get it?"

The woman laughed. "Oh, please. Call me Cin. Everyone else does, and with you around it'll make things less confusing, anyway."

"Very well, Cin." Cin was rather young to be the lady of such an estate. "Is the young man who brought us from the Radial Road your husband?"

Cin laughed, the sound raucous and unhindered. "Oh, Goddess, no! That was my husband's younger brother, Garald. My husband is over there." Cin pointed at a man currently speaking with Ocrestia. Cinzia was relieved to see that he did not seem to have a problem with a tiellan in a place of power. Ocrestia was still the only tiellan woman who had been appointed to the disciples. Cinzia had asked Jane to appoint more, but Jane had shrugged, as if the matter were out of her hands. "Canta will call whom She will," Jane had said. Cinzia did not see things that way. Appointing more tiellans would help their cause, help connect them with the tiellan people, and help the tiellans who had already flocked to the Odenites feel safer and represented. The thought made her glance back to the cliffs, and her heart froze. She did not know much about siege weaponry, but the arm of the weapon now swung back and forth, slowly settling into an equilibrium.

Had the weapon been fired?

"He's the ugly one, I know," Cin said, oblivious to Cinzia's realization. Someone—perhaps Eward—shouted something in the distance.

Cinzia gripped Cin's arm. "Perhaps we should—"

She stopped as another nearby shout split the air, this one much louder and more urgent. Cinzia had not heard whatever the person had said, but the tone… She only had a second or two to try to process what she had just heard when a deafening explosion rocked the earth beneath her feet.

Then Cinzia was on the ground. She wondered, for the briefest moment, whether this might be another earthquake caused by Morayne. But immediately she knew the truth. The trebuchet had struck Triah, and somewhere very nearby.

Cinzia slowly rose to her feet, looking frantically around her. Everything was hazy and shadowed, as if a tremendous dark cloud had overshadowed the sun. But the morning had been cloudless.

Many others rose slowly from the ground, while some remained there, hands covering their heads.

"Is everyone all right?" Cinzia called out, coughing. Coughing, she realized, because of the dust thick in the air. That was why it was so dark.

Apart from the choking dust, it seemed that everyone nearby was uninjured. Cinzia helped Cin to her feet, the woman coughing and spluttering, then walked quickly to Jane. Whether her sister had not fallen at all, or gotten up quickly enough to begin helping others up, Cinzia could not be sure, but Jane was already up and about, seeing to everyone around her.

"The trebuchet," Cinzia said. She had pointed out the weapon to Jane that morning, but Jane, in typical fashion, had chosen to go about their business, citing Canta's protection.

Jane nodded, coughing.

"Where did that explosion come from?" Cinzia asked, loudly so anyone in the courtyard could hear. Her gaze moved around the small area, but there was no damage that she could discern.

"Not sure." Eward came up to his sisters. "I've sent Prelates outside to see if they can tell what's going on, but… I think for now it's best we stay inside these walls."

As Eward spoke, the dust cleared a little more. Cinzia's gaze rose upward, following the outline of the Grinatans' manse through the settling dust. The house had been a three-story affair, with a small bell tower jutting up from the third floor. Or at least there had been one there when Cinzia had walked into the courtyard.

"Was there not a bell tower up there before?" Cinzia asked.

The others followed her gaze. Eward mumbled something under his breath.

Fast footsteps approached them from behind, and they all turned to see one of the Prelates running toward them, panting.

"Prophetess! Disciples!" he called. "I think you should come outside and see this."

Terris looked out across the battlements on the topmost floor of God's Eye. The city spread out around them in all directions, the harbor and the Wyndric Ocean beyond that to the west, and the great plains to the east. Terris knew it was an optical illusion, but it almost felt as if they were on a level with the plateaus atop the Cliffs of Litori. In reality, the cliffs stood another hundred rods taller.

"They're preparing to launch again," Hindra said.

"Our forces have engaged them," General Marshton said. "With any luck, they will push them back and destroy that cursed thing before it does any more damage."

A few moments before, they had witnessed the first missile strike the city. Those with sharper eyes than Terris had watched it arc across the sky to land in the nobles' district, where it had sent up a cloud of dust and debris. From their vantage point atop the Eye, of course, such things seemed small. Inconsequential. Normally Terris loved the feeling of detachment, the global sense of understanding he felt from observing so much from such a high place. Today, however, he felt sick. He'd been so busy thinking about the missile's trajectory, speed, and striking power that when the dust flew into the air, he'd watched dispassionately.

It took him a few moments to realize that the missile had destroyed lives—perhaps someone he knew. The next missile might strike his own district, his childhood home, or his parents.

"Where did it hit, exactly?" one of the general's aides asked.

"Looks to be…" Terris calculated the streets in his head.

"Around the Twenty-Fifth Circle, near the Radial Road," Hindra said.

Terris nodded, grateful for his assistant. He looked to General Marshton, the commanding officer, now, at the Eye. "What were they aiming for, do you think? That isn't a military area."

"The elves don't care who they kill, what they destroy." Marshton was a big man, not quite as tall as Terris himself but far broader in the shoulders. He looked perpetually hunched. His voice was low as he stared out at the city. "They have no honor, and no respect."

Honor and respect? Terris was not sure the Khalic Legion valued such things, either, when life and death were on the line.

Marshton looked over his shoulder. "What is the status of the harbor?"

"Still nothing, sir," one of his aides called back from the opposite side of the Eye. They had to shout around the Eye's apparatus itself; the brass circles, mirrors, and magnifying glasses were not in use, but Carrieri had ordered Terris to keep the weapon at the ready.

Wind whipped Terris's clothing against his body, and he was grateful for his goggles. Below, at sea level, it was a soft sea breeze, but at the top of the tower the effect was magnified to a strong, gusting wind.

"The trebuchet is preparing to fire again!" one of Marshton's men called.

"Chief Operator, we need to do *something*." Marshton's attention was on the brass mirrors now. "Are you really sure we can't—"

"I've already told you, General: the Eye's range is limited. It can reach anything on the ground for almost two-radials, but it cannot be angled above its own plane."

"You're telling me that a thing this complicated and expensive can't do something as simple as point *up*?"

Terris took a deep breath. He had explained the science of God's Eye to many generals, lieutenants, senators, and even priestesses in the past. Marshton wasn't a fool, and he was speaking out of pique rather than a failure to grasp Terris's explanation. "It is not a matter of expense, but of design," Terris said, as patiently as he could. "Had the original builders desired, they could have installed mirrors to angle the light upward. But their focus was on the sea. I don't think they ever expected an enemy to come from the cliffs. And we do not have adequate time to create a new mirror now, nor the machinery to install it."

Terris would have gladly pointed the Eye at the massive siege engine atop the cliffs, were it not for these limitations. The anger he saw so evidently in Marshton's creased eyebrows, his reddened face and clenched fists, slamming on the battlements every few moments, pressed within himself, too. He was simply better at masking it.

"Should we evacuate the tower?" Hindra asked, her dark eyes wide as she stared at the trebuchet atop the cliffs.

Terris hesitated. He had wondered the same thing, when he'd first seen the siege engine. God's Eye seemed a prime target for such a thing.

"Nonsense," Marshton said. "We're too far away. And even if we were struck by one of those missiles, the tower is strong. A little boulder would cause some damage, but nothing unfixable. Right, Terris?"

"Speaking strictly scientifically," Terris finally said, "chances are unlikely we'll be hit at all, let alone suffer any serious damage. Their weapon is big, but that means its aim is uncertain. And a clifftop is not a good site for such a weapon—they'd have to calculate for crosswinds and other irregularities. The first missile landed in a residential district—not exactly a strategic victory—so it is clear they are not practiced in this art. And, yes, even if one were to strike, it would likely not cause enough damage to…" Terris's voice trailed off. He cleared his throat before speaking again. "To be honest with you, General, I would strongly consider evacuation of God's Eye, if I were you. Even that small chance… if circumstances were to somehow allow such a thing, the consequences would be… Goddess, they would be catastrophic."

"It is a good thing you are not me, then, Terris," Marshton said, his face even more red than it was before. "The moment we evacuate this tower, the Rodenese fleet will come flooding through that harbor. We will thwart them with the power of God's Eye, just as we did two weeks ago. And this time, we will make sure they do not forget the lesson."

"Incoming!"

At the sound of the word, all eyes atop the tower turned to the trebuchet in time to see the great counterweight swing down. Despite the growing terror in his gut, Terris marveled at the feat of engineering. The counterweight had to weigh… Goddess, almost twenty tons, and he calculated the entire machine at close to a hundred rods tall when the beam was fully upright. He would never underestimate tiellan engineering again.

The counterweight swung beneath the trebuchet's frame and the beam flew above as the sling launched another projectile into the sky.

Terris's stomach dropped as the missile flew. He squinted to see it as best he could, but his eyesight was too weak. He sucked air through his teeth rapidly.

"Where—"

Then he heard the crash, and turned to the west to see another puff of dust, pitifully small from this height. Terris strained his eyes, trying to determine…

Goddess, where was the Glass Pyramid?

"Goddess rising," Hindra whispered.

The structure, while not quite as impressive in size as anything around the Trinacrya, or God's Eye itself, was nevertheless one of Triah's signature buildings. A giant triangular pyramid, made of glass and metal, eight stories in height. Construction had finished only recently, about three years ago, and it had been a major attraction for people all over the Sfaera. The structure had sat in the new arts district, at the Fifteenth Circle, along the Coastal Road.

But now, as Terris looked to where the pyramid should be, he saw nothing but dust and debris, and perhaps, if he squinted, the jagged remains of something that had once loomed large.

33

CARRIERI SNATCHED THE MAP from the aide's hand, his anger simmering just below the surface.

"Thank you, Ryven."

He unrolled the map, spreading it out on the nearest table, sending writing utensils and a few stacked books flying. They had commandeered the top floor of the Merchant's Tower, ten floors up. It wasn't the safest place for a war office in a bombardment, but it commanded a good view of the city. Carrieri and his aides now gathered around the table on which he'd placed the map. Wide windows ran along each wall. Sunlight streamed in; it was a beautiful morning, or would be under any other circumstances.

Carrieri placed his finger on the map, at the intersection of the Radial Road and the Twenty-Fifth Circle.

"The first missile struck here, between the old nobles' district and the current financial district."

"Canta's bones," one of his men whispered, "That's just three circles away."

That was true enough, but Carrieri didn't have time to acknowledge the obvious. They likely only had moments before the next—

The door to the room burst open, and a messenger entered, panting.

"Second missile. Direct hit on the Glass Pyramid."

Carrieri swore. The Glass Pyramid was another civilian target; it held no tactical or military meaning. What were the tiellans bloody trying to do?

Looking down at the map, his finger moved to where he knew the Glass Pyramid was—*was*—and he reached for the quill, marking the spot in dark ink. Twenty-Fifth Circle on the Radial Road. Fifteenth Circle on the Coastal Road. It was impossible to discern a pattern with only two points, but he tried, anyway. The exact center in between the two points was close to the Sinefin River, where it met the Twentieth Circle. Nothing of note there. Drawing a line using the two points, moving southeast, just led out of town. Drawing a line northwest, however, from the Radial Road to the Coastal Road…

…led directly to God's Eye.

"Canta's bloody bones," Carrieri muttered, shifting the map on the table so he had a better view of the Cliffs of Litori north of the city. "They're trying to hit God's Eye." The map was to scale, more or less, and made by the famous Gendri Dargania, so it was relatively accurate, too. He scratched another broad X on the map roughly where the massive trebuchet was stationed, and his suspicions were confirmed. The two shots fired so far looked to be calibrations, testing how far it could fire, and how accurately.

"Give me a report on the battle," Carrieri said.

Behind him, a psimancer in communication with the Hood Regiment stepped forward. "They have engaged the tiellan forces, sir, but the tiellans are strictly on the defensive. With the higher ground, they are holding their position."

"And the Rodenese Fleet?"

"A few ships have been spotted in the distance, Grand Marshal, but no significant movement yet."

Carrieri clenched his jaw.

"Illaran," he snapped. "What of the project we discussed?"

"They have engaged the enemy, Grand Marshal."

Carrieri exhaled, but he could not afford a sigh of relief. Not yet. Illaran's forces were their last hope at this point. If they could not stop the trebuchet…

Goddess, he could not consider that option.

"Tell General Gerundi to press the attack," Carrieri said, turning back to the psimancer that connected him with the general. "Send everything he has against the tiellans; *make* them react."

"Yes, sir."

"And…" Carrieri hesitated. Damn Kosarin for not giving him more psimancers; he needed to communicate more quickly. With everyone. "Get to the Eye as quick as you can," Carrieri told the lad. "Take… Oblivion, is there another psimancer here?"

"Here, sir." A young woman stepped forward.

"Accompany him. Keep in touch. Make sure God's Eye is completely evacuated except for essential personnel. And tell the ones who stay they must be prepared to exit the building as quickly as they can."

"Sir…"

"You heard me," Carrieri said. The Eye would remain operational, even with a skeleton crew.

The messenger and psimancer both saluted, and then ran down the stairs.

Carrieri turned back to the window facing the cliffs. He could already see the trebuchet reloading.

Goddess, he pleaded, *don't let me be right*. He had hoped, leaving Winter to fight those Outsiders herself, that he would destroy her. Instead, it seemed, he had created a monster, with an eye trained on his beloved city.

* * *

The second missile sailed toward Triah, and a suspicion shivered through Urstadt. Winter was fixated on the boulder, muscles tense and brow slick with sweat.

Urstadt had seen her like that before—mostly when she had used her psimancy during the battles against the Legion. Urstadt was willing to bet just about anything that Winter was using psimancy to… to what? Steady the projectiles? Propel them farther, or faster? *Aim* them?

"The Legion has redoubled their attack. They are pressing our forces back, Urstadt."

Rorie, half of her body slick with blood, the other half covered in sweat and dirt, approached.

"Goddess, I hope that gore isn't yours," Urstadt said, looking the woman up and down.

"Not most of it."

Urstadt glanced east, where the battle between the Rangers and the Legion's forces was underway. She could barely make out generalities in the chaos, but it did indeed seem the Rangers were losing ground. There was still quite a ways to go before the Legion reached the trebuchet.

"You're losing ground, but—"

"But we haven't broken. Not yet. If the Legion keeps up this way, though… ain't gonna be long."

Urstadt exhaled slowly. She could help, but there was little one woman could do—even a woman like Urstadt—to turn the tide of an entire battle.

Well, she corrected herself, a woman like *Winter* might, but the queen was otherwise occupied.

"We're moving too slowly," Winter shouted, and the team of engineers pulled harder, resetting the War Goddess's beam and counterweight.

"Better send in the reinforcements," Urstadt said. They'd kept a few hundred of their Rangers in reserve, on the chance that another attack might come from somewhere else. Urstadt was still betting Carrieri had something else up his sleeve, but they could not let the Legion Regiment through the front line. It would end everything.

Rorie nodded. "Will do."

"And stay safe, Rorie," Urstadt said.

Rorie offered a casual salute as she mounted her horse and rode off. "Under the sun and moon," she said with a grin. Then she spurred her horse onward, toward the reinforcements.

Urstadt turned back to Winter. The trebuchet's mechanism had nearly been reset, and the engineers were preparing to run in and ready the sling.

Urstadt was about to inform Winter of the battle's progress, when she noticed something out of the corner of her eye. A group of people, approaching from the cliff face.

Not tiellans.

Urstadt's instincts were all that saved her as she dropped. A crossbow bolt flew through the air where her head had been a fraction of a second before. She rolled, calling to Winter over her shoulder.

"We have company!"

Urstadt dove for cover behind one of the smaller trebuchets, and tried to get a better look at their new attackers. There were ten or eleven of them, both women and men. All were dressed in dark clothing, with boiled leather armor but no chain or plate that she could see. Swords, axes, and crossbows. And—

The trebuchet behind which Urstadt hid slid to the side, about one rod.

Urstadt moved with the trebuchet, cursing as she did so.

Psimancers.

Urstadt gripped her glaive, adjusting her armor. Winter, too, had her sword in hand, but had yet to take cover.

"You cannot stop me," Winter shouted. One of the smaller trebuchets nearby lifted into the air, and lurched toward the oncoming group, picking up speed as it went.

They aren't here to stop you, Urstadt realized. She glanced at the War Goddess, prepped for launch but without ammunition. Engineers fled from the siege engine as a pair of circular blades cut down two of the fleeing tiellans.

They're here to stop that.

Three of the advancing men had almost converged on Urstadt's position. She edged around the small trebuchet, which hadn't moved since that first initial attempt. Either the telenic with this group realized she wasn't powerful enough to move it fully, or she'd become distracted by other things.

Two of the men circled around the trebuchet one way, while the other took the opposite direction. They knew Urstadt was here, and these men meant to deal with her.

Urstadt did not give them the chance. She swept around toward the lone warrior, bellowing as she swung her glaive at his face. Her attempt to catch him off guard failed as he ducked and lunged toward her, and Urstadt immediately knew the types of warriors she faced. These were not simple soldiers; some of them, of course, were Nazaniin, while others were likely some of the Legion's top soldiers, reserved for covert operations of utmost importance. Like taking out a weapon of mass destruction targeting their city.

Urstadt twisted out of the way, yanking her glaive back to avoid embedding it in the wood of the trebuchet, and she and the other man faced one another just as his two comrades circled around behind her.

Urstadt sidestepped and turned, getting the three in front of her as best she could, but the men moved with her, widening their positions, keeping her within their triangle. Two swords and an axe. Crossbows were slung on the backs of the swordsmen, but she doubted they would utilize those weapons at such close quarters. The man with the axe was huge, a head taller than Urstadt and thickly muscled, while the two swordsmen were thinner, more sinewy.

She had no more time to consider. The taller swordsman lunged at her from behind and slightly to her left. Urstadt stepped to the side and parried with her glaive, dancing around a strike from the axe. At the same time, the other man charged.

It had been some time since Urstadt had fought more than one foe at once outside of a mass battlefield. She used to practice against three, four, even five expert swordsmen at the same time in Roden, emerging the victor perhaps half of the time. The bouts had gained something of a reputation in Roden before she left. Both victories and defeats were almost always by a hair's breadth, but a loss was a loss no matter how close the call, and a loss in an actual fight meant death. She could not afford a loss now.

Urstadt twirled her glaive, blocking, parrying, and dancing around the attacks of her three opponents. Instinct and muscle memory took over, and Urstadt moved with the wind, her glaive an extension of herself, obeying her every command. She was a blur as she whirled around and around, dodging attacks at lightning speed. Urstadt stayed on the defensive, parrying and weaving, while she looked for an opening.

She found it. The shorter swordsman and the axeman crossed paths just as Urstadt twisted around an attack from the third man, turning to face the other two, glaive prepped for a thrust. She stabbed with her glaive, impaling the axeman through the gut and the other through one shoulder.

She left her glaive where it was, pinning the two together, and drew her short sword as she slid away on the grass.

The uninjured swordsman did not miss a beat. He leapt at her, swinging down. Urstadt brought her sword up just in time to block, one hand on the flat of her blade.

With a grunt—her limbs and lungs burned with exertion and pain—Urstadt forced her body forward, sliding her legs beneath the tall swordsman's. While he did not fall, he stumbled, and that was enough for Urstadt to be on him, driving her sword through his neck. He gurgled as Urstadt withdrew her sword, but she could not afford to watch him die. She turned in time to see the axeman, her glaive still rammed through his belly, running toward her with a bellow of rage and pain.

But he was wounded, not thinking clearly, Urstadt could tell from the shuffle in his step as he charged. She ducked out of the way, her legs screaming with exhaustion, and stabbed her sword into one calf as she moved past him. She turned quickly, planting a kick in the man's back, and he fell, her glaive tearing a gaping hole in his back.

Urstadt took a step back, getting her bearings. The tall swordsman struggled on the ground on his hands and knees, gurgling and spluttering, but the blood pouring from his neck told her he had almost no time left. The short swordsman, however, was nowhere to be seen. Urstadt twisted around, her eyes darting back and forth, but she saw—

—a flash of movement above her. Urstadt brought her sword up too late, and felt the blade cut through her side, just below the ribs. Her own sword found a truer mark beneath the other's chin, ramming up through his skull. The two of them fell to the ground in a heap. Urstadt rolled the man's twitching body off of her.

She cradled her side, inspecting the wound. Her micromail had absorbed most of the blow, but the sword had left a long, shallow gash surrounded by deep bruising. It would scab over, and while it hurt like all Oblivion, the wound was far from mortal.

Urstadt stood, shaking herself to regain her senses, looking for Winter.

The queen was still by the War Goddess. One of the massive barrels, a 300-pound boulder, cotton, saltpeter, and buckets of pitch inside, rose up into the air, and moved slowly toward the open trebuchet sling.

Winter was moving it with her psimancy.

The tiellan queen was facing down five attackers; she must have dispatched two or three of them already. But she seemed to be concentrating almost entirely on the War Goddess and the missile she now carried with her *tendra*.

There were no living engineers in sight; a dozen lay dead on the ground, and the others must have fled.

The remaining attackers advanced on the War Goddess, three of them firing bolts, some at Winter, others at the war machine itself. Whoever the psimancer was apparently still lived, as weapons and debris flew toward the trebuchet, but Winter easily blocked and deflected all projectiles aimed at herself or the trebuchet.

For Canta's sake, why doesn't she just kill them? Urstadt wondered. What was so important about firing the trebuchet that made Winter all but ignore everything else?

Urstadt tugged her glaive from the axeman's gored body, wiping it on the grass. She secured her short sword in its sheath over her shoulder, and then advanced on the remaining attackers. She was approaching them from behind, and slightly to their right. Hopefully, they were too occupied with their offensive against Winter, and wouldn't notice her creeping up on them.

The thought came too soon. Another man was moving toward her stealthily.

He wore dark greens and browns, and was shorter than Urstadt. Brown hair, brown eyes. More or less nondescript. He carried a long black staff, likely made of blackbark.

Then she caught a glimpse of the sword at his waist. Long, slightly curved, with a bone-white handle and silvery blade.

A Nazaniin sword.

A psimancer.

The man realized Urstadt had seen him, and changed course to attack her more directly. Urstadt swung her glaive, the man readied his staff, and they both picked up speed as they clashed.

Urstadt's glaive *clanged* against the man's staff, and they both disengaged, twirling their weapons. The man wielded his staff expertly, his footwork and hand placement precise and easy. She mirrored him, matching him step for step, flourish for flourish.

But Urstadt did not have time for flourishes. Winter had placed the missile on the War Goddess's sling, but the five remaining attackers were practically on top of her.

Urstadt lunged at the psimancer, and quickly lost herself in the flurry of attacks, defenses, dodges, and feints that followed. Their movements were precise and purposeful as a dancer's. Urstadt had never met a person who moved the way this man did; she imagined, after a few moments of fighting, that she probably moved very much the same way. Their styles were different; where Urstadt went for the blunt blow when she could, he turned a twisting dodge into an almost impossible attack, contorting his body in a way she had never seen. He also used his surroundings, perhaps not better, but more creatively than she did. He launched himself against one of the smaller trebuchets, flipping over her while slipping a dagger from, Goddess, Urstadt didn't know, from *somewhere*, to throw it immediately at her when he landed. She deflected the blade with her glaive and charged, hoping to catch him off-guard, but he met her blow for blow.

The two of them *moved* as they fought, and Urstadt did all she could to direct the fight toward the War Goddess, where she could help Winter as quickly as possible, if she could ever free herself from this Nazaniin.

Nazaniin, and yet he seemed to not occupy himself at all with psimancy. Either he was *incredibly* good at hiding it, he was leaving it all to one of the other psimancers, or he had somehow run out of *faltira* or whatever other energy he needed to access the Void.

Blood trickled down Urstadt's side from her open wound. Her lungs would not last much longer, let alone her muscles. The Nazaniin stranger, too, seemed to favor one shoulder over the other. Every move she made screamed with agony, but this was what she had trained for. To outfight when she could, to outlast when she couldn't, and to outrun as a last resort. Every breath came as a struggle, a gasping wheeze from the pits of her lungs, but she fought through it all, darkness threatening the edges of her vision.

She and the Nazaniin warrior danced, twirled, and savagely attacked one another. Urstadt had learned a great deal about him during their short fight. His favored side, for one. His preference of finesse over strength, for another.

Strength was one of Urstadt's specialties.

In a final burst of power, Urstadt lunged at him, both hands on her glaive, ignoring the blade. She chose to do so at the exact moment his left side faced her, and in a surprising moment of weakness, the man crumbled beneath her. She was about to finish him off when he spun away. Urstadt stopped herself just in time to watch the Nazaniin impale one of Winter's attackers, who had turned from the War Goddess to rush at them instead.

Urstadt blinked, her breath leaking from her in ragged gasps.

"You…" she said, but could say nothing more. And, as she said it, another of the attackers turned on them, just as the man turned to look at Urstadt.

Hefting her glaive like a spear, Urstadt threw her weapon. It launched just over his shoulder, fingers away from his ear, and embedded itself in the chest of the other attacker.

The man looked back, then at Urstadt.

"You're… protecting her," he rasped.

Urstadt nodded, unable to form the energy to say anything else.

Without another word, they turned and took out two more soldiers advancing on the War Goddess.

Urstadt looked around for Winter, felt a moment of panic when she did not see the queen anywhere, but then she spotted the surviving attacker—who must be the psimancer, considering the weapons and debris still pitifully attempting to attack the trebuchet. She was climbing up the frame of the engine, toward the pivot.

Goddess, what was Winter doing up there?

But then Urstadt realized. The sling had been reattached to the trigger-hook. Winter had climbed up to buy herself time.

And to lure the last attacker onto the machine.

A slow, laborious cranking sound filled the air, and the

counterweight began to fall. The remaining psimancer woman realized this too late; she stood directly between the missile, slowly moving away from her now, and the counterweight, moving faster and faster down and through.

Several sounds at once assaulted Urstadt's ears. The deep *whumff* of the counterweight as it swung down and through the War Goddess's frame, followed immediately by a sickening *crunch* as it collided with the psimancer. The War Goddess's sling *snapped* as the missile launched high and far, toward Triah.

Then there was silence, and for a moment Urstadt wondered if she had gone deaf. The entire world seemed to stop as the missile sailed across the sky, almost disappearing.

Looking up at Winter, perched halfway up the frame of the War Goddess, Urstadt witnessed the exertion on the woman's face, the concentration, could almost see the sweat falling in great drops.

When Urstadt looked back to the city, she had lost track of the missile, until the bright, booming explosion erupted about two-thirds of the way up the tower of God's Eye.

Horror gripped Carrieri's heart as the trebuchet fired again.

"Should I give the order for the essential personnel to evacuate the Eye?" someone asked. He was not sure who.

"Yes," Carrieri whispered, knowing the order would come too late. Knowing that the people he'd already ordered to evacuate would likely not make it out in time, either.

It's too late, he thought.

It's too late.

Cinzia, Jane, and the other disciples rushed through the streets of Triah as quickly as they could. Few people had been injured by the impact at the manse, and other than consoling their hosts on the lost bell tower, there was not much to be done. At Jane's insistence, they headed toward the city center. On their way, the *crump* of another impact sent them diving for cover.

"Where did that strike?" Jane demanded, as they got to their feet again.

"Northwest of us, I think," Cinzia said. Goddess, why were they in the city when it was being *bombarded*, especially by something the size of that *monstrous* thing on the cliffs.

"You know the city," Jane said, her voice calm. "Think, Cinzia."

"I…" She met Jane's eyes. "Why do you want to know, sister? Surely we should get out of the city, back to the camp. Isn't our task to keep our people safe?"

"We should keep *all* people safe," Jane said. "We might be able to help, whatever is happening. Now, tell me. Where do you think it struck?"

Cinzia's cheeks burned. She knew her sister had not meant to shame her, surely.

"I think it fell close to the Coastal Road," she said. "I could not possibly say where exactly, but… maybe near the Fifteenth Circle?"

"Good enough," Jane said. "Take us there."

And that's where they'd been headed, when the third missile flashed above them, and slammed directly into God's Eye, not three circles away from where they stood.

Dark smoke poured from the side of God's Eye where the missile had struck, flames glowing brightly in contrast.

"It's still standing," Elessa whispered in awe.

"Thank the Goddess," someone else said.

"That's where we must go," Jane said. "Cinzia, quick! Lead us to that tower."

* * *

Terris knew where the projectile was headed the moment the massive trebuchet fired. The missile arced through the air at incredible speed, wavering slightly.

Anywhere from one to two thousand people occupied the tower of God's Eye at any given point in time; some worked or lived there, in the space leased by the city itself, while others—the Eye operators and military personal—worked there in a very different capacity. Civilians and senators often toured the structure, witnessing its grandeur and the apparatus at the top. And the fact that Carrieri thought it necessary to begin evacuating all but necessary personnel from God's Eye told Terris enough. An order that had just arrived only moments ago; too late, Terris realized, squinting, trying to discern the location of the projectile. It was impossible to truly tell where the trebuchet was pointed—it seemed to have hardly moved during the three launches, but each missile clearly struck a different location in the city—but as Terris looked up at the beastly machine before the third launch, he could have sworn to the Goddess it had been aimed directly at him. Not just the tower, but *him*.

A small sigh of surprise escaped his lips as he realized his legs were wet and warm.

He would have thought time would stretch at this moment, that he might see his life flash before his eyes, or think of the people he cared about most, and how if he'd lived differently he might not be a lonely old man, obsessed with his work, or wish that Hindra were not here so that she could live to be with her husband and children, but those thoughts were only the thinnest of shades in his mind as the missile streaked silently toward them.

An incredible crash and roar broke the world of silence. The stones beneath Terris's feet shook with such violence he felt it in his chest, in his testicles, in his throat.

As Terris came to, he realized he was lying prostrate on the floor. Scrabbling about, he grasped a brass ring of the Eye's apparatus, and hauled himself up. As he did so, a ringing in his ears he hadn't realized was there began to fade, and in its place he heard nothing but screams. Hindra, wide-eyed, crawled toward him. General Marshton lay with his back against another brass section of the apparatus, half seated, half lying down, bellowing at the top of his lungs, his eyes unblinking as they stared out at nothing. Other officers and aides screamed, and above it all, Terris's nose caught the whiff of something burning.

No.

Terris took a tentative step, afraid the entire floor, the entire tower, might buckle beneath him. But his left foot found purchase and stayed, and as he stepped with his right, he felt more solid. The impact had caused the tower to shudder violently, and while that initial quaking had stopped, Terris could not help but think the building still wavered, still trembled, almost imperceptibly. It took him far longer than he liked to finally make it to the ramparts.

"Terris!" Hindra called. "What are you doing?"

"I have to see the damage," Terris said, but the words came out in a whisper, and he knew they would not reach Hindra, not above the people still moaning and screaming, not above the dull roar of fire below them.

"You'll fall!" Hindra shouted.

Goddess, were his hands trembling that much, or was it the building itself?

His legs and hips hugged stone. He sucked air through his teeth as he leaned forward until his eyes barely peeked over the edge of the ramparts and down, down, down the tower to the city directly below.

This used to be a rite of passage. Young operators would

come out here the first night they were assigned to the Eye, to look out over the city they had sworn to protect. *I did this, once. Hindra, too.* He remembered her laughing when he told her how he had done it, too. How funny she found that.

It was difficult to see exactly what was happening. Smoke poured up toward him from the tower below. His lungs hacked, rejecting the haze. Beyond the smoke, bright flames licked the side of the tower—perhaps around the thirty-seventh, maybe the fortieth floor—and chunks of stone were falling, falling, falling the many stories down to the city below. The shot must have been filled with explosives, Terris realized. A simple boulder would never cause fire like this.

"Terris, get down from there, please!"

Terris listened to Hindra this time, and edged backwards.

"Are you two coming?"

Terris and Hindra looked up to see General Marshton had recovered himself. Every hint of his former terror was gone.

"Where—?"

"We're descending the tower, getting out of here before the whole thing topples."

We won't be able to, Terris thought, *not if that fire reached the tower's core.* But he and Hindra followed Marshton and his entourage anyway. They stumbled into the stairwell, running into the back of the general as he skidded to a halt.

The other officers and aides had stopped at the platform at the top of the stairs, all of them looking down, faces pale but the horror on them accented by a faint, flickering orange glow.

When Terris moved to the railing, he saw the fire. It was about ten flights down, and slowly licking its way up. Glowing orange-yellow embers burned where the flames were hottest, and blazing timbers and red-hot chunks of masonry toppled down the open spiral staircase at irregular intervals.

Smoke stung his eyes, and the smell of it was strangely chemical, somehow more toxic and irritating to his nose, eyes, and throat than typical woodsmoke.

"We're trapped!" one of the aides shouted. Someone else cried heavy shaking sobs.

"Oh Goddess, oh Goddess, oh Goddess…"

General Marshton's commanding presence once again deflated as he stared blankly at the impassable staircase below them. Terris saw Hindra blinking back tears, and took her hand. She looked at him, surprised but grateful, and squeezed his hand in return.

The entire tower shuddered, and Terris's stomach leapt into his throat. He felt as if he'd dropped a full two or three rods. He felt as if—

He had no time to think about what he felt like next, as the floor gave way beneath him, and he found himself falling, gripping Hindra's hand and falling, amidst stone and metal and debris and fire and smoke and awful, awful terror.

The trebuchet had already fired twice by the time Knot reached it. Knot had only confirmed Winter's presence with the tiellans two days ago, but based on what he'd heard of the Chaos Queen, what he'd seen of Winter in his vision, she had to be behind the war machine.

The first two missiles had both landed in the city, on seemingly inconsequential targets. Why use such a weapon if she couldn't control it? Why risk innocent lives?

Hadn't Winter learned her lesson from Navone?

But now he watched the third projectile sail toward the city. A weary hollowness grew within him when it slammed into God's

Eye, three-quarters of the way up the tower, in a burst of fire and debris.

Knot was surprised that the tower still stood. Whether or not it would remain that way for long he could not say, but there was a chance it might not fall. Goddess, how he hoped the tower wouldn't fall.

Winter was perched halfway up the frame of the big trebuchet. She remained there, gripping the wooden frame, the wind blowing stray strands of hair across her face.

She looks different, Knot thought. *She is different.*

Winter looked down. Their eyes met, but Winter showed no surprise, no anger, no joy. None of the emotions Knot had suspected. Instead, only sadness.

Knot heard a gasp behind him, followed by a distant rumbling, and turned.

Cinzia had not led the others very far when she heard a loud *crack*, followed by a low rumble. She stopped in her tracks, looking up at God's Eye, towering above her now, high above the other buildings around them.

The sounds were this: another crack, and then a series of them, moving progressively faster, closer together, louder and louder and more jumbled and becoming more and more a single, steady, ominous roar.

The sight was this: God's Eye, standing tall, a burning, gaping, smoking wound on its side in one moment, and then what appeared to be a cloud of dust and smoke circling upward, all around the very top floors of the tower. That cloud of dust descended, slowly at first, but picking up speed, and as it descended Cinzia realized the entire tower was falling with it. She watched God's Eye crumble to the ground, and she stood only a few hundred rods away.

Her reaction was this: Cinzia turned and ran. She grabbed Jane's hand and tugged her sister along with all her might, grabbed Ocrestia's hand, too. She screamed for everyone to *run* at the top of her lungs, and thank the Goddess they obeyed her for once, or they obeyed their instincts, because it was all Cinzia could do to keep control of her feet as they sprinted wildly away from the destruction. As they ran and as the tower collapsed behind them, a dark, billowing cloud of dust and debris pursued them, and soon Cinzia and all of the disciples and Prelates were encompassed by the dark. Grit dug into her eyes, Cinzia coughed in the thick haze, but she still ran, pressing on and on until she was free of the cloud, and out in the daylight once more.

A terrible, hacking cough folded her in half. Her dress, once a soft teal, was completely gray, caked in a thick layer of dust and ash. When she could finally stand, she saw the others looked the same, completely gray from head to toe.

"Is everyone all right?" Jane shouted, and the disciples began to respond. Eward helped Elessa up from the ground. He was nothing but a gray man with a small patch of pink on one cheek.

The dust cloud loomed, still thick and musty but slowly, slowly clearing. Above, Cinzia saw blue sky, and nothing, nothing at all, where God's Eye had once stood.

On the bow of the *Reckoner*, Cova stood watching the Triahn skyline. At first she'd found herself quite bored; a large trebuchet hurled missiles at the city, but it seemed to be firing quite slowly, and not hitting any targets worth noting. The third missile, however, had been different.

Cova gasped in shock as a great cloud of fire and smoke erupted from the side of God's Eye. She'd felt a sick sense of terror, at first, but beneath that a low thrill.

This was what Winter had promised her. This was what she and her fleet had waited for.

She wondered why it felt so much like a defeat.

Cova's shock turned to horror when the upper levels dissolved in a cloud of smoke, collapsing downward into the levels below them. One floor collapsed into another, and those two into the next, and this continued in an increasingly rapid chain reaction until the entire tower rushed down on itself, like a spring recoiling, but recoiling infinitely, losing all of its energy until it recoiled into nothing at all. A cloud of dust and debris belched forth through the streets of Triah, originating at the tower's base. The black, billowing monster, waves of dust and smoke and ash and rock and terror building and building upon itself, growing and spurting outward, hunting through the streets, seeking and annihilating everything in its path. Jetting from the collapsing tower like fire from the mouth of a dragon from the Age of Marvels.

She could not help but wonder how many people had been in that tower when it fell, and how many people the collapse crushed on the ground. She could not imagine the casualties.

And, most of them, she had to imagine, were civilian.

"What have we done?" Cova asked out loud, her voice seeming far too small against the lap of the ocean on the hull, the call of seagulls in the distance, and the low rumbling sound that sent a chill down her spine as it reached them, moments after the tower had actually fallen.

"We did not do this, Your Grace," Andia said. "The blood shed here—"

"It is as much on our hands as it is anyone's," Cova snapped.

But is this not what you wanted? You came here to conquer Khale. Conquering inevitably means casualties, sacrifices made.

"Not like this," Cova said aloud.

As the smoky haze cleared, Cova saw Triah's skyline, starkly different for the absence of what had once been the tallest tower the Sfaera had ever seen.

"What are your orders, Your Grace?" Admiral Rakkar asked beside her.

Cova wiped her cheeks, noticing for the first time the tears streaming down them. She cleared her throat, and took a few deep breaths to dispel the heavy pit in her stomach. She wanted to double over and vomit, and not because she was seasick.

They had come all this way. She could bring her forces back to Roden now, without doing what they came here to do. She could not tell her Ruling Council that she had looked victory in the face, and given it up.

The deep breaths did not help.

Ruling Council be damned. She was an Empress, and she would not act unless she was sure it was the best course.

"For now," Cova said, her breath catching, "we wait."

Carrieri's right palm pressed against the glass of the western window of the Merchant's Tower. His fingers flexed and strained, as if trying to break their way out.

Dust, smoke, and ash spilled upward into the air, a sickening contrast to the beautiful, bright blue autumn day. Not a cloud in the sky, but plenty on the ground.

"Illaran?" Carrieri asked, his voice hoarse.

When the man did not respond, Carrieri turned to face the Nazaniin.

Illaran stood behind Carrieri and to the right, staring out the window, his face so pale it could have passed for bone.

"*Illaran.*"

The Nazaniin started, his eyes slowly shifting toward Carrieri.

"Sir…"

"What of the black offensive?"

"I have no contact with them."

"What was your last report?"

"That they had found the Chaos Queen, and were converging on her position. That was before the trebuchet fired the last round."

And no contact since. They were dead, almost certainly. Captured in a best-case scenario, but Carrieri had not seen a best-case scenario in far too long.

"The Hood Regiment?" Carrieri asked.

"They are still engaged with the tiellan force," the man said slowly, "but they say the battle stopped for a full minute, between when the Eye was struck and when it collapsed."

"Is the trebuchet reloading?" Carrieri asked. Without the black offensive's eyes, the Hood Regiment offered his best intel on the weapon.

Silence. Carrieri looked back at the psimancer, annoyed, but the man's eyes were wide.

What now?

"The war machine has been disabled. Or perhaps destroyed, they cannot be certain, but it does not appear the weapon will fire again."

Carrieri blinked in disbelief. His men murmured excitedly.

"Say that again."

"The war machine has been disabled," the psimancer said, more confidently this time.

"By whom?"

"They think it might have been the tiellans themselves," the psimancer said slowly. "They say the sling and reloading mechanism have been removed, and the arm is about to be detached from the frame. They can see it happening."

Carrieri turned on his heel and walked quickly to the northern windows. Sure enough, as he looked up at the cliffs, the arm wobbled on the trebuchet's frame.

He allowed himself one short, wretched sigh of relief.

"And the battle with the tiellans?"

"The regiment has sustained minimal casualties, but has not gained any ground."

"Order the retreat," Carrieri said immediately, his mind made up. Enough blood had been shed today. With the Eye down, a larger foe was on the horizon.

"Are you sure, Grand Marshal?"

Carrieri could feel the tensity thick in the air around him. The viscous confusion. His men wanted revenge for what had just happened, Carrieri understood that. But they would not get it now. Not with such a small skirmish, that had accomplished so little. Not when the Chaos Queen herself could turn her attention to the battle, now, and slaughter every last Legionary on that cliff.

"Order the retreat," Carrieri repeated, calm leaking from him far too rapidly for his liking. "Man our ships, get them battle-ready. Man the…"The thought made him sick. "Man the war machines along the sea wall. Keep an eye on the tiellans on the cliffs, be prepared for any advance on their part, but now that the Eye is gone, the main threat is Roden."

Carrieri's throat caught, as the full weight of what he had just witnessed crashed down on him. The people who had been killed. What the entire city must have witnessed. The fear that surely roiled in the heart of every Triahn citizen.

"We fight the battles that need to be fought today," Carrieri's voice was firm. "We have a city to defend. After that…"

Carrieri turned to face everyone in the room: his advisors,

his aides, his lieutenants, the psimancers. "After that," he said, "we must... we *must*..." They must what? Respond? Retaliate? What in Oblivion sort of response did this situation call for?

"Rebuild," Carrieri finally said.

Because he'd be damned, he'd be damned to Oblivion a thousand times, if he let the tiellans defeat them like this.

Winter leapt down the last few rods, landing easily on the long grass. As she stood, three *tendra* snaked out behind her, each carrying a blade. One snaked to the War Goddess's sling, severing the thick rope from the beam. The other two sought the ropes holding the counterweight, slicing each load-bearing cord. The counterweight fell to the ground with an earth-shattering crash of splintering wood and cracking stone.

But Winter did not care about any of that, because she was already rushing to meet him, as fast as her feet would carry her.

She had seen him the moment she loosed the third shot from the War Goddess. She had sensed him before she saw him, on the lower edges of her vision, standing on the grass looking up at her. There was no explanation, no logic behind her thoughts, only feeling. How was he alive? How was he *here*? And, in all Oblivion, why *now*?

But here he was, nevertheless, and Winter could not stop the flood of emotions that bubbled up from her. For the first time since Eranda's death, she found herself sobbing as she launched herself into his arms.

Knot wrapped his arms around her as she barreled into him, but Winter immediately sensed his caution. And why wouldn't he be cautious? He had just seen her kill hundreds, perhaps thousands of people. Winter could not pretend the blame lay with anyone else; she did not *want* to pretend the blame lay with anyone else. She had done what she had done. Reasons and costs aside, Chaos and prophecies and Nine Daemons aside, *she* had done it.

She also knew Knot couldn't possibly see things that way, at least not now. And even if she explained everything to him, he might never forgive her.

But that was a conversation for another time, Winter had to remind herself. That time was not *now*.

Slowly they separated, standing awkwardly at arm's length.

This time, she was glad he did not kiss her. She remembered wishing he would, when they were together in Navone and Roden, but things were different, now. Goddess, *she* was different, now.

"I thought you were dead," Winter said.

Knot cocked his head to the side, and Winter caught a hint of quizzicality. "Thought the same thing about you. Up until… a while ago."

A while? Winter wondered what that meant, but dared not ask.

Winter shook her head, still in disbelief that this was real. Still in shock that Knot was standing before her. And, eclipsing those two sentiments, the ever-growing horror.

I thought I was alone, this whole time. I thought he was gone, I…

If she'd known he was alive, she might not have *survived*. She might have waited for him to rescue her from that cell in Roden, waiting for a man who didn't even know she was there…

"So… what do we do now?" Winter asked.

Knot closed his eyes, and for a moment Winter wondered whether he would respond at all.

"Don't know, darlin'," he said quietly. "But we've got a lot to talk about."

34

"WE HAVE TO GET out of here," Elessa said, pointing east, toward the Odenite camp. Dark rain clouds—so different from the horrible mass that had come from the Eye, and yet so similar in appearance—continued to roll across the sky, and Cinzia felt the first few drops of rain fall on her skin. The water was cold, even through the layers of dust that caked her. "We have spent far too long in this city already. It's too dangerous. We cannot risk our lives—we cannot risk *your* life, Jane."

Jane had been silent since they had run together from the oncoming dust cloud. That silence continued, as Jane stared intently at the ground.

"Is she all right?" Lucia asked.

Cinzia had her eyes trained on her sister. What would Jane have them do this time? Where would her sister's visions, or whatever they were, lead them after this?

A film of gray dust still covered all of them, even after vigorous brushing and patting. They stood huddled at the side of the road; people had been running back and forth along the street—away from the collapse of the Eye—generally ignoring their group. Eward and his Prelates stood forming a loose circle around the disciples, but their protection was largely unnecessary. There were much more important things for everyone else to focus on right now.

There were much more important things for them to focus on, too, Cinzia realized.

Seeing the fall of the Eye, the collapse of the tower and the falling debris and raging cloud of destruction and choking horror, a single image had come to Cinzia's mind.

Herself, on a rooftop in Roden, snow falling gently all around her, as she looked up at the sky and suddenly, unbidden, without requirement or prerequisite, had felt love.

She did not know what that experience meant anymore, not in the grand scheme of things. She was no longer even sure the love she had felt that day had come from a conscious being at all, let alone a goddess named Canta.

But she had felt it. The cause now blurred in her mind, but the feeling rang out clear like a morning bell.

She had felt love when she did not think she deserved it— when she needed it most, though she did not even know of that need at the time. It had been a tender mercy, a tiny salvation.

What if the disciples of Canta's Church could provide that, even to the smallest extent, now?

"We have to go back," Cinzia said. The rain fell faster, the drops increasing in size, pattering loudly into the city around them.

The other disciples, already engaged in a discussion on how best to get out of the city, all turned to look at Cinzia, dumbfounded.

"We have to go back and help," Cinzia repeated, this time with more confidence. The more she spoke, the more she felt the truth and power behind her words. "Many of us have healed others before."

You've only done it once, though, haven't you? a voice whispered in Cinzia's ear. For a brief moment Cinzia felt a very different sense of panic that threatened to overwhelm her. The voice, while Cinzia was *mostly* sure came from her own mind, had just the faintest echo of Luceraf's low, soothing tones.

"Many of us have healed," Cinzia repeated, shutting her eyes tightly, trying to focus her thoughts. Another roll of thunder in the distance, and Cinzia's eyes snapped open, fear enveloping her once more.

"And there is no more important time than now to offer that healing." Cinzia put a hand on Jane's arm. "We *must* go back."

As if Cinzia's touch awakened something in her, Jane looked up. "We must go back," she said.

A spark of hope awakened within Cinzia. The other disciples, who had been skeptical at Cinzia's words, now looked at Jane. Then, one by one, they all began to nod.

Eward looked at her, eyes widening in exasperation. *We cannot afford to go back,* Cinzia imagined him saying.

Cinzia moved to her brother, her head close to his. "We must do this, Eward," Cinzia said. She could not tell him to have faith; she was not even sure she knew what that was anymore. She could not tell him to trust in Canta; she did not know what that meant herself. "It is the right thing to do," Cinzia finally said. It was not eloquent, it was not complicated, but it was a truth Cinzia knew in her heart.

Eward looked like he was about to protest, but Jane and the other disciples were already backtracking toward the center of the catastrophe. With a helpless shrug, Eward gave in.

"Very well," he said. "I hope you are right, Cinzia."

If there was a place worse than Oblivion, Cinzia witnessed it on the trek back to the site of the tower's destruction. The malicious mass of dust and dirt stained everything. Black, muddy sludge covered the streets, beginning to run with the rainfall; the walls were an ugly gray. The air itself blurred brown everywhere Cinzia looked, and worst of all were the people, limping or crawling or prostrate or unmoving, covered in muck.

Corpses appeared far earlier than Cinzia expected, but among the dead were the wounded, too, and the able-bodied fleeing, or mourning, or wandering as they stared up or down or all around them with eyes incompatible with the chaos, death, and horror around them.

They came upon a young woman choking in the mud. She was struggling to stand, but her leg was broken. Elessa stopped at her side and laid her hands on the woman's broken leg. Her fingers crackled with energy and light. Cinzia felt the energy of it, the passing of something from Elessa to the woman, the gift of life and hope in the midst of death and tragedy, a gift not understood in a moment but understood in a lifetime. And with that first gift, a portion of Cinzia changed into something it was not before, the smallest parting of a curtain to allow entry for a streak of sunlight, stirring up dust, piercing through darkness.

The smile that formed on the young woman's lips was like the slow spread of watercolor on paper; it broadened and deepened into an expression of pure joy. She stood with Elessa's help, taking a few tentative steps. Her eyes widened in shock and she embraced Elessa impulsively.

The disciples were not the only witnesses to the healing. There were dozens of people in the street: the walking wounded and their rescuers, and others escaping the wreckage. But everyone slowed and stared as Elessa and the young woman embraced, as if drawn by an invisible thread.

As Cinzia took in the scene, she saw Ocrestia approach a middle-aged couple. The woman was helping the man to limp away from the disaster zone. Cinzia caught the shock on his face when he saw the tiellan disciple, with just a hint of disgust. For a moment she thought he would push Ocrestia out of the way, but the tiellan instead spoke to the woman, who indicated an area around the man's ribs, blood darkened by gray grime.

Ocrestia placed her hands at the wound, mouth moving as she did so. When she lifted her hands, the blood remained on the clothing, but the man's expression of thinly veiled hatred had turned to one of shock. He burst into tears, thanking Ocrestia, over and over again.

Cinzia felt a tight grip on her shoulder. "You were right, sister," Jane whispered in her ear. "*Thank you,* for doing what I could not."

Before Cinzia could respond, her sister moved to a group of people clustered statuelike around a small form on the ground, a man crying beside it. As she followed her sister, she saw it was a small boy.

One of them, a woman, held a hand up to Jane as she shook her head—the boy was dead. But Jane took the young woman's hand in her own, and the woman's face crumpled as she, too, began to weep, and let Jane through to the child's body.

She knelt beside the father at the center of the group, placing a hand on his shoulder, and inspected the boy.

He is dead, Cinzia thought. *We cannot heal the dead.*

But Jane placed her hands on the boy's head, whispered words rising from her ash-gray lips, up into the storm. The small crowd was perfectly still, as if they all took a collective breath and held it. Even the wind and rain faded to stillness.

When the rain resumed, and the breeze continued, once again heedless of the destruction and sorrow it passed through and around, Jane stood.

And with her, the boy.

The young father embraced his child with a sob, and the

other adults stared at Jane, the whites of their eyes wide and contrasting starkly with the grimy grayness of their faces.

Who says what we can and cannot do?

Tears streamed down Jane's face. "We will help all we can," she said, looking at each of her disciples. Her gaze rested on Cinzia. "We will *heal* all we can. We are Canta's disciples. We are Her servants, and we carry with us her power. We will be instruments in Her hands to alleviate this tragedy."

A warm feeling blossomed in Cinzia's chest as her sister spoke—a warmth she had not felt in a long, long time.

The next hour passed as if Cinzia walked through a dream. Each of the disciples healed in turn—broken limbs, bloody wounds, terrible hacking, choking coughs, all were made whole—and Cinzia found herself healing among them.

She did not question it, nor did she question herself. She tentatively placed her hands on the back of a man who lay broken on the ground; whether he had been broken by debris or somehow, miraculously, survived the fall from the Eye, Cinzia could not say, but his legs bent unnaturally beneath him, and when she asked if he could move, he said he could not.

This is not right, Cinzia thought to herself with sadness, horror, and overwhelming confusion at the tragedy before her. Not just the broken man, but all of it. Such healing should not be necessary, because such tragedy should never exist in the first place.

But, if she could help, she would. She could think about the logistics of it—about whether she even believed in a Goddess anymore, and whether that should affect her ability to heal—much later. For now, there was no option but for a Goddess to exist in the face of such tragedy. If there was not a power to alleviate this pain, then there was no hope at all.

Much, much later, she would question this line of thinking. She would wonder how a Goddess could exist at all in the face of such tragedy; the polarized nature of these thoughts would not escape her, and would only compound her confusion, frustration, and doubt.

But, for now, by some miracle, Cinzia placed her hands on the next broken man before her. His eyes flickered as she touched him. She focused on his wounds, and the sudden swelling of light that poured forth from her and into him.

The man shifted beneath Cinzia's hands, his legs twitching and moving, and when Cinzia looked at them directly she saw they were no longer twisted and broken. He used those legs, and Cinzia's shoulder, to help himself up, staring at his healed body in shock. Tears streamed down his face, making paths in the grime, and Cinzia realized she was crying too.

How could Canta, if She was indeed the power that caused this, use her as an instrument? Cinzia had been a Daemon's avatar; even now, she still questioned Canta's very existence. How could she be trusted with this power, wherever it came from?

Whatever power this is, Cinzia realized, *it must be good. It cannot be anything else.*

Cinzia and the others finally made it to Sky Plaza, but the location was completely unrecognizable. God's Eye, the Four Pillars, and the entire grounds around the structures were nothing but rubble, now. The only remnant of God's Eye was a broken ruin, pitifully small, jutting up out of the desolate mass. A gaping wound. Everything else was shattered stone, wood, and iron.

Senate apartments, housing the senators, their families and aides, had once surrounded the Eye, but entire swaths of those apartment buildings were gone, disintegrated by the tower's collapse.

The rain fell steadily, muffling the cries of the wounded and mourning. Cinzia caught the sharp whiff of smoke and fire and burning wood and stone through the dull smell of wet stone.

She glanced behind her. Jane and the other disciples stood with her, and just behind them, Eward and his Prelates. But, to Cinzia's surprise, behind the Prelates was another group. Cinzia recognized in it the man she had just healed, as well as the young woman Elessa had mended, and the many others the disciples had healed on the way along their trek toward the broken tower. Dozens of people, following behind them, looking up at them—looking up at Jane—expectantly.

Goddess, what can we possibly do for them? Healing the body was one thing. As someone trained in medicine at the seminary, Cinzia knew this. But healing the mind, the soul, was another thing entirely.

It did not take long for it to become clear that people were trapped beneath the rubble. Some of the shouts and moans came from within the rubble itself, and people immediately turned to Jane and the Disciples for help.

Cinzia turned to the Prelates, looking for Eward. When he met her eyes, she nodded to the group that had formed behind them.

"Organize them into groups that can start picking through and moving the debris. We must find as many of the people trapped down there as we possibly can."

Hours passed. The Triahn City Watch showed up, helping where they could. They looked at Jane and the disciples dubiously at first, but soon recognized the good they were doing—and the miracles they performed—and did all they could to help.

Legionaries joined them, adding their strength to the people clearing wreckage and debris, making space for both healers and doctors to help the wounded.

The Denomination arrived, too, with priestesses by the dozen ready to offer medical assistance and Goddessguards and Sons of Canta ready to help move bodies, rubble, and the injured when possible.

Cinzia had never thought of Triah as particularly welcoming, let alone a place where the people actually cared about one another. But here the City Watch, the Legion, priestesses, Odenites, Goddessguards and Sons of Canta labored alongside civilians, all looking to clear the rubble and help where they could. More than one Cantic priestess gasped at the miracles wrought by the disciples.

Senators even showed up, helping where they could. They all worked long into the evening, and as the storm above passed and night began to fall, one of the senators, someone Cinzia did not recognize, gave a speech about how this would band them together, about how this was why the Parliament had been formed, because contrary to the old monarchies and empires, Khale believed every life had value, and they would work and rescue and heal all they could.

The senator did not speak of the city's attackers, Winter and her tiellan army; Cinzia could understand why. There were many tiellan citizens in Triah. They worked alongside the humans to clear rubble at the disaster site, and their kind were also among the injured, dead, and dying.

The speech ended, but Cinzia hardly noticed. She had spent much of her energy healing another young girl, and quite suddenly a wave of exhaustion washed over her. She felt as if the muscles in her limbs had gone completely limp, and her bones themselves no longer had the strength to support her weight. She wasn't sure how many people she had healed that day—perhaps a dozen, maybe a few more—and she wondered how in the Sfaera she would manage to get back to the Odenite camp at this point.

"I've got you, sister."

Cinzia looked over to see Eward, a sad smile on his face, on one side of her, and another Prelate on her other side.

"I can handle myself, Eward," Cinzia said, between deep, ragged breaths. "See to Jane."

"Jane is fine, believe it or not," Eward said. "She is still healing people. Raising some from the dead, if you can believe it. But the disciples are collapsing."

Cinzia looked around and saw he was right. A Prelate was helping Ocrestia move slowly along, her body heavily supported by his arm around her waist and hers over his shoulders. Two more Prelates carried Elessa, lying prone on an impromptu stretcher.

"Is she—"

"Exhausted, and she'll need a great deal of rest. I imagine you all will. But they say she'll be fine."

"Eward—"

"I know, Cinzi. It's all right."

"Thank you, Eward." Cinzia could not bring herself to say anything else; the exhaustion bit deep, and she feared if she began sobbing she might actually use up what little remaining energy she had and die right there on the spot.

Her brother helped her move away as she faded in and out of consciousness.

35

"You went to Sky Plaza yesterday."

Code nodded, standing at attention. Kosarin faced him from across the great table at the center of the Heart of the Void.

"I did," Code said. After the Eye fell, he'd spent the entire day at Sky Plaza, recovering the injured and dead, clearing the rubble—both of which it seemed they had only faintly scratched the surface of.

And you weren't there, Code wanted to say. He refrained— Kosarin was his superior, after all.

"I trust you didn't use psimancy to help?"

"Of course not, sir." The Nazaniin were forbidden to use their powers for public use—for money or otherwise. But helping yesterday, Code had seriously thought about forgetting that rule completely. His telenic *tendra* could lift far more and far heavier things than he ever could on his own. If the Nazaniin donated a dozen telenics to the clean-up effort, it might only take months instead of years.

Code shivered. Years, months, all of those terms were meaningless. The fall of the Eye had changed everything. The next moment would come if they all survived this one. Code would go back to Sky Plaza again today, damn whatever it was Kosarin was about to say.

Which is why what Kosarin said next surprised Code so much.

"Good," Kosarin said, nodding. He finally saluted Code in return, and Code stood at ease. Kosarin slumped down in a chair at the large table. "That is good work you are doing," Kosarin said. "And I think you should keep doing it. I'll send some other Nazaniin to Sky Plaza today, and release all Citadel students from their classes and nonessential duties so they can help with the effort. We need solidarity more than anything else at a time like this."

Code tried to keep his shock under control. The old man could still surprise him, apparently.

"You understand that you still cannot use psimancy to help?"

Code managed a nod. "Yes, sir." The fact that Kosarin was willing to spare anyone at all was a miracle; he'd take what he could get.

Silence rested between them, and Code was about to ask Kosarin's permission to go when the Triadin spoke up again.

"While you're down there," Kosarin said, his eyes meeting Code's, "I have a small mission for you."

Code cleared his throat, willing himself to stop the frown that tugged at the corners of his mouth.

A small mission. Of course there was something.

"What is it, sir?"

"It won't interfere with your clean-up; in fact, it should go right along with it," Kosarin said slowly. "A *rihnemin* powered the Eye. One of the smallest *rihnemin* on record, but one of the only stones that had proved to exert power—until the Chaos Queen came around."

Code had suspected as much. Rumors circulated through the Nazaniin—especially since the Eye had demonstrated its power, in a relatively cloudy sky, no less—of what exactly it was that powered the weapon.

A part of him wanted to refuse Kosarin's order outright. Code was helping at Sky Plaza because people needed him— not because there was something to be gained.

"You think me callous," Kosarin said. Before Code could respond, he continued, "You may be right. But I will tell you one thing: we cannot let that *rihnemin* fall into the hands of the Cordier woman. Carrieri may have lost his edge, but removing all the *rihnemin* from the area was not a mistake. We must keep this artifact safe from the Chaos Queen until we can find a new home for it, or rebuild the Eye."

Code hated to admit it, but Kosarin had a point. Everyone in the Nazaniin had heard about what Winter did at the battle against the Daemon Mefiston; after what she had done to the Eye with nothing more than a big trebuchet, he did not want to see her get her hands on another *rihnemin*.

"And take the couple from Maven Kol with you," Kosarin said, waving his hand. "What are their names? Alain and Morayne?"

Code's eyes narrowed. "*You* sent for them."

Kosarin nodded. "Of course I did. The world is collapsing, Code, if you haven't noticed, and it's collapsing on *Triah*. We need as much power here as we can muster."

Code masked his anger as best he could. "Why not send for them in your own name? Or ask me to do so?"

"I was not sure they would respond to my summons," Kosarin said. "And I know you are fond of them, Code. You are a good agent, and a powerful psimancer, but emotion tends to cloud your judgment."

Inside, Code was boiling with rage. *So you went behind my back, deceiving all of us. Just to get your way.*

Code was under no illusions. Kosarin was the Venerato of the Citadel, the Triadin of the Nazaniin. He was one of the most powerful men in the world, and Code happened to work for him. For all Code knew, Kosarin was delving him right now, perceiving his every thought. His thoughts he could more or less keep in check, but he could not mask the anger seething beneath the surface.

"Very well, I'll take them," Code said, forcing a smile. "Next time, sir, do me a favor and just ask me first. I'm a Nazaniin, after all. I'll obey orders."

Kosarin smiled, his blue eyes twinkling. "Yes, Code," he said. "I have no doubt you will."

Sky Plaza had become a tomb, and Code, Morayne, and Alain helped to excavate it. The sheer immensity and force of the debris as the Eye collapsed had blown away the four smaller towers around it, and a large portion of the other closest buildings; only skeletal ruins remained; broken walls, defeated but still reaching upward; cracked foundations beneath mounds of crumbled stone, melted metal, and splintered, charred wood.

The destruction twisted Code's gut in on itself, as if his insides had turned to stone and now ground continually against themselves. The sick feeling had made it almost impossible to move, let alone help, yesterday when he'd arrived at the plaza shortly after the fall. Today, the sick feeling seemed partially alleviated, but Code hated the great, gaping emptiness that took its place even more.

He could not believe this had happened. And yet it had. He could not believe someone would do this, and yet someone had.

In a way, the impossible work of cleaning up was a welcome distraction from the thoughts that otherwise threatened to overwhelm.

They assisted all day long at Sky Plaza, lifting rubble, dealing with yet another unidentified, and often unidentifiable, corpse. Code wasn't sure what was worse: finding them individually, dead and alone, or in groups, dead and together. No more survivors had been found, and a feeling echoed around the plaza that they had likely found their last. They could not hear anyone shouting for help, and were rapidly approaching the point at which a person could no longer survive without water.

But retrieving the sunstone, however, was not as difficult as Code would have feared. As the sun sank lower in the sky, people began to return to their homes. By nightfall, only a few other people remained besides the three of them. And, by midnight, Code—with his gilded dragon piece—had made sure they were the only ones around.

Morayne's ability to move earth certainly helped in the search, as did Code's telesis, but what helped more than anything was the *tug* Code felt shortly after he took *faltira*, just as they began the search. As if something in the debris called to him, sought him out.

The pull made Code uncomfortable. He had ascended the Eye numerous times, and never remembered feeling anything like that tug. But he followed it anyway, and sure enough after a few moments, with their combined powers, they had unearthed a rune-covered amber stone from the rubble.

"That can't be it," Code said, staring at the thing. But this fit the description Kosarin had given: an amber stone just larger than a human head, covered in runes, and unexpectedly light. Very different from every other *rihnemin* Code had ever seen.

"What a strange thing," Morayne said, her eyes wide. Code wasn't sure, but he thought he saw the stone glow faintly as she regarded it.

"And now what?" Alain asked. "We take it back to your

superior? The one who summoned us here?"

Code scoffed. "Not a chance."

Arro had sparked something in him, and that spark had become a fire in Mavenil. After returning to Triah, that fire consumed him. There were things in this world that mattered more than the coin and power he got from the Nazaniin.

He'd watched the Odenites, Cinzia among them, heal countless people over the last few days. He'd even seen them raise a few people from the *dead*, for Canta's sake. Those actions stood in stark contrast to Kosarin's orders, and Kosarin's deceit.

Code was nothing but a tool for Kosarin; Alain and Morayne had now become tools in that bastard's hands, too. And while Code agreed that he didn't want the Chaos Queen getting a hold of a *rihnemin*, he had also realized, as he walked to Sky Plaza that day, that he didn't want Kosarin's hands on it, either.

"If we're not going to give it to him, then what are we going to...?" Alain's voice trailed off, and Code turned to see his friend glowering at three newcomers in Sky Plaza: a full *cotir*, approaching from the south. Code knew them well: Anthris, a lanky young woman, an acumen; Tarbin, the telenic, a thickly muscled man; and Methasticah, an elderly voyant, and one of the first psimancers on record in recent history. This *cotir*, in particular, was known for completing many of Kosarin's personal, most secret assignments. Which, more often than not, included hefty dirty work.

Code could hold his own against any one of them individually, but he knew he couldn't possibly take them all at once.

"Code..."

Glancing at Alain, Code saw sparks dancing around the man. He cursed. The last thing they needed was another explosion in Sky Plaza.

"Keep calm," Code said, speaking low and smoothly, "and

let me handle this."

If it came to a fight, he feared his friends would have no choice but to step in. But he hoped to avoid that.

"Give the stone to us, Code," Tarbin said, stepping forward.

"Afraid not," Code said, flashing his most winning grin back at them. "I'm under Kosarin's orders, you see, to bring it back to him. That's what my friends and I were just about to do before your little interruption."

"We know you weren't going to take the stone back, lad," Methasticah said, his voice high and jittery. "And Kosarin knew it, too. That's why he sent us."

Code looked down at the sunstone, teeth clenched through his smile. "You know, I haven't heard anything about passing the stone on to anyone else." *There are things more important than coin and power from the Nazaniin.* "But if you want it that badly, I'd be happy to hand it over."

With a grin of his own, Tarbin stepped forward, but Code continued. "*If* you let my friends and me go." He realized he didn't have much to bargain with, but he needed to at least make the appearance that he did.

Unfortunately, Tarbin's response was a soft chuckle, which didn't help their chances.

"Can't really grant you that either, I'm afraid. We need those two," he said, nodding to Alain and Morayne, "just as much as the *rihnemin*. Kosarin wants to add them to his collection."

The same boiling rage Code had felt in Kosarin's presence came rushing back. He knew that bastard had been up to something. Alain and Morayne were special; they controlled a form of magic the Sfaera had never seen before. Of course Kosarin would want to know more about them. He didn't know what Tarbin meant exactly by "collection," but he'd be damned if he was going to find out.

"Did Kosarin know about me?"

Another figure—the source of the new voice—walked out of the shadows and into the moonlight. A young tiellan man, with light, straw-colored hair and bright eyes.

Code tilted his head to one side. He'd never seen this lad before in his life, he was certain of that, and yet there was something oddly familiar about him.

Methasticah stepped forward, his movement urgent. "Tarbin, she's a—" He stopped speaking in mid-sentence as his head snapped backwards, and he collapsed to the ground.

She? What in Oblivion was Methasticah talking about? Code squinted. He'd been quite sure the tiellan was a man.

"*You*," Tarbin growled, but his head was shuddering violently.

Acumency. Code had suspected it with Methasticah, but someone—the tiellan man, it seemed—was killing the *cotir* with unrestrained psionic bursts, rupturing their brains inside their skulls.

Still gripping the sunstone in both hands, Code took a step back, glad to see Alain and Morayne do the same with him. They stood atop one of the smaller mounds of rubble, and had no solid cover to get to one of the street entrances to the plaza.

"We'll have to run for it," Code said. "I'll distract them as best I can, and you two get to safety. I'll meet you at the Blessed Storm."

This could not be the Chaos Queen—her description didn't match this young man at all. Then again, Methasticah had called the lad a *she*, so what did Code know?

"I am not sure running for it is in our best interests," Morayne whispered.

A half-dozen *tendra* exploded forward from Anthris, but she met the same fate as her companions, collapsing to the ground.

"It's our only chance," Code said.

Code.

Code blinked as the voice echoed in his mind. He knew that voice. A woman's voice, one he'd heard before. But it was still the young tiellan man staring at him.

Give me the rihnemin, the voice said, *and I will spare you and your friends. My quarrel is not with you, Code.*

And then, Code knew. Kali and Nash had been two of the most famous—and, among some circles, infamous—field operatives among the Nazaniin. Nash a telenic to be reckoned with—he'd taught Code everything he knew—and Kali a force rumored to be making even Kosarin nervous with her rising power. She'd even managed to transfer her sift into the body of another. But they had both died in Roden, on a mission to deal with Lathe and the tiellan girl.

But now it was Kali's voice Code heard in his head.

Give me the rihnemin, she repeated. *Do not try my patience.*

Code dropped the amber stone. It landed with a soft *crunch* on the debris at his feet.

"It's yours," Code said out loud, taking another step back. He didn't know what in Oblivion Kali wanted with it, but there was a delicious irony in her taking the stone instead of Kosarin. How she was still alive, and why she'd taken the body of a young tiellan man, were mysteries for another day.

"Let's go," Code said, walking as quickly as he could away from the *rihnemin*, while maintaining some level of dignity. "Before she changes her mind."

"Why is everyone calling him a she?" Morayne asked.

Code ignored her. His mind was already racing to think of how to avoid Kosarin—the master of the greatest spy network in history.

PART IV

WHO WE TAKE
WITH US

36

The Cliffs of Litori

THEY SAT AMIDST THE tall grass atop the cliffs. Despite nearly two years gone between them, Knot found the way they sat cross-legged next to one another familiar. They had sat like this lifetimes ago, in Pranna, before and after they were engaged to be married.

"And now you're here, Queen of the Tiellans," Knot said.

And now you're here, and you've killed thousands of people.

Winter had just told him her story, how she had indeed demolished the imperial dome in Roden as Astrid had seen, but how she had then survived and been imprisoned by the new emperor, Daval; how she had traveled back to her hometown of Pranna, where the tiellans had been pushed out by humans, and on to Cineste, to witness a massacre; how she had led the survivors to the ancient tiellan city of Adimora and taken control of their forces—with the help of Daval's former captain, Urstadt, the woman Knot had just fought in error. She told him of her victories against the Khalic Legion, capped by a battle against the Daemon Mefiston, where the Legion briefly allied with and then abandoned her army. And finally she told him of the path that led her here, to Triah.

The path that led her to fell God's Eye.

"And now I am here," Winter said quietly.

Knot shook his head. "Astrid saw the dome fall on you; she

told me you were dead, that nobody could have survived."

"I was the only one who did," Winter said with a shrug. "And I thought you were killed, too. How could we have known otherwise?"

She looked out over the cliffs, toward the sea. Knot's own gaze followed hers for a moment, but then he turned back to the city below them.

"And the Tokal-Ceno, the—the new one who became emperor, he told you I was dead as well?"

"He did," Winter said. "Although I now realize he had no idea what had happened to you. One more reason to hate him."

And yet, Knot sensed no hate in her voice. He sighed. "I am happy you are alive."

"And I you."

The wind moved between blades of grass, between Knot and Winter as they sat together.

I am so sorry I left you, Winter. That's what he wanted to say, but the words wouldn't form in his throat. Not after all that had happened, after all they had both done.

"But you are not happy to see me," Winter said after a moment.

Knot looked at her sharply. "No, darlin'." He exhaled heavily. "Circumstances make that impossible."

"You don't need to be sorry. We have both changed."

Knot shook his head. "It ain't that you've changed, it's…"

Goddess, how to tell her this.

The city below hummed and swarmed with movement, from this distance and height like a massive colony of ants making their way above ground. A pile of rubble marred the surface.

Knot nodded at the site of the collapse.

"You've killed many people, Winter. Why'd you do it?"

"It's a long story."

"You've told me your story, haven't you? Why don't I understand what you did here? Why is that still a mystery to me?"

"You don't understand," Winter said quietly.

"No I don't, that's exactly what I'm telling you. But if you have a reason, if you—"

"You aren't one of us, Knot."

He knew what she meant. He just hadn't expected that particular argument from her.

"I lived in Pranna for a year—"

"That year isn't worth a horse's ass, and you know it."

"I've *helped* you," Knot said, "and I've helped many other tiellans since you... since we parted ways." He'd fought Kamites in Tinska; he'd put his life on the line for Ocrestia and Cavil, the tiellan Odenites. But some had died. Been killed, rather, whether in Tinska or one of the two attacks at Harmoth.

Had he really helped anyone?

"You are still a *human*. You'll always be a human, Knot, so you can never fully understand what it's like."

He couldn't argue the point.

"But how does that," Knot said, pointing at the tiellan camp behind them, "lead to *this*." He pointed at Triah, at the crumbled scar on its surface near the sea.

"A long road," Winter said quietly. "My people were enslaved by humans for a thousand years. When we were finally freed, we weren't acknowledged as equals; we were banished to the smallest, dingiest corners of your cities, or the far outskirts of your towns."

Winter, who had been sitting straight and still, leaned forward ever so slightly. Knot would have hardly noticed the change in posture, but her eyes changed a great deal. Where a moment ago they had been deep, calm pools of darkness, they were now twin pits of black fire. "Tiellans are being beaten to death in the streets. In Cineste, I saw a field of bodies—tiellan men, and women, and children—all of them slaughtered for no better reason than that a few humans *did not want them to leave of their own will*. And outside Adimora, Riccan Carrieri fled with his army and left us to fight dozens of Outsiders, just like the ones we fought in Izet, alone. He could have helped us, and he *left* us to die."

Knot could say nothing to those things. Her account of what had happened outside of Cineste, and then at the Battle of the *Rihnemin*, had sent chills down his spine. A part of him wanted to tell her what he, too, had witnessed, of the persecution in Tinska, and the Beldam's preaching. But another part of him did not dare; not if another God's Eye would be the result.

"You killed tiellans, too, when you attacked the Eye."

Winter sat up straight, and while the fire did not leave her eyes, it calmed somewhat.

"I know I did," she said. "And I have wept for them. I will continue to weep for them, and for the innocent humans I killed that day, too. But I do not regret it, Knot."

Knot stared at her in disbelief. How could she not regret the slaughter of innocent people?

"I am using the only tactic the humans left me."

"And what tactic is that?" Knot asked, his throat dry. The words barely scraped past his lips.

"Fear."

Silence fell between them, a silence like that which followed a sudden clap of thunder, gently rumbling and ringing until all sound faded, and there was nothing but tension.

"Are you still taking *faltira*?" Knot asked. All but blurted it out, really; the question had been on his mind since the moment he knew she was on the cliffs with her tiellan force, since the moment he saw her through the Void. And, truthfully, he knew the answer. He knew a monstrously powerful psimancer traveled with the tiellan Rangers. It would be too much of a coincidence for it to be anyone else. He'd been resisting asking the question this entire time, thinking it was none of his business anymore. Winter was right when she had said they'd both changed; perhaps, for all he knew, she had changed for the better in this way. Perhaps she could take *faltira*, and it did not affect her the way it once had.

But now, hearing her talk this way, hearing her casual disregard for life, he asked the question anyway. It suddenly seemed very much his business.

Winter closed her eyes, and did not open them. She remained seated there, cross-legged, arms resting on her knees.

"You must know the answer to that," she said after a moment.

"I need to hear it from you."

"Then yes. I am still taking *faltira*."

Knot was surprised at the hurt that caused him. He remembered withholding frost from her before Kali and Nash confronted them at the fountain square in Izet. Perhaps, if he had given her a frost crystal, everything would be different now. Perhaps they might never have been separated. Perhaps they would have found those monks Astrid had mentioned, and this would all be done with. Perhaps she would not need it anymore.

"You killed a man in Izet for *faltira*," Knot could not stop the words from tumbling out of him. "You lied to me for weeks about it, putting all our lives at risk. You killed dozens of people, of *innocent people* in Navone, because you couldn't control yourself. How can you still be taking that shit, Winter?

All you do is leave a trail of bodies behind you. You think you're helping, but all you do is destroy."

Knot did not care about the tears running their way down Winter's cheeks from her still-closed eyes.

"You're right about me, Winter. I'll never understand what it's like to be tiellan. I can't begin to imagine the things you, or your people, have gone through. But I don't know anything— *anything*—that justifies mass murder," he said, pointing down at Triah, at the rubble that was once God's Eye. "At this point, I can only hope *faltira* has taken complete control over you. Because if this is who you truly are…"

Knot stood. Winter did not look at him. She remained seated in the grass, wet lines running down her cheeks.

"I don't want any part of it."

37

As Knot walked away from Winter, one emotion dominated all the others within her, plowing through the fear, the guilt, the horror.

Relief.

The hope she'd felt at seeing him again had slowly turned to a heavy terror. The tiellans she'd grown up with in Pranna were almost all gone: Eranda had been killed, as had Lian, and Winter's father; she'd never even known her mother. Everyone close to her died. As much as she yearned for him, as much as sitting next to him here on the grass had filled her with a sense of calm and an underlying desire, she could never be with him. She could not let him become another casualty.

And now she could not help but feel he had become one, all the same.

He was probably halfway back to the Odenite camp by now. She wondered if he would have a difficult time getting back down the cliffs through her army, but then she remembered who this was. Her husband. Lightning on dark water. He would make his way wherever he wanted to go just fine.

She did not know how long she sat there after he left. Long enough for her tears to dry. Long enough for the sun to set and the late autumn moon to rise into a starry night, the lamp and torch lights of the city below a poor facsimile on the ground of what she saw in the sky. Long enough for the air to cool and form goosebumps along her skin.

She was getting too used to the warm weather of the south. In Pranna, this weather would have been a pleasant summer's day.

As much as she wanted the fact that Knot was alive to change everything, in truth it changed very little. Knot *didn't* know what it was like to be a tiellan. None of the humans ever would. Winter did not want all humans to die for their wrongs. Now that Knot was alive, she could think of at least three humans worth keeping around, along with Urstadt and Galce. But none of that changed reality, or the situation she and her people found themselves in. Winter could not stop, not until the humans in power changed themselves—or different people came into power, people who *could* change. Not until the humans stopped viewing tiellans as something less than themselves.

Not until you have your revenge.

Murderer.

Winter stood. She needed to find Urstadt, to spar with her, get some of this aggression and energy out. Her muscles ached with the need to exert themselves.

And she needed some more *faltira*.

Slowly, Winter allowed her gaze to move from the sea— where she had been staring almost through the entire conversation with Knot—to the city below. She forced herself to look at the pitiful pile of rubble where God's Eye had once stood tall.

She did not know how many people had been killed in that attack. She did not want to know. She had done it to place a dagger of fear into Triah's heart, the center of human domination in the world. The consequences were too much to bear.

But her people *had* been wronged. Things *did* need to change. And, Oblivion, she *would* take revenge on Riccan Carrieri.

Winter *had* killed people, just to get frost. That dealer in

Izet. And she hadn't told Knot about Hirman Luce, the Izet High Lord she'd murdered in the council chamber at Daval's instigation. His name should be added to the list as well. And the people she'd killed *because* of frost was far longer than she cared to admit. Goddess, she had taken lives simply because she could not control herself. Navone's memory still burned within her, a hot shame that refused to die down.

Was Knot right? Was God's Eye just another Navone?

Winter fell to her knees. The creeping fear and worry that had caused hot tears to run down her face as Knot left now fully reared its head as the terrible terror and shame it truly was.

She knew she had done terrible things. But, this entire time, she'd thought she at least had some reason for her actions. But if Knot was right, and if this attack on God's Eye was nothing more than *faltira* driving her, what did that mean?

Or, worse, perhaps it wasn't *faltira* at all, but her own thirst for destruction.

As her sobs subsided, a sharp voice made her look up.

"Hello, Winter."

Winter blinked and stood up, her eyes sore, dry, and covered in crusty filth from her sobbing. She wiped her eyes and nose, squinting in the dark. Ghian was half-bathed in shadow. She did not need to access acumency to see his true nature. The black skull of Azael, wreathed in flame, was as much a part of him as his hair or eyes or the color of his skin.

All the softness she'd felt in Knot's presence, all the vulnerability, suddenly turned to cold black stone.

"My dear, are you all right?" Ghian asked, his voice concerned but his face still bathed in darkness. "It looks like you've been *crying*."

"What do you want, Ghian?"

He gave a slight shrug, barely perceptible in the moonlight.

421

"I've only come to check on you. I heard an old friend of yours had come calling."

"I'll believe you care about my well-being when the Sfaera flattens into a disk and people begin walking off the edge of it."

Ghian clicked his tongue. "Such venom. I've never hurt you the way that man has."

The cold black stone turned into a cold black rage.

"Are you going to tell me what you're doing here, or am I just going to leave you to whatever it is you do in the dark?"

"Whatever it is I do in the... I'm not some cultist, hiding in the shadows, Winter."

"Aren't you?"

Ghian scoffed. "Far from it."

"I don't have time for this." Winter turned and began to walk away.

"I know what you're feeling right now, Winter," he called after her.

Winter ignored that comment. How Ghian Fauz could understand what she was feeling right now was beyond—

"You're worried," he said. "You're worried what you've done has been for nothing. That you've killed innocent people, and it's all been for nothing."

Winter spun on her heel and marched back to him, until they stood face to face.

"You have no right to eavesdrop on my private conversations. I don't need you, Ghian. I don't need the Daemon that controls you. If you become a nuisance to me—" Goddess, he already *was* a nuisance "—I can get rid of you. Understand?"

Winter got the slightest bit of satisfaction at the fear in his eyes—this was certainly Ghian she was threatening, and not Azael—but that satisfaction quickly soured.

You get satisfaction from making people afraid? Is that what you have become?

"I see you, girl."

Ghian had said the words, but it certainly wasn't him. Not anymore. The man must have given up his body to Azael's control again.

"Why in Oblivion should I care?"

"You are on the right path. It is difficult and long, but this is where your road must lead you."

Winter resisted the urge to grab Ghian by his collar. She imagined the effect would be lessened considering she was a fair bit shorter than he was, but she wanted to do it all the same. She couldn't keep the anger from her voice, though. "What in Oblivion are you talking about?"

"This is what must be," Azael said, gesturing toward Triah. "This is all part of what I have foreseen. You are becoming the weapon the Sfaera needs you to be."

You are a weapon.

"I'm *not* a weapon," Winter said, but even she didn't believe the words.

"I have seen all of this. You have seen it, too."

"If you have seen all of this, then tell me more," Winter said, suddenly desperate. If there *was* meaning somewhere, *anywhere*, she needed it. "What am I a weapon *against?*"

Azael hesitated. Winter could see the frustration and struggle in Ghian's face.

"You will be the weapon the Sfaera needs," Azael said again, but his deep, rolling voice faltering slightly, as if…

"You already said that," Winter said, taking a step back. "What am I a weapon against?"

"You are what must be. *This* is what must be."

Winter shook her head.

"Let me put it for you in terms you will understand," Azael said, his voice back to normal. But Winter could not forget the waver, the moment of frustration and confusion.

"You have become an instrument in my hands. You have struck fear in the hearts of the people in that city below. But you need to do more."

Winter felt dead inside. The Daemon was right. She *had* done his bidding, or as good as. How had she not seen it?

If *that* was the deeper meaning… Goddess, she was no better than Daval. She was no better than Azael himself.

"They fear you," Azael said, pointing at Triah. "Just as they will soon fear me. You know what you have to do now, don't you, girl?"

Winter wanted to shake her head, wanted to deny it. She wanted to say no.

But when she closed her eyes, Chaos loomed, dark and inviting.

"I do."

There was nothing left inside her to argue, to fight. She wanted Azael to be wrong, but after what Knot had said, how could she think anything else?

She had used her lust for frost, and for power, to get this far. She had murdered and killed, lied and cheated, intimidated and deceived. She had done it under the guise of retribution and justice for her people, and a part of her still believed that, but… she had gone this far; what was a little further? She had killed so many people; what were a few more? What were a few *thousand* more?

If they wanted her to be a villain, perhaps she should become the villain they always thought her to be.

"Azael." Winter faced the Daemon in Ghian's body.

"Yes, child?"

"I am ready."

38

House of Aldermen, Triah

THE CONSULAR'S OFFICES CONSISTED of three large adjoining rooms: an anteroom, where Karina's secretary sat; a meeting room overlooking Trinacrya Square, filled by a blackbark desk and lined with paintings of previous Consulars; and the smallest of the three, the Consular's windowless study.

It was to this last room that Karina brought Carrieri. Bookshelves and scroll shelves lined the room, which was furnished with comfortable stuffed chairs and a long couch.

"The others—"

"Will arrive shortly." Karina made for the liquor table. She poured herself a glass of brandy, and raised another to Carrieri questioningly.

Carrieri shook his head. He'd normally make a comment about it being a bit early in the day for that sort of thing, but given the circumstances, he couldn't blame her. It was four days since the Eye had fallen, and the assembly was making slow progress in deciding how to house the displaced, where to treat the wounded and how to even start the clean-up operation. Even with a strong Consular like Karina running things, the senators were quick to argue and slow to make decisions.

In short time the study's population increased by three: Kosarin Lothgarde, Venerato of the Citadel, along with his second, Sirana Aqilla, and the Essera herself, Arcana Blackwood.

Together with Carrieri and Karina, they were the five most powerful people in Triah—perhaps the five most powerful people on the Sfaera.

The five most powerful people on the Sfaera, after Danica Winter Cordier.

"The trebuchet?" Karina asked.

"Still dismantled," Carrieri said. "We monitor it at all times of the day and night." It was the first question she asked every day since the attack, and for good reason. But the tiellans did not seem interested in rebuilding the war machines.

"What of the Rodenese fleet?" Karina asked.

"The blockade continues, but they have yet to mount an offensive."

"Why? The Eye is down. Their main deterrent is gone. With the tiellans inland and them at sea, they could overwhelm us from both sides."

Carrieri shook his head in frustration. "I cannot say for certain." This question had plagued him the past few days. The respite was welcome, but could not last. This had to be the eye of a storm; the Rodenese navy had not come all this way to blockade Triah, not when the city was at its most vulnerable.

"You have no idea why they hold back? Not even a guess?"

"I have guesses, of course, but—"

"Guesses are all we have right now, Grand Marshal. Tell me yours."

Carrieri pursed his lips. "The most likely scenario is that the alliance between the tiellans and the Rodenese has broken down. Rodenese prejudice runs deep; and if the tiellans hate us, who live alongside them, they must hate the Rodenese even more, who drove them out with pogroms and death."

"Good."

"Don't take comfort from my words," Carrieri warned. "They're just conjecture, and must be taken as such. We cannot assume anything about either enemy at our gates."

"I understand that, Riccan. And while I agree with you, time does not. Send messages to both parties. See if either will meet with us."

Those words brought splutters from the rest of the group, but Carrieri nodded. It was the inevitable conclusion. When outmatched and outflanked, negotiation was the only recourse.

"Yes, Consular," Carrieri said, with a small bow.

"Essera Blackwood," Karina said, pouring herself another glass of brandy, "we are honored by your presence. Would you give us a report on the numbers?"

"The death toll has risen to twelve hundred people," Blackwood replied. "We are still finding bodies in the rubble." In public, the Essera was all pomp and majesty, but here, she was all business. "We found a particularly large group of corpses beneath the rubble this morning. We think a lot of them were trying to escape down the stairwell of the Eye at the time of the attack."

"How many injured?"

"Over three thousand," Blackwood said, "and there are reports of a nasty cough going around. Our priestesses think it might have something to do with all the dust and debris people near the Eye inhaled when it collapsed, and over the following hours."

"How are your priestesses handling those numbers? Do you have enough people?"

"We could never have enough for something like this," Blackwood said, her voice calm with patience that Carrieri could not fathom. "Hundreds of priestesses have been recalled from outside the city to help with the recovery effort, but many of them will not arrive for days, perhaps weeks, and in the meantime we are stretched very thin."

"What of these Odenite priestesses?"

"Disciples," Blackwood corrected. "They continue to help where they can, but there are only nine of them and…"

"What?" Karina prompted.

"And they are being met with some opposition."

Carrieri sat up in his chair. "Why would they meet opposition? Who would *oppose* them? They've saved dozens of people, if the reports are to be believed."

"Hundreds, actually," Blackwood said. "But… some rumors began, early yesterday morning as far as we can tell, that the Odenites are in league with the tiellans."

"In *league* with the tiellans?" Karina angled a look at Carrieri. "Is there any truth to this?"

Carrieri shook his head—he had heard of no such connection—but it was Lothgarde who responded.

"There may indeed be some truth to it, Consular. There is an ex-Nazaniin, of sorts, with the Odenites," Lothgarde said. "He is married—or at least he was, at one point in time—to Winter Cordier."

Carrieri bristled. "Why weren't we told about this?"

"The Nazaniin deserter was our business," Lothgarde said, "we saw no need to bring him up. We only discovered his connection to the tiellan leader recently."

Carrieri imagined the Venerato was using the term "recently" rather loosely.

"But what has that to do with these disciples?" Karina asked. "All these women have done is go about healing the people of our city."

"The rumors," Blackwood said, clearing her throat, "say that the Odenites and tiellans planned the attack together, so that the Odenites could then show their power and gain the favor of the people. People are refusing the Odenites' help because they claim not to buy the ruse."

"They think the Odenites *planned* the attack?" Karina asked, her voice rising with incredulity.

"The theory is not completely unfounded," Lothgarde said.

Carrieri stared at Lothgarde accusingly. One thing was certain: The people wouldn't know about the Odenites' connection to the tiellans—unless that information had been *leaked*.

The question was, why?

39

Odenite Camp, outside Triah

"WHAT?" JANE ASKED. "WHY do you keep looking at me like that?"

She had woken Cinzia by dropping a knapsack on her bed not ten minutes ago, with the unusually sunny declaration that it was a lovely day, and they should go for a walk.

"You are hiding something from me," Cinzia replied. "I can tell." She had not felt this free with Jane since… Goddess, since before they left Tinska, surely.

Jane rolled her eyes. "I'm *not* hiding anything from you. I really think we need a break, after everything we've seen." She grew more serious. "And I want a few moments alone with my sister. It has been too long, Cinzia. Now come on, if you don't hurry up we won't get there in time."

"In time for what?"

But Jane was already walking out the door, and Cinzia had no choice but to follow.

"Have fun, girls," their mother, Pascia, said as they passed the campfire she was tending outside their family's group of tents.

"*Mother* knows where we're going?" Cinzia muttered. "Have you told the entire camp except me?"

"She suggested it, actually, but I agreed with her. This seems like something we both need," Jane said.

"I prepared some food and water for you in that knapsack.

You can argue between the two of you who gets to carry it," Pascia said with a sly grin.

"There will not be an argument," Cinzia muttered. "This is Jane's idea, so she will be carrying it. End of story."

Jane did not object, and Cinzia felt an unexpected wave of nostalgia. They had all been so busy with the Odenite movement, with taking care of the people in their charge—and Cinzia with her own secret life—that she had hardly felt connected to any of them recently.

Cinzia paused, turning to take in the family scene. Her mother and sisters, knitting by the morning fire. A little further off, Eward was teaching Ader how to chop wood.

She had missed so much of this, lately.

"Are you coming?"

Jane was waiting for her, knapsack on her back. Cinzia took one more glance at her family, then followed her sister out of the camp.

They followed a small trail in the direction of the Wild Cliffs, on the southern side of Triah. More than an hour later, by Cinzia's count, they stopped to refill their water skins from a spring. The hem of Cinzia's dress had been stained a dark brown from the dust, dirt, and mud of the trail.

"I know this place," Jane whispered. "We're almost there."

She led the way into a meadow. The tall grass was running to seed. Cinzia ran her hands along the top of the gilded blades. They whispered dryly against her skin, occasionally with a sharp, scratching accent. It was an unusually sunny day; Cinzia had the feeling it was the season's last go at warmth before another long winter. The brightness of the sun above her mixed with the chill of a strong breeze, fluttering her dress about her legs. To her right the meadow ended abruptly at a steep cliff. From where Cinzia stood, the grass seemed to end and then immediately give way to ocean.

"We're here," Jane said, her voice full with satisfaction. "It took a little longer than I expected, but I think we still made it in time."

Cinzia walked hesitantly to the edge of the cliff, the grass scratching against her legs. Her hair gusted in front of her face, her skirt flapping against her thighs. Here the grass grew in patches and in carved depressions along the rock face. A few paces beyond where she stood, the vegetation ended completely, revealing a small scar of rock. Beneath her was nothing but the foaming ocean.

As she looked down, an old fear rose within her. She remembered a night in Izet, the snow around her as she stood on the roof of an inn. A dagger in her hand, and the feeling that it would be easy—welcome, even—to plunge it into her chest.

She was close to the cliff's edge, now. So close. One step, and everything could end.

Another gust of wind whipped against her cheeks, her clothing. Someone grabbed her arm, and Cinzia flinched, taking a step back.

Jane pulled her from the edge. "What is wrong with you? I take you all the way up here and then you scare all holiness out of me? What were you thinking?"

What *had* she been thinking? What in the Sfaera would ever possess her to go anywhere near the edge of a cliff? She looked over her shoulder, shuddering. She did not relish the idea of going out there again.

"Sorry," she mumbled. The waves rolled gently far below. She tore her eyes away. "You said earlier you know this place?"

"I have never been here before, but I've seen it in a vision."

Jane's tone was matter-of-fact, as if there were no room for interpretation or argument. And, Cinzia supposed, at this point there was not. How many times had Jane suggested they do something because of a vision, dream, or direct communication with Canta herself, to have the thing eventually work out, more or less, to everyone's good?

Her sister looked almost regal, standing here above the ocean, the wind in her hair. In that moment, Cinzia made a decision. She could almost sense Canta's Heart, in its pouch at her belt, glowing with anticipation.

"I have something to tell you, Jane."

Goddess, where to begin?

Jane's eyes met hers, and for a moment the two remained silent, the wind whipping between them, but their eyes still and fixed.

"I thought you might."

Cinzia started with Luceraf. She told Jane how she had allowed the Daemon to occupy her mind in exchange for freeing Knot from the Black Matron's prison.

Jane didn't interrupt. Her eyes widened in surprise at first, but she eventually began to nod slightly now and again, and Cinzia began to wonder whether Jane already *knew* about her relationship with Luceraf.

"This is why I have not been able to translate," Cinzia said eventually, quoting the Codex: "*Any communication with one of the Nine is an abomination, and all those who interact in any way with the Nine are lost.*"

"I had wondered, but had not wanted to say anything."

"So you did not know, then?"

"Canta does not grant me omniscience, Cinzia, much as I would appreciate such a gift. But I knew something was wrong with my sister." Her face changed slightly, and she whispered, "Is the Daemon listening to us speak?"

Cinzia shook her head quickly. "I have only given you half the story. Luceraf is no longer with me, thank the Goddess. I knew I had to separate myself from the Daemon, but I hoped, too, to come across something that might help me understand how to defeat the Nine."

"You always seem to be grasping at that hope," Jane said flatly. "That was what got you connected with Luceraf in the first place, apparently."

Cinzia felt the color rush to her cheeks, but continued anyway. She told Jane of the team she had assembled: Knot, Astrid, Nayome, the Beldam, Code—and the two he recruited, Alain and Morayne.

Jane's eyes truly did widen at this, and her mouth fell open in shock. "You met with the Beldam? And a *Cantic Crucible?*"

"Nayome is the woman who came to Navone," she said.

"I remember the name. She was responsible for Nara's death."

Cinzia bowed her head. "Nara was dear to me too. But Nayome was my best connection to the Denomination. And she believed me when I told her about Luceraf and the imminent threat of the Daemons."

"And she agreed to help *you?*"

Cinzia stared at Jane, her jaw set. "Yes, she agreed to help *me*, Jane. Is that so difficult to believe? Even with me being a disciple in a new Church directly opposing theirs, and with a Daemon in my head... oh all right, fine, maybe it is difficult to believe. But I knew Nayome at the seminary. We were friends, years ago, before all this."

She went on to tell Jane the rest of the adventure, holding back only some parts of her conversation with the Essera, and the choice she'd been offered. And, finally, Cinzia told Jane about the gemstone. The Heart of Canta, her experience in the Void, and how she expelled the Daemon from her body through the stone. Again, she withheld some details; telling Jane that she used her own blood to expel Luceraf did not seem right.

When she finished, Jane had a wide smile on her face.

"Jane?" Cinzia asked. "I have not broken you, have I?"

In answer, her sister wrapped her in a long, powerful embrace. Cinzia stood stiffly, then forced herself to relax, melting into Jane's arms, eventually returning the embrace.

"You've done it, Cinzi! You've done it, you've done it, you've done it!"

Cinzia patted Jane lightly on the shoulder, not sure what it was she had "done" exactly. When Jane finally released her, she expressed as much.

"The gemstone!" Jane said, her eyes brighter than Cinzia had seen them in a long, long time. "Canta's Heart!"

Cinzia narrowed her eyes. "I'd never heard of the gemstone till I saw it in the Vault. How do you know what it is?"

"Don't you remember? The Codex mentions Canta's Heart," Jane said excitedly. "As a weapon to be used against the Nine."

"It… does?" Cinzia had always been frustrated at the book's conspicuous lack of information regarding the Nine Daemons. How had she not noticed that part?

Jane's smile faded. "I'm afraid I have something to tell you, as well. Since that night you were unable to translate… Canta's work had to continue, Cinzia. It is not dependent on you or me, and will go on without us if it must. You became so scarce, always gone from the camp, always up to Goddess knew what. And in this case…"

"You found someone else to translate," Cinzia said quietly.

She had known from the moment she accepted Luceraf's bargain that she would forfeit some of the power Canta had given her—in this case, her seership. She had been granted the ability to translate the Codex of Elwene; that had been one of the few things she had embraced in all that Jane had ushered in. Then she had lost it.

"Canta called Elessa to translate the Codex, yes. I am so sorry, Cinzi."

The loss ached, but she could not blame Jane.

"I made the choice," Cinzia said, "and I have to accept the consequences."

"Now that you are free of the Daemon," Jane said, her voice growing hopeful, "perhaps you can begin to translate with me again."

"Perhaps," Cinzia said, with a smile she did not feel. *If you are disappointed you no longer can translate, but no longer want to translate, what exactly is it you want?* she asked herself.

Silence was her only response.

"You were talking about the Codex," Cinzia said, changing the subject. "It says something about the gemstone?"

Jane nodded eagerly. "Do you remember the symbols occurring throughout the Codex?"

Cinzia nodded. Strange symbols cropped up throughout the book, usually near certain words. The symbols did not translate in Cinzia's mind; they remained as they were, and they did not look like symbols she recognized in any language, dead or otherwise. But she and Jane had made note of them as they went along, hoping their meaning would become clear at some point.

"Elwene includes a key for them at the end of her book," Jane said, speaking quickly, the words tumbling out of her. "They're endnotes, Cinzi. They clarify, expand, and even in some cases *change* the meaning of the words in the Codex. I can tell you the exact passage. It was partway through Elwene's own book, in reference to avatars.

> An avatar is powerful, but he or she can be stopped. Decapitation is said to have worked, but this is often difficult, as the bond with a Daemon physically enhances the avatar. The avatar grows stronger than any human, with skin like stone or steel. An avatar may not fully be under the control of one of the Nine, and might be swayed to break the hold the Daemon has upon him or her. But this is only a theory, and has never been known to happen.

Cinzia marveled at Jane's ability to recall passages of the Codex as if she had memorized them. She would have been quite skeptical of such a claim, if she had not heard Jane do it on many occasions, quoting lines they had translated, either recently or distantly, word for word.

"There was a notation there, a symbol," Jane said, "at the part saying an avatar might be able to break the hold the Daemon has upon him or her. The section it referenced at the back of the Codex was long, longer than most notes. Here, it is better if I recite it for you.

> I have researched these rumors, and there is indeed some truth to them. One documented instance tells us of the Daemon Samann, who infested his consciousness into that of a young nobleman. When the nobleman's friends, all heroes, became aware that he could hear a voice inside his head, telling

him to do terrible things—he killed many of his own people, once the Daemon came to him—they set off on a quest to find a cure. They had heard of an ancient gemstone called the Heart, and procured this stone for the young man. We know little of the stone, but most accounts agree that it had a reddish hue, and was perhaps egg-shaped. They brought the gem to the nobleman, and a struggle ensued. The moment Samann saw the stone, the nobleman later said, the Daemon broke into a panic. He begged his avatar not to touch the stone, wheedling and threatening by turn, but the nobleman eventually succumbed to his friends' insistence, and grasped the stone in both hands.

Three records recount what happened next, but they all differ. One says the nobleman died moments after touching the stone, his face frozen in a mask of horror, both his soul and the Daemon banished into Oblivion. Another states that, after a torturous struggle, the Daemon departed, leaving the avatar an incompetent, drooling facsimile of the man he once was. The final account states that, when the nobleman took the stone in his hands, his eyes closed, and he appeared as if asleep. When he woke, he was free of the Daemon, but still had a tendency toward cruelty, whereas before Samann's infestation such things had never been in his nature.

In any case, the incident fascinates me. Such a gemstone, if found, could change the entire course of life on the Sfaera. And, if the power of this gemstone can somehow be used to fight the

Daemons themselves, to imprison them or even kill them, then its potential is astounding.

Cinzia stared at Jane, caught in her own astonishment and growing excitement. She could not believe, first of all, that her sister could possibly recite such a long block of text, seemingly without effort. Jane did not stumble, stutter, or hesitate at any point while relaying Elwene's note.

And more importantly, could it be that she might actually be able to use Canta's Heart to *defeat* the Nine Daemons?

"If Luceraf is truly gone, as you say—"

"She is," Cinzia said quickly.

"Well, then, since Luceraf has truly been dispelled from you, to use Elwene's language, then it seems we can rule out the first two accounts. You seem, more or less, yourself. Would you agree?"

More or less myself. While she was confident Luceraf was gone, she still felt Luceraf's *absence* acutely. She heard the echoes of Luceraf's voice, on occasion, within the walls of her mind. But revealing such a thing to Jane did not seem wise.

"I think I am the same, more or less. Perhaps I spent less time with a Daemon than the man Elwene mentions?"

"Perhaps. Can you tell me what happened? How exactly you expelled her?"

Again, she felt she ought not to tell Jane about the blood.

Do not be a fool, Cinzia told herself. This was her sister, after all. This was a woman with a direct link to Canta. So Cinzia put away her hesitancy and described her experience in the Void, including the voice that had instructed her and what it had told her to do.

Take the dagger.

Draw your own blood.

Be rid of the shadow.

Cinzia shivered, the sound of the voice reverberating within her once more.

"Whose voice was it?" Jane asked. "Was it male or female? Could you tell?"

Cinzia thought about it. It had sounded a great deal like Luceraf's, in a way, but at the same time, it had sounded very different. She had heard a hint of Azael there, too. She would never forget the sound of the Fear Lord's voice as it came to her, through Kovac, in Izet. The deep sound of crackling fire and flame, burning deep into her mind and into her bones.

"It sounded like both, at times."

Jane frowned. "I do have a hunch as to who it might have been."

Cinzia met her sister's eyes. "Who?"

"Canta, of course," Jane said with a smile.

Canta. The thought had crossed Cinzia's mind, but would the Goddess—if she truly existed at all—actually deign to speak to a doubter like Cinzia? Who had let her faith dwindle and fade, until a stiff breeze could snuff it out completely?

"I do not know, Jane..."

"It *must* have been, Cinzia. Who else would think it so important to contact you, to tell you how to use the Heart? Who else would have reason to foil the plans of the Nine Daemons? Who else would have the *power* to speak to you that way, in the Void? To bring you there in the first place?"

"A great many people could speak to me in the Void," Cinzia said. "But... you are right, I do not know how I ended up there." Somehow, the explanation still did not seem right to her.

"We have to get you back there," Jane said. "We have to get you back to the Void, and you need to contact that voice again. You need to contact Canta."

Cinzia frowned. "Could she not just speak to me through you?"

Jane opened her mouth, but said nothing. Cinzia was about to ask if her sister was all right, when she noticed the silence. Trees rustling, birds taking flight, waves rolling and crashing against the rocks fifty rods below were sounds taken for granted, until suddenly they were gone, and a daunting, aching silence remained in their wake.

Looking around, Cinzia realized it was not just that they were silent; all movement around her had stopped. The trees were frozen; a few stubborn leaves hung in mid-fall. The sea below was still as a painting, white caps unmoving. She waved one hand through the grass that had scratched her legs; it moved with her hand, but did not return to its original position, instead remaining slightly bent over at an awkward angle. She breathed in the smell of the sea, the slow earthy decay of the quickly approaching winter.

"Hello, daughter."

Cinzia turned to see Jane, her mouth no longer forming a wide, frozen O, but rather smiling at her in a way Cinzia had never seen Jane smile before.

Instinct drove Cinzia one step away from Jane, and she was suddenly very aware of the cliff face she had so callously stood on the precipice of only minutes before. "Jane?"

"Jane is still here, worry not. I have only... well, I have stopped time, as you can see. In stopping time, I have created a tiny space in Jane that I could occupy, for this one, brief millisecond. And, in this millisecond, we must have a conversation, you and I."

"You are...?"

"Yes, Cinzia. I am Canta, the Goddess of the Sfaera."

"You are speaking to me through Jane?"

"Yes, but I do not have much time. It was indeed me who spoke to you in the Void, and I am glad you did as I suggested. I am glad you rid yourself of the Daemon Luceraf, and are once again worthy to speak to me."

"Once again worthy," Cinzia repeated. Had she been worthy, once? If she had, why had the Goddess not spoken to her before?

"I know you have questions, Cinzia, but we must be brief. You have been blessed with that gemstone at your belt. My Heart, some people call it, but there are other names, more ancient than you or I. Either way, it is the key to the coming conflict. You can use that stone to banish the Nine from the Sfaera, Cinzia. If you use it correctly, in the exact way I tell you, you can even use it to destroy them, once and for all."

Slowly, Cinzia reached for the pouch at her belt. "I could destroy them?"

"*Do not touch it!* Conserve its energy. Keep it away from your skin, or anyone else's, until the time is right."

Cinzia took another step back.

Why am I afraid of her? Cinzia wondered. She remembered the love she had felt from Canta, once upon a time on that rooftop in Izet.

What was wrong, here?

"How do I use the stone?" Cinzia finally asked, the words forming like a sunrise in her throat.

Jane's weird smile grew broad.

"The day soon approaches where you will need to put this knowledge into action, Cinzia. There is not much time left at all. So please, listen carefully. The stone you hold is a dagger in the Void, imbued with my own life-force; it is one of the few items that can be seen or used in the Void at all, and when it is used there, its effects can be felt in the Sfaera, and beyond it. With this dagger—this stone—you can rid the Sfaera of the Nine Daemons."

"This will banish them?" Cinzia asked.

"It will kill them, child, once and for all."

"But why me?" Cinzia asked. "Who am I to do this thing?"

"There is no time to explain," Canta said quickly. "Listen to me, Cinzia, and don't forget any of this."

Cinzia absorbed the information as best she could, beating back her wonder and awe and unease and confusion, trying to get to the point, the center, of what the Goddess in her sister's form told her.

She could destroy the Nine Daemons.

Cinzia blinked, and the sounds returned, the motion returned, and she lurched to one side as her feet suddenly felt very unstable beneath her.

"We need to find an—Cinzia, goodness, are you all right? What is wrong with you?"

Cinzia found her balance. There was concern on Jane's face—and that terrible smile was gone.

"Just a spot of vertigo," Cinzia said, looking at the sea. Sure enough, the waves continued on their paths, the grass around her wove gently in the crisp breeze.

"We should get you off this cliff," Jane said, her voice full with excitement. "I wonder if you will be able to translate tonight? Perhaps we can uncover something in the Codex that can clarify what to do with the stone."

Cinzia knew exactly what to do with the stone.

"And if that does not work?" Cinzia asked, more to keep Jane talking than anything so she could organize her own thoughts.

"And if that does not work, we might have to look up this acumen of yours in the Denomination. Because I think our only option at that point will be getting you back into the Void."

40

ASTRID WAS GLAD SHE did not mind the cold as she made it back to the Odenite camp, Knot at her side, an injured disciple in tow between them. Another disciple—Elessa—shivered beside them as they walked, pulling her cloak more tightly around her. The first snows would fall soon. The previous day had been sunny, but Astrid had a feeling in her bones it would be the last they would see for some time.

Cinzia rushed up to them as they approached. "Ocrestia! Is she…?"

"She'll be fine," Knot said.

"I can speak for myself, thank you very much," Ocrestia said. "And he's right," she said with a sniff. "I'll be fine."

"What in the Sfaera happened?" Cinzia inspected the black-and-purple bruise that webbed out from Ocrestia's left eye, and the accompanying wound on her cheek.

"You didn't seem fine when that man hit you," Astrid said. She turned back to Cinzia. "All she did was offer to heal a man's family—they're taken badly with the cough, so he said. And he just smacked her in the face! Knot stopped him."

Cinzia's face creased with concern. "Well, get something cold on it, and rest," Cinzia told Ocrestia. "There's some fresh water by our fire—clean the wound before you do anything else."

The rest of the visitors to the city had reached the camp

now, and Jane joined them. She wore a simple light-blue dress and a dark-blue cloak on her shoulders. Blue looked good on her; Astrid wondered why Jane did not wear it more often.

Two Prelates had also been injured in the altercation, and the Odenite group had been forced to move quickly out of the city before more Triahns ganged up on them.

"I think we must reconsider the benefits of going into the city, sister," Cinzia said, when she heard that.

Jane, lips pursed, nodded reluctantly. "I think you may be right."

"How could they have turned against us so quickly?" Ocrestia asked, nursing the wound on her head.

Cinzia frowned at the woman. "Didn't I tell you to clean that wound? Go on, for your own sake! Plenty of rest and water for you. The last thing we need is you collapsing."

Ocrestia grumbled something, but Elessa and Danica helped her off to find clean water.

When the three disciples were out of earshot, Astrid spoke. "Nobody's said the most obvious thing."

"But we've all considered it," Jane said quietly. "Ocrestia is the only tiellan disciple, after all. Considering it was a tiellan army that attacked the Eye, we should not be surprised at the violence being directed at her."

That was true enough. There were rumors of such things—tiellans being cornered, beaten, even killed, throughout the city. The disciples had even healed a few tiellans whose wounds looked nothing like those of the people injured in the Fall of the Eye. The Eye and the surrounding buildings had mostly been occupied by humans.

"There's more to it than that," Knot said.

Astrid glanced at him. "What're you keeping from us, nomad?"

"Had a conversation with Code in the city today."

Astrid looked at him out of the corner of her eye—an eye that was beginning to glow bright green now that the sun had set, but she paid it no mind, not even covering it with glamour. The Odenites knew who and what she was, by now. More or less, anyway. "When did you slip away for that?"

She'd hoped to draw a smirk out of him with that, or *some* kind of reaction, at least, but she got nothing. Knot had been completely stoic since the Fall of the Eye, and Astrid could not blame him. Not only for the shock of what had happened in Triah, but because of whatever had happened up on the cliffs as well. Knot had yet to talk to her about his encounter with Winter. Astrid imagined she'd have some apologizing to do— she hadn't thought anyone could survive the collapse of the dome in Izet, but she hadn't checked to be sure before she'd told Knot that Winter was dead.

"Rumors abound in the city about the Odenites," Knot continued, ignoring Astrid. "Most of them connecting us to the Chaos Queen's Rangers. Some people think we helped plan the attack."

Cinzia gasped, and Jane grew pale. Astrid exhaled a puff of air, but she couldn't say such news surprised her.

"But we helped *heal* people afterward," Cinzia said. "How could they suspect us of *planning* it?"

"They think we're in league with the Rangers, that we planned the attack so that we would have an excuse to demonstrate your ability to heal, and gain the favor of the people."

"That is madness!"

"Canta told me she counseled against us healing people after the Fall," Jane said. "She told me twice not to do it, but the third time I asked, she relented, and... this must have been why she forbade me from doing it."

"But we did something *good*," Cinzia said. "No matter what people think of it now, we helped people, Jane. Is that not good enough?"

"No," Jane said. "I do not think it is. Canta has plans for us, here in Triah. And we may have set them back."

Astrid snorted. "Can't your Goddess just... fix it?"

Jane sighed. "Canta's will shall come to pass, no matter the obstacles, no matter the human—or tiellan—interference. But we still have to overcome the immediate problem ourselves. We must discuss what to do about the tiellans, and about our apparent connection to them, at least in the minds of the Triahns."

Astrid looked around them. "Might be best to do that in private, at least?"

Jane nodded. "Yes, you are right. Let us retire to our tent. We need to find a resolution for this problem as quickly as possible."

The discussion lasted long into the night, with Elessa eventually joining them as well. The other disciples, exhausted from what healing they had been able to do that day, had retired to sleep.

It was just as well, Astrid figured. They needed to make a decision quickly, and the fewer disciples present to make that decision, the better. In her experience, if you got enough disciples together, they could take hours to decide whether to send one or two people out to fetch tea for the lot of them.

"Knot has already tried talking to Winter," Cinzia said. "She would not see reason."

Knot remained silent. While he'd said as much earlier, he didn't seem to like the direction the conversation was going.

Astrid growled in frustration. "And at this point I doubt she will. But if we cut off the head of the snake..."

Jane, Cinzia, and Elessa stared at her. Knot looked away.

Of course he knew this was the only recourse.

"You mean... you want to assassinate her?" Cinzia asked slowly.

"It is the only option we have," Astrid said, "if we want to end the problem the Rangers present for us. They're putting a bad name on the tiellans, on a name we have worked so hard to protect. They—*she*, rather—killed thousands of people. She's responsible for the persecution you face right now. Winter is unstable. She always has been. Think of Navone, of all the people killed and injured there. Think of the lies she told us, the destruction she's wrought since she left Izet. This woman..." Astrid trailed off. She could not say any more; she knew the pain it caused Knot, and despite the fact that she was *right*, that Winter *did* deserve to die, she hated herself for proposing such a thing.

Cinzia's response surprised Astrid. "Perhaps we should ask Ocrestia. As the only tiellan disciple, she would offer a perspective—"

"Ocrestia needs to heal, Cinzia," Jane said. "And besides, as a disciple, her will is aligned with ours."

Aligned with ours? What was Jane talking about? Cinzia and Jane were at odds all the time.

"Who are we to pronounce judgment on the Chaos Queen?" Elessa asked. "Is it not against Canta's teachings? We should leave the judgment up to her."

Cinzia shook her head slowly. "We cannot possibly be considering this. We *know* Winter. Or at least some of us do."

If anyone would go along with this, Astrid thought, looking at Jane, *it is you.* As much as the Prophetess pretended to have some sort of moral code, to be inspired by Canta, the source of *all* morality for Oblivion's sake, her morality seemed awfully malleable at times.

448

"I could do it," Astrid said quietly. "I'd be the best candidate. I could slip through their camp at night, surprise her. She may be a powerful psimancer, but if I catch her by surprise, it will be over quickly."

At least I would save Knot from having to kill Winter. He had once loved Winter—might still love her now.

Cinzia was still incredulous. "We cannot truly be considering this," she said. "We cannot decide to kill someone just because they are making things difficult for us. This should not be news to any of you, but things have *always* been difficult for us. We have always seen our way through, overcoming every obstacle in our way."

"*Canta* has always seen us through," Jane said gently. "And Canta always provides a way."

"If it is Canta's will, then so be it," Elessa said.

"Have all of you gone *mad*?" Cinzia asked. Astrid conveniently found the tent flap very interesting at that moment, not meeting her eyes.

"I'll have no part in this," Cinzia said. "And I cannot believe any of you would." She swept out of the tent.

Elessa looked from Knot to Astrid, then excused herself quietly.

Jane remained for a moment. Astrid still felt the woman's eyes on her.

"You two have a lot to talk about," Jane said. "Knot, you are married to this woman. I know you still have feelings for her. You probably believe she can be saved. She cannot. I have seen it, Knot. Her continued existence will visit endless destruction upon the Sfaera."

Knot's face was hard, and he did not meet Jane's eyes.

* * *

"I don't think it'll help to have the same argument again, nomad," Astrid sighed, some hours later. She'd escaped their claustrophobic tent and Knot had found her sitting on a small boulder near the outskirts of the Odenite camp. "But don't worry. I'm not going to kill her. Not while you don't want me to. The Prophetess can go shove her face in a wasp's nest, far as I'm concerned. You know Winter best; you know if this is really what needs to happen or not."

With a jump, he lifted himself onto the boulder next to her. The sky above was starless, blanketed by nighttime clouds. A pale smudge on the horizon bespoke the moon's position, but other than that the night was dark.

"It is," Knot said, after an uncomfortable silence.

"It is what?"

Knot took a long, slow breath. "It is what needs to happen. You are right, Astrid."

Astrid looked down, a heavy feeling growing in her gut.

"You've changed your mind, then?" He'd hardly been willing to engage with her at all on the subject, but he'd made it clear enough that he did not agree with the idea.

There was a part of her, she realized, that had wanted Knot to say no, to stop her from doing what she proposed. That had made her assassination idea seem safe. She wasn't worried about killing Winter. The woman deserved it. She had meant everything she had said. Winter was a mass murderer.

She did worry, however, what it would do to Knot.

"It's not that I want it to happen." Knot hung his head, shaking it slowly. "I only just discovered she was alive."

Astrid had the sense that something was wrong; the discomfort between them, the way Knot shook his head just now, something did not seem right.

"Are you all right, Knot?"

Knot's face contorted in the darkness. "No," he said, his voice gruff. "No, I'm not."

Astrid edged closer to him. Of course something did not seem right; *nothing* seemed right.

She put an arm around him, resting her head on his arm. "I am so sorry," she said. "Are you sure this is something you want me to do?"

"As sure as I can be," Knot said, his voice barely a whisper.

"All right," Astrid said. If Knot thought it would help, if he thought it was the right thing, she would trust him. That did not stop the heavy feeling in her gut increasing, swelling, until it seemed to fill her whole being with an immense weight.

"Do it tonight," Knot said.

Astrid blinked, raising her head from his arm.

"Tonight?"

"The sooner the better. Get it done, Astrid. The sooner it's done, the sooner we can..."

Heal? Move on? Deal with the next problem?

But Knot did not finish his sentence.

"Very well, nomad," Astrid said, sliding down from the rock. She looked back at him hesitantly. He remained there, head hanging low, barely illuminated by the filtered moonlight. "I'll see you when I see you."

Then she swept off into the night, moving as quickly as her powers would allow.

Had anyone been around to see the aftermath of that conversation, this was what they would have seen:

A young girl, speeding through the forest, a dark streak with bright, glowing green eyes making her way to the Cliffs of Litori.

And a man, head bowed, sitting still on the stone. After a

few moments, when the forest around was silent but for the chirp of crickets and the distant sound of the few Odenites still awake, chatting and singing at firesides, the man slid down from the rock, and moved into the forest.

It would be difficult to see what happened in the forest, given the darkness and the foliage cover, but anyone watching from a distance would have seen a man, average height, lean and muscular, features shadowed by darkness, trudge directly into the woods, neither searching for nor following a path, his boots crunching on leaves, twigs, and other detritus.

Moments passed.

Then, the crunching sound of boots on leaves and dead wood once more. The foliage parted, but the person who walked back into the clearing toward the Odenite camp was very different than the man who had walked out moments before.

A woman, hair long and the color of spun gold, tall, with bright, piercing blue eyes. She seemed to carry her own light with her, her features much more discernible than the man's had been. Nothing like the glow of the young girl's eyes, of course, but a soft, faint radiance, hardly noticeable except in contrast to the previous man's dark form. She wore a simple, light blue dress, and a long dark blue cloak, the hood down around her shoulders.

"Canta forgive me," the woman whispered, as she walked back toward the Odenite camp.

But, of course, there was no one around to hear it, or to see her, and the night was none the wiser.

41

ASTRID CREPT THROUGH THE underbrush, keeping to the tree line. The gleam of her eyes would give her away if she moved out into the open, but she knew well how to use the shadows to her advantage.

But when she reached the clifftop, Astrid stopped in disbelief. The tiellan army was gone. The camp that had once held over two thousand tiellan Rangers had been reduced to waste.

Had the Legion gotten the drop on the tiellans? Perhaps someone had done her job for her. But there was no sign of combat; if anything, it appeared like the tiellans had simply... left. No tents remained, no bedrolls, fires had been extinguished. They'd left the siege engines: the colossal trebuchet had been dismantled, but the others—a few smaller trebuchets and a ballista or two—remained intact. And, curiously, the tiellans had left weapons: swords, axes, shields, and spears littered the ground—hundreds of them.

Why would the tiellans depart—and leave so many of their weapons behind? They were winning the war, despite their small numbers. This must be a ruse, to lull Triah into a false sense of security before thrusting the knife deeper. But if that were the case, surely they had underestimated the Khalic Legion. And anyway, she could not imagine anything *more* devastating than their attack on the Eye. Why dismantle such a weapon?

Then she noticed a figure standing alone, near the cliff's edge. A woman, with a single long, thick, loosely tied dark braid trembling in the wind. Astrid had not seen Winter since that day in Izet, but her form was unmistakable.

Astrid tensed. Whether the rest of the tiellans were here or not—and why they might have left—was beyond her, now. All that mattered was that Winter was alone. Unprotected.

Her claws extended to their full length. She had not brought any other weapons, but she did not need them. With any luck, this would only take a moment.

Astrid sprang into a sprint, but even as she did so, doubt clouded her mind. Knot had given her permission, but what did that really mean? Permission to do something she hated the idea of doing in the first place? What good did that do her?

And what did her good matter when so many lives were at stake? Winter had proven her unpredictability; she had proven her disdain for life. Whether it was frost or Winter's own nature no longer mattered. Winter was a threat to the Sfaera itself.

Or she was a woman driven to the edge, fighting for what she believed was right. Funny how Knot actually giving her his permission was what made Astrid question the act all the more.

Hadn't Astrid proved her own disdain for life, many times over? Who was she to pass judgment on someone else for that reason? She had gone for decades completely past feeling, not caring who she killed or why. But, at some point, that had changed. She had started to care. She had started to regret what she had done. She had begun to seek redemption.

What stopped Winter from experiencing the same change?

Something was not right, she knew it as she ran. Winter should have noticed her by now. But Astrid was committed now, flying too fast and powerfully to stop, all of the momentum of the past few days—of the past few *years*—behind her, propelling her, and she leapt at Winter, claws extended, ready to make the kill.

Everything stopped.

Or, at least, Astrid did: she hung frozen in midair, claws extended toward Winter's neck. She struggled against the force that held her, but none of her muscles responded. Even her eyes refused to move, locked straight ahead on her prey.

"Hello, Astrid," Winter said. Her voice was… small, as if she were speaking from the bottom of a very deep hole. "You may know that telesis is not able to move living things." She turned slowly, observing the razor-sharp claw so close to her neck. She met Astrid's frozen gaze. "But then, vampires are not living things, so we are told. And telesis seems to have some effect on you, wouldn't you say?"

Astrid managed a low moan. She strained her muscles, but it was as if they were no longer her own; they refused her commands, and she remained there, stationary, levitating above the clifftop. Winter began pacing a slow circle around her.

Beyond her alarm and confusion, Astrid was not afraid. There was no animosity in Winter's dark eyes. But, as Winter came to stand in front of her once more, she *did* see fear in the tiellan. Astrid had learned, over the years, decades, and centuries, to recognize fear. The quickening of the pulse, dilated pupils, the sheen on her skin—and a particular *smell* that accompanied fear-sweat, something sickly sweet, almost as intoxicating to her as the smell of blood. But beyond all of those things, there was something else altogether that she had learned to sense: a change in the air around someone who became afraid, dark and crackling and volatile. Astrid sensed it all around Winter.

Winter had Astrid at her mercy; what in Oblivion did she have to fear?

"I will not kill you," Winter said. "I know how much you mean to him."

Astrid dropped to the ground, her muscles suddenly back under her control. She fell in an undignified heap with a short squeal. She jumped up, dusting herself off. She didn't pounce. Her appetite for murder had gone.

"Do what you came here to do, Astrid. I have to imagine Knot would condone it, given my last conversation with him."

Astrid didn't move.

"Do it," Winter's voice cracked. The fear that Astrid sensed around the woman grew.

Do it. This was what she had come here to do, after all. Kill Winter Cordier, the Chaos Queen. End the conflict, hopefully save the Odenites and countless lives in the process.

And yet, she hesitated.

"*Do it,*" Winter said again, her voice wavering but louder.

Astrid took a step forward, one clawed hand flexing. "You... want this?"

"*Kill me.*" Winter raised her chin, baring her neck.

Astrid could sense the blood pumping beneath Winter's skin, could almost smell the sickly sweetness of it... but it was hardly a temptation.

Her claws slowly contracted.

Winter noticed, and her fear and anger grew still more. "Do what you came here to do! Kill me!"

Slowly, Astrid shook her head. "I'm not going to do that," she said quietly, not even sure if Winter heard her.

"You want to make me suffer? Fine. Torture me? Fine. Just do it, Astrid. End it."

End it.

"I..." Astrid hesitated. "Winter, I know what you mean to Knot. I cannot do this to him. It doesn't matter whether he agreed or not; if Knot won't be selfish once in a while, someone has to do it for him."

"I can't live any longer," Winter gasped. "I can't be this. I don't want to be what I am."

Astrid, for all the anger she felt at the injustices to the Odenites, to the innocent lives lost, could understand that much, at least.

"And... what do you think you are?" Astrid asked.

"A murderer."

"You've killed a lot of people," Astrid said.

"And I deserve to die."

Don't we all?

"You have all this power," Astrid said. "You've become a leader. You've caused all this pain, you've *felt* all this pain, and yet you don't know the first thing about it."

"What do you know about my pain?"

"I've felt pain, too. If you think you're alone in that, you're mad."

"But—"

"Yes, *just* like you've felt it," Astrid said, anticipating her protestation. "Believe it or not, Winter, there are a *lot* of people who have lost fathers, mothers, husbands, friends. A lot of people who've lost themselves to addiction, or felt trapped. A lot of people who felt helpless in the face of oppression. None of this is new. This is *life*. Some people take their entire lives to figure it out; others never get there at all."

And it takes some people a few lifetimes, Astrid realized.

"But if you can," Astrid said, "Then your life is worth

saving. Even if you think it's just a possibility, then you're worth keeping around."

Winter looked down at her hands, her face pale, eyes dark.

Oblivion take it, Astrid thought, and moved toward the woman. Perhaps she moved too quickly, because Winter started, her head snapping up to look at Astrid, perhaps thinking she had changed her mind, that she actually was going to kill her.

Surprise, bitch. Tentatively—Astrid was not about to throw her arms around the woman, this wasn't exactly a family reunion—Astrid took Winter's hand. Winter stared at their hands, her dark eyes wide, Astrid's small fingers holding hers. Astrid squeezed once, and then Winter's facade—the one Astrid had hqqqoped was there, had hoped she could penetrate—finally crumbled, and she began to cry.

"I understand," Astrid said, and she meant it.

Winter pulled Astrid in toward her. Astrid felt the woman's arms around her, and stood there uncomfortably for a moment before she made herself return Winter's embrace.

They remained that way for a long time—Goddess, at least it *felt* like a long time to Astrid, but when she looked up, the hazy bright spot in the clouds where she knew the moon hung in the sky had hardly moved at all.

"So," Astrid said, extricating herself from Winter's arms, "now that we've decided neither of us is going to kill the other, I have to ask you something."

Winter laughed, but the sound still seemed forced, sad, and she wiped some of the tears from her cheeks.

"Erm... what happened to the rest of the tiellans?" Astrid asked.

Winter looked back at the tiellan camp vaguely. For a

moment Astrid wondered whether she'd noticed the other tiellans had left at all.

Winter pursed her lips. "I might have made a poor choice," she said.

Astrid frowned. *Don't make me regret not killing you.*

"I sent them away."

"Away where?"

"I did not specify. I simply told them they could not be here."

"And why did you send them away?"

But Winter was looking over Astrid's shoulder.

"You need to leave, Astrid."

Approaching from the forest was a tiellan man, perhaps a few years Winter's senior, leading three humans: a noblewoman with a pink bow in her hair, a tall, sinewy elderly man with sunken eyes, and a very old woman with long wiry hair, who muttered to herself as she walked.

An odd assortment, indeed.

Winter's aura of fear had grown even larger, spreading out from her like an ocean, flowing in every direction.

And, Astrid was surprised to find, she felt a twinge of fear, too.

There are daemons even daemons fear.

"Go, Astrid. I must handle this myself."

Winter meant what she said. Without thinking of refusing, Astrid bolted east, along the cliff face, carefully avoiding the strange group.

She did not look back.

42

WINTER TURNED AWAY FROM the green blur of Astrid's eyes as she streaked away in the darkness. She had Daemons to face.

Ghian came first, his visage torn between Azael's terrible smile and Ghian's own terrified, pale mask.

"You are doing the right thing, Winter," Azael told her. Ghian whimpered, but Azael shut that down quickly. "This is how you become the hero the Sfaera needs."

"Let's get this over with," Winter said. She didn't look directly at Azael after that first glance. The dark, burning skull, even after all this time, still terrified her, although it also filled her with an immense sadness.

But now she saw more movement behind Azael-Ghian and their followers. Four more humans emerged from the trees: a short merchant, his eyes shifting back and forth, a beautiful woman with thick red hair, a hugely fat fellow, and a Cantic priestess, her robes soiled and filthy, her brown hair disheveled in a frizzy halo about her face. When they saw the priestess, the noblewoman and the tall, wiry man grabbed her by the arms, holding her tightly between them.

"What is this?" the priestess said, blinking, as if she had just awoken from a dream. Her eyes came to rest on Winter. "Who are you? Where am I?"

Her gaze must have taken in the lights of the city far below behind Winter, and her eyes widened.

"Goddess, are we on the Cliffs of Litori? Are you taking me to the Chaos Queen? Please, she wouldn't want anything from me, I can—"

"That's enough," Winter said, stepping forward.

"I give the orders here," Ghian said, but she ignored him and looked at the others, the seven who seemed to have no qualm with being here, atop the Cliffs of Litori, at night, with the Chaos Queen herself. She could guess who they were, pieced together from what her experience, research and spies had told her: they were avatars. The tall, elderly man would be Hade, defeated on the island of Arro almost an entire year ago. The mumbling woman was Nadir, defeated in Maven Kol only months before. Between the fat man and the merchant, one of them must be Iblin and the other Samann. The beautiful woman was Estille, and between the noblewoman and the Cantic priestess, one would be Bazlamit, and the other Luceraf, but she was not sure which.

"This is all of you?" Winter asked. She couldn't help but notice there were only eight of them; perhaps Mefiston's death had been final, after all.

"They are all here," Ghian said, his voice hard, the echo of Azael's running beneath it.

The priestess stared at Ghian. Perhaps she had heard the echo, too.

"Our mistake was taking people of power as our avatars, thinking to use their stations and abilities," Ghian said, but Azael's voice grew more and more loud as he spoke, the deep, harsh sound of fire. "We failed multiple times, for that." His eyes darted to the remains of the War Goddess. "And now we need a place of power, such as that—endowed only recently by you, my dear.

And, by your leave, tiellan blood, from a tiellan queen."

Winter drew a dagger from her belt, and the noblewoman whimpered. Also at her belt was a pouch full of *faltira*, nine crystals to be exact. She hoped that would be enough.

Ghian looked at her expectantly. The old muttering woman could hardly focus on anything at all, while the old man's eyes were completely unreadable, sunken into the dark pits below his forehead. Winter half-wondered whether Hade had eyes at all.

She closed her eyes.

Chaos was there, huge and black. A shiver ran down Winter's spine. She tried to mask the quake it sent through her body.

When she opened her eyes, Ghian was no longer smiling.

"If you do not do this, we will find someone—"

"I'll do it." She raised the dagger. The priestess cowered as Winter recited the words Ghian had taught her.

"My blood for the blood of Aratraxia. My blood pays the price of passage, from their realm to ours." She slid the blade across her palm. "My blood for the blood of Aratraxia." She smeared the blood along the noblewoman's forehead.

"Yes," Ghian said, but the voice was completely Azael's now, echoing over the cliff face.

Winter turned to Ghian, and ran her bloody palm along his forehead, too. She caught a flash of Ghian—*just* Ghian, not Azael—and saw his eyes darken with horror, but there was nothing she could do for him. She did the same for each person there, the looks on their faces ranging from anticipation to confusion, to terror.

Nine of them in total, including the frightened priestess.

The moment she smeared her blood along the forehead of the last person—the priestess—the air around her crackled and sparked, but with light and heat that she could neither see nor feel.

Bursts of dark light surrounded her, issuing forth from each person. The priestess screamed, a few of the others moaned, but the faces of the rest were silent, contorted masks. Ghian's eyes pleaded without words, until blackness completely took them over. His mouth opened wider and wider, and inside housed neither tongue nor flesh, but a gaping, horrific darkness. Ghian's jaw snapped and his mouth expanded, far past the point it should be humanly possible.

The darkness swallowed Ghian whole, and in his place towered the cloaked figure of Azael, the Fear Lord.

His cloak was of a deep, infinite darkness that consumed everything that came near it, absorbing the light that filtered down from the overcast night sky above and the city below. The cloak fell in long jagged torrents over Azael's arms, spilling to the ground in a black mist.

When Winter had seen Azael before, his presence had been closer to a nightmare than reality. Now she felt the same unreasoning, unstoppable fear and knew it was real, a relentless weight threatening to crush her into the ground, into the cliffs below her, or an impossible heavy blanket that had just been thrown over her, dragging her down and down into the earth below.

"It's about time," Azael said. His voice still had that strange rolling, burning quality to it, but less penetrating, not quite all-encompassing in the way it had been before. He looked at the others, who were also beginning to twist and morph. "Let's get this over with." A beam of *something* shot up from Azael into the night sky; it was not light, Winter was sure of that, because it was black and dark, but neither was it darkness, as it dispelled and warped the night sky around it.

The hand that emerged from Azael's robe was nothing but

black bone, pointing one lone, skeletal finger at Winter.

"You," Azael grated, his voice like fire, "have just saved the world."

Astrid sprinted through the Odenite camp, knocking aside makeshift stools and scattering campfire ashes in her wake.

When she reached their tent, she shook Knot awake.

"Winter's still alive," she told him, "I let her live—" not entirely true, considering the fact Winter could have killed her easily, but still, "—but I think now she's done something incredibly stu—"

"You've been up there? What in Oblivion…?" Knot growled. But he was already awake, alert, and throwing on his armor. He followed her out into the night, and they both looked up at the cliff face.

It looked… Goddess it looked like…

Eight strange columns of light jutted up into the night sky. Red, orange, gold, green, blue, violet, silver, and a dirty shade of white. And another column, darker even than the night sky, pulled the other lights toward it, around it, so that they began to lean inward and eventually spiral around one another as they rose upward.

White flakes had begun to drift slowly down around her. She held out her hand, and a tiny snowflake landed, perfect and unmelting on her palm.

The first winter's snow.

"Come on," Knot said, stalking away. "We need to find Cinzia."

Cinzia and Jane were together, awake and fully dressed, when Astrid and Knot ran up to them. They'd been watching the spectrum of color on the cliff too, and the strange, dark light bending them all into itself.

Cinzia counted eight lights. Nine, including the dark pillar.

"It's happening, isn't it?" Cinzia asked.

"I didn't kill her, if that's what you mean," Astrid said.

"I am sorry you didn't, Astrid," Jane said. "If you had, you might have prevented this."

"And what *is* this?" Cinzia asked.

"This is the Rising," Jane said. "The Nine Daemons are here."

"How is *Winter* involved?" Knot asked, his eyes searching the clifftop as well.

"I think she's planning to fight them," Astrid said. "Or kill herself trying."

Knot swore. "I've got to get to her."

"I think…" Cinzia's hand strayed to the gemstone in the pouch at her side. She half-expected it to shine through the pouch itself, perhaps even burn through it, but the pouch was as dark as ever. She could sense it, however, sense the connection between the gemstone and those lights on the clifftop.

"I think I need to be up there."

Jane's eyes widened. "Why on the Sfaera would you…?"

"I know how to use Canta's Heart," Cinzia said. She met Knot's eyes. "The gemstone I procured at the Fane. I think I can use it to stop…" She glanced up at the lights on the clifftop again. "To stop that, I hope."

"But you said you did not know how—"

"I've figured it out, sister. But I need to get up there, to where they are."

"It's too dangerous," Knot said, shaking his head.

"Did you hear what I said?" For a moment she almost forgot Jane and Astrid were there. She took his hands in hers. "I can stop this."

Knot scowled. "Then I go with you. To help you, somehow. And to help Winter."

"If I can do this right," Cinzia said, "I think I can help her, too."

465

"Then let's go!" Astrid was pacing back and forth like a jungle cat, waiting impatiently.

"There's something else up there," Jane said. Her face was an illumination of color, yellow and orange and green and violet. Each of their faces, Cinzia realized, was lit up in a rainbow of color. It would have been an incredibly beautiful sight, had the portents not been so dire.

A faint shimmer in the light show above them caught her eye. And then another. And then another, and another, and suddenly she realized why she had not been able to see what it was Jane saw. She had been looking too narrowly. In the sky above the cliffs, a massive, roiling blackness shimmered and twisted. A blackness all too familiar to her. And, if she squinted, she could see dozens of large, dark forms pouring down from the darkness, and onto the clifftop.

"Outsiders," Knot said.

"There are so many of them." Cinzia had only ever seen three at a time, at the most. Canta's bones, there had to be a hundred of them up there already.

Astrid laughed nervously. "Maybe going up there isn't the best idea," Astrid said.

Cinzia squeezed Knot's hands tightly. "It is the only way," she said. "But how in the Sfaera am I going to make it past all those Outsiders?"

"I believe I can guide you, sister."

"I'm coming with you both," Knot said.

"Oblivion," Astrid muttered. "If you're all going to go, then I might as—"

Something *thumped* loudly to the ground behind them: an Outsider, twice the height of a human. Fangs the size of Cinzia's forearm jutted at all angles from its mouth, and a half-dozen black horns and spikes ran the length of its head.

Astrid looked back at the others. "Go. I can handle this one."

With a supernatural burst of speed, the vampire leapt on the monster, burying her claws deep in its neck.

Cinzia pulled Knot along gently. She could not imagine the conflict in him, but they had to move.

"Astrid can handle herself," Cinzia said to him quietly.

Jaw set, Knot nodded, and the three of them moved toward the cliffs.

As the Nine Daemons formed, coalescing in rays of light around Azael, Winter could not help but wonder what in Oblivion she had done. She ducked back behind a pile of timbers, shielding herself from the monsters as they formed, unable to tear her eyes away.

It was too late to change her mind now.

Outsiders rained down all around her, falling heavily to the ground, their dark forms in stark contrast to the gently falling snow. Given what had happened when Mefiston took his form at the Battle of the *Rihnemin*, she had expected these Outsiders to appear. That was why she had sent her Rangers away.

But the Outsiders were the least of her concerns at the moment.

After Azael took shape, each of the nine people around him began to change. The fat man ruptured, his flesh exploding outward. Gore splattered everything around him, giving way to a *hugely* fat monster of a man. Bald, hairless, his skin pasty and pale pink and covered in the guts of his former host. The fat hung in loose folds, like a set of clothes several sizes too large. The man was naked as far as Winter could tell, but his rolls of fat kept him as modest as any item of clothing might. This was Iblin, the

Daemon of Greed and Gluttony, standing at least four times her height. As Winter stared up at him in horror, she noticed for the first time the Daemon had only a single eye at the center of its head, bloodshot veins around an iris of sickly yellow.

The noblewoman appeared to be slowly melting, her skin sliding off her muscles, her muscles sliding off her bones, her bones melting into a viscous, slimy substance. The woman's face was last to liquefy, even then not quite being absorbed into the horrific substance, her eyes, nose, and mouth elongating and warping, almost straining to escape the blob they had become a part of, but never quite succeeding.

The old woman, mumbling to herself all the while, began to morph into the Daemon Nadir, Insanity, elongating until she stood even taller than most of the Outsiders dropping to the ground around them, though not quite as tall as Iblin, or a feathered serpent Winter recognized as Bazlamit, both of whom stood at least twice the height of most Outsiders.

The old woman's head split into three, like a flower blooming with three large petals. Her true face remained at the central head, but her eyelids peeled back revealing bright orange glowing eyes, red-ringed in blood. The heads that split to either side had all four eyes sewn shut with ragged, uneven stitches. All three of the heads converged at the mouth which had morphed into something like the center of a flower, though the mouth had now opened wide into a near-perfect circle, rows of sharp teeth lining the entire circumference's interior. The scalp and top of the skull of each head was missing, as if torn away, revealing a mush of gray matter amidst jagged bone and bloody flesh. The noblewoman's arms lengthened till they formed long, uneven claws that scraped the ground.

A chill ran through Winter as the rest of the Daemons

formed. Each one sent a ray of colored light up into the sky: orange from Nadir's horrifying visage; gold from Iblin's corpulent bulging sack of a body; green from the huge werewolf Samann; blue from Luceraf, the feathered serpent; violet from Estille, the Lust Daemon, who was still a beautiful woman, but with curling horns, the leathery wings of a bat, and a long, barbed, swaying tail; the pile of viscous flesh that Winter now recognized as Bazlamit sent a silvery light up into the night sky, through the falling snow; and, finally, Hade, who had taken the most nebulous form of all, hardly more than a billowing cloud of crackling smoke, sent up a pale gray light, almost white, but lacking the purity.

"Where is the woman?" Iblin bellowed, his voice deep and booming.

"She is close," Azael said, "but she is not our immediate concern. Our immediate concern is—"

"Solidifying our power," Bazlamit hissed. "Claiming our true forms."

True forms. Were these not the Daemon's true forms?

Winter looked down at her pouch. The *faltira* that she had used when Astrid attacked her had faded moments ago, and she'd been stopping herself with all the willpower she had from taking more of the drug. Now was the time. She took two crystals. She needed all the help she could get, consequences be damned.

The frost took effect almost immediately, and power rushed through her. As the drug burned, the nearest Outsiders turned to face her, dark eyes staring.

Winter ignored them, and came out from her hiding place.

"Honestly, I'm insulted." Her voice shook. She was terrified. "I thought I'd be just *slightly* higher on your threat list."

She was minuscule in their presence. She was nothing.

And yet she wasn't.

She was a murderer, yes. She knew she was that.

But she was a tiellan woman, too. She was a wife, however estranged. She was a daughter, and a fisherwoman, and a huntress. She was a queen, now, too; a warrior. She was the Harbinger. She was all of these things, and yet she was one thing more.

She was a weapon.

"Let's see if we can do something about that."

With every *tendron* available to her—hundreds, so many she could not count them—she sought out the weapons she had ordered her Rangers leave behind. Axes, daggers, circular blades, swords, spears, sharpened shields. The *tendra* that did not find weapons found other things instead: a wooden beam from a shattered trebuchet, one of the stones from the War Goddess's unused ammunition. With all of these *tendra*, all of these weapons, she moved forward, attacking, in what she knew would be her final battle.

43

Triah

"Sir, another one has appeared near the Trinacrya, at the center of the city."

Carrieri held up a hand to the man who had just approached him, and turned back to his conversation with Captain Deregard. "Split your platoon. Take half of them to the Fiftieth Circle, the other half to the Thirty-Ninth by the shore. Take out those two threats."

Carrieri stood in the courtyard of the Legion's central barracks, soldiers and officers and messengers swarming around him. Snow fell gently from above. Normally, he took joy in the first snows of winter. While the cold and inconvenience got old quickly, their first appearance was always welcome.

Tonight, he had no time to notice such things.

"Yes, sir." Deregard saluted, but before he turned Carrieri gripped him by the shoulder.

"If more of those monsters show up, take them down. Understand, Captain?"

"Yes, sir." Deregard's face was pale, but his eyes were hard with determination. If Carrieri had a hundred more men like Deregard in his army, he could conquer the Sfaera.

"Good. Now go."

Carrieri turned to Illaran. "How many does that make?"

"Five inside the city, sir."

"Five." Carrieri swore. He wiped sweat and snow from his brow. "And we have no idea what is causing them? How to stop them raining down on us?"

"No to both accounts, sir. Although the lights at the top of the Cliffs of Litori continue to shine."

"Can we get a squadron up there?"

"Sir... there are five in the city, but there are over a hundred on the cliffs."

"Canta's bones," Carrieri muttered. There hadn't even been that many at the Battle of the *Rihnemin*.

"Is the Chaos Queen causing this?" Carrieri demanded. "I thought the Rangers retreated yesterday. Isn't that what our scouts told us?"

"Yes, sir. But perhaps she didn't go with them."

"What about the city walls? No attacks?"

"Not from the tiellans, no, sir. The Odenites battle their own monsters; two or three have dropped in among them as well."

Carrieri swore again. "Is there anyone these daemons *aren't* attacking? What of the Rodenese fleet?"

The fleet had begun moving inland earlier that night, when the light show had started up. "They've changed course, and were last seen heading toward the northern pass. We think they're going to attempt to scale it and fight the monsters atop the cliffs."

"What in Oblivion is going on?" Carrieri muttered. "What regiments haven't been deployed yet?"

"Root, Orb, and Thorn."

"Send the Root Regiment to the cliffs," Carrieri said. "But don't let them engage that nest of monsters, not if they can avoid it. We must see what the Rodenese are up to. Goddess, we must see what in Oblivion is going on up there." He knew it might be a suicide mission. It could be a trap; the tiellans might fall on them from the trees, and the Rodenese from the cliffs. All while daemons slaughtered them.

He remembered, bitterly, when he had retreated from the Battle of the *Rihnemin*. He hadn't thought the tiellans had enough left to counter the dozens of monsters they had been fighting together. He hadn't counted on Winter being… whatever in Oblivion she was. Perhaps she had called the Outsiders down on his city as revenge.

Carrieri could not help but wonder how things might have been different if he had stayed to help the tiellans fight, instead of leaving them to die.

"Get the Orb Regiment as well," Carrieri said. "I'm sure we'll get more reports of…"

Carrieri trailed off. In the midst of the falling snow, a strange blackness twisted above him—a blackness very different from the night sky around it, and not just for the absence of falling snow. This blackness glistened, oscillating.

Both Carrieri and the psimancer dove out of the way as a black shape dropped from the portal, contorting around itself until it coalesced into a sinewy black form with claws and teeth and jaws that seemed far too big for its already massive stature. A long, snaking tail whipped out from behind the monster, covered in black barbs.

"Form up behind me!" Carrieri shouted. His disoriented soldiers backed away from the monster, staring up at it in terrified awe. "*Form up!*"

This time his order galvanized the soldiers into action.

"Loose ranks," Carrieri said, "spears and shield up front, archers in the back. We'll turn this thing into a bloody pincushion. Illaran, you have no place in this fight. Get my

473

orders out, and inform me of any updates."

Illaran nodded, unable to take his eyes off the roaring monster.

"*Go*," Carrieri said, and then Illaran was off.

The monster roared so loudly it made Carrieri flinch, the sound some twisted hybrid between a deep, booming bellow and a high-pitched inhuman scream.

Carrieri drew his sword and rushed at the monster with a war cry of his own, his soldiers charging behind him.

Snow continued to fall lazily, dissolving in the water of the bay below, as Cova and her Reapers marched up the mountain pass. Beasts as big as small ships roamed the clifftops. Her scouts reported some in the city, as well as the Odenite camp. What Cova had seen through the spyglass on her ship, and the way the monsters were described to her, reminded her of a rumor she had heard in Izet, from the time the old Emperor Grysole had been killed: massive daemonic bodies had been found beneath the rubble of the imperial dome alongside that of the emperor. Her father had kept the whole thing quiet.

Whatever her father had been involved with—daemons and monsters and Scorned Gods—had something to do with what was happening now.

And atop the cliff, in a twisting array of colorful light, even more terrifying monsters battled a tiellan women—which must be Winter Cordier. Cova knew enough of legend to know that the Nine Daemons, in their true forms, were on top of the cliff.

If the tiellans were still up there, they did not stand a chance. Cova had heard nothing from Winter or Urstadt of any plans for such… Goddess, what even was this? The end of the Sfaera?

Once she had read the signs, she knew it was in her best

interest to help. She prayed Carrieri would recognize the threat, too. If the Daemons defeated Winter and the tiellans atop the cliff, they would barrel down toward the city and destroy Triah completely—eventually, they would destroy the entire Sfaera. The Nine had no good intentions for the Sfaera, or its peoples.

The pass narrowed quickly as it curved into the cliffs, taking a series of switchbacks before reaching the top, about half a radial from where the center of the clifftop battle was, near the southern edge of the cliffs that faced out over Triah.

Cova ducked her head and marched, worried her troops would not arrive in time.

Knot, Cinzia, and Jane had only been able to find two horses quickly. They galloped up the path to Litori. Cinzia rode behind Knot, her arms wrapped tightly around his middle.

"Mind sharing with me what exactly it is you're planning on doing once we get to the clifftop?" Knot asked, turning his head so Cinzia would hear him. He hoped they weren't riding into the jaws of death for nothing.

"I just need to hold the gemstone, and it will take me into the Void."

Knot frowned. ? How would Cinzia possibly get into the Void? She wasn't a psimancer.

"The gemstone provides a connection to the Void for me," Cinzia said, either sensing or anticipating his worry.

"And once in the Void?"

"Once in the Void, I'm going to kill the Nine Daemons."

Knot spurred his horse onward, eyes narrow.

"I can tell you all about it," Cinzia said, "after it's done."

Assuming we survive all this.

Cinzia's arms tightened around his waist.

The nearest Outsiders turned their sleek heads, each one full of fangs and a pair of dull eyes, to take in the approaching riders.

Knot took the reins in one hand and drew his sword. The Outsiders would make quick work of the horses; he debated whether or not to tell them all to dismount when Jane rode out ahead of them.

"Jane!" Cinzia called out, but the Prophetess did not look back.

Jane's blonde hair streamed behind her as she spurred her horse, one hand raised, palm forward. For a moment that was all there was: a woman riding toward a dozen monsters.

Then a hot, white light blasted forth from Jane's palm. Knot remembered a similar beam of light at the Odenite camp outside Kirlan when Outsiders attacked; he had only seen the light from a distance, but the white heat was the same, and outside of Kirlan it had obliterated one of the Outsiders.

As it did here.

The beam cut directly through two Outsiders caught in its path; anything caught in the light disintegrated. The arm and tail of one Outsider evaporated, and it roared in pain, while the head and torso of another did the same, and the beast's remaining parts fell lifelessly to the ground.

"How close do we need to get?" Jane shouted back at them.

"Canta Rising," Knot whispered. For a moment, he had the tiniest hope that this might work.

"Eward! Now!"

Astrid pulled both claws from the Outsider's back and flipped backwards into the air, clearing the monster just as a volley of three dozen arrows turned it into a pincushion.

476

She landed in a crouch, ready to pounce again, but the beast wavered, then tumbled to the ground. The earth shook with the impact. She grabbed the sword that Eward tossed her and drove it into the Outsider's eye to be sure it wouldn't get up again.

"Nice work!" She and the Prelates had become a decent team; this was the third Outsider they had taken down that night. Astrid provided a distraction—something she could do easily enough, given her enhanced speed at night—dealing what damage she could, while Eward's Prelates stuck it with as many spears and arrows as possible.

"Wish there was time to celebrate it," Eward said, looking east, "but we've got another one near the river."

Astrid followed his gaze. Sure enough, another dark form rose, and she heard the low rumble of its roar, felt it in her chest.

"Shit," she whispered. When would they stop?

She glanced up at the cliffs. The spiraling lights were no longer organized and symmetrical; they flickered, dancing around the clifftops. There was a fight going on up there. She needed to be a part of it.

But the people here needed her, too. She could not very well abandon them.

A large shape—far larger than any of the Outsiders she had seen thus far—dropped from the shimmering portal in the sky, falling toward the cliffs. When it finally struck the cliffs, the entire Sfaera seemed to shake.

She had seen one of these, once before. Beneath the dome in Izet, a massive Outsider, perhaps ten times the size of the others, had risen. Winter had pulled down the entire dome on the thing's head to defeat it.

And now one stood atop the cliffs.

Another whistling sound, and another dark shape plummeted

toward the cliffs. The Sfaera shook again, and another colossal form rose.

These huge Outsiders were slightly different in form than their smaller counterparts; while the Outsiders Astrid was used to fighting walked on two legs, using their fore claws as weapons, the huge ones rose on all fours like gargantuan lizards; jaws large enough to swallow the smaller Outsiders whole sat atop thick necks, and tails wove back and forth, covered in dark spikes.

One of them snaked its head up toward the sky and issued a bone-shaking roar, the likes of which Astrid had never heard. The Prelates around her clapped hands over their ears, cowering away from the sound.

"*Shit*," she whispered again. They were barely holding their own against the Outsiders down here; there was no way they could do anything against those monsters.

Astrid attempted to summon Radiance, as she had many times already, but the blade still did not come.

Goddess, what good was the power if it took her a dozen more lifetimes to learn to control it?

"Astrid…" Eward stared up at the cliffs.

"We can't do anything about them right now. Let's get to the river. Take care of the Outsider there. Then we'll see what we can do about…"

Astrid shook her head, a quake running down her spine as another beast roared.

"…then we'll see what we can do about that."

44

URSTADT FLINCHED AS ANOTHER horrific roar thundered through her, then spurred her spooked horse on. She caught glimpses of the bright colors of the Nine Daemons through the trees on occasion, heard the sounds of fighting, and was hungry to join it.

She rode at the head of fifteen hundred Rangers, with Rorie at her side. Winter had ordered them not to come back under any circumstances, but once they had seen the supernatural lights in the sky, Urstadt had said to Oblivion with circumstances. Rorie had quickly agreed. Loyal as they were to their queen, the Rangers were not a force to mindlessly follow orders, especially when it put their leader, who had done more than most to free them from tyranny, in danger.

A few hundred Rangers had chosen to stay behind; some under the pretense of holding their position, others stubbornly holding on to Winter's orders, while a few admitted freely they had no desire to ride back into a battle where monsters roamed. Every single one of the Rangers present with their company had been there for the Battle of the *Rihnemin*. Every single one of them knew what they were facing.

When Urstadt broke through the forest onto the plains of Litori, she had no time to take in the battlefield. Three Outsiders snaked their heads around, sensing the movement from the forest. The moment they saw Urstadt and the Rangers, all three of them took a running leap toward the tiellan forces.

"Form squads!" Urstadt shouted. After the Battle of the *Rihnemin*, the Rangers had prepared almost daily for another fight with Outsiders. She hoped the training would hold up now.

Snow drifted down around her as she he spurred her horse forward, the Rangers fanning out behind. Urstadt gripped her glaive but even through her gauntlet she could feel the cold of the weapon. Such things did not bother her so much, but she worried how the tiellans would fare while fighting in the cold. Her horse whinnied, shaking its head, but she leaned forward and patted the animal, whispering soothing sounds, unsure whether the horse could even hear her through the cacophony. Tiellan clan horses were well trained, but even they could only handle so much.

Urstadt and Rorie, along with eight other Rangers, formed a squad, and Urstadt took point, rushing at the nearest Outsider that had just leapt in front of them. Urstadt leaned in the saddle, spurring her horse to the side just as the creature clawed at her. She jabbed it with her glaive, and Rorie followed with her lance.

Outsiders swarmed around the clifftop, hundreds of them. At least two colossal monsters, far larger than any of the other beasts that swarmed around Litori, roamed the cliffs, towering above the others. To the east, something else was happening. A beam of white light, some kind of weapon, sliced through Outsiders as if they were paper; Urstadt could not discern much else than that. Near the edge of the cliff, a swirling battle of color raged. Eight colors, to be precise; for eight remaining Daemons.

Winter had to be there.

Urstadt spurred her horse forward and thrust her glaive into the closest Outsider's ribs. Her squad had already stuck the thing a dozen times over; hot red blood dripped from a dozen wounds. Urstadt's horse reared as the Outsider turned to face them. With a tug, Urstadt used the horse and the Outsider's momentum combined to tear her glaive from the side of its chest in a wash of fresh gore. She struck again, this time where the neck met the jawline, and her glaive pierced deep. As she pulled it out, the Outsider stumbled, then toppled to the ground.

The other squads had made quick work of the other two Outsiders that had attacked them. They had also attracted the attention of half a dozen more.

Out of the corner of her eye, Urstadt saw movement toward the north. Movement that was not the shining, sinewy black bodies of Outsiders. Soldiers crested onto the cliffs from Litori's Pass.

She doubted Triah would send troops by that route; if anything, they'd send another regiment up the wider pass to the east.

That had to be Cova.

The distance between the Rangers and the Rodenese was greater than the distance between the Rangers and the swirling battle of colors where Winter must be, but the Outsiders between the Rangers and Rodenese were far fewer and more spread out; no more than two dozen, all told, while they would have to fight their way through five or six dozen, including the two immense devils, to get to Winter. The beam of white light to the east still shone, and seemed to be on the move, but that was an unknown quantity.

Roden, at least, was Roden.

Another roar from one of the massive beasts shook the ground beneath Urstadt's feet.

Oblivion, she would be deaf before this battle ended. If she didn't die first.

"Fight to the west!" Urstadt shouted when the roar subsided. "Unite with those forces!"

As they rode toward the approaching soldiers, Rorie rode up beside Urstadt.

"Those are the Rodenese forces."

"They are," Urstadt said.

"They hate tiellans."

"Not all of us do, Rorie."

"But Winter—"

"*We* need help first," Urstadt said, "if we want to help the queen. We will stand the best chance of reaching her if we unite with Roden. Even if they only sent a tenth of their soldiers, that more than doubles our numbers."

And we'd better pray to whoever might listen that they sent more than a tenth.

Rorie nodded reluctantly.

As Urstadt spurred her horse onward—the animal, given the option, certainly seemed more optimistic about this trajectory than she had going toward Winter—she hoped she had made the right decision.

She patted the horse's neck again. "Don't worry, girl," she said. "We'll be heading to Winter soon enough. I hope you build up the courage by then."

She hoped the same for herself.

Cinzia and Knot rode behind the Prophetess, Jane's white light disintegrating any Outsider that dared cross their path.

Goddess, why hasn't she used this power before? We could have destroyed the Outsiders easily, Cinzia thought.

But even Jane could only wield so much power for so long. Already the light was starting to fade.

"Jane, stop here!" Cinzia shouted. This would have to be close enough. She dismounted, and Knot followed, his sword drawn. He looked down at it, eyes wide. It was, perhaps, the first time Cinzia had seen him at a loss as to what to do.

"I don't know what I can do to help," he said.

Cinzia took his face gently in both her hands, and brought it to hers. They kissed, and a light, airy elation filled her, as if, for the briefest moment, the weight of all that happened around them, the doom and the death and the Outsiders and the Daemons, was lifted from her, and in their place she was filled with light, and with love.

When she pulled away from him, she could not stop the smile spreading wide across her face. The weight was already returning—the weight of what she was about to do, of what she *had* to do if they wanted the Sfaera to survive—but it was not as bad as it had been moments before.

"I've let Goddessguards protect me for most of my life," Cinzia said, stroking his cheek as she stepped away from him. She reached for the gem in the pouch at her belt. When she withdrew it, a bright red glow burst from the stone, illuminating everything around them in a vibrant crimson.

"It is time I returned the favor."

Urstadt and the Rangers made solid progress, driving their way west through the Outsiders toward Cova's army. Cova—or whoever was leading the Rodenese—must have noticed what they were trying to do, or had the same idea, and Roden made headway toward them, too, the Reapers in dark blue tunics and dark gray lacquered armor leading the vanguard.

The Rangers cut through the monsters efficiently; they suffered inevitable casualties, but Urstadt would be surprised if they lost more than one tiellan for each monster taken down by a Ranger squad. Some squads, including her own, took down monster after monster repeatedly without losing a single Ranger. There were a few squads, however, who met with disaster, losing half a dozen or more Rangers in a confrontation, almost always because another Outsider blindsided them from the south.

Although their progress drew more beasts to them, hundreds of the monsters didn't engage at all. Instead, they clumped together in great groups, some stalking about, others standing perfectly still. This included, thankfully, the two massive Outsiders.

A shape, much larger than the other Outsiders the Rangers had been fighting, fell from above. The more common, relatively smaller Outsiders fell from just a half dozen rods in the air or so, but the huge ones toppled down and down from at least a hundred rods, if not more. The enormous shapes had time to pick up speed, and gave everyone around time to notice, to hear the great whooshing whistle as it careened toward the ground, screaming with momentum. This one's impact shook the very foundations of the Sfaera, and Urstadt's horse stumbled, then almost immediately panicked, practically sending Urstadt flying. She calmed the animal, as did the Rangers all around her with their own horses to varying degrees of success, but they were all painfully aware of where the massive beast had landed: almost exactly between the Rangers and the Rodenese Reapers.

Their way was blocked.

The Outsiders that stalked the ground between the two armies were dwarfed by the rising shape that had just landed among them.

The new Outsider was different than the other two who had landed and now milled about farther south on the cliff; it was perhaps just a touch smaller than its two massive cousins, but instead it rose on its hind legs, and looked very much like one of the smaller Outsiders in appearance: long, muscled arms with a set of claws on each the size of spears; powerful hind legs, and a long, swinging, spiked tail, with an unspeakably large head at the end of a twisting, sinewy neck.

The dragon was Roden's sigil, and Urstadt had seen many depictions of the legendary creatures from the Age of Marvels, in paintings, tapestries, sculpture, and more—serpentine winged beasts, with great claws and teeth, spouting flames from their mouths.

These massive Outsiders were not unlike dragons. Twisted, misshapen, perhaps—the Outsiders had none of the elegance of the artistic depictions she had seen, but instead were lopsided, malformed versions, without wings or the breath of fire. It seemed physically impossible that the Outsider that had just landed should be able to lift a head of such size, even on a neck as large and powerful as that. And its teeth, which protruded at all angles, were absurdly long; perhaps twice as long as a man, and thicker at the base than a man at the shoulders.

Snaggletooth stood slowly, rising to its full height—taller than the other two behemoths because it stood on its hind legs— and issued forth a roar the likes of which Urstadt had never heard, or imagined she would hear, in her worst nightmares, let alone in her lifetime.

But, unlike the other two behemoths, this one wasted no time. It lowered its gaze at the tiellan forces and charged forward, sprinting toward them.

Urstadt felt a warm trickle run down her legs, wetting the underclothes she wore beneath her armor.

"Regroup!" she screamed, her instinct kicking in as she wheeled her horse around. "Form a line! Get ready to—"

But it was too late. Snaggletooth was upon them.

The monster roared again, a deafening ringing in Urstadt's ears. As its jaws opened, Urstadt met the blackness inside.

One moment Cinzia was on the Sfaera, looking at Knot, gripping Canta's Heart in both hands, and then with a puff of red smoke she was back in the starry Void.

Just as Canta had told her, the Nine Daemons did not appear anything like the other star-lights in the Void. Instead of tiny points of light, they were more like great burning suns, or multidimensional eclipses, more accurately: bright spheres of light whose outer edges burned with color, but inside were black, far blacker even than the Void itself. The closer Cinzia got to them, the more clearly they appeared. That was why Canta had told Cinzia to get as close to the Daemons as possible in the Sfaera before sinking into the Void.

Nine of those dark suns burned before her now. And there was a tenth: a dark burning star, different and larger than the others. Cinzia would have thought it more powerful if she did not already suspect what—or who—it was.

It had to be Winter.

The lights moved about one another in a strange dance, sometimes colliding, sometimes weaving around one another, with Winter's dark star always the catalyst, the center of everything.

A white mist outlined Cinzia's hands, her body, her feet, even her dress; it was as if she was looking down at nothing but a glowing silhouette of herself. Instead of the gemstone she had been holding in the Sfaera, she now gripped a dagger, with a shining gold blade and bright red jewel in its pommel.

Take the dagger. Strike down your enemies. Let light back into the

Sfaera.

Canta had told Cinzia those words, so similar to the ones she had heard when she cut her own hand, ridding herself of Luceraf.

But now, Cinzia's hands shook as she moved.

For all her talk, for all her fear, she still hesitated now, when it came to the possibility of killing. Even if the being she was about to kill was a Daemon.

In her mind's eye, Cinzia suddenly saw a face: her old Goddessguard, Kovac, the way she remembered him, gray-brown beard and bright blue eyes, smiling at her. But, in an instant, that face changed. The eyes shifted into something horrible, something evil, leaking iridescent green smoke—how she had last seen him, possessed by Azael, trying to kill her.

A dagger appeared, protruding from one of Kovac's eyes, and the light in the other went out—both the evil green light, and the calm blue that Cinzia had loved as much as her own father.

Do it for Kovac.

Cinzia stepped forward, finding the nearest glowing sun. This one was a black gaping wound surround by burning green light: Samann. Envy. All of the rage and loss Cinzia had felt in the moment of Kovac's death came rushing back to her.

Gripping the dagger tightly, Cinzia thrust the weapon into the black center of the burning green orb. Just as she had thrust Kovac's own dagger into his eye, killing him.

She had been half afraid the green light would burn her, but her ethereal limbs felt nothing as her hands passed through the flame, burying the dagger in the dark center of the light.

For a moment, nothing happened. Had Canta sent her on a fool's errand? Or, worse, did Cinzia's doubts hinder her ability to do what was necessary?

Samann's light trembled, the movement increasing until it vibrated intensely, so quickly it almost became a blur. In a silent, fierce explosion, the light burst outward in an angry, flaming ring of bright green. Again, Cinzia felt nothing, *heard* nothing, only saw the light ripple outward. But the light did not return or reform; after the explosion, nothing was left. The strange sun-like light was gone, completely dissipated.

Cinzia stared at the space where Samann's light had been. Had she just killed one of the Nine Daemons?

45

THE SNAGGLE-TOOTHED OUTSIDER smashed into the tiellan forces, sending men and women flying as it rammed into them with its head, then swept up a good half-dozen at least in a single chomp of its jaws.

It roared again, and even from behind the sound was devastating. Cova covered her ears, cringing until the roar died away and the monster swiped at the tiellans' front line with one of its massive clawed arms, taking out another dozen soldiers. A group of Rangers rallied, throwing spears at the beast, but their weapons had little effect.

"Your Grace, we must get you away from the battlefield," General Horas said. "You cannot be here, not with a monster like that. I recommend a full retreat." He nodded to his second, who turned, about to relay the order, but Cova stopped him.

"No," she said, with as much confidence as she could muster. Horas was the better tactician by far. She had little experience at all in the matter. But she knew what they needed to do. "We press on. Form up archers, and have them concentrate all fire on that Goddess-damned snaggle-tooth. We are going to help those tiellans."

"But, Your Grace—"

"If we don't take care of that mammoth creature now," Cova said, meeting her general's gaze, "it might come after us next, and then we will have two thousand fewer allies to fight alongside us. It is now or never, General. If you don't agree with me, you can leave."

The general opened his mouth, but Cova spoke right over him. She was not about to let him off that easily.

"And if you choose to leave, I'll have you executed on the spot for refusing to follow orders, and desertion." She raised her sword. "I'll do it myself if I have to."

The general, face pale, looked from Cova to the Snaggletooth, then back to Cova again. Slowly, he nodded.

Before Cova could say anything more, a very different sound echoed through the night. A single, all-encompassing *thump*, like the boom of thunder but louder and felt in the chest and bones far more than heard by the ears.

Canta Rising, what was that? Was there not enough going on already? The sound seemed to have come from the light-battle ensuing to the south.

General Horas, also shaken by the strange blast, nevertheless saluted. "Yes, Your Grace."

"Press the attack."

"Right away." Cova's army reformed, focusing on the Snaggletooth.

She hoped to Oblivion she did not live to regret her decision.

Winter did not know what had happened. One moment, she was fighting the Nine Daemons, hundreds of weapons at her disposal. Fighting the Nine, even with the arsenal she controlled, was like attacking wisps of smoke. Literal smoke, in Hade's case, but no matter who she attacked, they managed to evade almost every strike.

Strangely, the Nine did not seem focused on attacking

her, only on defending themselves. As they entwined, Winter noticed they had begun to look more human. Their forms diminished, their monstrous features fading. Samann's wolf-like face softened, shedding some of its hair, the nose shortening and ears shifting and shrinking.

When Winter first attacked, the Outsiders seemed *surprised*. It did not take them long to recover; Iblin barreled forward, but his actions were strange. He didn't try to crush her, or pummel her to death. Instead, he seemed more interested in stopping her, grabbing hold of her, although Winter could not imagine what he would do to her if he was successful. Similarly, Samann and Luceraf sought to disable Winter with their claws and talons, but never attempted a killing blow.

Winter found it far too easy to avoid all of them.

Bazlamit, on the other hand, tried a much more roundabout method. Her bulbous, globular form shimmered and vibrated, and then split into two separate halves, and suddenly Winter faced her old mentors, Kali and Nash.

"Stop what you are doing, Winter," Kali said. She wore what Winter always recalled her wearing: black leathers, tightly fitted, with her curved Nazaniin sword at her side. This was the version Winter had best known her as, the tall version with dark hair and striking blue eyes.

"We only want to help you," Nash said, and the emotion that bubbled up at seeing him surprised her. He looked exactly the same, including the scar on his cheek, the circular blades at his belt.

With an effort, Winter ignored them, fighting on.

Hade and Estille evaded her advances, but didn't attack at all.

Nadir's onslaught worried Winter the most, though it, too,

seemed far from lethal. Winter could not see the Daemon's attacks, but she felt an immense pressure in her mind, building and building and building, as if her brain were expanding in her skull and there was no way to release the force. As if her own blood were boiling her brain alive. As if she were losing control not only of her grip on reality, but on herself and everything it meant to be her.

Fortunately, Winter discovered that her acumenic *tendra* came in handy when defending herself from Nadir's attacks.

Azael was the most mysterious of all of them. He simply stood still at the center of it all, unmoving, as the fight blazed around him.

Something is not right. Winter could feel it in her marrow. The Daemons should be trying to demolish her, send her to Oblivion, but they seemed far more interested in something else, something Winter could not discern.

As she fended off Nadir's attacks with her acumency while simultaneously keeping up her telenic offensive against the others, she noticed new arrivals getting closer.

Her eyes focused immediately on Knot, walking up toward the Daemons as if he hadn't a care in the world. Winter's heart twisted in her chest—he would be crushed before he even understood what was going on. Winter fumed with fury, concern, and confusion all at once. What in Oblivion had brought him here, anyway?

Jane, the priestess's sister, was with him, an almost blindingly white light bursting forth from her hands. Stranger still, she caught a glimpse of something else: a flash of movement, a trick of the eye, a woman who was there and then was not there, and looked vaguely familiar.

Finally, as Samann twisted his lupine form to swipe his

large paw at her, something else happened.

The Daemon disappeared.

The battle all around her stopped, the Daemons turning to stare at the place their brother had been in confusion.

Winter was sucked toward the space Samann had once occupied, as if his sudden absence pulled everything around it inward, desperately trying to fill the space that was now empty. A peculiar sound accompanied the shift, a soft, grating *pop*, the way her ears had popped when she had climbed the Sorensan Mountains.

The power of Samann's disappearance—his *death?*—affected the other Daemons, as they skidded toward the vacant location until the power dissipated.

In that moment, Winter saw another shady flash of movement, as if the falling snow had settled on someone's head and shoulders for a brief moment, and then rethought the fact that there might be a person there at all, and continued drifting toward the ground.

Winter closed her eyes, and let herself fall into the Void.

In the Void the woman sees the sun-stars, the residue of the Daemons in the space she has come to know and love. But there is something else there, too, unexpected.

A woman.

The priestess, Cinzia Oden.

Is she a psimancer? No. Cinzia Oden drifts through the Void, not as a typical star-light, nor the ersatz version of herself, the way the woman or Kali or other psimancers appear in the Void, more or less similar to how they appear on the Sfaera but ever so slightly transparent, with footsteps echoing ripples of light with each step.

No, this is like looking at a sketch of the priestess, of pale white light, stuttering through the Void, on occasion not even visible at all.

The priestess moves toward one of the nine—*eight* remaining suns, and suddenly the woman notices her dagger of gold and crimson, almost giving off its own light in the Void. Unlike the priestess, and even unlike the woman herself, the dagger looks *real*; not a sketched outline of light like the priestess, nor a projection of itself like the woman, but something that exists completely and wholly.

With a lunge, the priestess thrusts the dagger into one of the dark suns, and for a moment nothing happens. Then, in a bright explosion the sun sends out a shockwave of silvery burning light.

The silvery sun is gone. Bazlamit is gone, just like Samann had gone before her.

"*What are you doing here?*" the woman asks, and the priestess turns to respond, the white outline of her face fading in and out of the Void.

"I am killing Daemons," the priestess says, her voice echoing as if she were speaking from the bottom of a long, deep well. "Keep distracting them, and I will kill them all."

But how? the woman wants to ask. *And with* what?

But there is not much time. The priestess, it appears, has the same goal as she does. They must end the reign of the Nine before it begins. They must save the Sfaera.

So, she nods to the priestess. "Work quickly." And then she goes back to her body, battling Daemons.

Urstadt blinked into consciousness.

It was night. It was snowing. Cold bit at her face, pain split her skull and burrowed through her shoulder. She tried to move, but something held her down. Snowflakes drifted down, the shimmering darkness straight above, and over an unmoving hump a massive shape roared, the sound piercing through the already loud cacophony of battle.

The damned Snaggletooth.

Urstadt's head cleared, and she remembered the monster's mouth gaping before her. How was she still alive? She tried to move the dead weight on top of her. It took her just a moment to realize it was Rorie, or part of her at least, torn in half at the waist by Snaggletooth's teeth or claws or Oblivion knew what.

Rorie must have been, at least in part, why Urstadt was still alive.

A very different pain pierced through Urstadt's body, more acute than the pain in her head, and far deeper than the pain in her shoulder. Rorie had been a good soldier, but more than that, Urstadt had grown fond of her.

With an effort that sent a jolt of fresh pain through her shoulder, Urstadt rolled Rorie's torso off of her, and kicked away another tiellan corpse on her feet. Urstadt struggled to stand, breathing in the fresh, cold air, in time to see Snaggletooth's huge foot stomp down on three mounted tiellans, crushing all of them at once, and then swiping at another squad advancing on it.

Canta Rising, the Rangers did not stand a chance against that thing.

Urstadt had to regroup the tiellan forces, but the battle had moved north of her, where Snaggletooth now dealt with more tiellan squads. In the distance, a small ray of hope showed itself in the form of the Rodenese Reapers, now advancing on Snaggletooth in a loose formation, archers continually peppering it with arrows that glanced off its hide. They could likely overwhelm the gargantuan beast eventually with sheer numbers, but that assumed very little intervention from other

Outsiders, or the two—no, Urstadt realized as she looked south, *five* more towering dragon-like beasts lingering around Litori. Three more must have dropped while she was unconscious.

Urstadt swore, looking about for her glaive, but found nothing. Her sword rested intact at her hip, but that would do little good here. She needed something else, something…

Her gaze found what she sought. When making the war machines to assault Triah, the tiellan engineers had made a few ballistae as well. After dismantling the War Goddess, the tiellans had left most of the other siege engines intact; they'd posed no threat to Triah from atop the cliffs, anyway. This ballista still appeared operational.

The bolts were scattered across the grass, knocked flying by a dead tiellan Ranger. She picked up one and carried it to the ballista, then lined up her shot.

Snaggletooth twisted around to claw at a group of approaching Reapers, snapping its tail out behind it at the same time and cutting through a line of tiellans.

Urstadt pulled the ballista's trigger.

With a deep *snap* of the drawstring the bolt shot forward. Urstadt squinted but lost track of it in the night. For a moment she thought it had hit Snaggletooth but had no effect; then, an Outsider behind and to the side of Snaggletooth shuddered and fell, the bolt protruding from the side of its head.

Urstadt cursed, and retrieved another bolt. This time she waited until Snaggletooth turned sideways, swiping its tail at a squad of Reapers, and then she fired. The bolt plunged into Snaggletooth's shoulder.

The colossal monster snapped its jaw down on a group of Rangers, leaving shredded body parts and horses where tiellans on horseback had once been, and Urstadt was worried the bolt would have no effect, when Snaggletooth shuddered and craned its massive head around to look at the wound. Upon seeing the bolt, Snaggletooth snaked its head upward toward the stars and roared so loudly the snow seemed to stop in fear.

Snaggletooth's head lowered, and its gaze scanned outward from its wound, settling on Urstadt and the ballista.

Urstadt swore and cranked the winch lever as fast as her fatigued muscles would allow. She slid a new bolt into place as Snaggletooth thundered toward her, its giant maw open.

"Rot in Oblivion, you son of a bitch," Urstadt muttered, then pulled the trigger mechanism.

The bolt shot up and forward, but did not have much room to travel. It embedded itself in Snaggletooth's eye the full length, only a few fingers of wood and fletching protruding from the now rapidly leaking gooey surface. The gargantuan beast fell to the ground with the sound of a deafening thunder clap; Urstadt only just managed to leap out of the way as it slid to a stop, and was still.

Between Jane's cascading beam of white light, Winter's onslaught against the Nine, and Cinzia as she wove in and out of reality, assassinating Daemons, Knot felt incredibly useless. He attempted to attack an Outsider once that got too close to Cinzia's position, but Jane's beam of light had swept over the beast before Knot could get within reach.

And yet, he had never been more proud.

Jane's power mystified him. He had no inkling of how she did what she did, but she clearly wielded great power. He and Jane had certainly had their differences, but he was grateful to be on her side.

Winter's power astounded him. He knew of all she had

done, knew she was behind the massacre in Navone and the destruction of the imperial dome in Izet, but she had to be using not just dozens, but *hundreds* of weapons at the moment. More than any living psimancer could conceive, let alone control. But Winter's attacks on the Daemons were both fierce and masterful.

What Cinzia did made his hair stand on end. He only caught glimpses of her, but her shadow moved from one Daemon to the next, and the orange, yellow, and red lights winked out, one by one. Each imploded in another reverse thunderclap, drawing everything near it inward before it collapsed into nothing. At times Knot glimpsed the gemstone Cinzia carried around in both hands, but at others he could swear she held a dagger, bright golden blade glinting.

"*Enough!*" Azael shouted, his voice burning deep. "I thought you were going to save the Sfaera. Instead, you have doomed it." The Daemon turned to the remaining three. "Hade, Estille, Luceraf. We must regroup. Salvage what we can." The black, hooded figure, once so imposing, seemed hardly more than a man in a dark cloak, now.

"I hope you understand what you have done before it is all over," Azael said. He indicated the Outsiders all around them. "I could have managed the destruction these would wreak, had you let us continue. But now I cannot. I leave you to reap what you have sown." Azael hesitated, then spoke again. "They will be drawn to the largest congregations of people nearby. Protect them if you can."

Then, in a cloud of dark smoke, Azael, Hade, and Nadir were gone, and Jane, Knot, and Winter were left facing a field of Outsiders.

In an instant, Cinzia's visage flickered, then reappeared

completely, as she shoved the gemstone back into the pouch at her belt.

"What happened?" she demanded. "Where did the others go?"

"They left," Knot said, his voice quiet. To his side, Jane teetered, then collapsed. Knot barely caught her before she hit the ground.

"Where? Where did they go? I have to—"

"We have more immediate problems," Knot said, nodding at the Outsiders.

Whatever had kept the beasts relatively passive, whatever had kept them from grouping and overwhelming their attackers, was gone, now. They all turned to look at Knot, Cinzia, Jane, and Winter, black eyes gleaming, maws dripping rancid saliva.

"Oh Goddess," Cinzia whispered.

"We've got to get out of here," Knot said, already suspecting there was no hope. Jane was incapacitated in his arms. He looked to Winter.

She shook her head slowly. "I cannot handle this many, even at my strongest. I'm practically burned out, Knot. Any further use, and I'm afraid... I don't think I would make it."

Knot growled in frustration. There had to be something. "Cinzia, can you—"

"There might be something else I could try," Winter said, her eyes darting toward the Outsiders enclosing on their position. "Gather close to me, all of you..."

Astrid took a running leap and launched herself into the night, everything slowing around her. Snowflakes almost froze in place in the air, only disturbed as she crashed through them. The Prelates below and behind her became momentary statues, drawing bows, thrusting spears, shouting orders. And the

Outsider that stood tall before her slowly turned its head to meet Astrid's attack.

It turned too slowly.

Astrid collided with the side of the Outsider's head, her claws digging in to the monster's flesh for purchase. Prelates jabbed spears up into the monster's ribs from below as Astrid scrambled to the top of its head. She gripped herself in place with her feet, raised both hands high, and brought them down on the top of the Outsider's skull with as much force and strength as she could muster.

Both fists pierced the Outsider's flesh, then with a sickening *crunch* smashed through its skull, bits of bone and gore flying.

The monster went limp beneath her, and Astrid leapt away as it fell, landing awkwardly in a roll of mud and snow and blood. When she pushed herself to her feet, she looked for Eward.

"What's next?" she asked, shaking filth from herself as she approached.

Eward looked around, then met the eyes of an incoming group of Prelates.

"No more reports, sir," one of them said.

No more reports. Had they killed all the Outsiders in the Odenite camp already?

Astrid turned to look at the cliffs. The raging war of colors was gone, as was the shimmering portal that had once twisted above the cliff.

"Did they actually *win?*" Astrid asked, to no one in particular. But it couldn't be true. Hundreds of Outsiders still swarmed the clifftop, and a few, three or four at least, of the massive monsters.

"There don't seem to be any more Outsiders appearing in the camp," Eward said. "I think the portals have closed."

But as he said the words, the air around them crackled with energy.

"What the Goddess-damned Oblivion," Astrid muttered, taking a step back. Something was coming.

A cloud of black smoke billowed out of nothing. Astrid braced herself to pounce, glancing at Eward, who nodded, sword raised, signaling the remaining Prelates to form up.

Three shadows emerged from the smoke. Three shadows, but four people, Astrid realized. Knot, carrying an unconscious Jane, Cinzia walking beside them, and behind them both, the Chaos Queen herself, Winter Cordier.

Astrid couldn't stop the wide grin spreading across her face.

As Winter stepped into the Odenite camp, tendrils of black smoke wisped between her fingers, trailing along her arms.

She glanced at Knot, but he did not return her gaze.

At least I got us out of there. She honestly had not thought it would work, but after using the travelstone, something had itched within her, until she'd attempted weaving all three *tendra*—her telenic, acumenic, and voyantic *tendra*—together. In doing so, with some practice, she had managed to recreate whatever force the travelstone allowed her to access. The act had taken every last bit of power she had; it was all she could do to remain standing without help, but she'd be damned if she showed weakness now.

Before Winter could process what had just happened any further, a small form rushed past her, colliding with Knot. It was Astrid. The girl pulled Knot and Cinzia close to her, hugging them both tightly.

They looked for all the world like a pristine little family finally reunited. A stab of jealousy pierced Winter's heart.

"That's the last time I let you two go anywhere without me," the girl said.

A young man, not far behind Astrid, hovered over Jane.

"What happened? Is she all right?"

"She'll be fine, Eward," Cinzia said woodenly. Then she seemed to notice her tone, and added with more compassion in her voice, "I think she just exhausted herself."

"Doing what?" A group of women had gathered around Jane, taking her from Knot toward some kind of makeshift field hospital.

"Protecting me," Cinzia said.

"What happened here?" Knot asked. "Did you defeat the Outsider?"

Only then did Winter become aware of the massive dark corpse just a few rods away.

"Oh…"

"That wasn't the only one, I'm afraid," Eward said. "We've killed a half-dozen of them at least. We've lost a lot of people. The disciples have been healing, but even still… many Odenites are dead."

Winter clenched her jaw. Many were dead because of the Outsiders. The Outsiders were here because of the Nine Daemons.

And Winter had summoned them.

"There are four Daemons left alive," Cinzia said through gritted teeth.

"You killed five of them?" Winter asked.

Cinzia only nodded.

"Wait," Eward said, "what are you talking about? Cinzia, *you* killed the Nine Daemons?"

"Five of them," Winter said. "Perhaps."

Eward did a double-take, and now stood dumbstruck,

staring at Winter.

"You're... you're the Chaos Queen."

Immediately, the Prelates around them all shifted, reaching for weapons. Winter herself tensed. She had not thought about what her presence here might mean; she had only wanted to get everyone out of there as quickly as possible.

"Put down those weapons," Cinzia said. "She helped us defeat the five." Then she turned to face Winter and Knot. "But we need to find the other four. We have to finish this."

Knot inclined his head, but Winter was not so sure.

"Something is not right about all of this," Winter said, wavering slightly. Bloody Oblivion, she needed to rest. "Did you hear what Azael said? He said, 'I thought you were going to save the Sfaera.'"

"Because you summoned them in the first place?" Cinzia asked, a sharp edge to her voice.

"*Regardless*," Winter said, her voice hard, "something was not right, even from the beginning. They seemed to think summoning them would do something *good* for the Sfaera, not cause its destruction."

"Of course they would want you to think that," Astrid said, "They're the Nine Daemons."

"Perhaps," Winter said, "but I think there was more to it than that. What they said, how they acted... they hardly even attacked me, even when I went after them with everything I had. They mostly just defended themselves, and one another."

Winter remembered Azael's frustration, his *sadness* as he and the remaining three Daemons left.

"Azael did say something about managing the destruction the Outsiders would cause," Cinzia said, "but I do not know if that means anything."

"We can discuss details of the battle later," Knot said. Winter followed his gaze to the cliffs, where the remaining Outsiders—hundreds of them, including the huge ones—were working themselves into a frenzy, moving toward the cliff's edge. "But we have to keep in mind the war is far from over."

As he said the words, something changed in the Outsiders on the clifftop. Their frenzy stopped, and they all stared down at the city. An eerie silence filled the night, accented by the softly falling snow. Dawn was close.

"Azael said that, when left to their own devices, they would seek the largest congregations of people," Cinzia said.

The moment of stillness did not last long. With a roar, one of the Outsiders leapt from the cliff. Cinzia stared, wondering whether the thing had just leapt to its death, but as she squinted into the dark, the shape *sprinted* down the cliff face as if it were a horizontal plane, as if the force of the Sfaera did not pull it down toward it—or did not pull it down fast enough.

Two more followed that first Outsider, and then three, and then dozens were sprinting down the Cliffs of Litori, roaring as they went.

Winter was vaguely aware of Knot and Eward giving orders, forming the armed men into ranks. She felt Cinzia's gaze on her.

"You are powerful," Cinzia said. "You are the Chaos Queen. Can you stop that?" she asked, pointing at the charging Outsiders.

Winter followed Cinzia's gaze, her eyes wide. Slowly, she shook her head. "I… with a *rihnemin*, perhaps I could, but the humans destroyed all the *rihnemin* here. I have some crystals left, but I could only do so much against them before I burned myself out, or died in the process." Even that was a generous estimate; Winter would not last more than a few minutes in her current state.

"So burn yourself out, or die in the process," Cinzia said quietly, her eyes uncharacteristically dark.

But Winter recognized the pale horror on Cinzia's face, the sense of sheer hopelessness. Hundreds of Outsiders remained, including at least five or six of the huge versions of the beasts. Now that they were charging, she did not know how they could be stopped. The entire Khalic Legion could stand in their way, and the Outsiders would slice through them like sickles through wheat.

They did not stand a chance. None of them did. It did not matter that Cinzia had killed four of the Daemons today; the Odenites and the people of Triah would all die anyway, and there was nothing any of them could do to stop it.

Cova oversaw the retreat of her soldiers with mixed feelings.

The monsters that had previously been uninterested in the fight had changed their tune when the light-battle had ended. The portals had snapped out of existence, at least—but the remaining Outsiders had threatened to overwhelm her people, even when they managed to unite with Urstadt's group.

The tiellans were a spent force. They had brought a few hundred Rangers with them, all wounded, an injured, weary Urstadt the only human among them. Tiellans had been outlawed from Roden for decades, and she wondered whether her people knew how to act around them—in the aftermath of battle was one thing, but once they had recovered, how would things stand? She had ordered those taking the tiellans onto their ships to treat them as they would any ally, but she worried nevertheless. It might have been a poor decision on her part.

But what else could she have done?

Cova boarded her ship, watching as the last of her soldiers boarded theirs. Then, they hauled up anchor and made their way out to sea, the snow drifting all around them, melting into the waves.

"Grand Marshal…"

In the courtyard of the Legion's barracks, Carrieri inspected the body of the Outsider. The hide was like a shark's skin: smooth to look at, but rough to the touch. He half expected his hand to be covered with dozens of tiny lacerations when he pulled it away, but he was uninjured.

"Grand Marshal, you need to see this."

"Another one?" Carrieri sighed wearily. He had received no reports of new Outsiders dropping from the sky in the city for the last half hour or so. That seemed a good sign, but he was far from ready to dismiss the threat.

Carrieri followed Ryven up the barracks' observation tower. It was not that high up—at five stories, not even as high as the Merchant's Tower—but enough to see over most of the buildings in the city. The lad pointed to the cliffs, where the lights of the Nine Daemons had burned only moments before. Now, Litori was dark.

"What is it I'm supposed to be…" but then, as his eyes adjusted to the darkness, he saw it. The cliffs appeared unusually dark. But as Carrieri squinted, he saw the cliffs *moving*.

The hundreds of Outsiders at the top of the cliffs poured down toward the city, sprinting vertically down the cliff face itself, packed so tightly the cliffs became a swarming waterfall of dark horror.

The daemons were coming, and Triah stood helpless in their path.

46

SNOW FELL ON THE trees, grass, and stones around Astrid as she sprinted toward the cliffs, a cold winter breeze in her hair. Sprinting was an understatement, not only because of her advanced speed, but because of what she knew she had to do. Jane was unconscious. Cinzia's strange gem-weapon could do nothing against the Outsiders. Winter had nothing left to give.

She deliberately looked down at her claws as she ran. She had always hated looking at herself, but now felt a sense of gratitude. If her friends had nothing left to give, she would give what she had to help them. She tried summoning Radiance again, expecting nothing, and again, nothing was what she got.

She had slunk away silently, as Knot and Eward organized the Prelates, as Cinzia and Winter argued over what to do. She had wanted to squeeze Knot's hand, to tell him thank you, to tell him so many things.

She remembered sitting with him by the banks of the River Arden, not long after they'd met. *If you've kept it, after all these years, you've managed something incredible. Never let it go.* He'd said that to her, and it had changed everything.

"All my life, I've run away from trouble," Astrid whispered. There was no one but herself around to hear it, but she whispered it to Knot, across the growing distance that separated them. "Since I met you, I've begun to run toward it. What have you done to me, nomad?"

The first Outsiders were just reaching the base of the cliff as Astrid approached them at full speed, her eyes glowing, claws ready. A large field separated the cliffs from the city, a few hundred meters wide. The Odenite camp lay at the easternmost edge of that field, spilling south toward the river, while the city stretched south and west.

Astrid burst forward, her muscles tensing, and she leapt onto the back of the nearest Outsider as it scrambled down the cliff face. With a scream she tore her claws through its hide, but she did not remain long. Another monster turned with a low growl and swung its own massive claw—as large as Astrid herself— but she leapt onto a new victim. The Outsider who had turned to strike her instead gouged the monster on which she had first landed. The injured beast growled, turning on the one that had attacked it, and the two tumbled to the snow-covered grass below in a biting, clawing ball of rage.

Astrid felt the weight of more and more Outsider eyes on her, but their momentum carried them down the cliffside too quickly for them to do much about it other than take the occasional swipe at her, more often than not injuring one of their own kind. Astrid leapt from beast to beast, zipping in and out and around and between them, using her nighttime power and agility. While the Outsiders were quick, they could not match her.

Astrid ran on pure instinct, slashing and clawing here and there, but it wasn't enough. Not even close. At best, she managed a light distraction as the Outsiders made their inexorable way toward the city, and toward the Odenites. Toward Knot and Cinzia; toward Jane, Arven, Ehram, Pascia, and Ader; toward everything in the Sfaera that Astrid cared about.

She was almost halfway up the cliff, now, leaping and sprinting from Outsider to Outsider. Some of them tried to turn and go after her in anger or confusion, but going up the cliff was much more difficult than going down, especially with the momentum of dozens of other Outsiders pushing in the opposite direction.

Astrid growled, the sound low and coming from her gut. *A flaming sword sure would be useful right about now*, Astrid thought, but she had to come to terms with life without the blade. It had been an iridescent miracle when she needed it most, and for that, she was grateful, but Eldritch had emphasized how slowly such powers grew, how difficult it was to control them. Astrid had no choice but to accept that.

But, then again, she'd never been one to settle. She looked down at one of her hands again, *willing* Radiance to appear there. But as she did so, she distracted herself just enough to miss a huge Outsider's claw snapping toward her, knocking her off the back of the one on which she stood, out into the snow falling through the night, and down toward the field below.

"Knot, where is Astrid?"

Knot turned from the Prelates. He had been about to give them some kind of motivational speech, but he'd be damned if he could think of a single thing to say when it was just this Prelate force against a mass of monsters that large, racing down the cliff toward them.

Cinzia walked toward him quickly, her hair blowing in her face, covered in flakes of snow.

"Thought she was with you," he grunted.

"She is not," Cinzia said, and the worry in her voice made his gut twist. "Nor with Winter, nor anywhere else I've looked."

Knot frowned. "She was here when we came through the traveling cloud. That was only moments ago…"

The twist in his gut compounded, wrapping in on itself over and over again, churning in the pain that came with realization and terror. He looked toward the cliffs, dreading what he might see.

Cinzia followed his gaze.

"That… cannot be her," she said softly.

A green streak of light moved across the fields, and leapt high into the night and onto the Outsiders racing down the cliffside.

"What in *Oblivion* is that girl doing?" Knot growled, but he'd known, deep down, the moment Cinzia had asked where she was.

She had gone toward the bloody trouble.

The green light bounced up the cliffs like a tiny firefly. A few Outsiders fell in its wake, and despite his horror, despite the worry in his gut, a flash of pride burst in his chest.

But then something happened. The green firefly fell from its height halfway up the cliff, plummeting toward the base of the rock.

Knot rushed forward, but Eward was suddenly there, holding him back.

Knot whirled on the lad. He knew Eward's intentions were good, but he didn't care. He punched Eward full on in the face, and the lad swung around, almost losing his balance. But he came at Knot again, gripping his arm tightly.

"You can't do anything about that, Knot!" Eward shouted. "We need you here. We need you with the Prelates. You can do the most good with us, not out there with her. Astrid can handle herself. We've seen her do it, time and time again."

Eward looked to Cinzia for help, but Cinzia said nothing.

Her mouth was open, but she remained silent and staring at the spot where Astrid had fallen.

Knot turned back. He could not see the green light anymore. Had he missed it when she struck the ground?

He was about to shove Eward off him again, Prelates be damned, Odenites be damned, everything and all Oblivion be damned, when a bright flash of light lit up the night sky, momentarily blinding him.

Astrid fell, and dreamt, drifting down with snowflakes, Outsiders raging and racing downward but unable to touch the stillness that surrounded her as she fell.

She dreamt she was on a ship. The dark sky, full of twinkling stars behind her, slowly converged with the pink rosy light of dawn. The sun's bright rays kissed her face, the warmth pleasant and welcome and something for which she had yearned her entire life. Astrid smiled in response, without fear and without question. This was right. This was what should happen.

Astrid looked over her shoulder, and noticed something on the ship she had never seen before.

It was just Knot, at first, but then Cinzia was there, too. They both stood close behind, standing next to one another, smiling at Astrid. Knot and Cinzia were there, but then so was Jane. And then Trave was there, too, but Astrid felt no animosity toward him, no anger, only a steady warmth, as if the sun that shone on her face filled her to the brim and overflowed toward him, too. And next to Trave, the Homemother, and again Astrid felt that same overflow of warmth. Some of these people had betrayed her, had hurt her, but they were all still her family. And then next to them…

Astrid's father. Her papa, smiling at her, and the same

warmth she felt from the rising sun also emanated from him, and in Papa's arms, a little boy, and a baby girl, that same incredible warmth all around them.

She had never felt more loved, or more capable of it.

Family is not about what we remember, or where we are. It's about how we feel, Cinzia had once said to her.

And here, on this ship, with these people behind her, Astrid knew she was with family.

A bright light burst into the night sky, temporarily blinding Cinzia, all colors at once and yet no color at the same time.

As her vision slowly returned, she scanned the field for Astrid's faint green light, but it was nowhere to be seen.

Knot struggled against Eward and the Prelates holding him back, but it was Cinzia's hand on him, her fingers closing tightly around his, that finally calmed him.

There was no green light, but there was something else. A great burning rainbow of color, in the shape of a sword as tall as a man. Illuminated by that fire, a small girl stood, her shadow flickering, her hair blowing in the winter breeze, snowflakes falling around her. The army of Outsiders still rumbled down the cliffs, all of them switching direction like a flock of birds, aiming their charge directly at the girl with the flaming sword. The monsters towered over the girl as they charged, but she stood her ground. The five gargantuan Outsiders rumbled to the base of the cliffs, all swinging their unfathomably large maws toward Astrid.

Knot returned Cinzia's grip tightly, and the two watched as their friend—their little girl—danced.

Astrid struck the ground, disoriented, but immediately rose to her feet, whatever pain accompanied her fall and the impact completely forgotten, overtaken by the memory of the ship, of the sun, and of her family.

When she looked down at her claws, she realized Radiance burned in one hand, the giant, flaming blade reaching high above her.

If you've kept it, after all these years, you've managed something incredible. Never let it go.

She heard their voices in her mind, mixed with her own. She heard their voices, and they were with her, even though they were not.

Family is not about what we remember, or where we are. It's about how we feel.

She felt them burning inside of her, felt their love and their hope and their fears and their forgiveness.

I love you. It doesn't matter what you are. It doesn't matter where you've been...

"All that matters," Astrid whispered, "is what we do."

Just like her dream, Astrid knew the sun was about to rise. Both what was at stake and what she faced were as clear to her as a bright, clean brook.

Astrid swung Radiance, slicing into the first Outsider that reached her, and the b east immediately burst into an explosion of color and fire.

She dashed to the side, striking the next, and the next. Astrid bounced from Outsider to Outsider, demolishing each one with great, broad swings of Radiance. One, five, fifteen, thirty. Monster after monster fell to her blade in showers of burning color. Outsiders roared all around her, enough of them on the ground now that they could surround her completely, but she did not care. She was fast—nothing on the Sfaera had ever been so fast as she was now; she darted between them, around them, dashing everywhere at once, and they could not touch her. She was strong; she swung her great flaming sword, cutting through her enemies one by one. The roars pierced through her, but they were nothing compared to what she felt, compared to what she was, and compared to what she could do.

After the blinding flash of light, Carrieri focused on the tiny figure, holding an impossibly large flaming sword as it met the oncoming Outsider horde.

When she had begun to fight, slaying Outsider after Outsider with each stroke, swift and sure, a tiny seed of hope sprouted from somewhere deep within Carrieri. He had once seen an Alizian master calligrapher display his art, creating a document in moments with sharp, confident, brisk strokes of the arm-sized brush he wielded. This tiny illuminated being wielded her flaming sword the way the Alizian master calligrapher had wielded his black paintbrush. Each stroke had a purpose, the flaming edge creating arcs of colorful fire in its wake, leaving afterimages in patterns that Carrieri could not have imagined in his wildest, most creative dreams.

"What is that?" Ryven whispered beside him.

"That," Carrieri said, the spread of hope slowly blossoming, "is a Goddess-damned miracle, son."

Cova had descended to her cabin to think about what had happened, wanting to be alone. When someone came knocking on her door, insisting she come to the deck, she had almost lost it and sentenced the man to death right there. Fortunately, after a few deep breaths, she had gotten a hold of herself, and reluctantly walked out onto the deck, fully prepared to throw the man overboard if it was not something worth seeing.

It was, as it turned out, absolutely something worth seeing.

From their distance, far out into the bay, it was difficult to discern much. But what Cova did see was a blinding bar of light swinging in arcs, circles, spirals, and jagged lines, leaving burning afterimages in the dark behind it, causing every Outsider it connected with to burst into a fan of chromatic color and sparks. One of the massive, dragon-like beasts approached the zipping luminescence, but the light skidded back, then burst forward, gaining speed, running directly toward the underbelly of the beast. The Sfaera went dark once more as the light disappeared within the monster, but immediately illuminated again as it burst out of the monster's back, flying high into the air. The gargantuan Outsider started to collapse, but burst into an immense cloud of fire and color before it hit the ground.

Cova had gone into her cabin to think about their next move, and to deal with the crippling shame she felt at taking her forces away from Triah, leaving the city at the mercy of the Outsiders.

And here was someone, or some*thing*, doing what she could not.

Saving them all.

Cova wept openly at whatever it was that moved behind that bar of burning light, dispatching monster after monster. She wept until the tears streaming down her cheeks soaked the thick scarf at her neck, until her eyes were sore and dry, and her hands trembled from hope, worry, and gratitude all at once, until the snow finally stopped falling and the clouds in the sky began to part, revealing the first rays of a sharp winter dawn.

Astrid dreamt she was on a ship, and she dreamt she fought daemons, daemons that even daemons feared. She dreamt of swelling sails, and an ocean so still it could have been glass.

She dreamt a delicate dance of death as she flickered from one Outsider to another, Radiance bursting every one of them into flame and fire and sparks and shadow. She dreamt of the sun rising in the east, the pink, purple, and orange hues rising slowly above the waveless sea. She dreamt of the sun rising in the east, the rosy peach rays breaking through the dissipating clouds of an extinguished winter storm, reaching across snow-covered fields, the Sinefin River, the Cliffs of Litori, and finally across the Outsiders, the fields, and Astrid herself as they reached for the great city of Triah and the ocean after, and everything else that lay beyond.

The sun is rising, Knot thought, unable to voice it, unable to speak at all, unable to move. He gripped Cinzia's hand more tightly as they stood together, watching the incredible display of fire, color, combat, and destruction.

"Canta has sent an angel."

Knot would not have been able to tear his eyes away from Astrid if he had not immediately recognized the voice as Jane's. Conscious now, and standing next to him. Winter was there, too, her face illuminated by both Astrid's light and the sunrise, watching wide-eyed as Astrid fought for them all.

"Can't you do something?" Knot pleaded, looking to Jane.

"All is happening that must happen," Jane said. "This is Canta's will."

Knot almost lost it then. He struggled again to break for the cliffs, but the Prelates held him back again.

The sun is rising. The sun is rising, Astrid.

Dawn's rays reached out, out and out and out, farther and farther from the east, until they swept over Knot and Cinzia and everyone else silently, onward toward the cliffs and toward

Triah and toward Astrid, and the moment the light struck her, she transformed. In another burst of light, the girl ignited into a column of pure white flame.

"No!" Cinzia screamed beside him, and her grip on his hand broke as she fell to her knees.

Knot's throat was raw, his voice heavy, and all he could think was *the sun is rising, the sun is rising,* over and over and over again. Knot could no longer see Astrid, and he could no longer see her sword, but the great column of light and color still *moved*, leaping and striding from Outsider to Outsider, eliminating them, large and small alike, until they were all gone, and nothing remained on the field but snow, sunlight, and a single, tiny form.

Astrid dreamt the sun rose, and she did not burn. She dreamt of becoming one with the light. She dreamt of those she loved, and of those who loved her. She dreamt of her ship taking a turn, and in that moment, Astrid knew where she was going, and the word rang in her mind and in her heart like the tolling of a great bell.

She was going home.

47

THEY FOUND HER BODY amidst the freshly fallen snow.

Winter accompanied them, though she felt a stranger. Knot, Cinzia, Jane, Eward, and some of Jane's other disciples all walked together, while Winter remained a few paces behind, Astrid's words in their final conversation echoing in her mind.

There are a lot of people who have lost fathers, mothers, husbands, friends. A lot of people who've been addicted, or felt trapped. A lot of people who felt helpless. None of this is new. This is life. It's what living is.

Knot knelt beside the girl's body. Winter knew from the hope she'd felt as they had walked toward the girl—the hope that she might still be alive, that the miracle of light and fire had somehow preserved her—that Knot and Cinzia must feel it, too, far stronger than she did, and that the sharp pain of disappointment at the lifeless corpse they found must be infinitely stronger for them, too.

Cinzia fell to her knees at Knot's side, but neither of them moved, neither of them touched the body. Everyone behind them sensed the importance of the silence and the stillness, and did not move at all.

Later, Knot bent down, wrapping his arms around the girl, and lifted her. She dangled loosely from his embrace, and with Cinzia's help he adjusted his hold on her, so he carried her across his arms and body.

"She looks like she was just a girl," someone remarked, someone Winter did not know. No one responded.

He was right, whoever it was that had said it. Astrid had no trace of vampirism on her: no fangs, no claws, no glowing eyes. It was daylight, of course, but Winter suddenly could not imagine what the girl looked like *with* those things. Even at night, the image seemed strange, something that had only happened in a nightmare, or in a dream. The girl Knot carried was just a girl, nothing more.

And that was all anyone said. They walked back to the Odenite camp together in silence, with only the sound of boots crunching on snow and the occasional gust of wind to accompany them. Even Triah itself loomed oddly silent in the distance, without bells or shouts or anything of the sort.

Knot and Cinzia walked ahead with the body. The disciples, Jane, and her family followed.

And Winter was left alone, standing in the middle of the Odenite camp.

Were the rest of the tiellan Rangers all right? Had they stayed away as she had ordered? She had noticed some commotion at the edge of the battlefield, and thought she saw some of Roden's banners, but could not be sure. She had been too absorbed in her struggle with the Nine Daemons.

A growing sense of unease seeped through her, like ink slowly soaking through paper. What the Daemons had said to her, what *Azael* had said to her, still bothered her. How they had acted around her still bothered her. It had almost felt as if she were not truly facing Daemons at all, but people. Had she made the wrong choice? Perhaps she should not have summoned them at all. Perhaps she should have left it alone, and Cinzia and Jane would have solved the problem with whatever plan they were concocting.

If she had left it alone, Winter knew, if she had not done anything for the Daemons, Astrid would still be alive.

The hate she felt for herself because of that understanding was beyond description, beyond bounds. She was responsible for Astrid's death. She was responsible for the terrible grief Knot and Cinzia must be feeling, that anyone who had been close to the girl now felt. And, more than that, she was responsible for the fact that Astrid would never again make another sarcastic comment, fight another battle, help someone in the way she had helped Winter not twelve hours earlier.

In that moment, Winter wanted change. She no longer wanted to be the person she was. She no longer *could* be the person she had been.

She did not know what she could possibly become, but she knew the only option left was to try.

48

CINZIA SAT IN HER tent, unable to move. The events of the last day were hazy and blurred together. She had left Knot alone to grieve in his tent. She wanted to give him that space.

And here she was in hers.

A knock sounded at her doorpost. She might be asleep, she reasoned. This knock might be waking her from a terrible nightmare, and she would rise up and it would be Astrid waiting for her, a grin on her face, ready to—

"Yes?" Cinzia asked, sitting up. You're not dreaming, she had to remind herself, despite her exhaustion.

"I am so sorry… someone is waiting to see you, Disciple Cinzia," the Prelate outside her tent said.

Someone to see her. The thought of seeing someone else, of even having a conversation, multiplied the weariness in her bones many times over. She was about to open her mouth and ask that whoever it was return another time, when she saw the pouch on the table, partially open, a red multifaceted gem partially exposed. The gem reminded her of the dagger, and the dagger the Daemons, and the Daemons the Outsiders, and the Outsiders the vampire, the little girl, the—

Cinzia stood, a burning energy filling her limbs. Whoever it was at her door, whoever actually thought seeing her at this time, at this hour, at this moment in her life was remotely a good idea, would pay to Oblivion and back.

"Show them in," she said evenly.

The person who walked into her tent at that moment was the last person Cinzia would have ever expected, but it did nothing to alleviate the rage that boiled inside of her.

"Nayome," Cinzia said. "What in Oblivion are you doing here?"

"Cinzia," Nayome said, entering the tent. Cinzia had not seen her since their infiltration of Canta's Fane. Between all that had happened, with the Fall of the Eye and all of the healing and miracles, and the Nine Daemons and the Outsiders and—

And, for the briefest moment, the red gem in her belt pouch, now resting on a small table by her bed, called to her.

But Nayome was much more put-together than the last time Cinzia had seen her. Not a single blonde hair out of place, once again pulled tightly behind her head in a wide bun. She wore a dark cloak—Cinzia would have been shocked if even Nayome had the brashness to stride through the Odenite camp in full Cantic robes—but she did see the cream and crimson hem beneath, albeit tattered and muddy.

"Cinzia, I—are you all right?" Nayome asked.

I cannot believe you would visit me, Cinzia wanted to say. *What would lead you to think such a thing would be a good idea? What idiocy overtook you, or are you always this stupid?*

But, while the anger still clamored inside of her, she knew it was useless. She knew it meant nothing, would do nothing.

So Cinzia slumped back into her chair. "What do you want, Nayome?"

"Some tea would be in order," Nayome said quietly. "I believe I may be here for some time."

"Bloody ask for it yourself," Cinzia said.

Nayome cleared her throat, but the woman did not seem

nearly as taken aback or angry at Cinzia's language as Cinzia would have thought. If anything, Nayome seemed nervous, fiddling with the hem of one sleeve. She looked over her shoulder.

"Tea, please," Nayome said, her voice loud and sonorous.

"Right away." Footsteps walked away from the outside of the tent.

"I sense Luceraf has left you," Nayome said. "Such news would have delighted me just a few days ago," she muttered. "But now…" She met Cinzia's eyes. "The gemstone works, then? You've tried it?"

How Nayome could possibly know about the gemstone was beyond Cinzia. And what did she mean, 'but now?'

"If you are wondering how I know such a thing, I followed you into the Vault after all. I couldn't help myself. I heard your conversation with Arcana." Nayome looked over her shoulder as she said the Essera's name, as if the woman might be inside the tent with them.

"And now… what is it you want?" Cinzia's mind and body were exhausted. Goddess, she did not want to deal with this tonight.

"I think we need to share information with one another."

For the first time, Cinzia noticed a large pack at Nayome's feet. Had she carried that in? Cinzia could not remember the woman taking it off, or setting it there, but it had to belong to her. Cinzia rubbed her eyes. Perhaps she was so exhausted that she had not noticed.

And, suddenly, Cinzia realized what this was. Whatever Nayome had come here to do or to say did not matter; whatever was in that pack did not matter. None of it mattered, except that it was a distraction. A distraction from—

Cinzia tried to think of a way to retrieve the small pouch

with the gemstone in it without being too obvious, but could think of nothing, and settled for striding purposefully over to it and grabbing it in both hands. Or, at least, that had been her plan. The moment she tried to stand, she almost buckled. She steadied herself on the arms of the chair, and then ended up limping over to the small table where the pouch lay. She picked it up, and hobbled back to her chair, settling down into it with a long sigh.

"What kind of information?" Cinzia asked.

A distraction.

Nayome stared at her, blinking for a moment, then continued with a tiny shake of her head. "You healed people, near the Eye, after what happened. The dead and the dying."

Cinzia inclined her head. "I did what I could, but it was only Jane who raised people from the dead."

Nayome appeared to process this information for a moment, then nodded quickly. "Well, whatever has happened between us, and whatever else might happen in the future, I thank you for that. What happened to the Eye…"

When Nayome did not continue, Cinzia looked up to see the woman blinking back tears.

A knock sounded at the doorpost. "Your tea, Disciple Cinzia."

"Yes, yes," Cinzia said, shutting her eyes tightly in an attempt to reset her mind. "Please bring the tea in, thank you."

The tent flap pulled back, and the Prelate entered, a tray with a clay teapot and two cups held in both hands. He did a double-take at Nayome, seeing her in her full Cantic robes, before he placed the tray on a small table between Cinzia and Nayome.

"Er… is everything all right, Disciple Cinzia?"

"Everything is fine," Cinzia said, although nothing was fine, and nothing would ever be fine. "Thank you."

"Would you like me to pour?"

Nayome took up the teapot, filling their cups. "Thank you, but no," she said, inclining her head toward the Prelate. Then she turned her attention back to Cinzia. "It would benefit our conversation if you dismissed your guard."

The Prelate frowned. "I am sorry, miss, but I do not take orders from you—"

"It is quite all right, Hennic," Cinzia said, smiling up at the man. *A distraction.* "A private conversation would do us good. Nothing to worry about. You can still keep guard over the tent, but… please do so at a distance."

"Disciple Cinzia, I really—"

"If Eward has a problem with this, tell him he can take it up with me."

Hennic glanced back and forth from Cinzia to Nayome, obviously flustered. But he could not very well disobey a disciple. Eward had trained his force well, and with the exception of Jane, disciples held ultimate authority throughout the camp.

"Very well, Disciple Cinzia," Hennic said with a small bow. "If you need me, or need anything at all, just—"

"I shall call out very loudly. Worry not, Hennic," Cinzia said.

Then she and Nayome were alone.

Cinzia reached for her cup of tea on the table. The clay was warm in her hands, and the tea was strong, with a bitter edge to it. Sugar, of course, had become quite scarce for the Odenites.

"Nayome," Cinzia said, placing her cup back down on the tray, "you have yet to actually share anything of note."

"I am aware of that. I had to make sure that silly guard was gone. What I am about to tell you should not fall on anyone else's ears."

Cinzia frowned. "What could you possibly have to tell me that

I would not want to share with the other Odenites?" The moment she asked the question, however, she realized how silly it was. She had kept plenty of things from the Odenites, both for their good and her own convenience, or shame, depending on the day.

Nayome took a long draught from her cup.

"Before you left the Vault, Arcana gave you a choice. You could take the gemstone or the pages."

"And…?"

"You took the gemstone. But after you left, I glanced around. The other artifacts in the Vault frightened me. But the pages, on the other hand… Arcana had implied they could be read by anyone who chose them. So, I chose them."

A distraction from—

"You are telling me that you, a Holy Crucible of the Denomination—" Goddess, no wonder she did not want anyone eavesdropping on this conversation "—stole the pages from the Denomination's secret vault?"

"Yes," Nayome said, sitting back in her chair. "That is exactly what I am telling you."

Cinzia glanced at the pack at Nayome's feet. "And there…"

"I have them with me, yes."

Cinzia's exhaustion was all but forgotten, now. "Why did you bring them here, Nayome?"

"I already told you," she said. "We need to exchange information."

"What information do I have that would benefit you?"

"You have that gemstone," Nayome said, nodding at the pouch now sitting in Cinzia's lap. "Once you read this manuscript, you will understand why I want to know more about it."

"Very well then," Cinzia said, unable to keep the eagerness from her voice. "Let me see it."

"I will," Nayome said, "but first you must understand something. What I've read in these pages… they have changed the way I view the world, Cinzia. They have changed the way I view Canta. And, to be completely honest, not for the better. If you truly want to read them, I need you to understand that your views may also change."

My views are already changing, Cinzia wanted to say. But the truth was, she did not think her faith, or whatever had happened to it, was any of Nayome's business.

"I understand," Cinzia said.

"You used to wear the Trinacrya," Nayome said.

Cinzia's jaw clenched. "Thank you for pointing that out."

"I am not trying to be petty, Cinzia. You used to wear the Trinacrya, but did you understand what it meant?"

"Nayome, I have neither the time nor the patience—"

"I don't mean that in a figurative sense," Nayome said, clearly frustrated, "I mean it literally. Do you know why the Denomination used the Trinacrya as its main symbol?"

Cinzia pursed her lips. "It was the symbol Canta chose, first of all." But no, that would not be the answer Nayome sought. "The circle represents the eternal progression of things, how one event always leads to another, and one generation to the next, always in patterns."

"And the triangle?"

"The triangle… has always been less clear," Cinzia admitted. "Some say it is the unity of mind, body, and spirit. Others the symbiotic relationship between Canta's children, the Denomination, and Canta Herself. Others the triplicity of all things."

"Yes," Nayome said, "and yet others the triplicity of Canta's own nature."

Cinzia frowned. She did not think she had heard that particular interpretation.

"I hadn't heard of it either," Nayome said, anticipating Cinzia's thought. "Until I read the pages."

Nayome's eyes darted down to the backpack at her feet, and then back to Cinzia.

"Canta's existence spans three phases," Nayome said. The excitement, the anticipation on her face were gone. In their place, a deadly seriousness. "Destroyer, Lover, Creator."

Cinzia had never heard this before. But at least it was—

A distraction.

"More accurately, at least according to history," Nayome continued, "you might order them Creator, then Lover, then Destroyer."

Cinzia glanced again at Nayome's backpack.

"Very well," Nayome said with a sigh. She reached down into the pack, but instead of pulling out a pile of pages, she retrieved a small, leather-bound book. She tossed it to Cinzia, and Cinzia nearly knocked over her tea trying to catch it. The book landed awkwardly in her lap, and Cinzia stared down at it, crooking her head to read the title that was currently upside down. She turned the book around.

Poems and Verse.

"Don't worry," Nayome said, "we will get to the pages soon. I know you are chomping at the bit, as it were. But first… what do you know of the poet Cetro Ziravi?"

Cinzia blinked. She remembered a missing copy of Ziravi's works from her family's library in Harmoth—

A distraction.

"Everyone knows of him," Cinzia said. "Everyone familiar with poetry, at least. His epic was famous for challenging the

Denomination itself at the time."

"Exactly," Nayome said. "And do you know why his poetry was so controversial?"

"Because it placed the Essera contemporary with Ziravi in Oblivion," Cinzia said. She might have found that humorous, once. "And criticized the functionality and, according to some, the legitimacy of the Denomination."

"His epics did, yes. But his poetry…?"

Cinzia shrugged. "What about his poetry, Nayome?" A part of her wanted Nayome to just leave, to be done with this conversation, with all conversation, but at the same time—

A distraction.

"He often wrote poetry as if from the point of view of Canta herself," Nayome said. She nodded at *Poems and Verse*. "Turn to page seventy-nine."

Cinzia frowned, but did as Nayome requested. Anything was better than being alone with her thoughts.

"'Wild Calamity'," Cinzia read.

> *I do not control myself,*
> *I do not hold back, hoping my rage and*
> *power spare the deserving,*
> *I do not weep through eternity, nor do*
> *I scrape my knees along the floors of*
> *time, atoning.*
> *Because I love what I love, and I love*
> *all things.*
>
> *I destroy all things,*
> *Just as I create them.*
> *I could not destroy that which I did*

not first love,
And so the circle spirals onward.

To destroy, I must first know love,
And to create, I must first know
destruction.
And to love, create.
Meanwhile, the needing, the touching
skin, the welding
bodies, the connecting of every pair of
lost children,
soft in body and young in mind,
continues my pattern
and life's wild calamity.

Cinzia's eyes narrowed.

...I destroy all things, just as I create them...

Slowly, everything began to click into place in Cinzia's mind. The Codex of Elwene. Elwene's footnotes. The Nine Daemons, the Betrayer... Canta. Canta, who created the Sfaera. Canta, who loved the Sfaera.

To destroy, I must first know love, and to create, I must first know destruction.

"Canta... the Destroyer," Cinzia said quietly.

"Yes," Nayome whispered, tears streaming down her face. "I wish I had never agreed to go with you, to help you get into that vault. I wish I had never followed you, because now I cannot unlearn what I have learned. I cannot go back to what I knew. I cannot reconcile my faith with what has been revealed to me."

Finally, Nayome hefted the backpack onto the table between them, heedless of the tea tray.

"Read it," Nayome said, taking the pages out of the pack. "Read it, and you'll understand. You'll know what I know."

And what is it you know? Cinzia wondered, the answer already echoing in her mind.

"The Nine Daemons were never going to destroy us," Nayome said. "That was Canta's duty. And now, I fear, she will soon come to let her sword fall on the Sfaera."

"Canta the Destroyer," Cinzia whispered. She picked up the pages, words forming out of nothing on the first document she took up, and began to read.

ALAIN, MORAYNE, AND CODE finally made it to the Odenite camp. Code had been leading them out of the city when monsters began raining down from the sky, and the rest of the night had passed in a dark, violent, snowy cold blur.

Alain hated the snow. He had never seen it before, and had been reserving judgment on the stuff his entire life. Now that he'd experienced it, however, he'd be quite happy if he never had to see it, feel it, shiver in it, kill in it, or die in it ever again.

Morayne, walking beside him, had not said a word since they left the city. Neither he nor Code had said much, either, but they had at least exchanged a few words between them. Alain recognized this sort of silence from Morayne. He reached out a hand to hold hers, squeezing it tightly. He barely felt a squeeze from her in return. He was about to ask her what was wrong, when Code swore beside him.

"You've got to be kidding me," he said. The Nazaniin had stopped, staring ahead of them. Or ex-Nazaniin, Alain was no longer sure; Code had said something about going to the Odenites first, and then perhaps traveling with Alain and Morayne to Maven Kol again, because he had no more business with his former associates in Triah. Alain had no idea what exactly that entailed, but it did not seem to indicate an ongoing relationship with the Nazaniin. He hoped whatever had happened did not have to do with himself or Morayne; he would hate to think they might have disrupted Code's life. He'd said as much to Code, and Code had insisted otherwise, but Alain nevertheless felt something was off.

But now, Code had stopped, and stared at a campfire ahead of them. The Odenite camp stretched on for quite some time—if anything, it looked even larger than it had when he and Morayne had first arrived in Triah—with tents, campfires, gathering areas, and more. But straight ahead of them was a tiellan woman, sitting alone at a fire pit that no longer burned. She seemed oblivious to the cold, her breath puffing visibly from her mouth, but she did not shiver nor pull her dark leather overcoat more tightly around her.

"You," Code said, walking toward the woman.

Her long black hair was braided tightly on either side of her skull, while a looser braid ran from her forehead, over her scalp, her neck, and halfway down her back. When Code spoke, the woman looked up at them, and Alain looked into twin black pools.

"Months of waiting to meet you," Code mumbled, walking more quickly, "and I run into you in the bloody *Odenite* camp? What are you doing here?"

"Do I know you?" she asked, standing, a hand straying to the hilt of her sword.

"Not yet you don't," Code said, stopping in front of her. "But you're about to. My name is Code. Was a Nazaniin, now I'm not so sure. Was assigned to gain your confidence, but now that I've found you, ironically, I don't much care to do that. But I figured I'd meet you anyway, considering… everything. I'd kill you right now for what you did to the Eye, if I didn't think you'd strike me down long before I made the move."

"I will not strike you down," the woman said, bowing her head.

Alain felt Morayne squeeze his hand. She was staring at the woman intently.

Something was certainly off, here. The woman had basically just invited Code to kill her, and Code wanted to kill her because…

Because she had destroyed the Eye.

"Ah," Code said, when he noticed the woman looking at Alain and Morayne, "where are my manners? Alain, Morayne, may I introduce you to Winter Cordier, the Goddess-damned Chaos Queen."

Alain would have thought that now would be the time his anxiety struck him hardest. That now he would have to begin counting, or stretching, or take a moment to excuse himself and just surrender everything he had no control over, like whether or not the Chaos Queen would kill him on the spot.

But instead, he simply met her eyes, those deep, dark pools, and holding Morayne's hand tightly, said, "Hello, Winter. I think I might be able to help you."

Kali, atop the Cliffs of Litori, held the small amber *rihnemin* tightly in both hands, the chill of winter creeping through her overcoat.

The fields at the base of the cliffs, almost pristinely white with snow save for a few lines of footprints, stood in stark contrast to the scene of violent horror on the clifftop. Humans, tiellans, Outsiders, and a single gargantuan beast all lay dead on the snowy grass. Blood, coagulated and frozen, coated the ground and the corpses alike. Hundreds of weapons and the dozen or so remaining siege engines littered the clifftop, the instruments of death scattered among death itself. The hundreds of other daemons who had poured forth toward Triah, sprinting down the cliffs, were nowhere to be seen, burnt into Oblivion by the mysterious burning light.

More than the horror behind her, and more than the emptiness immediately before her, two things drew Kali's attention: the great scar marring the face of Triah, and the overwhelming presence she felt, both in the Void and through her voidstone, in the Odenite camp.

Kali had been hesitant to return to the Void, at first. Having just escaped, she'd been worried she might find herself unable to leave once more. But the inevitable call of the star-light-speckled blackness drew her back in, and there, as always, she saw Winter's great burning dark.

After the Fall of the Eye, and knowing Winter was behind it, Kali could not bring herself to take the stone to her former student. Kali had watched the Eye fall from the Trinacrya at the center of the city along with hundreds of other Triahns, and she had never known such terror, such wanton destruction, in all her summers. She remembered, more than anything else, turning to see the faces around her, pale and slick with sweaty shock, all staring up at the Eye as it burned, eyes wide but still unable to take it all in.

If Winter got her hands on the *rihnemin* Kali now carried, what greater destruction could she cause?

Fortunately, Winter had been busy. Between the aftermath of the Eye, and whatever in Oblivion had happened atop this cliff, Winter had yet to contact Kali since she'd procured the *rihnemin*, and that was just as well.

But the respite would not last long, and Kali could not stand against Winter. She could still bring her the *rihnemin*, and save her own life, at least. And, after all, what was Kali if not one to follow orders?

Kosarin was the other option; he clearly wanted the *rihnemin*, though for what reason she could not fathom. A part of Kali relished the idea of holding that power over the *Triadin*'s head, but another part of her knew the man was just as dangerous as—perhaps the only person on the Sfaera who might be *more* dangerous than—the Chaos Queen herself.

With a deep, calming breath, Kali sat down on crossed legs, placing the *rihnemin* in her lap. The stone was a power piece in the ongoing warsquares match; for her next move, she would need to use it to her greatest advantage.

Knot knelt in his tent, unable to sit, unable to stand, unable to lie down or sleep. He knelt by her body, every trace of vampirism now gone, every hint that she had once been an incredible warrior, that she had once held a burning magic sword twice her own height, every hint that she had once been his friend, someone he cared about, gone.

A funeral was planned. A funeral had been planned by other people, not him. Truth was, he had no idea what she would've wanted done with her body. Truth was, he didn't think she thought there'd be a body that remained when she died, especially if she died by exposure to sunlight. Truth was, he had no idea what the bloody truth was when it came to what had happened, to what she had done, to the pillar of white burning light she'd become and why she now lay before him, unmarked, unburnt, unbroken.

A cruel joke is what it seemed. Like she could still be alive, somehow, because her body was not destroyed or marred or burned into nothing.

But she was not alive. She was not alive.

She was not alive.

Every part of her was gone, and he could not bring himself to look at the face of the body that lay on the cot in his tent.

So, because it was the only thing to do, the only thing he could do, he knelt there, holding the girl's lifeless hand, and cried.

ACKNOWLEDGMENTS

To say the process of writing these books has become like that of a well-oiled machine by now might be an overstatement, but efficiency and smoothness seem to increase with each volume. That's been doubly true for the book you hold in your hands, and that's in large part due to a very fine cadre of folks who continue to help me through the work.

Rachel, I could never thank you enough, but I'll keep thanking you every time anyway in the hopes that I one day might come close. You believe in me, you encourage me, and I'm pretty sure sometimes you just tolerate me, and I'm grateful for it all. Your love, support, and counsel make these books possible. They also help me be a relatively sane writer and person, which is nice. (Also, I'm sorry about what happens in this book. Um… I'll make it up to you?)

To my little ones, Buffy and Arya: You teach me every day about an infinite facet of love that I never knew existed. You inspire me. I thank God and the Universe and every power out there that could possibly listen every day for the two of you. I'm so grateful to be your father. Also, thank you for getting me into MLP.

Speaking of my littles, we have a huge list of folks who help take care of them, which means I actually have time to write these books, so a huge THANK YOU to you all. Maren, you get a specific shout-out this time around. You are awesome, we love you, and B loves you, so thank you so much for taking care of her! (She still wants to do a hot-chocolate date with you, by the way, so let's make that happen.)

Thanks to Dave Butler for hosting the best writing retreat this side of the Laniakea Supercluster (I hear Ophiuchus has some pretty good ones, though), and touring around the country with me like a rockstar. Edward M. Kovel will forever live in our hearts.

Thanks to Accidental Erotica for being the best writing group ever—and Janci Patterson for her freakish brilliance and offering amazing feedback on this book.

A HUGE thank you to my editor, Sam Matthews, for helping me make this book the absolute best it could be— and thank you to the whole team at Titan Books, particularly Hayley, Craig, and Joanna, for making every aspect of the Chaos Queen Quintet so awesome.

Sam Morgan, my agent, is the best agent. If he isn't your agent, I am sorry for you, because he's amazing. Sam, imagine the rest of this note as an artfully drawn T-Rex thanking you on my behalf. Seriously, thank you.

Lastly, thank you to Chris Welton for letting me talk his ear off for hours at a time about the seed ideas that became some of the most dramatic points of this novel (and this entire series) while walking around Brindisi, Italy, about thirteen years ago. 10/10, would recommend. I love you, old man.

ABOUT THE AUTHOR

CHRISTOPHER HUSBERG GREW UP in Eagle River, Alaska. He now lives in Utah, and spends his time writing, reading, hiking, and playing video games, but mostly hanging out with his wife, Rachel, and daughters, Buffy and Arya. He received an MFA in creative writing from Brigham Young University, and an honorary PhD in *Buffy the Vampire Slayer* from himself. The first novel in the Chaos Queen Quintet, *Duskfall*, was published in 2016 from Titan Books, followed by *Dark Immolation*, *Blood Requiem*, and *Fear the Stars*.

www.christopherhusberg.com
@usbergo

DUSKFALL

THE CHAOS QUEEN QUINTET

CHRISTOPHER HUSBERG

Pulled from a frozen sea, pierced by arrows and close to death, Knot has no memory of who he was. But his dreams are dark, filled with violence and unknown faces. Winter, a tiellan woman whose people have long been oppressed by humans, is married to and abandoned by Knot on the same day. In her search for him, she will discover her control of magic, but risk losing herself utterly. And Cinzia, priestess and true believer, returns home to discover her family at the heart of a heretical rebellion. A rebellion that only the Inquisition can crush…

Their fates and those of others will intertwine, in a land where magic and daemons are believed dead, but dark forces still vie for power.

"A delicious mix of Jason Bourne, dark fantasy, and horror. The kind of debut that has me thrilled for the future of fantasy."
Steve Diamond, author of *Residue*

"A fascinating mystery that slowly unfolds, and cultures and religions in conflict. Enjoy."
Melinda Snodgrass, author of *The Edge of Reason*

TITANBOOKS.COM

THE SILENCE

TIM LEBBON

In the darkness of an underground cave system, blind creatureshunt by sound. Then there is light, there are voices, and they feed... Swarming from their prison, the creatures thrive and destroy. To scream, even to whisper, is to summon death. As the hordes lay waste to Europe, a girl watches to see if they will cross the sea. Deaf for many years, she knows how to live in silence; now, it is her family's only chance of survival. To leave their home, to shun others, to find a remote haven where they can sit out the plague. But will it ever end? And what kind of world will be left?

"A truly great novel with a fresh and original story"
Starburst

"A chilling and heart-wrenching story"
Publishers Weekly

*"The Silence is a chilling story that grips you
firmly by the throat"*
SciFi Now

ANNO DRACULA

KIM NEWMAN

It is 1888 and Queen Victoria has remarried, taking as her new consort the Wallachian Prince infamously known as Count Dracula. His polluted bloodline spreads through London as its citizens increasingly choose to become vampires.

In the grim backstreets of Whitechapel, a killer known as 'Silver Knife' is cutting down vampire girls. The eternally young vampire Genevieve Dieudonne and Charles Beauregard of the Diogenes Club are drawn together as they both hunt the sadistic killer, bringing them ever closer to England's most bloodthirsty ruler yet.

"Compulsory reading... glorious"
Neil Gaiman

"Essential for any fan of Gothic literature"
The Guardian

"Up there with Bram Stoker's chilling original"
Daily Mail